ONCE UPON an Accidentally Bewitching KISS

#6 The Whickertons in Love

BY BREE WOLF

Once Upon an Accidentally Bewitching Kiss by Bree Wolf

Published by WOLF Publishing UG

Copyright © 2022 Bree Wolf
Text by Bree Wolf
Cover Art by Victoria Cooper
Paperback ISBN: 978-3-98536-048-2
Hard Cover ISBN: 978-3-98536-049-9
Ebook ISBN: 978-3-98536-047-5

Also by Bree Wolf

The Whickertons in Love

The WHICKERTONS IN LOVE is a new series by USA Today bestselling author BREE WOLF set in Regency-era England, portraying the at times turbulent ways the six Whickerton siblings search for love. If you enjoy wicked viscounts, brooding lords as well as head-strong ladies, fierce in their affections and daring in their search for their perfect match, then this new series is perfect for you!

#1 Once Upon a Devilishly Enchanting Kiss

#2 Once Upon a Temptingly Ruinous Kiss

#3 Once Upon an Irritatingly Magical Kiss

#4 Once Upon a Devastatingly Sweet Kiss

#5 Once Upon an Achingly Beautiful Kiss

#6 Once Upon an Accidentally Bewitching Kiss

Prequel to the series: Once Upon A Kiss Gone Horribly Wrong

Acknowledgement

A great big thank-you to all those who aided me in finishing this book and made it the wonderful story it has become. First and foremost, of course, there is my family, who inspires me on a daily basis, giving me the enthusiasm and encouragement, I need to type away at my computer day after day. Thank you so much!

Then there are my proofreaders, beta readers and readers who write to me out of the blue with wonderful ideas and thoughts. Thank you for your honest words! Jodi and Dara comb through my manuscripts in an utterly diligent way that allows me to smooth off the rough edges and make it shine. Thank you so much for your dedication to my stories! Brie, Carol, Zan-Mari, Kim, Martha and Mary are my hawks, their eyes sweeping over the words to spot those pesky errors I seem to be absolutely blind to. Thank you so much for aiding me with your keen eyesight!

ONCE UPON an Accidentally Bewitching KISS

Prologue

Near Fartherington Hall, summer 1798 (or a variation thereof)
Five years earlier

L ady Leonora Hurst, sister to the new Earl of Lockhart, clung
tightly to her mare as they thundered across the green
meadow. Wildflowers of all colors were in bloom, and above
the drumbeat-like sound of hooves, Nora could hear the soft buzzing
of bees and the gentle chirping of crickets.

The sun shone brightly overhead, and a mild breeze tugged upon
her mahogany curls. She swept her eyes sideways to the man riding
head-to-head with her. His name was Troy Beaumont, son to the Earl
of Whickerton, and he had been a dear friend for as long as she could
remember.

His family's estate bordered Fartherington Hall, and whenever
both families happened to be in the country, they seldom spent time
apart. While Nora had grown up with two brothers—one of whom had
sadly passed away a year past—Troy was the only son in his family,
eldest brother to five younger sisters. Indeed, Nora could not
remember a single day of boredom throughout her entire childhood.

Always had there been someone around with whom to play, with whom to get in trouble, with whom to explore the world.

"Do you think the others already figured out the last clue?" Nora called over the whipping wind as they raced along toward the ancient watchtower in the distance.

Troy laughed, amusement sparkling in his blue eyes. "How am I to know? I am here with you, am I not?"

Nora rolled her eyes at him, urging her mare closer, threatening to cut him off. "Don't tease me, Troy. You know I don't care for it."

His sharp eyes narrowed dangerously as he met her gaze before his hand flew out, attempting to grab her mare's reins.

Only in the last moment, Nora managed to pull her horse around, well-aware that the tips of his fingers brushed against the reins' leather. Her eyes narrowed, shooting daggers in his direction. "How disagreeable of you!" she called, fixing him with a challenging stare. "Was I wrong to expect loyalty? Are we not a team?"

A wide smile came to Troy's face before he threw back his head and laughed. "Why should there be?" he challenged, the look in his eyes telling her that he was once more teasing. "Neither one of us chose the other. We drew straws and found ourselves matched in this hunt. Why, I ask you, should that inspire loyalty?"

Nora fought to maintain a disapproving frown; yet she could feel laughter bubbling up in her throat. Troy simply was someone she could not be angry with for long. Although she disliked the way he sometimes teased her, he always did it in a good-natured way, his words never insulting or degrading.

As they neared the ruins, both slowed their horses, their breaths coming fast as they surveyed the ancient watchtower, now little more than a heap of rocks strewn about. One wall still stood erect, but crumpled away to its sides, fading away a little more each year.

"Would you have rather been matched with another in this scavenger hunt?" Nora inquired with a sideways glance at Troy. "Are you displeased that we find ourselves tied to one another on this quest?"

He grinned, and she could feel his eyes come to rest upon her, daring her to face him. "Now, I did not say that, did I?"

Huffing out a deep breath, Nora turned to look at him. "Does that mean that the moment I turn my back, I can expect to find a knife plunged into it?"

Again, Troy laughed, almost roaringly. "My dearest Nora, I've never known you to be so dramatic. Pray tell, what did I say that riled you so?"

Pressing her lips together, Nora tried not to laugh; however, this time, her efforts were futile. "Oh, I cannot be mad at you. I cannot even pretend to be," she chuckled, delighting in the wide smile that came to his face. "You are one of my dearest friends, and I would not hesitate to trust you with my life."

Although Nora had spoken lightly, perhaps even a little teasingly, her words chased the smile from Troy's face. Something serious, something almost shocked, now rested in his blue eyes as he stared at her.

"Oh, Troy," Nora chuckled good-naturedly, "do not worry. I have no immediate plans of placing myself in danger and expecting you to rescue me." She saw the hint of a smile crack through the tense expression upon his face. "All I meant to say is that we are dear friends, are we not? I've known you all my life, and I shall miss you." Her breath suddenly shuddered past her lips, making her realize how much she would miss him.

How much she would miss them all.

Indeed, this was her last scavenger hunt. Soon—in fact, in a matter of days—she would travel to London to be married and then move to her new husband's estate. She would be a wife and expected to behave accordingly. Gone would be the carefree days of chasing the wind, of playing daring games with her friends, of being simply Nora.

Soon, she would be Lady Hayward, wife to the Earl of Hayward. It would be a new life, a different life, and although Nora was looking forward to it, part of her could not help but wonder whether it would be exactly how she imagined it.

Her betrothed was a most suitable match. He was young and handsome, and when he smiled at her, Nora could not help but wonder what a kiss would feel like. From the first, he had been charming and attentive, and although Nora had only recently turned nineteen, she was certain that he would make her a most wonderful and exciting husband. Oh, how she longed for this new adventure to begin!

Yet a hint of sadness continued to linger. Sadness she ought to have expected. Perhaps she had been a fool not to see it coming. Of course, a drastic change—even a desired one—always came with a joyful as well as sorrowful eye, did it not?

A deeply affectionate smile claimed Troy's lips. "I shall miss you as well," he told her in a voice that, for once, held no teasing note. Riding side by side, he held out his hand to her and waited until she took it. "I cannot imagine this place without you. It will be utterly strange to ride these fields without you next to me. Indeed, we shall all miss you dearly."

Determined to hold the tears that threatened at bay, Nora returned his smile. "Let's not speak of my departure," she insisted, nodding toward the ruins up ahead. "Indeed, I am determined to win this last scavenger hunt." She glanced over her shoulder but could spot no riders upon the horizon. "Even if the others found the last clue, it seems they are having some trouble figuring it out. This is our chance!"

Clearing his throat, Troy nodded to her. "Then let us go see where the next clue could be hiding." They spurred on their horses and made their way across the last stretch of land before they found themselves standing in front of the ancient watchtower.

The rocks were covered in moss, and here and there, Nora glimpsed a bird's nest built into a crevice. Her eyes swept over the rubble and then flew up the one remaining wall, towering over them both. The beginnings of an old staircase made of the same rock sat nestled against the inner side of the wall, and the grass grew tall and wild all around the ruins.

"In order to remain safe from the elements," Troy remarked as they drew closer, his gaze sweeping over the rocks as well, "I suppose the clue must be hidden somewhere in a crevice."

Nora chuckled. "I thought the very same thing."

Turning to look at her over his shoulder, Troy grinned. "You know what they say, great minds think alike." Then he threw one leg over his horse's neck and dropped to the ground. "Where do you suppose we should begin to look?" he asked as he strode over to her.

Nora shrugged, gathered her reins, and placed them securely atop her mare's neck. Then she moved to slide out of the saddle. "I'll search along the inner wall and you the outer."

Troy grinned as he stood in front of her, holding up his hands to assist her down as he had countless times before. "What if *I* want to search the inner wall?"

Rolling her eyes at him, Nora sighed, once again fighting a grin. "You're impossible!" she chided as she leaned forward, ready to brace her hands upon his upper arms. "You're truly and utterly impossible! The most vexing man I've ever m—!"

Her mare suddenly shifted upon her hooves, and that small movement somehow upended Nora's balance. Her eyes widened as she fell forward, feeling her heart tighten in her chest and her stomach lurch into her throat. "Troy!" she called, her hands clutching at his arms.

Instantly, Troy surged toward her, pulling her from the saddle and against his chest. His arms wrapped tightly around her, and she could feel his heart beat wildly against her own. "I've got you," he gasped against her ear, his warm breath brushing over her skin. "I've got you."

Pinching her eyes shut, Nora tightened her arms around his neck and inhaled a deep breath. Then she released it as well as her iron grip, feeling Troy's hands upon her waist as he gently lowered her to the ground.

"I've got you," he murmured once more, and the moment Nora lifted her head and their eyes met...

...the world was suddenly a different place.

A shudder surged through Nora as she stood in Troy's embrace, their gazes locked, as though time had been suspended.

Countless times had he assisted her off her horse. Countless times had she looked into his eyes. Countless times had she looked at him and seen a friend.

Only now, Nora saw something else.

Someone else.

And so did he.

Nora could see it upon his face.

Although Troy possessed the ability to shield his thoughts and emotions like no other she had ever met, the look that now stood upon his face echoed her own emotions loud and clear. She saw stunned disbelief as he stared down at her, his breath coming fast and his hands holding her to him, as though he never wished to let her go.

Her own hands clung tightly to him as well, and although Nora wanted to believe so, it had nothing to do with the moment of fright she had just experienced. Indeed, that moment had been nothing. Nothing more than a second of panic, instantly soothed by Troy's protective embrace.

Nora swallowed, feeling goosebumps chasing up and down her legs and arms as Troy's breath teased her lips. He stood close. He stood so very close, his head slightly bent and his wide blue eyes looking down into hers. "I've got you," he murmured once more before his gaze dropped lower for a split second. "I've got you."

In answer, Nora's heart seemed to falter in her chest, and she licked her lips as her own gaze darted to his mouth.

Troy drew in a sharp breath, and his hands slid to the small of her back, urging her closer. He dipped his head ever so slightly, his eyes never leaving hers.

Nora lifted her head, her eyes wide and disbelieving as she watched him move closer.

And closer.

Closer still.

And then his gaze fell to her lips, and he dipped his head, brushing his mouth against hers in a feather-light touch.

Nora flinched, as though lightning had struck her, and Troy's head flew back up. Both stared at the other, eyes wide and breaths coming fast.

For a moment, Nora thought he would retreat, but he remained where he was, his arms wrapped around her as before. Long moments passed as they stared at one another, unable to move in either direction.

Apart.

Or closer.

And then Nora felt her gaze flicker to his lips once more, curious, tempted, and she could see an answering shimmer in Troy's eyes the second she looked up at him. When he leaned closer, her heart sped up, and she grasped his arms, pushing herself onto her toes, raising her chin to meet him.

His lips felt soft and warm against hers, and although Nora could not help the sense of disbelief that still clung to her mind, the jolt of shock they had experienced before failed to materialize. Instead, a warm tingling sensation came to her lips and then moved farther out into every region of her body.

Overwhelmed, Nora returned his kiss, guided by instinct alone. She knew not what she was doing; yet it felt wonderful, almost intoxicating, and she knew she did not want this feeling to stop.

Pulling her closer, Troy tentatively deepened their kiss. His hand reached to grasp her chin, then moved farther back until it cupped the back of her head while his other arm remained slung around her middle. He held her gently; yet Nora could feel his longing for more grow...

...in tandem with her own.

The world around them vanished, and all that mattered was this feeling, right here, right now. The way her heart beat strong, and yet seemed to trip and stumble every so often. The way his warmth appeared to reach for her, touching her skin and sending shivers across it. The way his lips moved over hers with urgency and caution alike.

And then his teeth nipped her lower lip, and Nora gasped. Her lips parted, and she froze in utter surprise as she felt him touch his tongue to hers for only a split second.

Panting, they stared at one another, and for a moment, Nora reeled from the shock of finding herself staring up into Troy's face. Had he truly just kissed her? Had she—?

His hand on the back of her neck tightened, bringing her mouth once more closer to his. His eyes were dark and looked into hers with such intensity that Nora felt a shiver dance down her spine. Was this Troy? The neighbor she had known all her life? How could this—?

Again, his lips touched hers, and Nora closed her eyes, her hands reaching out to slink around his neck. All thoughts vanished, slipped from her mind as though they had never been. All that mattered was Troy and the feeling of his lips against hers, of his heart thundering as wildly as her own. Never had Nora felt so alive. Never had she—

A shout drifted to her ears, and Nora froze.

As did Troy.

Their eyes flew open, and they stared at each other in complete shock as reality returned with full force, ripping away this moment of intimacy they had shared.

"Over there!" someone called from beyond the wall, and they both recognized his sister's voice.

"Louisa," Troy murmured absentmindedly, still staring at Nora with a rather dumbfounded expression.

In the next instant, they both surged apart.

Nora tried her best to breathe as Troy shook his head, no doubt to shake off the lingering emotions that had found them so unexpectedly. He raked a hand through his hair, pacing away and then back to her, his eyes wide and unblinking.

Louisa's voice once more echoed to their ears as the sound of hoof-beats grew louder. "Do you think we're the first ones here?"

"I don't see anyone," Leonora—or Leo—replied in her usual matter-of-fact kind of voice.

Troy stared at the watchtower's remaining wall that still concealed them from his sisters' eyes before returning his gaze to Nora.

Only a moment later, Louisa and Leo came riding around the edge and pulled up short, their eyes going wide as they saw them. "Someone *is* here," Louisa exclaimed in surprise, pulling up the reins before jumping out of the saddle. "Don't tell me you already found the next clue?" A touch of displeasure came into her green eyes.

Troy cleared his throat. "No, we...we haven't." He swallowed hard, and his eyes darted to Nora. "We...We only just got here."

"Good!" Louisa exclaimed eagerly, then turned and dashed back to Leo. Together, they began searching the watchtower's ruins, eagerly peeking into every gap and crevice.

All the while, Nora and Troy stood rooted to the spot, unable to move, unable to look at each other but equally unable to *not* look at each other. Nora could see his breath still coming fast as his eyes returned to her again and again, the memory of their kiss etched into his face.

"Why are you only standing there?" Louisa called over from where she was searching the ruins.

At the sound of her voice, Nora and Troy both flinched. It seemed their minds kept slipping away to that one moment that had been different from all the others, forgetting what was around them, who was around them this very minute.

A deep frown came to Louisa's face as she exchanged a quizzical look with Leo. "Or did you already find it? But if you did, why would you still be here?" She tapped a finger to the corner of her mouth, thinking.

Tearing his eyes away from Nora, Troy moved toward his sisters. "We have not found it yet," he said in a voice that did not sound like his own. "We were merely...taking a break."

Louisa laughed, her watchful green eyes darting back and forth between Nora and her brother. "You're acting...strange," she remarked thoughtfully, exchanging another glance with her sister, who nodded along an agreement. "Has something happened?"

Troy snorted, a smile coming to his face that looked just a little bit strained. "Oh, you are just trying to distract us from finding the clue." He fixed her with a challenging stare. "Trust me. It will not work."

Instantly accepting her brother's challenge as Troy had no doubt known she would, Louisa dashed away and rather frantically continued her search. Leo joined her while Troy moved to the other side of the wall. As he stepped around it, his gaze moved to Nora for no more than a split second before he vanished from sight...

...but it was enough.

Nora felt his gaze like a jolt that shocked her entire body, as though the earth beneath her feet was no longer steady but trembling and rumbling, seeking to throw her off. A tremor surged through her, and she clasped her hands around her arms, willing herself to breathe calmly and regain the peace of mind that had been hers only minutes earlier.

Still, her mind kept replaying the moment she had spent in Troy's arms, the moment he had kissed her. It was but one moment, and yet she knew she would never forget it. It had changed everything, had it not?

9

All of a sudden, Nora's eyes widened, and she clasped a hand to her mouth as a gasp escaped her lips. "I am to be married in a few days," she murmured to the wind tugging upon her curls. "I am to be married." Her eyes moved to the wall, behind which Troy had disappeared. What was she to do now? Had this kiss meant something? Ought she...?

Oh, dear heaven, what was she to do?

Chapter One

THE HEART REMEMBERS

London, late summer 1803 (or a variation thereof)
Five years later

The streets of London were dark as Troy left his club. Stepping out onto the pavement, he rolled his shoulders, then breathed in deeply the soothing night air. Here and there, a carriage rolled by, the sound of its wheels on cobblestones drifting to his ears. Murmured sounds echoed in the night, reminding him of the buzz of voices he had just escaped. Indeed, it had been a long night, and Troy longed for the solitude of his own chamber.

Just as he turned toward his waiting carriage, an acquaintance rounded the corner, quickening his steps as he spied him. "Leaving so soon?" Lord Kinsley inquired, an excited glow in his eyes. "The night has barely begun."

Offering no more than the barest of greetings in return, Troy nodded. "Be that as it may, I must return home." He was in no mood to hear another one of Lord Kinsley's tall tales. Indeed, the man was the worst tattletale of London, putting any and every gossiping lady to shame.

"Have you heard?" Lord Kinsley rushed to ask as Troy turned toward his carriage.

Troy sighed. "No, nor do I care to." He took another step, but the man was not to be discouraged.

Clearly, the thought of sharing this latest gossip emboldened Lord Kinsley, for he rushed forward and all but stepped into Troy's path, his eyes sparkling with eager delight. "Lord Hayward finally breathed his last," he blurted out, eyes expectant, no doubt eager for Troy's reaction.

Indeed, as much as Troy wanted to disappoint the man, it proved impossible this night. "Lord Hayward...is dead?" he gasped, eyes widening in shock as he stared at Kinsley.

Pleased by Troy's reaction, Kinsley straightened, puffing out his chest. "That he is," he confirmed with a smug smile. Then he laughed, shaking his head. "It comes as a bit of a surprise, does it not?" He frowned. "Although considering the many drunken accidents the man's had throughout his life, I suppose one should have expected such an outcome. Do you not agree?"

Troy had expected no outcome at all, for he had done his utmost these past five years not to think of the man at all. After all, any such thought would have inevitably turned Troy's attention from Hayward to the man's wife.

Nora.

"Poor man broke his neck," Kinsley exclaimed, the look upon his face both pleased and marked by a hint of dismay. "Fell off his horse." Clucking his tongue, he shook his head. "Truly, he ought not have tried to ride home after a night of drunken stupor. Very unwise, that is."

Troy barely heard a word of Kinsley's recounting of how Lord Hayward had met his end. The shock of the news still echoed in his bones, waves of disbelief flooding him. Never had Troy contemplated such a scenario.

Never.

Ever since that day five years ago, when Nora had chosen to wed Hayward, Troy had done his utmost to banish all thoughts of her from his mind. He had not attended the wedding; how could he have?

That one moment by the ruins had changed everything for him.

All his life, Nora had been a friend. *Only* a friend. Nothing more than a friend. And then, from one second to the next, the world had shifted upon its axis, turning everything upside down.

All of a sudden, Troy had become aware of her in a completely different way. That kiss—that one kiss!—had been his undoing. Where before he had been perfectly content to spend the occasional afternoon in her presence, to chat with her and laugh with her, he now wanted more. He no longer sought to be one friend among many. He no longer wished to be *only* her friend. As much as he tried to steer his thoughts back on to familiar ground, they continued to stray, urging him to remember the moment they had shared by the ancient watchtower.

To this day, Troy recalled in excruciating detail the shock in her wide brown eyes the moment they had found themselves in each other's arms. Troy had simply meant to catch her as she fell. He had not intended anything beyond that, and yet the moment she had looked up and their eyes had met...

Closing his eyes, Troy swallowed hard. He could not explain it, for it did not make any sense. He had certainly tried to make sense of it these past five years but failed each and every time.

The devastating truth was that he loved her. Of course, Troy had always loved her in a way. After all, she had been a dear friend. Now, however, the love he felt was different. It was tied to other desires and wishes and longings.

Indeed, this love urged him to remember the softness of her lips and the warmth of her body as they had stood so close that their hearts had beat as one. This love made him wish to hold her again, to run his fingers through her mahogany tresses and gently trace the elegant column of her neck. This love turned his stomach when he thought of her as Hayward's wife.

His wife!

Troy's hands balled into fists as he forced his breathing to even and his emotions back under control. Yes, whenever his thoughts were not sufficiently occupied, he occasionally lost himself to the pain that still lingered. It struck at him then, drilling its talons into his body until he ached all over.

No! He would not think of Nora as Hayward's wife. He would—

Troy paused, his brow furrowing as a dangerous thought surged through his mind. Had he been capable of calm, rational thoughts in that moment, he would have shaken his head at himself that it had taken him so long to realize something so very obvious.

"She's a widow," Troy mumbled under his breath, staring at Kinsley but not seeing the man. "She's no longer his wife."

Kinsley chuckled, a vile sound that made Troy's head snap up. "Yes, Lady Hayward is indeed a rare beauty," he mused, an appreciative glow in his eyes that made Troy want to plant his fist in the man's face. "Damn shame! Young and fetching, she should have no trouble finding herself another husband." Grinning, he winked at Troy. "I wouldn't mind finding her in my bed, mind you." Before Troy could explode, Kinsley shrugged. "If only she weren't barren."

Troy stilled. "Barren?" he echoed, his thoughts still slow to keep up.

Kinsley nodded eagerly. "Five years of marriage, and yet it's Hayward's cousin who inherits. Unfortunately, the fault must lie with her." He leaned closer, conspiratorially. "After all, it is no secret that Hayward has too many bastards to count, and I'm certain he was most eager to get his heir on the lady the moment they were wed." He laughed, another vile, sickening sound. "I doubt he wasted any time seeing her to their marriage bed."

A wave of nausea rolled through him causing Troy to think he would be sick. "Good night, Kinsley," he gritted out, turning away. A few quick steps carried him to his carriage, and he dropped onto the cushioned seat with a groan of agony.

As the carriage pulled away, his hands were still balled into fists against the tremors that seized him, shaking him almost violently. Over the past months, he had successfully dodged each and every reminder of Nora and her husband, and now, it had taken Kinsley no more than a few words to bring forth this raging monster Troy turned into whenever his thoughts went rogue.

Still, this time, a ray of sunshine seemed to fight its way through the dark thunderous clouds of his heart. And as much as Troy tried to close his eyes to it, to ignore it until it went away, a sliver of hope blossomed in his soul.

She's a widow, something whispered to his treacherous heart. *She's no longer Hayward's wife.*

No! Troy brought his fist down hard upon the carriage wall, briefly concerned that he might have caused some damage, completely oblivious to the pain that seared up his arm.

Then he closed his eyes and rested his head against the seat, forcing himself to remember the truth.

The ugly truth that had overshadowed his life these past five years.

Indeed, after their encounter by the ancient watchtower, Troy had paced his chamber like a caged lion, raking his mind about what to do. She was to be married in a matter of days, and yet...

Eventually, Troy had sat down and written her a letter. A letter revealing his love. A letter begging her to call off her nuptials. And he had delivered that letter to her parents' townhouse the morning of Nora's wedding.

Grudgingly, Troy admitted that he ought to have acted sooner. He ought not have waited until her wedding day. Perhaps he ought to have sought her out himself. Yes, all these points were true, and yet he doubted that she would have married Hayward that day if she had cared for him, Troy, the way he had so unexpectedly come to care for her.

The ugly truth was that Nora had not even responded to his letter. Not in any way. She had simply married Hayward...and broken Troy's heart.

She had chosen another, and her being a widow now did not change that fact.

"Forget her," Troy growled into the dark interior of the carriage. "Forget her and move on." Only he had been telling himself to do so for the past five years. Yet his heart was still hers to command.

What was he to do?

Chapter Two

RETURNING HOME

Leighton, early autumn 1803 (or a variation thereof)
A few weeks later

"Please remember to pack the tea from the kitchen, the one the Dowager Countess of Whickerton sent to me," Nora instructed her maid before she stepped back, lingering in the doorway as her gaze swept over her bedchamber.

The view of the lake was breathtaking, and she adored the light blue curtains that perfectly complemented those upon her four-poster bed. The light wallpaper was cheerful, and the tall windows allowed light to flood her chamber, bathing it in a warm glow that had more than once soothed her mind.

Indeed, it was a beautiful chamber, and yet Nora had spent the past five years wishing to be elsewhere.

As her maids continued to pack her things, Nora cast one last look around the room and then turned and walked down the hall. As familiar as the house had come to be to her, it had never felt like home. She had found sanctuary here, away from London, away from her husband, away from his scandalous behavior. Yet it had never been home.

No, she would leave and return to her childhood home, Farther-ington Hall.

At the thought, Nora could not help but note a slight twitch that came to the corners of her mouth. *Could it be a smile?* She wondered if she had become altogether unfamiliar with such an expression. But why would she smile? What reason was there for a smile?

None.

Five years ago, Nora had married a man she thought she had wanted and been bitterly disappointed. For five years, she had shut herself away, existing from day to day with no hope for life to change.

And yet, it had.

Her husband's death had been unexpected, to say the least. Of course, it had been! Never had Nora contemplated the notion of becoming a widow so soon. She had thought herself trapped in this marriage until the end of her days. Yet here she was, a free woman once more. What was she to do?

Out of the distant recesses of her mind, an image arose. One that made the corners of Nora's mouth twitch once more. One that warmed her heart. One that whispered of longing.

Troy.

Over the past five years, Nora had not caught more than a glimpse of him here and there. Whenever they had attended the same event, he had quickly turned away and left, his eyes meeting hers for no more than a split second. Clearly, he disliked the reminder of what had happened between them by the ruins. Indeed, he had not spoken to her since that day.

Not one word beyond required pleasantries.

Not one.

Clearly, that day had meant nothing to him. It had shocked him, certainly; yet it had not turned his world upside down as it had hers. For days, Nora had fought with herself about what to do. After all, she had promised to marry Lord Hayward. She had waited and prayed that Troy would come to her, but he had not. She had told herself that if he would, she would call off her marriage, risk her family's reputation, risk her own future because the simple truth was that her heart wanted him.

Him and no other.

Only he had not come. He had not even attended her wedding. He had left London altogether, running as far as he could from the memory of their ill-advised kiss.

And so, Nora had resigned herself to her fate.

Stepping off the large staircase in the hall, Nora turned toward the drawing room. She had spent countless hours within but would no more. No sadness filled her heart at the thought, only a mild twinge of uncertainty assailed her. What would life be now?

As Nora approached, the sound of soft footfalls drifted to her ears from within. Frowning, she moved forward and then stepped over the threshold. Across the room, she spied a tall, somewhat lanky gentleman pacing up and down in front of the fireplace. "Mr. Clarke?" she exclaimed, noting the way the furrows upon his forehead disappeared as he beheld her. "I had not known you had arrived." She tried her best to smile at him. "Please be assured that I shall be gone by tomorrow. Leighton is all yours."

Brushing a curl of his blonde hair from his forehead, Mr. Clarke strode toward her. "Oh, my dear, that is not why I'm here. I assure you." He grasped her hands, and Nora tensed, fighting the urge to retrieve them. "I came to assure you that Leighton is still your home and always shall be." He swallowed, and a shadow fell over his face. "I know my cousin's passing has come as a shock; however, I have no intention of uprooting you." He sighed and squeezed her hands in what Nora assumed was meant as a reassuring gesture. "These are dark times, and I believe it will do all of us good to hold on to each other."

Nora swallowed, still holding on to her smile—although it was beginning to feel a bit strained. "You are too kind," she told him, then gently extracted her hands, her feet carrying her to the window. "However, I wish to return home."

"Home?" her late husband's cousin exclaimed, a good amount of shock ringing in that one word as he followed in her wake. "But *this* is your home. Nothing has to change. We are...We are family, and you will always be welcome here."

"I do thank you," Nora told him sincerely, remembering the many kind words he had always had for her. Always had they stood in stark contrast to her own husband's dismissive ways. "However, I cannot accept." She looked around the room. "Leighton is yours now, and I hope you and your son will find happiness here." She sighed. "I wish to return home, to Fartherington Hall."

Mr. Clarke's brows drew down, and a frown slowly spread across his face. "I admit I am surprised," he said, his head giving a slight shake. "Why do you wish to return? You told me you spent many happy years there; however, today, Fartherington Hall is no more than an empty place, is it not?" A sorrowful expression came to his eyes. "Your father and eldest brother are dead, and as far as I know, your other brother has chosen a life of touring the continent, has he not?" He shrugged, incomprehension marking his face. "Why then do you wish to return? Would you not be much more comfortable here?"

Nora sighed, reminding herself that only she knew that her brother Christopher had never toured the continent. Instead, he had found a new home in Ireland, choosing to leave England to protect his illegitimate son from wagging tongues. Of course, that also meant he would not be welcoming her back to Fartherington Hall upon her return. Indeed, Mr. Clarke was correct, was he not? Only Nora's mother remained, a woman who knew how to keep to herself. Why then did she want to return?

Pressing her lips together, Nora fought the impulse to speak his name. Alone in her chamber, she had done so every once in a while over the past few years. It had caused an odd thrill to course through her body, always accompanied by a sense of deepest loss and regret, though. Still, she could no more stop these thoughts than she could stop herself from drawing breath.

Meeting Mr. Clarke's gaze, Nora squared her shoulders. She could not shake the impression that only if she appeared determined would he finally relent. "Of course, you are correct. However, my mother, who is very dear to me, asked me to return, and I must admit I long to see her." She willed a smile upon her face. "Yes, I believe it would be wonderful to see my childhood home again. It will give me comfort during these hard times."

Nora could see that Mr. Clarke did not approve of her decision; however, he nodded in acceptance. "Of course. I understand." Again, he took a step closer, his gaze strangely imploring. "However, I want you to know that you are always welcome here."

"Thank you," Nora told him with gratitude in her heart. "You've always been very kind to me. I shall not forget it." She inclined her head to him. "Farewell, Mr. Clarke." Then she turned and walked out of the drawing room, her feet carrying her back upstairs. Yes, even though the dark cloud of her husband's presence no longer lingered here, Nora felt a deep desire to leave this place behind.

Indeed, only when the carriage finally rumbled down the drive early the next morning did she feel a sense of relief, as though a burden had been lifted, one that had been weighing on her for the past five years. She looked out the window at the large estate, the sun glinting off its windows, and knew that she would never return. Whatever life held in stock for her now, it would not include Leighton.

Turning in her seat, Nora left behind her past and tried her best to look toward the future. Yes, she would return home. But what would she find there? The only family she had left in that place was her mother, and they had never been close. Not that her mother was a cold person, but there always had been *something* that stood between them. An invisible barrier that Nora had never been able to make sense of. Still, at least, her mother would be someone to talk to, someone who knew her.

That thought felt comforting.

The thought to not be alone in the world.

Still, now that the carriage was on its way back to her childhood home, Nora could not help but think of all the hopes and dreams she had entertained upon leaving it five years ago. Of course, life did not always provide what one wanted; however, Nora had never thought about it going so horribly wrong. She had been so hopeful, and now, everything was lost. She had neither love nor a family of her own. Nothing to bring her happiness.

Nevertheless, Nora could not help but feel relieved she had not borne Hayward's child. He had blamed her, of course. After all, he already called countless bastards his own. Never had he tried to hide that fact from her. He had never pretended to be faithful. The man she had once thought him to be had quickly vanished after their vows had been spoken.

Oh, what a mistake she had made! Only now, it was too late. She would never be a mother, and she would never marry again. All that awaited her now was loneliness, was it not?

And yet as the wheels turned upon the hardened ground, Nora's thoughts strayed to Whickerton Grove.

Fartherington Hall's neighboring estate.

Troy's home.

Chapter Three

TRAPPED IN TIME

earing his gaze from his sister and his oldest friend, Troy
marched back down the path he had come and headed
toward the stables. He was uncertain why the sight of them
together irritated him so; yet he refused to dwell upon it. He had his
reasons. Sensible reasons, of course.

Calling for his horse to be saddled, Troy paced up and down in
front of the stable doors. He raked a hand through his hair, his gaze
drawn back to the gardens where somewhere inside Juliet and Christopher were going for a stroll. Indeed, he had seen his sister's eyes light
up the moment Christopher had reappeared in their lives. People whispered that he spent his time touring the continent; however, Troy
knew better. Not because his old friend had told him so, but because
Troy had made it his business to find out the truth.

Pulling himself into the saddle, Troy urged his gelding down the
slope toward the open land surrounding Whickerton Grove. He
needed distance. He needed to get away. Usually, the estate's business
kept his mind busy, shutting out all concerns and questions he might
otherwise foolishly entertain. However, since Christopher's return, his
mind had been most adamant in drawing him back to matters past.

To the man's sister.

To Nora.

Gritting his teeth, Troy spurred his mount on, eager to feel the chilling wind tear on his clothes and whip in his face. He had promised himself he would not think of her. He had done his utmost to distract himself, and yet...

A dark growl rose from his throat as his gaze locked upon the far horizon, white clouds drifting overhead across a light blue sky. If only it would rain! He thought. If only it would pour as though buckets of water were dumped upon the earth!

Perhaps it was simply Christopher's return that made thoughts of Nora linger. If only he would leave again! However, if he did, Juliet's heart would break once more.

Troy was certain of it. He had seen it happen once before. Although the eldest of his five sisters had always known how to hide her pain behind a polite expression, Troy had seen the depth of her despair. The thought still made his blood burn with anger. How could Christopher have simply left? Without a word? How could he have done that to Juliet? Although there had been no understanding between them beyond that of friendship, Christopher ought to have... He should have...

Closing his eyes, Troy bowed his head, trusting his gelding to find his way. Yes, he was furious with Christopher for hurting his sister. But that was not why control was repeatedly slipping from his grasp lately, was it? Yes, he liked to believe so; however, deep down, Troy knew better. It was not only Juliet's pain he remembered. It was not only her pain he feared to see spark to life again.

It was his own.

To this day, a part of Troy could not believe that Nora had not sought him out after receiving his letter. She had not even had the courtesy to pen a brief reply. She had simply...married another.

Without a word.

Without an explanation.

Without...

Troy's eyes were unseeing as he thundered along, his thoughts drawn back to that day five years ago. He still remembered how the two of them had charged down the meadow side by side, Nora's mahogany tresses billowing in the wind. It had been a wonderful afternoon, filled with joy and excitement, a dear friend by his side.

And then Troy had suddenly no longer seen the friend who had been in his life since the day she had been born.

From one moment to the next, he had become aware of her in a completely different way...and he had not seen it coming. Countless times, he had looked at her, talked with her, even danced with her; and yet he had never seen what he had seen in that one moment.

If only it had never happened!

A muttered curse flew from Troy's lips at the thought of Nora's hold on him, even after all these years. Could she not simply have remained a friend? But it had been his own bloody fault, had it not? *He* had kissed her, not the other way around. Perhaps she had simply been too shocked by his actions to put him in his place.

The thought turned Troy's stomach. He could have sworn she had kissed him back, but perhaps it had simply been his addled mind that had made him see things the way he wanted them to be.

The memory of their kiss still lingered, as though no more than five minutes had passed since. More than anything, Troy remembered that sudden need to feel her, to hold her in his arms and taste her lips. He recalled the warmth of her skin and the softness of her mouth with excruciating detail. A groan slipped from his lips as longing barreled into him once more. Would it ever stop?

Running a hand through his hair, Troy all but flinched when his gaze fell upon the ruins of the old watchtower. Instantly, his hand jerked on the reins and his gelding tossed up his head, irritated by Troy's erratic behavior, forcing him to drop his gaze and reassure the animal.

When Troy looked up again, his eyes were drawn to the spot where he and Nora had stood five years ago. The spot where he had kissed her. The spot where everything had changed.

At least for him.

Not since that day had Troy come here, and he had not meant to come here today, either. Was it a mere coincidence? Or had his subconscious mind somehow guided him here? It was more than likely, was it not? After all, as much as he hated to admit it, Nora was the most prominent thing on his mind these days.

In truth, she always had been.

Ever since that day.

Yet ever since she had wed Hayward, Troy had been unable to bear thinking of her. Every glimpse of her had been torture. Every thought of her had threatened to drive him mad. Every day had pushed him a little closer to the edge of a dark, endless pit.

In the end, only his father's interference had brought Troy at least some piece of mind—if one could call it that. By handing over the estate's affairs into his care, his father had given Troy something to focus his thoughts, to anchor them to a safe topic. From that day on, the study had been Troy's domain and the ledgers his to watch over. His father's trust in him had felt good, soothing, and Troy had given everything to his family's estate.

Every moment of every day.

Every thought.

Every bit of strength.

Indeed, he had believed himself in control of his feelings, of that pit of fury deep inside, that well of pain. Perhaps he had been fooling himself.

Perhaps the past five years had made no difference at all.

Dismounting, Troy let his gelding graze freely, his own legs carrying him closer to the crumbling wall. A cold wind blew across the meadow, stirring the tall grass and tugging upon his coat. Autumn was well on its way, and leaves everywhere were changing color. Another year was drawing to a close.

Another year, like all the others.

Troy knew well that his life stood still. These past five years, he had done what was expected of him, as a son, a brother, heir to his father's title; yet he had not lived. He no longer knew how.

He suspected the same of Juliet.

After Christopher's departure, she had retreated from the outside world, suddenly content to merely serve as their grandmother's companion. Indeed, Troy had always known that his eldest sister was the most maternal of them all, and to see his four younger sisters married while Juliet remained unwed seemed wrong somehow.

If anyone ought to be a mother, it was Juliet.

Heaving a deep sigh, Troy leaned his shoulder against the rough stone wall, the last remnants of the old tower that yet withstood the ravages of time. Perhaps there was still a chance for Juliet after all. As much as Troy feared she would be hurt again, as much as it pained him to see Christopher and feel himself reminded of Nora day in and out, he knew he could not be selfish. If there was any chance for Juliet to find happiness, he needed to ensure that she would. Was that not what brothers did?

Troy inhaled a deep breath, his molars grinding together as he fought the urge to simply turn his back on this matter. Yet he could not. It was his responsibility and, also, his desire to see his sister happy. And she needed him. She needed him to assure that Christopher's intentions were indeed honorable. He needed to ensure that Christopher had returned for a reason that would not once again shatter Juliet's heart.

However, if Juliet finally received her happily ever after, it meant that Christopher would remain. He would become Troy's brother-in-law, and they would see each other often. Although Troy could not deny that he missed his old friend, something deep inside twisted and turned painfully at the reminder of their shared past. How could he look at Christopher and not think of Nora?

Pushing off the wall, Troy raked his hands through his hair, his fingers grasping, tugging, making his scalp tingle. Somehow, he needed to make his peace with the past. Yet it had been exactly what he had tried his utmost to do for years now and found himself unsuccessful. He paced back and forth, stepping around the boulders strewn about, his gaze blind to his surroundings, his eyes unseeing as his heart thundered wildly, painfully in his chest.

Indeed, where was the calm he had managed to hold on to for so long by burying his head in the earldom's affairs? Had it simply slipped away? Had it taken no more than the mere mention of her name? The mere thought...of her?

Troy felt his hands ball into fists, the desire to plant them somewhere, anywhere, almost overwhelming. His teeth ground together painfully, his steps growing larger and more forceful as he walked aimlessly through the ruins. Every once in a while, he would spin around and walk back the way he had come, as though some kind of enclosure existed around the watchtower, not allowing him to leave, keeping him in this very place.

This one place that had been the site of his doom.

A frustrated growl rose from his throat, and once again, Troy jerked around, his feet moving without thought, his eyes snapping to the horizon.

And then he saw her.

For a moment, Troy was certain he had strayed into a dream. He was certain that he was hallucinating, that he was imagining seeing her. Perhaps the turmoil of the past few years had somehow addled his brain. Perhaps he was no longer capable of rational thought, of seeing what was real.

Blinking, Troy stared across the small stretch of grassland, the stalks swaying softly in the autumn breeze. He blinked again and again, and yet she remained.

Seated atop a honey-colored mare, Nora looked back at him, her eyes wide and her lips slightly parted, as though seeing him had come as an equal shock to her. She wore black from head to toe, and Troy once more heard Lord Kinsley's words echo through his mind. Indeed, Hayward was dead, and Nora was a widow. Unbidden, joy blossomed in Troy's heart; only the feeling was quickly subdued when he reminded himself what her black attire meant. She was in mourning.

Nora was mourning her husband.

His loss.

Was her heart broken?

Troy knew he ought to simply turn and leave. Yes, it would be rude, incredibly so, but it would still be wise. He should not step closer. He should not meet her. He should not speak to her, and he should definitely not look into her eyes.

Yet...

...Troy did not move.

Chapter Four

DARE TO DREAM

After five years, Nora once again stood in her old bedchamber. The room seemed to echo with the memories of a wonderful childhood and youth, reminding her of the dreams she had once harbored, the hopes for a beautiful future she had often entertained. Simply standing in the doorway brought tears to Nora's eyes, and she pressed her lips together to keep them at bay.

"It is good to have you back here," her mother said, her voice lacking the warmth and devotion Nora had hoped for. "It's been a long time."

Nora turned to look into her mother's eyes, wishing she saw something there that would allow her to sink into her arms and feel comforted. Her heart ached to be held, to have her mother's arms close around her and feel safe in her embrace.

However, while Elizabeth Hurst, Dowager Countess of Lockhart, wasn't cold and unfeeling, Nora had always felt as though an invisible wall surrounded her mother's heart, not allowing her to fully engage with her children the way Lady Whickerton always had with such natural ease. As they had all grown up side by side, Nora had often found herself comparing the two mothers. She had always longed for the natural way Lady Whickerton often drew her children into her arms, even if it was only for a quick embrace. The way her hand would occasionally brush their cheek or down their arm, a devoted smile upon her face. The way her eyes would glow, warmed by love and devotion; and a sigh would drift from her lips whenever her gaze fell upon her children.

Nora knew that her mother loved her, and yet, somehow, she did not know how to show it. Sometimes, Nora thought that the love her mother felt for her children was something that bothered her, as though it made her weak and vulnerable. Sometimes, Nora even thought her mother did not *want* to love them.

Especially Christopher.

For some reason, it had always seemed that she loved him least of all.

"You must be fatigued from your long journey," her mother remarked, stepping back instead of closer. "Rest and then meet me later in the drawing room for tea." A small smile flashed across her face, but disappeared quickly, as though it had never been.

Standing in the doorway, Nora watched her mother turn and walk away, her heart aching at the emptiness of Fartherington Hall. Indeed, her father and eldest brother were dead, and while her mother still lived, she did not seem quite here, either.

The only one that remained was Christopher.

To Nora's surprise, her remaining brother returned home to Fartherington Hall not long after. Indeed, it was the Dowager Countess of Whickerton—fondly referred to as Grandma Edie by all who loved her!—who had called him back to attend her youngest granddaughter's wedding.

And his path had crossed Juliet's once more.

Nora could see how deeply her brother still cared for the eldest Whickerton sister and was not in the least surprised that Christopher had no intention of staying at Fartherington Hall. Of course, Nora could hardly blame him. His eagerness to return to Juliet's side was written all over his face, the besotted look upon his features making her smile. Nora loved her brother dearly, and whenever they had seen one another over the past few years—which had not been often—he had looked regretful.

He did not now. Hope shone in his eyes, and Nora felt her heart pause in her chest as she remembered what that felt like.

"Come with me to Whickerton Grove," Christopher exclaimed all of a sudden, his hands holding hers tighter within his own. "Please! Grandma Edie insists I visit. Come with me!"

Shocked by the thought alone, Nora stared up at him. Before she could even form a clear thought, her head began shaking from side to side. "I cannot. I'm still in mourning. I—"

"That is out of the question!" Nora flinched at the sound of her mother's harsh voice. Her eyes seemed cold as they swept over Christopher. Then she turned to look at Nora, all but ignoring her only remaining son. "You cannot attend any events while you're in mourning!"

Before Nora could say anything more, their mother started berating Christopher. Somehow, she always found fault with him, never assuming anyone else could be responsible. Nora could see that her mother's harsh treatment pained him. Indeed, all his life he had done his utmost to earn her respect, her love, but for a reason neither one of them understood, he never had.

"I did not suggest she attend a ball or similar event," Christopher sought to defend himself against their mother's accusations. "I merely think that seeing old friends will do her good." Nora felt his gaze drop to her face, a caring look coming to his eyes. "She does not look well, and I am concerned."

At his words, Nora felt something deep inside her warm. It had been a long time since anyone had spoken to her or about her in such a manner. Indeed, life had been cold lately, absent emotions that sustained the heart. Yes, it felt good to be loved.

A harsh scoff left their mother's lips, and Nora could not help but wonder why she always seemed almost heartless whenever Christopher was nearby. "She looks as any young widow is supposed to look during her year of mourning. Do not lead her astray. Any wrongdoing on her part will severely harm her chances on the marriage mart once her year of mourn—"

"I will not marry again, Mother," Nora interrupted, her gaze hard as she looked at her.

Clearly taken aback, her mother blinked. "Pardon? Why ever would you say that?"

"Whether you like to hear it or not, Mother," Nora insisted, needing her mother to understand that there was no use in trying to seek another match, "no one would want me."

As though slapped, her mother flinched. "Why? What have you done?"

Nora swallowed, remembering this look in her mother's eyes. Always had she been afraid that some kind of scandal would arise that would ruin their family. Yet she had always found excuses for their eldest brother's scandalous behavior. "I failed to give my husband an heir." The moment the words left her lips, Nora felt...relief. Victory perhaps. Indeed, she wanted to be a mother; however, she had not wanted her husband's child. Not after the way he had treated her, betrayed her, destroyed her. "I was married five years, and yet I did not conceive once. I'm barren," she blinked away tears, "and everyone knows or at least suspects it." Holding her mother's gaze, Nora shook her head, needing her to understand that this was not something that could be remedied in any way. "No one will want me, and...I am fine with that." Not wanting to give her mother any chance for a reply, Nora turned upon her heel and left.

Blindly, she walked through the house, well aware that her bedchamber would not give her comfort. No, she wished she could leave, her heart aching for a place that felt...like home. For people that looked at her the way Christopher just had.

A sob tore from her throat, and she pressed her hand to her mouth. Tears collected in her eyes, and yet in that moment Nora could not have said what had brought them on. She did not want to pity herself, yet her life had turned into a series of regrets and longings disappointed. Was this it? Would she now forever wander the halls of Fartherington Hall with nothing to look forward to and no one to love?

Eventually, Nora found herself in the drawing room, her gaze drifting out toward the gardens. She watched as a strong autumn breeze whipped down leaves and sent them dancing through the air. In her mind's eye, she could almost see them all as they once had been:

Sebastian, Christopher and herself as well as Harriet, Christina, Leonora, Louisa, Juliet...and Troy.

Once, long ago, they had been the dearest of friends. Oh, if only they could be again! A desperate longing awakened in Nora's heart, and she wished she could simply saddle her horse and ride over to Whickerton Grove.

Her brother's words continued to echo in her head, urging her to accompany him. Oh, if only she could! Her gaze moved downward and swept over her black gown. Instantly, anger swept through her veins at the thought of this pretense. Why was she forced to mourn her husband when, in truth, she felt nothing but relief at his passing?

Never had Nora thought of herself as someone pliable. Yet with no one to fight for, she did not have the strength to go against convention, against her mother. What good could possibly come of that? After all, even if she were to ride over to Whickerton Grove, she would simply be in the way, would she not? Christopher needed time alone with Juliet, and the other four Whickerton sisters were now happily married and living in their own homes.

Closing her eyes, Nora rested her forehead against the cool windowpane. Envy gripped her at the thought of her old friends, and she wished she had possessed the foresight to choose more wisely. How had they done it? How had they found the one man they could love? The man who loved them as well?

Once, life had seemed so easy, so simple. Perhaps it had been a naïve thought, but Nora had always imagined meeting someone and falling in love and then living happily ever after.

A wistful smile came to her face. Yes, it was nothing more than a fairytale. Perhaps that alone should have told her the happily ever afters were impossible to find, should it not? Yet others had found it. Why not her?

Days passed in painful loneliness as Nora continued to walk the halls of her childhood home. Everything seemed dark and gray, devoid of color, devoid of life. Every day, this gloom weighed a little heavier upon her shoulders, and she felt herself begin to give in under its pressure. Her legs grew weak, and her hands started to tremble.

"What am I to do?" she mumbled to herself. "Should I have

remained at Leighton?" The moment the thought entered her mind, Nora cringed. Even though Mr. Clarke had always been kind to her, he did not feel like family. Nor did her late husband's estate feel like home...or ever would.

No, it had been right to return home to Fartherington Hall. Yet if she remained locked away here every moment of every day, Nora had no doubt she would lose her mind. No, she needed to get out, which, of course, posed a bit of a problem as she was still in mourning.

For a long time, she simply moved from one window to the next, looking outside at the world passing her by. And then a few whispered words dropped from her lips. "Perhaps I should take a quick ride across the fields."

The ghost of a smile tickled the corners of her lips, and Nora knew she did not have a moment to lose.

Indeed, the second she felt her mare's strong body beneath her, felt the wind tug upon her curls and chill her skin, something deep inside Nora broke free. With no regard for anything besides her own need to lose herself in the moment, she gave her mare free rein, leaning forward in the saddle as her horse's hooves thundered across the ground.

Time lost all meaning.

Her regrets slipped away.

And then she saw it.

The old watchtower.

At the mere sight of it, her heart began to dance in her chest, and although it had been a long time, Nora instantly recognized the feeling that swept through her as joy. It was short-lived and quickly replaced by a more familiar one called regret. Still, it had been there, even if only for a moment.

And even though her dreams would forever remain that, dreams, Nora no longer saw any harm in indulging them. Perhaps it would do her good to dream for a little while.

And with that thought in mind, she urged her mare toward the watchtower, eager to relive the moment she had long ago experienced there...

...with Troy.

Chapter Five

INTO A DREAM

S tanding among the ruins of the old watchtower, Troy stared
across the small distance toward where Nora sat atop her horse.
He didn't move. He barely even dared to breathe. Somewhere
deep down, a voice whispered that this had to be a dream while
another, fairly rational-sounding voice reminded him that as a new
widow, Nora had in all likelihood returned to her childhood home. So,
it made sense that she would be here.

But *here*? In this very place?

Of course, it was not Fate that had brought them both here this
day. That was a ludicrous thought. It was nothing more than a coincidence that had their paths cross here today.

Yet did it matter if it had been coincidence or Fate? It froze Troy's
limbs all the same, his heart elbowing aside all rational objections to
his presence here, urging him to remain. Ill-advised or not, he could
not seem to bring himself to leave.

And then Nora dismounted.

Her brown eyes remained locked upon his as she moved as though
through a fog. Troy watched as she brushed her hand down her mare's
neck, her chest rising and falling with a long, deep breath. Her lips

were slightly parted, and her eyes blinked almost rapidly, as though she, too, was uncertain whether this was a dream or not.

And then Troy abandoned his spot.

Only he moved in the wrong direction.

Not away from her.

But toward her.

Slow steps carried him closer, his hands still balled into fists at his sides. He knew not why he was approaching her. They had nothing to say to one another. And yet he could not stop himself.

Nora was certain her knees were about to buckle as she stared at the mirage in front of her eyes. Of course, he could not be here. No, her dreams had to have conjured him. He was not real. He could not be!

And yet the dark look in Troy's eyes cut through her as it had before. She saw the hard twist of his lips and the tension that held him rigid. It was a familiar sight.

Whenever they had crossed paths before, he had always looked at her thus. Anger and something unknown blazing in his eyes, as though she had wronged him in an unforgivable way. Even when she and Christopher had visited Whickerton Grove a year ago, Troy had not looked at her differently. In fact, he had not looked at her much at all. Almost the entire fortnight he had spent locked away in his study, avoiding her, ignoring her. She had understood the message his behavior had been meant to convey with perfect clarity.

Yet here he was, walking toward her. Nora had all but expected him to turn upon his heel and leave without saying a single word. Why was he still here?

With one hand upon her mare's neck, Nora watched him approach, her whole body trembling, as though all strength had left her. What was it about him that did this to her? Why was it only the sight of *him*, the thought of *him*, that made her heart beat stronger in her chest while at the same time stealing the breath from her lungs?

Closer and closer, he came, his steps slow and the look in his eyes unwavering. He barely blinked; his gaze focused upon her in a way that sent a shiver down Nora's back.

It had been so long since she had felt something, anything. All she had known were loneliness and regret, living alone upon a large estate with only servants to speak to. And yet, Nora had preferred loneliness to her husband's company.

While at first, she had found herself blush and smile at Hayward's attentions, she had soon learned that the man rarely thought of anyone but himself. Once, she had thought him kind and considerate, only he had been anything but.

Nora blinked, urging her mind to return from the past to look upon the present standing now barely an arm's length in front of her. "Troy?" she whispered, feeling a deep frown descend upon her forehead. "Are you truly here?"

Looking into his face, Nora felt disbelief mingle with something utterly overwhelming, something warm and joyous. "It is you, is it not?" Nora could not help but feel like a fool for asking this question.

Yet it did not matter.

Linking his arms behind his back, Troy stared down into Nora's face, a myriad of emotions tugging upon his heart. Too many to make sense of. Too many to even sort.

The moment she spoke, he all but flinched. "Troy?" Her voice rang with disbelief. "Are you truly here?" She blinked, and to his utter surprise, he saw something wistful in her eyes. "It is you, is it not?"

Without thinking, Troy nodded, his thoughts for once not crowded by what once had been. No, right here and now, he only knew what was right in front of him.

A gasp left Nora's lips, her eyes widening as they swept over him. "Troy," she mumbled as the corners of her mouth tugged upward.

The sight of her surprised Troy. However, what surprised him even more was the look of her.

The look upon her face.

The look in her eyes.

As much as he had always avoided her presence, she had seemed to do the very same. He remembered well the shocked look upon her face whenever they had stumbled upon one another at an event. Granted, the last time had been long ago. However, Troy remembered it clearly. She had seemed displeased to see him.

She did not now.

Nora's face glowed as she stood before him, and the moment she lifted her hand and reached out toward him, Troy thought he would faint then and there.

His breath lodged in his throat as he watched her hand move closer. He did not understand what was happening, but whatever it was, it shocked him to his core.

And then her hand softly settled upon his arm, just below his shoulder.

Instantly, the glow upon her face intensified and the corners of her mouth curved into a deep smile. "It *is* you," she breathed, disbelief still etched into her voice. "I had not expected to find you here."

"Neither had I," Troy heard himself reply, his voice hoarse, for despite the layers of clothing separating them, he could all but feel her hand upon his arm. He all but felt the warmth of her skin, its softness and gentle touch, and it was driving him mad.

For so long, he had done his utmost to keep away from her, to avoid her presence, to banish her from his thoughts. Now, she stood right here in front of him, her hand still resting upon his arm, as though it were the most natural thing in the world. How was he to make sense of this?

Chapter Six
FRIENDS OF OLD

L ooking up into Troy's face, Nora felt completely at a loss about how to address him, how to speak to him. One second, she was certain she saw her friend of old while in the next...he was suddenly the man who had kissed her.

Here, in this very spot.

Her eyes swept their surroundings, and rather belatedly, Nora realized that, yes, it had been in this very spot that Troy had kissed her more than five years ago. Did he remember that day?

Her gaze returned to his, and the way he suddenly drew in a sharp breath, his eyes widening ever so slightly, told her that he did. But was it a good memory or a bad one? Filled with longing or rather regret?

Nora did not know. She had always thought he had quickly come to regret their kiss. Yet the way he was looking at her now reminded Nora of *that day*.

His pale blue eyes seemed to burn into hers as his chest rose and fell with rapid breaths. She could see his pulse hammering in his neck, his jaw clenched as though he too wished to reach out and...

Nora swallowed, completely overwhelmed by this unexpected moment.

Exactly like the one five years ago.

She withdrew her hand, her palm still tingling with the sudden contact. She had touched no more than his coat, and yet it felt over-whelmingly intimate after the distance that had existed between them thus far.

"What brings you here?" Nora asked abruptly, feeling the need to fill the silence.

Again, his shoulders rose and fell with a deep breath, and for a moment, Nora thought he would not answer, that he would simply turn and leave. Then, the muscles in his jaw relaxed and his lips drifted apart. "Nothing," was all he said, his gaze still fixed on hers.

Nora swallowed, her hands trembling as she fought to think of something else to say. She did not wish for him to leave. In fact, the thought of watching him walk away would no doubt bring her to her knees. She wanted him to stay. She *needed* him to stay. If only for a few moments longer.

"You?" Troy surprised her by returning the question. Again, his lips pressed into a tight line, as though something unpleasant had suddenly resurfaced in his mind.

Nora shrugged. "I simply went for a ride. I needed to get out of the house," she continued, her mind stringing together words in order to keep him here. "There is not much entertainment to be had for a widow." The moment the last words left her lips, Nora knew them to be a mistake.

They served as a reminder for them both, and his face darkened. "My condolences," Troy seemed to grit out through clenched teeth, "on the loss of your husband."

Her words felt like a punch to his chest, and Troy fought to remain upright when all he wanted to do was give into that feeling of overwhelming rage. He wanted to grab her and shake her, snarl into her face and demand she acknowledge what she had done to him.

He did not though.

To his utter surprise, Troy managed to hold on to what flimsy control he had left over his emotions. He pushed thoughts of her and her husband away, knowing they would not serve him.

"Thank you," Nora whispered as she bowed her head, a shuddering breath leaving her lips.

Troy's muscles ached with the tension that lingered in his body. And the moment he saw a dark shadow fall over Nora's face, they almost snapped in two. She had loved Hayward, had she not? Indeed, her husband's loss had shattered her.

Troy scowled. Clearly, she had not known her husband. Clearly, she had not known the man he had been, for she could not have loved him then, could she? Had he been different at home with her? Had he been kind and devoted and—?

Gritting his teeth harder, Troy shook his head, trying to dislodge these torturous thoughts. "I bid you a good day," he forced out and then stepped back, determined to end this torment.

"No! Please!" Nora's hand shot out and grasped his arm, holding him in place. Her eyes were wide and filled with longing as she looked up at him pleadingly. "Please stay! Please don't go!"

Even though Troy knew it to be ill-advised, the sorrow he saw upon her face tempered the anger in his veins. Sadness overshadowed her eyes, and the need in her voice, the pleading tone, made his heart twist painfully. The sensation awakened emotions that had been long dormant. Emotions that felt for another.

The need to protect another.

To soothe and comfort.

Troy had not thought of her in that way in a long time. "Why?" he demanded, his voice harder than he wanted it to be as his insides waged a war about how to respond.

Her hand tightened upon his arm. "I missed you," she said simply, despair heavy in her voice. She looked so vulnerable, almost broken. "We used to be friends. Can we not be friends again?"

Troy's eyes closed. *Friends?* Indeed, they had been friends...once. Yet, he had not thought of her as a friend in a long time. Ever since *that day*, she had not simply been his friend. Ever since that day, she had been nothing to him...

...but still she meant everything.

Would it be wise to accept her back into his life as a friend? Troy knew from the way his heart twisted and twitched as he stood only an arm's length away from her that he could not look at her and simply see a friend. Could he pretend?

Perhaps.

Perhaps not.

Still, the thought to simply walk away, to return to that distance that had been between them these past few years, felt utterly painful. Troy could not deny that he desired to have her back in his life as ill-advised as it was. It was the truth, nothing more. It was what he wanted, and want was rarely rational and quite often far from wise.

It simply was...what it was.

Nora could see a myriad of thoughts drifting across Troy's face. He looked torn, and that gave her hope. After everything she had lost, Nora needed this.

Needed him.

Looking up into his blue eyes, now thunderous and overshadowed, she realized only in this very moment how deeply she had missed him. Before, she had not allowed herself to think of him much, perhaps sensing deep down that it would be too painful. Yet now, he stood right here in front of her, and she could no longer imagine simply letting him walk back out of her life.

"How is your family?" Nora asked, once again to fill the silence, to prevent him from suddenly whipping around and walking away.

Troy's gaze focused on hers once more. "They are well," he told her, his words somewhat hesitant, as though he was uncertain whether he should answer, whether he wanted her as his friend once more.

Nora nodded, trying her best to smile at him. "I heard Harry was recently married," she continued, fighting the urge to reach out and touch him once more. Was he truly here? Was this truly happening? "I suppose that came as a bit of a surprise to everyone, did it not?"

The expression upon Troy's face remained serious; yet he nodded. "It did," was all he said.

"How are your new brothers-in-law?" Nora inquired, wishing she knew them, wishing she was still a part of this life they had once shared. "Are they good men? Are your sisters happy?"

Once again, Troy's head gave a quick nod before a muscle in his jaw twitched and then hardened. "And your husband?" he all but snarled. "Was *he* a good man?"

Shocked by his anger, by this question, Nora stared up at him. "Why would you ask me that?" She shook her head, wondering how he could not know, wondering about the reasons for his anger. Had he not been the one to turn from her? Could he truly blame her for trying to move on?

Troy shrugged. His gaze remained hard, and Nora could see that, for some reason, he was furious with her. But why?

Inhaling a deep breath, knowing that if she wanted him to stay, if she wanted him to speak to her as a friend would, she needed to reach him somehow. She needed to remind him of who they used to be to each other. "Why are you angry with me?" she asked bluntly. "For I can see that you are. I know we have not been close these past few years; however, I still look at you and see a friend. Why can you not do the same? Please, talk to me."

To Nora's relief, the look upon Troy's face softened. Not much, but at least a little. It gave her hope once more.

"Christopher told me," Nora continued, hoping that this time he would answer her, "that Grandma Edie invited him to visit you at Whickerton Grove." She cast him a tentative smile. "I've heard it whispered that she has become quite the formidable matchmaker."

A scoff left Troy's lips, and to Nora's surprise and relief, it echoed with a hint of humor. "I suppose one can say that," he agreed and heaved a deep breath. "In fact, I doubt any of my sisters would be married today if it wasn't for her."

Nora's heart beat hard against her rib cage as she watched the anger drain from Troy's face. She did not quite understand why, but she was grateful. "Is that so? Indeed, I would've loved to be there, to see her work her magic."

Troy frowned down at her. "Magic? Would you not object to someone meddling in your affairs? Would you actually welcome it?"

Nora considered his words carefully. "I suppose, in general, I would object, yes. However, I know that her heart beats for you, for all of you, and she would never do anything that wasn't for your own good."

Still frowning, Troy shook his head. "Do you truly believe that? Do you truly believe it right that she should do as she did? I cannot help but think that another can never know what is best for one as one can for oneself."

Nora smiled up at him, delighting as much in the way they now spoke to one another as she did in that feeling that caused the corners of her mouth to curl upward. "Is her success not proof enough? Are your sisters not happily married?"

Again, Troy scoffed, and again, the sound seemed to hold humor. "They are," he admitted. "However, as far as I observed, they were not too happy with our grandmother's interference."

"Perhaps not at the time," Nora suggested with an arched brow. "However, I cannot help but think that they are grateful now."

Troy regarded her thoughtfully. Then a muscle in his throat tightened. "What of you? Did you choose on your own? Or did someone *meddle* in your affairs as well?"

Nora swallowed. "My mother approved of the match and welcomed it," she admitted, knowing she could not lie to him. Not to Troy. "But he was my choice." She closed her eyes for a brief second before looking up to meet Troy's gaze once more.

Chapter Seven

BETWEEN THE LINES

At Nora's admission, Troy turned away, his feet carrying him away from her. It had been foolish of him to ask because deep down, of course, he had known the truth. Hayward had been her choice, and he needed to make his peace with that fact.

"What of Juliet?" Nora blurted out, a few quick steps carrying her forward until she stepped around him and into his path. "What of Juliet?"

Troy frowned, oddly relieved that she had stopped him. While his mind knew he needed to get away, his heart thought differently. "What of Juliet?" he returned the question, well aware of what she was asking.

Nora sighed, her wide brown eyes sweeping over his face. "You know very well what I'm asking," she said, as though echoing his thoughts. Accusation swung in her voice, and somehow it reminded Troy of conversations they had had long ago. "Do not pretend you do not. I know you've seen the way they look at one another."

Sighing, Troy nodded, trying his best to ignore the tingle of delight that danced across his skin. "I have."

"And?"

"And what?"

Huffing out an annoyed breath, Nora shook her head. "Why do you pretend you do not know what I'm asking?"

Troy looked down into her face, feeling a strange sense of familiarity. Indeed, long ago, they had known how to speak to one another. "Because I do not care to think on it."

Frown lines came to Nora's forehead. "Why not? Christopher is your oldest friend. You've always been like brothers." Her frown deepened. "Do you object to him?"

Troy hung his head. It had been a long time since he had shared his thoughts with another. And Nora's reappearance in his life had him thrown. Her being here, merely an arm's length away, felt so familiar and, at the same time, so very strange.

Nora's gaze softened. Then she once more reached out a hand and placed it upon his arm. Troy almost flinched. "What happened between the two of you?" she inquired thoughtfully. "You know he cares for your sister. Why would you object to him? He has done nothing wrong."

Clearing his throat, Troy stepped back, welcoming and regretting the loss of her touch immediately. "He broke her heart," he snarled, looking at her with accusing eyes. "He left without a word, without an explanation."

A shadow fell over Nora's face, and she nodded. "He did," she confirmed, her head slowly bobbing up and down as she seemed to be searching for words. "But it was not because he did not care for her. You must believe me. There were other...circumstances that... I think...I think he may have realized too late how much she meant to him."

Squinting his eyes, Troy searched her face. That odd tone in her voice had not escaped him, and he could not shake the notion that... "Do you know?" he asked, watching her most carefully.

Nora's eyes slowly grew round, and although she hesitated to speak, Troy saw his suspicion confirmed. "Know what?"

"You know where he's been these past few years, do you not?" Troy asked, still watching her most carefully. "You know about...Ireland." He paused, unable to speak the words clearly, wondering if he had misunderstood.

Then, however, Nora's eyes flew open, and she stared at him with a bit of shock. "You know about his...," her voice dropped to a whisper, "about his son? Did he tell you?"

Troy's lips pressed into a thin line, and he shook his head. "He did not." Only too well did he remember how Christopher had vanished from one day to the next. "That is precisely the point, is it not? He made his choices without saying anything...to anyone."

Nora drew in a deep breath. "I think...I think he wanted to, but he was afraid of what...she would say." Something odd rested in her eyes, as though she were no longer speaking of her brother and Juliet.

Troy swallowed hard. "So, he simply left and broke her heart? Is that the man he is?"

Staring at him, Nora shook her head. "I admit what he did was wrong, but we all make mistakes, do we not? No one is free of mistakes. He tried to do the right thing." Her gaze fell from his, and her teeth dug into her lower lip. "It was...an impossible situation, and he did the best he could. I think he always regretted what happened."

Raking a hand through his hair, Troy felt as though his head were spinning. He was beginning to have trouble telling the difference between when they were speaking of Christopher and Juliet and when they were speaking of themselves. And they were speaking of themselves, were they not? Like Christopher, Nora, too, had one day simply disappeared from Troy's life.

Without a word.

Without an explanation.

"Then why is he back now?" Troy asked, then he held up a hand to stop her when she was about to reply. "I know my grandmother invited him. However, I refuse to believe that that is the reason. Yes, I admit I was happy to see him when he first arrived. It felt...familiar." The ghost of a smile tugged upon the corners of his mouth, surprising him as much as her. "I miss those times. I do. However, if life has taught me anything, it is that regrets and wishes have no bearing upon what is."

Nora blinked her eyes, her lashes fluttering up and down as tears collected in the corners. "I know," she whispered, her voice sounding choked all of a sudden. "Believe me, I know regrets and I know what it means to wish for something you know you will never have." Her shoulders drew back as she inhaled deeply, her chin lifting in determination. "However, is this truly the case here? Are you saying that there is no chance for Christopher and Juliet?"

Troy wanted to insist that there was no chance whatsoever; however, he could not. "I am uncertain," he finally said, torn about what to do. "I know that...Juliet loves him, but I also know that sometimes love is not enough. I do not want to see her hurt again. Yes, if there is a chance for them to be happy again, I will not stand in their way. Still, right here, right now, I cannot help but have doubts."

Chapter Eight

IN THE ARMS OF ANOTHER

" I have doubts as well," Nora admitted, wondering if he could see the truth of it upon her face. "However, I also have hope. I looked into his face when he spoke of her and..." Smiling, she shrugged. There were no words, were there? Indeed, Christopher had seemed like a different man. How does one explain something like that? "Did you not see it as well?"

With a begrudging look upon his face, Troy nodded. "I know he cares for her, and that she cares for him, but as I said, sometimes, that is not enough."

Nora nodded in agreement. "At least, their affection is not one-sided," she could not help but whisper, wishing that her own heart had chosen as wisely as her brother's. "That would be most tragic, would it not?"

Troy stood very still, as though those words had left his lips and not hers. His gaze narrowed, and he breathed in deeply. Then he blinked and took a step back. "Do you know what his intentions are? Why did he return? Why is he at Whickerton Grove as we speak?"

Nora shrugged, wishing she too could accept such an invitation. "I do not know. He did not speak to me of his intentions."

"Then I shall speak to him," Troy replied with a bit of a growl. "She is my sister, and as her brother, it is my duty to protect her heart."

The way he phrased his concern warmed every fiber of Nora's being. Indeed, Troy had a way of pushing people away, of holding them at arm's length. He knew how to act cold and distant in a shockingly convincing way, as though he truly wanted nothing to do with those concerned.

However, it was only a mirage, was it not?

Deep down, Troy loved most ardently and with all his heart. He was fiercely loyal, and she had often seen him act without regard for his own well-being when someone he cared for was at risk. Once, he had done so for her as well.

"Do you remember," Nora whispered, looking deeply into his eyes, "the day that wild dog charged me?"

She had been barely sixteen at the time, and Troy, at three-and-twenty, had seemed far too grown-up to engage in silly pranks. Yet when she had asked him to accompany her to the pond because she wished to catch a frog and put it in Sebastian's bed after he had hidden a small garden snake in her vanity, Troy had come along.

He had rolled his eyes at her and grinned in a highly indulging way, but he had come along.

Taken aback, Troy cleared his throat. "I remember, yes," he finally said, and his features hardened as he undoubtedly recalled the attack.

After a short walk, they had been in the meadow behind Fartherington Hall. While their siblings had turned to a game of cricket, the two of them had gone to hunt for a frog. However, before they had ever reached the pond, a scraggly and malnourished dog had rushed at them. Nora had been terrified at the sight; her limbs unable to move as the animal had charged her.

At the time, Troy had been a good bit behind her—for she had skipped ahead of him, picking flowers and humming to herself. However, the moment he saw the dog, she heard him call out to her.

Still, frozen in shock, Nora had been unable to move. She had stared at the animal, watched its approach.

Closer and closer.

Her fear rising with each leap the dog made toward her.

When the creature had been almost upon her, Nora had shrieked and stumbled backward, falling into the high grass. She had held up her arm to ward off the attack, had felt perhaps a nick of the creature's teeth upon her arm before Troy had suddenly been there.

Without a moment of hesitation, he had yanked the snarling animal away from her. The dog, however, would not be deterred. Immediately, it attacked again.

Only this time, Troy had shielded her from the desperate creature. The dog's teeth had sunk into Troy's arm, the arm held up in a defensive gesture as he had pushed Nora behind him, telling her to run.

Wiping at the tears in her eyes, Nora held Troy's gaze, the expression upon his face suddenly free of pain and anger despite the gruesome memory her words had conjured. Instead, his gaze swept over her almost lovingly, that Nora felt a gasp slip from her lips.

Her jaw quivered, and her knees trembled, but Nora managed to place one foot in front of the other. Her eyes held his, and her hands reached out to touch his arm.

Seeing her intention, Troy's breath seemed to freeze in his chest, and yet he did not move to stop her. He stood stock-still and waited.

Her fingers brushed over the fabric of his coat before one hand grasped his wrist while the other slowly pushed up the sleeve of his coat as well as the shirt below.

Troy jerked the moment her gloved fingers touched his bare skin, yet his eyes never veered from hers as she revealed the scars he had retained from that day.

Nora remembered how profusely the wound had bled; now, only a few silver lines remained where his skin had been cut upon the dog's teeth.

Fortunately for them both, the animal had been driven by desperation, its body weak and failing; and so, Troy had managed to kill it with a swift stroke of the blade he always kept tucked in his right boot. Nora had teased him about it once or twice, about his insistence to always be prepared as one never knew what the day would bring.

After that day, she had not done so again.

Lifting her eyes, Nora swallowed as she found his gaze fixed upon hers, an intensity showing there that took her breath away. The pulse in his wrist beat wildly below her fingertips, and Nora wished in that moment that she wasn't wearing gloves. What would his bare skin feel like against hers?

A shuddering breath lifted Troy's chest, and Nora sensed that he was about to retreat.

Instantly, panic flooded her and without another thought, she all but surged forward, wrapping her arms around him and laying her head against his shoulder. She held on tightly, ignoring the rigid stance of his body, as though he weren't a living being but a stone column instead, part of these old ruins. "Will you come back?" she whispered into the folds of his coat, not daring to look up at him. "Tomorrow perhaps or the day after."

Silence stretched between them, and Nora feared that any moment now she would feel his hands settle upon her arms and urge her back. In her mind's eye, she could see him step back, his expression hard, before he turned and walked away, never to return. The image made Nora's heart ache, and she squeezed her eyes shut against the pain, against the loneliness that threatened to return, drawing her back into its clutches.

And then Troy's chest rose once more with a deep breath and before Nora knew what was happening, she felt his arms close around her. He held her tightly, all but urging her closer, something almost possessive in the way he crushed her against him. Yet at the same time, his hands were gentle as they brushed up and down her back, soothing and comforting, exactly what she needed.

Tears slipped from her eyes, and her fingers clawed into the fabric of his coat, holding on as though for dear life. How long had it been since anyone had held her?

It felt as though a lifetime had passed since.

Never had there been any tenderness between Nora and her late husband. He had never looked at her with any depth nor sought to offer comfort when she had needed it. Neither had she had any close friends after she had retreated from society to Leighton, her husband's country estate. She had sought to put distance between her husband and herself, but in doing so, she had also lost touch with everyone who had ever meant anything to her. Her brother had been in Ireland, and her mother had remained at Fartherington Hall, refusing to leave the estate as always, not even willing to make an exception to visit her only daughter.

And now, after all this time, it was Troy who held her tightly in his arms. Troy who offered comfort. Troy who rested his chin on top of her head and breathed in deeply, as though he cherished this moment as much as she did.

When Nora had left for her ride today, she had not expected, not even dared to hope for anything meaningful to alter the dreariness of her life. And now, here she was.

Back at the old ruins.

Back in Troy's arms.

Was this a dream?

If so, she never wanted to wake.

Chapter Nine

A CLEAR LINE

Returning home from the old ruins, Troy felt as though he was still caught in a dream. Nothing seemed real. Not the crunch of leaves beneath his horse's hooves. Not the chilling breeze reaching out its icy fingers. Not even the cold air he drew down into his body. Everything felt muted and far away as his mind turned and his heart ached.

A dark curse left Troy's lips. Of course, his heart would ache. After all, he had barely used the thing in years. He had tried his utmost to keep everything away, every emotion that might prove his undoing. Of course, he had not always been successful. Yet, today had been wildly different than those few moments he had felt close to losing control.

Today had been...

He shook his head, unable to find the words. "Nora," he whispered to the wind, barely seeing the world around him, trusting his mount to carry him home. "Nora."

Blinking, Troy shook his head, wondering if this truly was a dream and he would wake from it at any moment. He was not certain whether he liked that thought. Had she truly been there? At the ruins, of all places? Had he truly held her in his arms today? After years of barely catching a glimpse?

His gelding tossed up his head, neighing softly and thus drawing Troy's attention to his family's estate as it slowly appeared from behind a large grove of trees. Smoke crawled out of the chimneys into the overcast sky. Yet even from this distance, Troy glimpsed two figures strolling through the gardens. Juliet and Christopher? He wondered, uncertain how he felt about this development. Was there truly a chance for them to find happiness despite everything that had happened? Or would it be wise for him to interfere before Juliet invested more of her heart?

Troy hung his head, knowing beyond a shadow of a doubt that it was already too late for that. Juliet loved Christopher. She always had. There would be no saving her heart if he were to leave again.

Nora.

Inevitably, Troy's thoughts circled back to her. That sense of disbelief still lingered, and yet he could still smell the soft scent of her hair as she had stood in his embrace. He could still feel the warmth of her body leaning into his. He could still feel his heart beat in a slightly different rhythm, as though this one moment had changed everything.

Changed him.

Raking a hand through his hair, Troy muttered a curse under his breath. No matter how he felt, nothing had changed. Not truly. He knew that, and he would do well to remember it. Indeed, he had been a fool for venturing to the ruins in the first place. He ought to have paid better attention to his surroundings. At the very least, he ought to have left immediately the moment Nora had appeared upon the horizon. He ought to have turned and left. He ought to have exchanged not a single word with her.

And yet he had, his heart weak for her, unable to resist that look in her eyes. Those wide, round eyes of hers had looked at him in a way that still made his heart falter in his chest. He had felt transported back to that moment five years ago, the deep longing for her reawakening, that odd sense of belonging with her.

He had been a fool then, and he had been a fool again today. Whatever he thought he had seen in her face, in her eyes, had never been there. She wanted to be his friend again. Nothing more. That was the truth, but was it a truth he could live with?

That weakness inside him urged him to consider continuing their friendship, answering that desperate need to keep her in his life, to not lose her all over again. Yet another part, one perhaps more rational, urged him to consider the consequences of seeing her beyond the glimpses he had caught over the past five years. What would it do to him to be her friend, but nothing more?

Returning his gelding to the stables, Troy stepped into the house. With his four younger sisters now married, Whickerton Grove seemed quiet these days. He could not deny that he missed all the silly antics, especially those his two youngest sisters had often been up to. He missed the laughter and silliness children brought to a home, wondering if he would ever hear it again.

Indeed, he ought to consider marriage. Troy knew that, had tried hard not to remind himself of that fact the past few years. Yet every once in a while, the thought had registered, loud and clear, making him want to turn and run from it.

Troy drew up short when voices echoed to his ears. He turned toward the drawing room and found the door ajar. As he stepped closer, he was able to make out not only his grandmother's voice but also that of the Scotsman, Keir MacKinnear. The man was the grandson of Grandma Edie's oldest friend. Decades ago, she had married a Scot and moved to the Highlands. Why Keir was here now, no one quite knew, except for Grandma Edie, of course. Apparently, she had called him down for some reason she insisted on keeping from them all.

In the next moment, the door opened all the way, and none other but his grandmother stepped out into the hallway. A shrewd look rested in her pale eyes as they swept over him. Then she moved toward him, lifting a hand, and giving his arm a slight pat. "Are you all right, dear boy? You look as though you've seen a ghost." Then she chuckled and, without waiting for him to reply, hobbled down the hall.

Frowning after her, Troy wondered about the knowing look in her eyes, as though she had seen right into his head, worse, right into his heart. Was it possible that she somehow knew he had seen Nora today? It seemed impossible. And yet Troy knew that with regards to his grandmother, that word held no meaning at all.

"She has a way of unsettling one, does she not?" Keir asked in his Highland brogue, a bit of a grin upon his face as he stood leisurely resting his shoulder against the door frame. His long hair was, as always, tied at his nape, his attire not that of a gentleman, but rather reminding Troy of a huntsman, trailing prey in the woods.

Pinching the bridge of his nose, Troy nodded. "I don't mean to be rude," he began, "but why are you here?"

Keir laughed. "I wish I could tell ye, but I've given my word." A bit of a frown came to his face, yet that good-natured grin remained. "Perhaps I shouldna have done so. I admit I had no idea yer grandmother was such an elaborate schemer. Next time, I shall be more cautious."

Troy nodded. "I believe that to be wise." He regarded the Scotsman carefully, then shook his head. "So," he said slowly, watching the other man with care, "she is planning something, is she not? I must admit, it makes me a bit nervous."

In a surprising show of companionship—considering they had only met a few weeks past—Keir grasped Troy's right shoulder and gave it a reassuring squeeze. "Dunna worry. I assure ye it has nothing to do with ye."

Troy frowned, relieved but wishing he knew more. "Is there anything you can tell me?"

Keir's eyes narrowed, and he reached back with one hand to rub the back of his neck, thinking. "Ye know yer grandmother as well as anyone in this house, so I suppose I could tell ye that she asked me to aid a friend of hers and it wouldna come as a surprise to ye, would it?" A bit of a wicked grin came to his face. "I hope that helps."

Troy returned the man's smile. "No, it does not. However, it is not much to go on." Indeed, who could be that friend? Was it someone he knew?

Over the course of the past year, his grandmother had seemed rather busy matchmaking. Troy was absolutely certain that she was the reason his four youngest sisters were now married. Who had she set her sights on next? Juliet?

Quite possibly, considering Christopher's revelation that his return to English shores had been due to a letter from Grandma Edie. Of course, it had been her. Of course, she was the one once again meddling in their affairs, clearly believing that Juliet and Christopher belonged together. Although Troy worried she might be wrong, he could not deny that knowing his grandmother's opinion on the matter soothed his concerns. As much as he disliked admitting it, the woman was rarely wrong.

In that moment, Troy could not help but wonder if his grandmother would seek to match him next, once she had succeeded in seeing Juliet wed to Christopher. He shuddered at the thought. Yet he knew he could not prolong a decision much longer. He had already passed his thirtieth year, and as his father's only son, it was his duty to provide an heir, to continue the line and pass down his family's title and estates. It was his responsibility to ensure his family's future, their happiness and well-being, to see them provided for and wanting for nothing.

In order to do that, he needed to wed. Closing his eyes, Troy wondered whom his grandmother would choose for him. Thus far, he knew she had chosen matches of the heart, not based on fortune or standing or reputation. No, at the core of all his sisters' unions was a deep, all-consuming love.

Nora.

"Are ye all right?" came Keir's voice as though from far away, concern in the way he once again squeezed Troy's shoulder. "Ye look shaken."

Clearing his throat, Troy moved so the other man's hand slipped from his shoulder. "I am fine," he insisted, steeling his voice and drawing back his shoulders. "It is nothing."

A knowing look came to Keir's eyes as he nodded his head slowly. "In my experience, when people say 'tis nothing, 'tis always something. Something rather profound, I might add." His brows rose slightly as though in encouragement, and for a moment, Troy felt tempted to speak honestly.

Then, however, he shook his head, reminding himself that the man was essentially a stranger. Yet, truth be told, he could not imagine speaking about this matter to anyone in his family, either. Perhaps it was simply who he was. Not one to share with others what went on deep inside his heart and soul. He never had been.

"In my case," Troy finally said, "it is truly nothing. I assure you."

Keir nodded. "Verra well." Still, the look in his eyes held doubt, emphasized a moment later as he continued, "If ye change yer mind, ye know where to find me." Then he walked away down the hall.

Troy stared after him, knowing that words would change nothing. Facts remained what they were, and it was a fact that Nora only saw him as a friend. Troy needed to accept that and move on.

Remembering the way she had been in his arms not long ago, he knew he could never be her friend. It would be torture, unbearable and crushing. No, he would not return to the ruins, no matter how many tears had glistened in her eyes as she had begged him to meet her again tomorrow.

He needed to end this, now. Draw a clear line. Protect himself.

Chapter Ten

AN UNEXPECTED VISITOR

Seated next to her mother on the settee, Nora carefully added another few stitches to her embroidery before looking up.

Her mother's head was bent over her own work, eyes focused, her mind elsewhere. Why would it not be? Nora wondered as she allowed her gaze to sweep over the drawing room.

In the corner, a tall grandfather clock counted out each moment that passed, never to be seen again. A sharp wind rustled the leaves outside, carrying them up before suddenly dropping them to the hard ground. The sun only peeked through the dark clouds here and there, fighting a losing battle.

Nora sighed, her gaze once more returning to her mother. Was this it? She wondered. Was this all her mother did day in and out? Rise early and dress for a day spent in loneliness? Hours of embroidery? Meals eaten in silence? Long moments staring out the window, wondering, wishing?

At Leighton, at least, Nora had seen to their tenants, to the village nearby. She had been the lady of the house, and while it had been her duty, she had also appreciated the task it set her. It had given her a purpose, something to do, to accomplish, to keep her mind from wandering to her husband's philandering ways.

Especially with Christopher still unmarried, their mother was still in charge of Fartherington Hall. Did she not care for it? Did she truly not wish for more?

The mere thought pained Nora.

In her youth, Nora had never paid much attention to her mother's daily routine. She had not seen that resigned look in her pale eyes, the way her lips often pressed together as though to hold at bay some harsh, torturous emotion. Yet the signs had to have been there, did they not? After all, Nora could not remember her mother being any different than she was today. Of course, when her father had still been alive, life had seemed...somewhat different. She remembered the occasional look shared between her parents, something that whispered of deeper emotions, of shared longing. Yet all that had ended, the day her father had passed away, leaving her mother behind in a world of regret. Was that not so?

Although Nora did not know the exact circumstances, she could not imagine it to be anything different. Indeed, what she saw in her mother's face was regret.

Closing her eyes, Nora inhaled a deep breath, wondering if she was looking at her own future. Would this be her life from now on as well? Now that she was a widow? Now that every chance for love was gone?

Troy.

At the thought of him, Nora felt a soft tug upon the corners of her mouth. It was involuntary, and she loved it. Yet, it also brought sadness. She had asked him to be her friend again, and yet even in that moment she had wanted so much more. Surprised, she found that this was a far greater torture than the marriage she had borne for five years.

Seeing Troy again so unexpectedly had swept Nora away into a dream where no rules existed, where nothing was impossible, where hope could still prevail. Now, however, she knew she had been a fool to allow herself to dream, even if only for a moment.

The day after she had met Troy, Nora had returned to the ruins, hoping, praying that he would be there. She had waited for as long as she could, but he had not come.

Neither had he come the days after, and with each disappointment, Nora's heart had broken a little more. Loneliness crowded around her, threatening to suffocate her, and she desperately clung to the memory of his warm embrace.

Tears pricked her eyes, and she drew in a sharp breath when her needle accidentally broke the skin of her finger.

Her mother looked up, a slight frown coming to her face as she watched Nora draw the tip of her finger into her mouth. "Are you all right?"

Nora nodded, fighting to blink back the tears that threatened. She was far from all right. Yet speaking of it would change nothing, would it? This was her life now, sitting on this settee, in this very room, day after day.

A voice deep inside chided her for entertaining such gloomy thoughts, for pitying herself the way she did. Yet the problem was that Nora had nothing to throw in the balance. Nothing to look forward to. Nothing to comfort her. How was she to convince herself that her life was not meaningless if she could not name a single thing that brought her joy?

But that was not true, was it? There was something, or rather someone, who brought her joy. Heartache as well, yes, but also joy. Despite her disappointments, despite his failure to appear, Nora could not help but smile and sigh every time she thought of him.

Abruptly pushing to her feet, Nora dropped her embroidery on the settee and then rushed toward the door.

"Where are you going?" her mother called after her, an indignant tone in her voice. "What is the meaning of this?"

Nora paused at the door, torn between the foolishness of seeking out the ruins yet again and the desperate need to try, to cling to that last shred of hope. "I need a bit of fresh air," she told her mother, willing her voice not to tremble as she looked back at her over her shoulder. "I shall be back shortly." Then she left without another word, afraid her mother would find some reason to detain her.

Nora could not say why, but she needed to leave right this second. A desperate need to see Troy burned in her veins, the need to at least lay eyes on him. But what if he did not come? It was very likely that he would not; after all, he had failed to appear all the days prior. Would she be tempted to ride to Whickerton Grove? Nora wondered, flinching at the thought. It was a place she had always loved, but also a place she had not seen in a year. It was Troy's home, and by not appearing, he had stated quite clearly that he did not wish to see her. Was she a fool to think about it?

Or simply desperate?

After changing into her riding habit, Nora rushed outside, welcoming the crisp air upon her heated skin. Dark clouds still loomed overhead, and yet they could not detain her. *Let it rain*, she thought, smiling despite the heavy weight upon her heart.

Guiding her honey-colored mare away from the house, Nora flinched when she suddenly heard her name called. One precious moment, she thought it might be Troy, but then she turned in the saddle to see that it was not. Instantly, her heart sank. "Mr. Clarke?" she exclaimed as he rode closer, and she could make out his face. "I am utterly surprised to see you here."

Bowing his head at her, Mr. Clarke smiled, his clothes travel-worn and his boots far from spotless; yet he appeared in good spirits. "Perhaps I ought to have sent a letter ahead," he remarked with a shrug, a hint of self-reproach coming to his eyes. "I apologize. I assure you I had no intention of startling you."

Trying to hide her annoyance with his sudden appearance at Fartherington Hall, Nora waved his concerns away. "Do not worry, Mr. Clarke. All is well. Pray tell what brings you here?" She glanced toward the far horizon, hoping he would not detain her for long.

The smile upon Mr. Clarke's face seemed to brighten. "I came to bring you this," he said, then rummaged in his inside coat pocket and drew out a small pouch. Holding it out to her, he said, "You seemed to have forgotten this at Leighton. It looked important, and so I took it upon myself to return it to you immediately."

Frowning, Nora took the small pouch from him. She loosened the string and then poured the contents into her palm. When her eyes fell upon the delicate pearl necklace her parents had given her on her sixteenth birthday, her frown deepened. "This is odd," she mumbled, then looked up into his still smiling face. "I am certain my maid packed this. I saw her put it away myself. How do you come to be in its possession?"

Shrugging, Mr. Clarke glanced down at the necklace. "That, I cannot say. After you left, one of the maids found it in your bedchamber. However, I cannot speak to how it came to be there. It must've been an accident."

Nora nodded, still confused. "Well, whatever the reason, I thank you. Thank you very much for returning it to me." Again, frown lines creased her forehead. "I'm surprised you brought it over yourself. You should not have taken that burden upon yourself, Mr. Clarke. Could you not have sent someone else instead?"

"Nonsense!" Mr. Clarke exclaimed, a determined look coming to his face. "I know how dear it is to you. So, I set out to return it to you immediately. I assure you it was no bother."

"You are too kind," Nora replied, tightening her holding on her reins as her mare danced nervously, no doubt eager to be off.

"Are you headed somewhere?" Mr. Clarke inquired with a curious look. "Perhaps I can accompany you?"

Nora tensed. "Oh, I am just going for a quick ride. I've been stuck in the house all day, and I believe some fresh air will do me good. But please, return to the house and have some refreshments. You must be weary from the long journey." She pulled her mare around. "I shall see you shortly." Unfortunately, before she could ride off, Mr. Clarke once more spoke.

"Nonsense!" he repeated himself, urging his horse closer to her. "I shall be happy to accompany you. After all, a lady of your standing should not be riding out alone." A rebuke sounded in his voice. "Where to?"

Nora gritted her teeth, fighting to hold back an agonizing groan that wanted to burst free. "There truly is no need—"

Mr. Clarke held up a hand. "Please. It is my pleasure."

But not mine, Nora grumbled inwardly.

Unfortunately, no matter what she brought forth, Mr. Clarke would not be deterred. Ultimately, Nora gave up, disappointment sweeping through her. She tried to tell herself that in all likelihood Troy would not be at the ruins anyhow. Yet, it was a small comfort.

Riding hard across the meadow, Nora tried her best to leave Mr. Clarke behind, to forget that he was there. She tried to retreat into her own mind, enjoy the chilling wind and the occasional ray of sunshine that peeked through the dark clouds overhead.

Yet the man by her side insisted on speaking to her, asking one question after another, inquiring after her days, her pastimes, her family. He spoke of Leighton, once more extending an invitation, insisting that she was dearly missed.

By whom, Nora could not fathom.

Listening as best she could, Nora allowed her gaze to sweep over the landscape. With no hope to meet Troy, she had simply allowed her mare to venture where she wished, now surprised to realize that they were drawing closer to the ruins after all. Had she subconsciously given her mare signs to return here? Or was this merely a coincidence?

Whichever it was, Nora could not keep her heart from dancing in her chest with eagerness, with anticipation...with dread. Would he be here? Even if he was, there was no way they could speak to each other now. But perhaps, if he was here, she could at least catch a glimpse of him.

One glimpse to sustain her...

...until the next time.

A smile teased Nora's lips, and she turned her mare toward the ruins.

Chapter Eleven

A FATHER'S COUNSEL

Walking the length of his study, back and forth, back and forth, Troy raked a tense hand through his hair. His pulse thudded wildly, and he gritted his teeth against the urge to growl at something or someone or nothing at all. His gaze returned to the window again and again, judging the clouds, before sweeping halfway across the room to the clock in the corner, reading the time yet again.

Barely a minute had passed since the last time he had looked.

Balling his hands into fists, Troy stopped in his tracks, feeling as though there was something crawling under his skin. It drove him mad, for he had found himself unable to rid himself of that sensation for days. At first, he had tried to ignore it. Yet with each day that had passed, he had come to realize more and more where its origin lay.

Nora.

Of course, it was Nora!

Although Troy had decided not to see her again, it was not as simple as that. Despite his efforts, his thoughts continued to linger with her. Asleep or awake, she seemed to be all he could think about, his heart quickening every time he recalled that moment by the ruins.

He cursed and berated himself for his inability to keep her from his thoughts; however, it did no good.

She was always there.

She was *simply* always there.

But more importantly, was Nora at the ruins at this very moment? Troy found himself wondering as he had all the days before. Each time, he had felt compelled to rush outside, see his horse saddled and take off. He had fought the impulse, of course. Yet with each day it had gotten harder to fight, the impulse more urgent in its insistence he comply. Right now, he felt like a caged lion, glancing at the door again and again, knowing that it was not locked, that it would not keep him in.

Keep him from going to her.

As though to prove his point, the door suddenly swung open, revealing his father in its frame. His warm brown eyes met Troy's and then narrowed as they took in his son's agitated state. "You look troubled," he remarked, then stepped inside and closed the door. "What's happened?" Long strides carried him closer, concern marking his features despite the full beard hiding the lower half of his face.

Staring at his father, Troy paused. Again, he felt the sudden desire to speak honestly...but pushed it down once again. No, no good would come from speaking of this madness. "It is nothing," he snapped, instantly regretting his harsh tone of voice. "I apologize, Father. I'm in a foul mood today."

"I can see that," his father remarked, arms crossing over his chest as he eyed him curiously. "The question is why?"

Troy wished he possessed the calm that always rested in his father's eyes. All throughout his life, Troy had found it soothing, comforting, his father's steady hand an anchor he had held on to more than once.

Only now, it failed to reach him.

"It is nothing," Troy said once again, remembering Keir's words from a few days ago.

His father chuckled, the sound warm and affectionate. Then he stepped forward and placed his hands upon his son's shoulders, his gaze insistent as it sought Troy's. "You're a grown man," he said unexpectedly, the hint of a smile curling up the corners of his mouth, "and I have no right to lecture you or tell you what to do, how to live your life." He squeezed Troy's shoulders. "However, I'm also your father, and it pains me to see you so troubled."

Troy heaved a deep sigh. "I apologize. I had no intention of causing you dist—"

Wrapping a hand around the back of Troy's neck, his father pulled him closer until they were almost nose to nose. "Don't," he whispered, his brown eyes fierce as they looked into Troy's. "Don't apologize. No situation was ever made better by an apology. It will not lessen my distress at seeing you thus."

Troy briefly closed his eyes and inhaled a deep breath. "I don't know what to do," he mumbled, his voice strangely hoarse, as though he had been screaming at the top of his lungs for the past few hours.

A compassionate smile flashed across his father's face, and his hand tightened upon the back of Troy's neck. "I know the feeling," his father replied in that deep, soothing voice of his. Then he lifted his head, his dark eyes searching his son's. "Who is she?" he asked abruptly, his brows arching up meaningfully as he saw the look of shock upon Troy's face. "Don't be surprised, Son. Believe me, I've been where you are. Tell me what happened."

Troy stared at his father, a man he had known all his life. All of a sudden, though, he glimpsed something in his gaze he had never noticed before. "How can you—? But I always thought—" He shook his head in confusion.

His father's hand slipped back onto his shoulder, a faraway look coming to his face. "You thought that, for your mother and I, it was love at first sight, did you not?" He chuckled, as though the thought was ludicrous.

Troy's frown deepened. "Why would I not?" he demanded somewhat indignantly. "That is the story you've always told us. I remember you telling us countless times, even as children, how you saw her and knew in an instant that she was the one for you." Again, he shook his head, feeling as though someone had just jerked the ground out from under his feet. "Was it all a lie?"

His father chuckled, giving Troy's shoulders another squeeze. "Don't be so quick to condemn others for their weaknesses. No one is perfect. I am not, and neither are you." His father's eyes looked deep into his. "No one expects you to be perfect, Troy. You're allowed to make mistakes. You're allowed to be weak. Do not place this burden upon your shoulders, for it'll only make you unhappy. Do you hear me?"

Still confused, Troy nodded, uncertain what exactly it was his father was trying to tell him.

His father heaved a deep sigh, a hint of reluctance in his eyes despite the warm-hearted smile that continued to linger upon his lips. "It was love at first sight," his father finally said, "but only for me. Your mother, quite frankly, wanted nothing to do with me when I first approached her." He chuckled, as though the memory was a happy one.

Rather dumbfounded, Troy stared at his father. "Why have you never told us this?"

His father shrugged. "Because...it does not matter. I was determined to win her heart, and I did." He shook his head, a broad smile upon his face. "It didn't matter how adamant she was or how disheartened I felt at times; the only thing that did matter was that I knew we belonged together." A questioning look settled in his eyes as he held his son's gaze.

Troy cleared his throat, trying to evade his father's eyes. "You are mistaken if you think that there is someone who—"

"You don't have to say anything if you don't want to," his father interrupted him before he could continue his lie. "But know that no matter what happens, I will always be here for you." His father's hands squeezed Troy's shoulders once more before he straightened and stepped away. He moved over to the door, one hand on the handle, but then he turned back and looked at his son. "Whatever it is that distresses you," he said gently but firmly, "trust your heart to know what's right. Yes, it might seem foolish at times, but ultimately, no advice is better. Honestly, I've always found myself regretting something that was done for the right reasons but felt utterly wrong." He held Troy's gaze for a moment longer before stepping outside and closing the door behind him.

Staring after his father, Troy found himself at a loss. Quite obviously, he had not hidden the turmoil within his heart as well as he had hoped, leading his father to offer advice he did not care to hear. Yet it circled in his head, fueling that urgency within him, that need to find his way to the old ruins as fast as he possibly could. Would she be there? Would she *still* be there?

For the thousandth time, Troy raked a hand through his hair, growling beneath his breath. He felt frustrated beyond all measure, unable to decide, torn in different directions. *Listen to your heart*, his father had counseled, but was that wise? Of course, Troy knew what his heart wanted. He had always known, ever since that fateful day five years ago. That had never been in question. However...

And then, before Troy knew what was happening, before he realized he had even made up his mind, he found himself striding down the hallway, quick steps carrying him outside, long strides eating up the distance to the stables. Within the blink of an eye, he was pulling himself into the saddle and urging his gelding into a gallop, eager, almost desperate to reach the ruins...

...and see *her* again.

It was foolish to do what he was doing, to be out here, to be riding toward her. It was foolish, so very foolish, and yet, the anticipation that built in his heart at the thought of seeing Nora tugged him onward, made him daring, even painted a smile on his face.

The moment the ruins came within sight, Troy felt a deep breath rush from his lungs. His hands tensed upon the reins, and his gelding tossed up his head. Troy tried his best to focus his thoughts, to calm his heart, but neither would obey. He charged across the meadow; his eyes fixed on those crumbling stones that had been there for as long as he could remember. But was she here?

Rounding the remnants of the last wall, Troy pulled up short, his gaze sweeping over his surroundings as he jumped out of the saddle. His pulse beat wildly, thunderously in his veins, and he could barely catch his breath.

Deep down, a voice whispered that he was being a fool, urging him to leave before it was too late, reminding him of the past few years and all that he had suffered. But strangely, that voice now rang no louder than a whisper when before it had been almost deafening.

Tension traveled through Troy's body, gripping his arms and legs, even his heart. He jerked his head from side to side, eyes still wide and searching. He could not keep still, pacing endlessly, cursing himself at the same time.

And then he caught a glimpse of movement on the horizon.

Troy's whole body snapped around, his heart pausing expectantly in his chest as he stared at the small slope.

A honey-colored horse stood up there, a woman upon its back, her dark tresses billowing in the wind.

A shuddering breath left Troy's lips, and as though on their own accord, his feet started to move toward her...only to pull to an abrupt halt when another rider appeared beside her a moment later.

It was a man Troy did not recognize.

His teeth ground together at the sight, and something dark and almost menacing swept through his chest. Who was that man? And, more importantly, who was he...to her?

Chapter Twelve

LOST TIME

Even before she glimpsed him, Nora knew he was there. It was as though she could sense Troy nearby, as though she could feel the wild beating of his heart and the emotions that raged within him. Had she simply imagined them? Lately, Nora did not feel certain of anything. After all, she had not doubted the course her life would take after becoming a widow. She had felt absolutely certain that she would follow in her mother's footsteps, living day in and out as a mere shadow of the young woman she had once been. And then, absolutely unexpectedly, Troy had returned to her life...and not in a passing manner, not as two acquaintances glimpsing each other from across a crowded ballroom.

Despite his failure to meet her here at the ruins at her request, Nora refused to give up hope because...because they *were* more than simply two acquaintances. Indeed, he had returned to her life in a way that made her want to hold on to him and never let him leave again. So, yes, perhaps she was a fool. Perhaps she was simply imagining this connection between them. But did it matter? After years of feeling nothing but hollowness inside her chest, Nora finally felt alive again... and she would not give this up easily.

"Perhaps we should return," Mr. Clarke suggested, casting a worried look up at the clouds above. Dark and gloomy, they loomed in the sky, threatening to drench them should they be foolish enough to remain outdoors. "I think it would not be wise to continue on much farther."

Nora could not help but smile, for she did not intend to be wise. There was an almost fearless tingle beneath her skin as she looked down toward the ruins and spotted Troy standing there, staring up at her. She had only meant to catch a glimpse of him, but now that they were so close, she knew she could not leave without *seeing* him.

"Ah, I see, there is another soul foolish enough to venture outdoors today," Mr. Clarke remarked as he caught sight of Troy. "An acquaintance of yours?" he asked, his voice suddenly tight and filled with disapproval. "From a neighboring estate, perhaps?"

Wishing Mr. Clarke had not arrived today of all days and was not right this moment ruining the very day Troy had finally returned, Nora drew in a deep, calming breath. Then she reluctantly moved her eyes from the man down below and looked at the one beside her. "In fact, he is an old friend. We grew up together."

Mr. Clarke's teeth seemed to grind together, as though he was trying to hold back words that wanted to burst forth. "Do you see him often?"

Nora steeled herself at the tone in his voice, lifting her chin, her gaze unflinching. "I'm sorry if you disapprove; however, whom I meet is none of your concern." She gave him a pointed look.

Mr. Clarke's jaw tightened, and his lips thinned. "I am merely thinking of your reputation, my lady," he grunted out before casting a dark look at Troy, his lips curving into a snarl. "After all, you are still in mourning, and I cannot help but be concerned with what people might think if they knew of your conduct. My cousin may be dead, but as I have told you before, you are still family."

Nora felt her hands tense upon the reins. "I thank you for your concern, sir," she replied on a hiss, surprised by her own behavior. It had been a long time since she had spoken so bluntly, with so little regard for how she was being perceived. Indeed, it reminded her of her former self...and it felt good. "I assure you, it has been duly noted." She held Mr. Clarke's gaze in a way that seemed to unsettle him. "And I would be much obliged if you returned to Fartherington Hall now. Be assured that I shall follow shortly."

For a moment, Mr. Clarke simply stared at her, a dumbfounded expression upon his face. "But…But I cannot," he stammered, slowly shaking his head as though still in disbelief about what she had said. "It wouldn't be right. I cannot possibly leave you alone here with," he jerked his head around to stare in Troy's direction, "him!"

"Yes, you can," Nora insisted, enjoying the way her heart beat powerfully within her chest. "He is a friend, and I will be safe with him." She jerked her head in the direction of Fartherington Hall. "If you please, sir."

Mr. Clarke's teeth ground together once more, his eyes narrowed and screaming with disapproval. Still, after a moment of hesitation, he pulled on his reins and turned his horse in the direction she had indicated. "Very well, *my lady*. If you insist." He cast her another dark look before spurring on his horse and riding off.

Nora wasted no time looking after him. She kicked her mare's flanks and quickly made her way down the small slope toward the ruins.

Toward Troy.

With his arms linked behind his back and his shoulders pulled back, he still stood in the very same spot he had occupied these past few moments. Not unlike Mr. Clarke's, his face looked dark, his eyes narrowed and hard as he watched her approach. Yet beneath Troy's anger, Nora could read something soft and caring. She saw the man she had known long ago, and a smile flitted across her face.

She liked the way he made her smile, the way a mere thought of him made her smile.

Pulling her mare to a halt, Nora jumped out of the saddle, eager to be near Troy, her eyes feasting on the mere sight of him. "I am so glad to see you," she exclaimed, rushing to his side. "I was so afraid you wouldn't come."

Her open words seemed to shake him out of this angry stance he had adopted. "I…I wasn't certain it would be wise," he murmured, and she could see that he still had doubts. Yet he was here.

For a moment, they merely looked at one another before Troy nodded toward the horizon, his jaw tensing. "Who is he?"

For a split second, Nora thought to see jealousy flash in his eyes, and it sent a shiver of delight through her. Was it possible that at least a part of him thought of her in that way? Or was he merely being protective? Concerned for her well-being?

"His name is Milton Clarke," Nora replied, loath to speak of him. "He—"

Recognition showed on Troy's face, and he nodded.

"You know him?"

Troy gave an almost imperceptible nod. "I doubt we have ever crossed paths; however, I am aware that...he is your late husband's cousin, his heir."

Nora almost flinched at the way Troy spat the word *husband*. It sounded like a snarl, harsh and accusing; yet it made her wonder once again if it had indeed been jealousy she had glimpsed in his eyes before. "He is," she simply confirmed, waiting, wondering what he would say next.

Troy's blue eyes lingered upon her face, and she could see that more questions coursed through his head. The muscles in his jaw tensed and then relaxed before they tensed once more. Finally, he asked, "What is he doing here? Does he not have better things to do now that he has an earldom to see to?"

"I would've assumed so as well," Nora replied honestly. Then she heaved a deep sigh. "He arrived just when I was about to ride out and invited himself along. I tried to dissuade him, but he was insistent."

Troy watched her most carefully, the words she had spoken clearly not satisfying him. "Why did he come in the first place?" he demanded, as though she owed him an answer.

Nora could not help but smile at him, her old self reawakening after lying buried for too long. "Are you jealous?" she teased, stepping closer and looking up into his eyes.

As before, Troy remained immobile; yet his throat worked as he swallowed, a hint of unease now lingering in his eyes. "I am... concerned," he insisted in a voice that made Nora want to hug him.

Not wanting to let him off the hook so quickly, Nora sidled closer, watching the way his eyes widened ever so slightly at her slow approach. "I assure you," she whispered sweetly, "there is no need for you to be jealous. Mr. Clarke is nothing more than an unwanted relation."

Troy's gaze burned into hers as the muscles in his jaw twitched furiously. She could sense that he was close to losing control and wondered what it would take to snatch what little he still possessed from his grasp. "He would not have come for no reason," Troy growled, that deep rumble in his throat teasing Nora's nerve endings and making her shiver in a dangerously compelling way. "Tell me."

Nora longed to bridge that last small distance between them. She wanted to step back into his embrace and feel his arms close around her. But she did not, because more than anything, she wanted to see what *he* would do. "He came to return a necklace I seemed to have left behind at Leighton."

Troy's frowned deepened. "He could have sent a servant," he echoed her earlier thoughts. "There was no need for him to deliver it personally."

"I agree."

"Then why did he?" Troy snapped a split second before his arms swung forward and his hands seized her by the arms, yanking her closer.

Nora gasped, her heart speeding up with the rush of emotions tumbling head over heels through her body at the feel of his touch. "I don't know," she whispered breathlessly, staring up into his thunderous eyes. "He said I was family and asked me to return to Leighton. He said it was still my home."

Another low growl rumbled in Troy's throat, and his hands tightened upon her arms possessively. "What will you do?"

"Why do you care?" Nora asked with a smile she could not suppress. "You cannot even bring yourself to be my friend again. I've been waiting here for you for the past few days, and you didn't come." An accusatory tone sneaked into her voice, and she felt the sorrow she had experienced upon realizing that he would not show resurface. "You left me here!"

"I never said I would come!" he argued, giving her a shake, one fueled by frustration and perhaps...

"I waited for you!" Nora insisted, aware of the way he flinched every time she did. "I missed you! Do you hear me? I missed you!" Tears collected in her eyes. "We used to be so close, and then you vanished from my life! I missed you! Do you hear me? I mis—"

With another tug, she flew against his chest, and a surprised gasp escaped her lips. Then the day suddenly darkened as Troy's head swooped down, blocking out the last few rays of the sun before his mouth closed over hers...fulfilling her wildest dreams.

Here.

Now.

So unexpectedly!

A shock wave shot through Nora at the touch of his lips, and her mind instantly went back to that day five years ago. Back then, however, Troy's kiss had been tentative—at least, at first—his heart and mind as confused as her own by the sudden desire that had caught them both off guard. Now, she sensed an almost desperate need in him, as though he was determined to make up for lost time.

As though he did not regret the kiss they had shared years ago.

As though he, too, had missed her.

Missed her with a vehemence that threatened to consume them both.

His hands held her crushed against his chest as his mouth devoured hers, nothing tentative in his need for her, every touch possessive, every kiss claiming her as his.

Nora's head spun and her heart soared as she clung to him, overwhelmed by the way he revealed his innermost emotions. He had always been rather closed-off, determined to hide his true self, lest it might make him vulnerable. He had trained the expression upon his face into an indifferent mask, making it all but impossible to guess his thoughts.

Now, the mask was gone, and Nora finally realized how wrong she had been. How very wrong! Troy had never regretted their kiss. He had not stayed away because the sight of her served as an unwelcome reminder of that day.

Tears shot to her eyes when she realized that their kiss had meant to him as much as it had meant to her. He cared for her, not as a friend, but...

Then why had he not come to her before her wedding? Why had he not said a word?

Did you? A chiding voice deep down whispered, making Nora cringe at the thought of what they had lost because... because...

Jerking backward, Troy stared down into her face, his blue eyes suddenly wide with shock. A tremble shot through him, and a sickening expression came to his face. "I'm sorry," he breathed, then stumbled backward, still staring. "I'm sorry. I shouldn't have..."

Heat still simmered beneath Nora's skin as the look in Troy's eyes sent an icy chill down her back. "No, Troy, listen! You didn't—"

His lips sealed shut, and he shook his head as he continued to stagger backward, putting more distance between them. Then he suddenly spun around, reached for his gelding's reins, and swung himself into the saddle.

"Troy, wait!" Nora called as she rushed toward him, wiping tears from her eyes, knowing that he had misunderstood them. "Don't go! You didn't—"

"You should stay away from me!" he snapped, such pain in his eyes that the sight of it cut Nora right down to her core. "I should never have come here!" Then he pulled his gelding around and thundered down the way he had come, leaving her behind, her heart aching in such a way that she thought it would split in two.

Chapter Thirteen

A LINE IN THE SAND

Blindly, Troy sat atop his gelding as they thundered along the narrow path that led back to Whickerton Grove. His eyes stared straight ahead, and yet they were unseeing, locked on to the memory of Nora standing before him, her lips swollen from his kiss and tears streaming down her face.

The image made him cringe, and a sickening sensation spread through his body. What had he done? Again! As much as he had wondered about what their kiss had meant to her before, he now could no longer ignore the truth.

Nora had asked him to be her friend, and he had crossed the line, unable to control himself. His blood had boiled with jealousy at the thought of Mr. Clarke's intentions toward her because clearly the man wanted more than to see to a former relation.

Far more.

Troy was certain of it, and the thought felt like torture. Years ago, he had been forced to stand back and let her marry another, and now he could not help but wonder if history would soon repeat itself. Yes, Nora had stated that Mr. Clarke was an unwanted relation; however, who knew what would happen down the line?

Indeed, he had been a fool to go against his better judgment and seek out the ruins today. Perhaps his father had been able to win his mother's heart, but by now, it was clear that Nora would never feel about him thus. She was his friend, always had been...or at least until he had lost control. Had he now lost her forever?

The thought felt like a stab to his heart, and Troy felt his shoulders fall, all strength draining from his body as he hunched over his horse's neck. Yet at the same time, he knew it would not change anything, would it? They had barely seen each other these past few years. She had not been a part of his life, and he had not been a part of hers. The only thing that would be different from now on was that Troy now knew how she truly felt about him.

As Troy drew closer to Whickerton Grove and then rounded the stables to approach from the front, his ears picked up the sound of carriage wheels rumbling closer. He turned to look over his shoulder and spotted several familiar carriages coming up the drive.

Gritting his teeth, Troy tried his best to compose himself, then handed the reins to a groom and moved toward the front entrance. He saw the front door open, and his parents step out, closely followed by Grandma Edie and the Scotsman. Smiles rested on all their faces, and Troy felt a small stab as he saw his mother slip her arm through his father's, moving closer, a tender look in her eyes as she gazed up at him.

In the next instant, carriage doors were flung open and within moments his sisters and their husbands swarmed out, embracing his parents and grandmother, as though they had not seen each other in years. Joy glowed upon all their faces, and for a moment, Troy stood back and watched them, envy burning in his heart. What he wouldn't give to be as happy as they were! To find himself married to the one he loved!

The thought made Troy flinch, for until this very moment, he had not dared admit even to himself that Nora was the only one he wanted as his wife. It shocked him nearly witless; and it made the moment by the ruins even harder to bear.

"Troy!" his youngest sister Harriet exclaimed, her flaming red hair billowing around her head. "Why the gloomy face? Are you not happy to see us?"

Troy swallowed hard and met his father's gaze across the sea of faces. His brown eyes were watchful and seeing, and it only took him a moment to understand. "Let's all go inside," his father called to his children and their spouses, gesturing toward the door. "It seems you brought an icy wind with you, and I, for one, do not care to catch cold." He laughed, casting another look in Troy's direction, and giving him a small nod. Then he continued to usher everyone inside, giving Troy the space he needed to compose his thoughts.

To Troy's relief, his siblings for once heeded their father's word, and before long, everyone was inside, Troy the only one who remained standing by the stoop, his legs heavy as lead. He waited there for as long as he dared. Then he walked up the few steps and slipped inside, relieved to find that the others had already retreated to the drawing room.

Silently, he slunk off to the study, knowing he would be missed soon, but needing a moment of solitude before he could face his siblings.

Seating himself at the large desk, Troy stared ahead at the wall, not seeing the portraits that had been hung up there nor the large bookcases that stood to their sides. He once again saw the scene up by the ruins until a groan escaped his lips and he buried his face in his hands. What had he done?

Moments passed as the clock on the mantle ticked out one second after another. Troy did his best to breathe in and out calmly, doing what he could to relax and loosen his muscles. He did his utmost to think of his sisters and their families, of the joyous days that awaited him in their company. He focused his thoughts as best as he could, not allowing them to stray, to venture back to *that moment*.

When he felt he had sufficiently recovered his composure, Troy rose to his feet and then left the study. He followed the soft hum of voices down the corridor and to the drawing room. Inhaling a deep breath, he stepped inside and was greeted by raucous hellos. His sisters flew forward and embraced him, smiling, and commenting as they always did.

"Are you all right?" Leonora asked gently, her wide blue eyes filled with kindness as she smiled at him. "You seem upset?"

Troy cursed under his breath and then doubled his efforts to appear at ease. Yet Leonora had always been one to read others almost effortlessly, her quiet disposition perfectly suited to a most keen observer.

"I would hug you," Louisa stated from where she sat near their grandmother, one hand resting atop her rounded belly. "However, I just sat down, and I don't think I have the strength to get up just yet." She grinned at him, then looked up and smiled at her husband. "Phin, go and hug my brother for me."

Phineas chuckled. "As you wish, dearest." Then he crossed the room in a few quick strides and clasped a hand on Troy's shoulder. "It's good to see you."

Louisa laughed. "That was a hug?" She turned to look at her sisters. "Men are strange creatures, are they not?"

Everyone laughed. "I've always thought so," Harriet exclaimed, blinking her lashes teasingly at her husband. "But utterly fascinating nonetheless."

Jack smiled at her, reaching out an arm to wrap around her middle, and pulled her close. He whispered something in her ear that made her turn around and hug him, resting her head against his shoulder.

Standing in the corner of the room, Troy watched as his siblings chatted happily, catching up on everything that had happened since they had last seen one another. He smiled when he saw little Sam, Christina's and Thorne's adopted little girl, that talking parrot Harriet had given her perched upon her shoulder. She was feeding it biscuits, occasionally brushing a gentle finger along its beak. As Troy looked up, he met his father's gaze, answering the question he saw there with a silent nod. Yes, he was all right...or he would be.

The day wore on, and Troy had just realized that neither Juliet nor Christopher were with them when Christina suddenly exclaimed, "Oh, no! What happened?" Eyes fixed out at the garden, she shot forward, hands reaching for the terrace doors.

Instantly, everyone's heads swiveled around, their gazes following her, finally seeing what she had seen: Christopher carrying an unconscious Juliet toward the house.

Troy felt his heart slam to a halt as he stared at his sister's closed eyes, her head resting against Christopher's chest, his arms holding her tightly. For a moment, he could not move, remaining where he was as the rest of his family surged forward, through the French doors and onto the terrace. He heard concerned voices, echoing here and there, asking questions, demanding to know what had happened.

Clearly shocked to see them, Christopher stopped on the terrace, eyes wide as he stared at their expectant faces. Troy could see that he was overwhelmed, yet at this very moment he did not feel too kindly toward his friend. What on earth had happened? Why had Juliet fainted? Had it been some kind of accident? Or...?

Loud thumps quickly silenced everyone, and all eyes turned to Grandma Edie. She was leaning on her walking stick, its end now resting calmly upon the tiles of the terrace. "You sound like a beehive," she commented, once again picking up her walking stick and gesturing with it toward Christopher and Juliet. "Give the man a moment to catch his breath." Casting a stern look around everyone on the terrace, she settled her pale eyes once more on to the man holding Troy's sister in his arms. "Now, dear boy, tell us what happened."

Troy tensed as he waited. Then Christopher merely said, "She... fainted," as though that were explanation enough. While his parents and sisters fluttered around Juliet and his father lifted her out of Christopher's arms, Troy stood back, quietly watching the scene.

Only when they had all left, rushing upstairs to see Juliet settled, did he step forward, his eyes hard as they met Christopher's. "In the study," he growled at his friend. "Now." Then he spun on his heel and marched away, trying his best to hold on to his composure until they were alone, for he did not relish the thought of discussing this matter with his brothers-in-law watching them.

Entering his study, Troy walked over to the windows and focused his eyes on the world outside, arms linking behind his back. He breathed in once, then twice, trying his best to clear his head. Yet the moment he heard Christopher step across the threshold, he growled, "I warned you, did I not?" Despite the calm he sought, Troy felt anger coursing through him as he slowly turned around to face his friend. "What happened? Why did she faint? What did you do?"

Anguish stood on Christopher's face, and he briefly closed his eyes. "I...I overstepped." Troy saw his friend's hands ball into fists at his side.

"She told me she had...chosen another, and I did not want to hear it so—"

Surprised, Troy frowned. "She did?" He took a step toward Christopher, completely taken aback by his friend's words. "Are you saying she is to be...married?" Indeed, deep down, Troy had always thought that Juliet did not seek marriage, at least not to anyone who was not Christopher.

Pain, raw and crippling, stood upon his friend's face.

"Who?" Troy inquired, wondering how he could be completely unaware of the fact that his sister intended to marry someone.

Christopher's jaw tensed. "Mr. MacKinnear."

Eyes widening, Troy thought of the tall Scotsman. "That...is a surprise," he remarked, unable to shake the feeling that...this was not true. Had Juliet truly agreed to marry Keir? Troy had seen them together upon occasion; yet there had never been...a spark between them, had there? Or had he simply missed it? "She told you that?" he asked, wondering if perhaps Christopher had misunderstood her.

His friend's head bobbed up and down, pain still resting in his eyes.

Troy frowned, unable to shake the feeling that something did not add up. "And she fainted because...?"

Drawing in a deep breath, Christopher closed his eyes as though himself in disbelief about what had happened. "I tried to kiss her."

His friend's words felt like a slap in the face. "You did what?" Troy heard himself growl as his mind recalled the moment earlier today at the ruins...with Nora. Rapid footsteps carried him closer as he stared at his friend. "Without her consent?"

Deep down, Troy knew that part of the anger he felt was directed at himself. Yes, he was appalled by what his friend had done; yet he had done the very same thing. Troy cringed at the thought, remembering the tears upon Nora's cheeks.

Misery lay in Christopher's eyes. "There is no excuse," he mumbled, raising his gaze to Troy's. "I will apologize to her, and then I shall leave." Something utterly hopeless rang in his voice, something that echoed within Troy's own chest. Indeed, his friend looked crushed, shocked, disgusted with himself, but most of all he looked forlorn.

Troy wondered how things had come to be like this. Once, they had all been friends, and now? He sighed deeply and then nodded. "I believe that would be wise," he finally said, knowing that his words would break his friend's heart all over again. No matter what had happened, he could see that Christopher loved Juliet, and although Troy thought she loved him as well, he clearly had been mistaken. Why else would she have fainted?

Yet there was nothing to be done. Perhaps it would indeed be wise for Christopher to leave, to not see Juliet again, to begin a new life on his own.

Yes, the same held true for Troy. He knew he had made a mistake venturing to the ruins today. It had been a mistake kissing Nora, one he would not repeat. Yes, he needed to keep his distance.

They both did.

And they both would.

Chapter Fourteen

WHAT BEFITS A LADY

Seated in the drawing room with a steaming cup of tea in her hand, Nora glanced over its rim, her eyes moving from her mother to Mr. Clarke. Although she loved the aroma—it was the very tea Grandma Edie continued to send to her—she flinched slightly as the hot liquid touched her tongue, then swallowed it before setting the cup back down. Indeed, she had known to wait; however, the quiet tension lingering in the room had made her reach for her cup, almost desperate for something to occupy her attention.

"How is everything at Leighton, Mr. Clarke?" Nora inquired, doing her best to appear interested. "Managing such a vast estate surely takes up a lot of your time, does it not?"

Mr. Clarke cleared his throat. "Not at all. I've retained my late cousin's steward."

"Mr. Heston?"

Mr. Clarke nodded. "Indeed. The man is most diligent in his duties. In fact, my cousin hired him upon my recommendation."

"How wonderful!" Nora exclaimed, giving him a small smile. "Then I suppose you shall have ample time to enjoy your new estate. Does your son not miss you? I would've thought he would object to you being gone for a prolonged time."

Mr. Clarke was a widower, whose wife had passed away after giving birth to their son roughly seven years ago. Occasionally, Nora had met the little boy, who possessed a rather quiet demeanor, his wide eyes always looking at the world in a disconcerted fashion. She remembered the way the boy always tried his best to stay near his father, as though losing sight of him would plunge his world into darkness. She had seen a bond there, between father and son, which made her wonder even more about Mr. Clarke's visit to Fartherington Hall.

As Mr. Clarke spoke about his son, Nora felt her mother's eyes upon her, something inquisitive and almost calculating in her gaze. Although she did not know what it meant, Nora did not care for it.

"You must long to return to him," Nora reasoned, trying her best to ignore the way her mother's gaze kept moving back and forth between her and Mr. Clarke. It was the kind of look that sent chills down her back.

"At present, I am enjoying your company," Mr. Clarke told her with a smile that almost made Nora flinch. "I am aware that this must be a very difficult time for you, and I am determined to remain at your side for as long as you need me." He heaved a rather dramatic-sounding sigh. "I cannot help but think that mourning my cousin together might make it easier on both of us."

"That is a very kind thought, sir," Nora's mother commented with a polite smile. "Please, feel free to stay for as long as you wish."

Nora barely managed to suppress a groan at her mother's words, fighting to hold on to her composure. Yes, this was a difficult time for her, but not because she was mourning her husband's loss. And Mr. Clarke's presence was not making anything better; quite on the contrary, at present, he was interfering with the one thing that gave Nora's life meaning and hope and joy.

Indeed, why was he here? During her husband's lifetime, she could not recall seeing Mr. Clarke all that often. He had stopped by Leighton upon occasion, staying on for a few days before returning to London. He'd always been kind and considerate, taking the time to speak to her. She had thought him amiable, and yet there had never been a closer connection between them. He was not a friend or confident, and even if she were grieving her husband, he would not be someone she would turn to. Could he not see that?

A short knock sounded on the door before their butler stepped in and handed Nora a letter. "This was just delivered for you, my lady." With another respectful bow, the man left quickly.

Surprised, Nora turned the letter in her hands, catching a glimpse of a scowl on Mr. Clarke's face out of the corner of her eye. Indeed, his shoulders seemed to tense, his features once more marked by disapproval. Did he think this letter was from Troy?

Nora sighed. If only it were! "It's from Christopher," she exclaimed with a smile, turning to look at her mother.

As always, her mother showed very little reaction. "Is he still in the country?" she asked in a rather disinterested tone.

"He's at Whickerton Grove, as you well know, Mother." Giving her mother a pointed stare, Nora then turned her attention to the letter in her hands, opening it quickly. Indeed, after the dreadful afternoon she had had thus far, whatever Christopher thought important enough to inform her of would no doubt be more entertaining.

"Whickerton Grove?" Mr. Clarke asked with a bit of a frown.

"A neighboring estate," Nora's mother informed him, speaking as though the people there were of no consequence when, in truth, they had once been the dearest friends they had ever had.

A dark sound rumbled in Mr. Clarke's throat. "I see," was all he said. Nora, however, sensed that he had just put two and two together, realizing that Whickerton Grove was Troy's home, the man he had seen her with a few days ago—seen and disapproved of, to be precise.

Dearest Nora,

Have you already died of boredom? I cannot help but wonder how you spend your days. Embroidery? Tea? Embroidery again?

. . .

Nora chuckled under her breath, unable not to. Indeed, she missed her brother. They had always had such a wonderful way of communicating, speaking honestly and without pretense.

"Is something humorous?" her mother inquired, a frown drawing down her brows in a rather suspicious manner.

Nora cleared her throat. "No, Mother, nothing."

Quite frankly, I do not truly expect you to change your mind; however, Grandma Edie insists I invite you to the autumn ball here at Whickerton Grove. She claims it will do you well and urges you to come. Of course, I agree with her.

Please, dear sister, forget duty and obligation for one night and come and dance with me.

Christopher

Nora could not deny that she longed to *change her mind*. Indeed, the thought of attending the autumn ball at Whickerton Grove drew a sigh from her lips and stirred wistful longings in her heart. Not only was she drawn by the memories she cherished of that place, but also by the people who lived there, people she loved despite the distance that now stood between them. Troy, of course, but also his sisters. They had once been the dearest of friends, and now, they were all but strangers, knowing nothing of each other's lives.

"What does he write?" Mr. Clarke asked in a strained voice.

Lifting her eyes off the letter to look at him, Nora swallowed a curt remark, annoyed with him for interrupting her musings. "He writes of the autumn ball," she said in a hard voice, wanting him to know that he was overstepping. "He's inviting me to attend."

"That is out of the question!" her mother exclaimed right away, anger and disappointment flashing in her eyes. "You cannot!"

Nodding along, Mr. Clarke fixed her with a determined stare. "I quite agree, my lady. After all, you are still in mourning, and it would not be fit for you to attend any social event." He looked at her mother, and they both nodded to one another in agreement. "Indeed, I must urge you to heed to your mother's counsel." He cleared his throat. "I must say I am rather disappointed with your brother's conduct. Why on earth would he invite you to such an event?"

Nora wanted nothing more than to defend her brother—as well as herself. However, she knew that any word from her would only launch her mother into another tirade, voicing her disappointment with the only son left to her. "I never planned on going," Nora stated clearly, though reluctantly. "However, I appreciate him thinking of me." She sighed. "It is nice to know that there is someone who cares."

"Surely, you know he is not the only one," Mr. Clarke exclaimed, exchanging another glance with her mother. "I am here for that very reason...because I care and want to see you well." He smiled at her, and yet his smile did nothing to warm Nora's heart.

"That is very kind of you, sir," Nora's mother replied. "Indeed, my daughter is most fortunate to have you here to help her through this trying time."

Nora wanted to scream!

Fortunately, in the next moment, their butler returned once more. This time, he delivered a letter to Mr. Clarke, who, upon reading it, quickly excused himself.

The moment the door closed behind him, Nora sighed in relief. "Oh, I can't stand the man! I wish he would leave."

"You cannot be serious," her mother exclaimed, a dumbfounded expression upon her face as she looked at her daughter. "Are you not aware of why he is here?"

Nora almost laughed. "To help me through this trying time," she said in her best imitation of Mr. Clarke's voice.

Her mother rolled her eyes. "To state his intentions."

"His intentions?" Nora frowned, feeling somewhat disconcerted by that look of delight that had come to her mother's face.

Delight was replaced by indulgence as her mother shook her head at Nora like a tutor, severely disappointed with her pupil's lack of understanding. "He wishes to marry you."

Shocked nearly witless, Nora stared at her mother, her thoughts immediately drawn back to the dark look upon Troy's face as he had glared at Mr. Clarke a few days ago by the ruins. *Are you jealous?* She had teased him, and yet she had not for a second thought that Mr. Clarke...

"Did you truly not know?" her mother asked with a chuckle. "My dear child, why else would he be here? To return your necklace?" She laughed. "That is ludicrous! Honestly, it wouldn't surprise me if he himself had *ensured* that the necklace was left behind, thus giving him the opportunity of returning it to you."

"But...But I'm still in mourning," was the first thing that came to Nora's mind.

"Which is why he has not proposed yet," her mother explained, as though it should be obvious. "However, he is making his intentions unmistakably clear, expecting you to accept him once your year of mourning is over." She took a sip from her tea. "I can only advise you to do so, my dear." A smile claimed her mother's lips. "You'd be mistress of Leighton once more."

Repulsion rippled through Nora at the mere thought of it, and she fought to suppress a shudder. "I will not marry again, Mother," she said vehemently, doing her best to shake off the lingering effects of the shock she had just received. "I told you that before."

"Oh, do not be so dramatic," her mother chided. "I quite understand your...apprehension; however, you need to think of your future. You ought to be relieved to receive an offer so quickly after losing your husband. Accept him as soon as your year of mourning is over, and you'll be set for life."

Nora scoffed. "That is precisely what you said to me last time, Mother. And see what happened."

"No one could have foreseen this," her mother exclaimed, disregarding Nora's concerns with a dismissive wave of her hand. "Truly, I urge you to think on it."

Nora heaved a deep sigh. "I will not marry again, Mother. I did not care for it the first time, and I doubt I shall care for it the second, especially since I do not care for Mr. Clarke."

Her mother gave her a long, stern look. "If you truly believe yourself incapable of providing your husband with an heir, that is all the more reason for you to accept Mr. Clarke. The man already has a son and although he might wish for another, he does not need one." She clasped her hands together, and for a second, a dark cloud seemed to darken her face. "Indeed, it is the perfect solution."

Glaring at her mother, Nora shot to her feet, impatience coursing through her veins and carrying her over to the window. Outside, golden leaves swirled about, being tossed here and there by a strong north wind. Inside, Nora felt her heart stumble and trip as though assaulted by unseen forces. "Perhaps he doesn't know," she mumbled, wishing her mother would drop the subject. "I don't think he would want me if he knew."

Indeed, in a society where reputation and standing were defined by a prosperous male line, a woman unable to bear children was of no use. No man would want her, Nora was certain of that.

Nora's heart broke when she realized—rather belatedly!—that that assessment included Troy. He, too, was the heir to his father's title. On top of that, he was the family's only son.

He needed an heir.

Nora had always known so; however, for a moment, she had allowed herself to ignore that fact, getting swept away in a dream. Only this was reality, and she could ignore it no longer. After all, by now, she knew that dreams never came true, did they?

"Perhaps you're worried for nothing," her mother remarked, unaware as it seemed of her daughter's suffering. "Perhaps it was Hayward who could not father children."

Nora almost scoffed. Perhaps her mother truly did not know, living her life far removed from London. However, so had Nora, and even out at Leighton, she had heard the whispers about her husband and his mistresses. On top of that, Hayward had never even tried to shield Nora from his amorous activities. More than one affair had resulted in a child, and he had always seen fit to inform her thusly, berating her for failing him as a wife. Fortunately, once he knew her to be barren, he had stopped visiting her bed.

Nora closed her eyes as she remembered the many lonely years of her marriage, years filled with regret and shame, and she found her thoughts inevitably drawn to Troy, to the moment they had shared only a few days ago.

Yet it no longer held hope for a shared future. It was like a taunt, an image of what her heart longed for but would forever be denied.

However, later that day, when night was beginning to fall, Nora sat down at her vanity and penned a few quick words. She knew she would never marry Troy, but perhaps they could have a few more stolen moments. Moments that would help sustain her once loneliness would dig its claws into her again.

It was selfish of her, but Nora didn't care.

For once in her life, she would be selfish...

...and she would enjoy every moment of it.

Chapter Fifteen

LONELINESS

He was weak. So very weak. Yet not until this very moment had Troy realized just how weak he was.

Weak for her.

Ever since that day by the ancient watchtower, Troy had been determined not to see Nora again. He had reminded himself again and again of the myriad of reasons why it would be a most awful idea. He had felt convinced that he was doing the right thing, that he was acting with consideration and foresight.

And then Nora's note had arrived...and changed everything. A few short words—nothing more!—and yet they possessed the power to move mountains.

To move him.

Meet me by the ruins. Please!

Six little words, almost insignificant-looking; yet the last one had done him in. He had once more seen those large, round eyes of hers filled with tears, begging him to come.

And now, here he was, riding along the narrow path that led straight to the ruins, his heart beating so fast that he feared it might jump from his chest and race ahead, unable to wait. His hands gripped the reins tightly, and his gelding once again tossed his head in irritation. Willing himself to loosen his grip, Troy angled his head and spied the crumbling wall of the old watchtower through a large gap in the dwindling foliage. More and more leaves were falling, their colors changed, and their strength gone as they drift down to the forest's floor. A nip lay in the air, and Troy wondered how soon temperatures would drop below freezing.

His gelding stepped onto the open plain, and Troy's gaze swept over the ruins. He held his breath until his eyes came up empty and his heart sank a little. Then he urged his gelding closer, his breath quickening as they made their way toward the ruins. Had she changed her mind? Would she not come?

Troy was surprised at the despair he felt at the thought, knowing he ought to feel relief instead. After all, he should not be here.

"I was afraid you wouldn't come."

At the sound of Nora's voice, Troy wheeled around in the saddle, his gelding stomping his hooves nervously as he tossed up his head and snorted.

Standing on the other side of the wall, leading her honey-colored mare by the reins, Nora smiled at him. The look in her eyes, though, held something tentative, and Troy wondered if she, too, felt doubts with regard to the wisdom of their meeting. Was she nervous about being alone with him after what he had done? Why then had she asked him here?

Dropping out of the saddle, Troy stepped toward her, uncertain how much distance to maintain so as not to make her feel uneasy. "I... I...," he began, feeling like a fool for his inability to produce a coherent sentence. "I need to apologize," he finally gritted out after a deep breath.

Nora frowned, patted her mare's neck, and then she stepped toward him. "Apologize? For what?"

Troy's teeth ground together painfully as heat shot to his cheeks.

Seeing it, Nora smiled in that sweet, slightly teasing way of hers. "Are you embarrassed?"

Linking his arms behind his back, his right hand gripping his left wrist almost painfully, Troy closed his eyes, unable to look at her. "I should not have kissed you," he forced out, all but pinching his eyes shut. "I apologize. You deserve better, and I—"

Soft hands touched his face, and before Troy knew what was happening, he felt Nora's lips brush against his. It was no more than a fleeting touch, and Troy pinched his eyes tighter, unwilling to let go of the illusion his wayward mind had conjured.

"Look at me, Troy," came Nora's voice from right in front of him, and instantly, Troy's eyes flew open. He stared at her as her hands still cupped his face.

With the blood rushing in his ears, he had not even heard her approach. Shocked, he would have stumbled backward if she had not tightened her hold on him, something fierce sparking in her brown eyes. "You need to understand something," she told him with a stern tone in her voice. "I...I did not mind your kiss."

Swallowing hard, Troy held her gaze, watched the stern look disappear and something imminently gentle and caring replace it. "You... You were crying," he whispered, almost entranced by the suddenly so vulnerable look in her eyes.

A deep sigh left Nora's lips, and she turned away.

"Nora," Troy whispered, reaching out a hand to touch her shoulder, but then he stopped himself, uncertain what stood between them here in this moment, what she was trying to tell him. "What is it?"

"I was crying because," the words shuddered from her lips on a sob, "because..." She turned back around, and he could see her eyes were swimming in tears yet unshed. "I...I've been so lonely." Shaking her head as though in disbelief, she threw up her hands, a hint of anger sparking in her eyes. "These past five years, I've felt as though...as though I were alone in the world." A tear spilled over and snaked down her cheek.

Troy stared at her. "Alone?" he echoed, completely overwhelmed by this moment. Whatever he had expected to happen, it was not this.

Nora lowered her chin, her eyes falling from his, as though she did not dare look at him a moment longer. "First, Sebastian died and then my father," she murmured, her hands wiping almost furiously at her eyes. "Then Christopher left and..." Slowly, she lifted her chin, her eyes returning to his. "I never loved my husband. I was a fool to marry him."

Her sudden admission slammed into Troy with such force that he stumbled a step backward, his eyes fixed upon her face, certain she was a mirage.

"Neither did he ever love me," Nora continued, shaking her head as if she were contemplating her life and the turns it had taken. "It seems ours was a marriage of convenience, only I had no idea until the day I married him." A scoff left her lips, and her hands flew up, as though she wanted to rake them through her hair. "I thought he cared for me," she continued, her eyes distant, "and I truly thought I cared for him, but..." Her eyes snapped up, and she stared at him. "I don't know what happened. One moment I thought I was happy, and then..." She swallowed. "And then you kissed me."

Troy flinched, and for an endless moment, they simply stood there and stared at one another.

The wind tugged upon Nora's curls, whipping her hair around her head. Her cheeks shone rosy from the cold of the season, tears glistening along a trail upon her skin. Her skirts billowed behind her, as though she would take flight at any moment and be lost to him forever.

Then Nora took a step toward him, and her lips parted. "You were my friend, Troy, and then...then you were gone." She held up a hand when he tried to speak; although, he did not know what he would have said. "No, I did not mean to accuse you of anything. All I'm saying is that...I felt alone. I have been feeling alone, and now that I'm back here," her gaze swept over their surroundings, the place of their youth, and the ghost of a smile tugged upon the corners of her lips, "I'm starting to feel things again. I'm starting to remember what it is like to have someone to lean on, someone to talk to, someone to...to hold me." Heartbreaking sadness rested in her eyes, and all of a sudden, she looked so vulnerable that Troy felt himself act without thinking.

Two large strides carried him to her, and he pulled her into his arms without a moment of doubt or hesitation.

And Nora came to him willingly.

Troy felt her hands curl into his lapels, holding on tightly, as she buried her face against his shoulder. Her own shook as she cried out the loneliness of the past five years, clinging to him as though she were drowning and he the only means to keep her head above the water.

And Troy held her as tightly as he could, for once not concerned with overstepping a line. Suddenly, life was simple again. She was his friend, and she needed him. His arms wrapped around her, tugging her closer into his embrace, as he rested his chin on top of her head, murmuring words of comfort he no longer remembered the moment they left his lips.

How long they stood like this, Troy did not know. However, eventually, Nora's sobs began to lessen, replaced by deep breaths. Yet she did not release him, not even when she felt calm again. Instead, she held on, snuggling closer.

Troy froze when a smile stole onto his face.

"Am I making you uncomfortable?" Nora asked, that knowing tone in her voice Troy had missed these past few years. Then she tipped her head back and looked up at him.

Even though Troy could not look into her eyes, for she kept her head against his shoulder, he could feel them upon him like a caress. "No," he lied.

Nora chuckled. "Yes, I am." Still, she did not step back. "Unfortunately for you, I've decided to be selfish today." Her head moved perhaps an inch away from his shoulder so she could peer into his eyes. "And I want you to hold me just a little bit longer."

Swallowing, Troy nodded, not trusting himself to speak.

With a sigh, Nora sank back into his embrace. "You're good at this," she whispered, and involuntarily his arms tightened around her. "You always were. I remember whenever you held me like this, the rest of the world fell away. Whatever had disconcerted, angered or upset me before, no longer seemed important." Her left hand slipped up to his shoulder and then curled around the back of his neck like an anchor, holding him to her. "How do you do it?"

Troy exhaled a deep breath. "I don't know." Slowly, the turmoil in his heart quieted and an old calm spread through his body, reminding him of the years when life had been simple between them.

"Christopher wrote to me," Nora mumbled against his coat. "He said Grandma Edie insists I attend the autumn ball at Whickerton Grove."

Troy chuckled as an image of his grandmother flashed through his mind, a rather mischievous look in her pale eyes. "I can't say I'm surprised."

In his arms, Nora's shoulders trembled as she, too, laughed. "I miss her. She was always so kind to me." Nora looked up at him. "She still keeps sending me that tea I always loved when I came to visit." Her eyes blinked as though to discourage tears. "She always writes a few words that... I don't know what I would have done without those words."

Now, Troy could see tears in her eyes as clear as day, and his hand moved to cup the back of her head, pulling her close again and urging her to lay her head against his shoulder once more.

As though it belonged there.

"How are things between Juliet and my brother?" Nora murmured after a while, inhaling a deep breath as though determined to speak of more joyous matters.

Troy tensed.

"What is it?" Her head rose, her eyes wide as she looked up at him. "Is something wrong?"

Troy cleared his throat. "Christopher...he left last night."

"Left?" Nora exclaimed, surging out of his embrace to better look at him. "What do you mean *left?*"

Troy regretted the loss of feeling her lean into him instantly. "Did he not tell you?"

Still staring up at him, Nora shook her head. "I have not seen him since he first left to visit you at Whickerton Grove. He has written to me, but..." She shook her head. "What happened? He wrote to me only a few days ago, inviting me. What could have possibly happened within the course of a single day to make him leave?"

An image of Christopher carrying Juliet in from the gardens rose in

Troy's mind, and he felt himself tense. Of course, he was concerned for his sister. Had been concerned for his sister. Yet Troy knew deep down that what had happened between Christopher and Juliet felt all too familiar. It was like an echo of the moment he had kissed Nora, also against her wishes. Or—?

Troy blinked, remembering vaguely that only moments ago she had told him she had not...minded his kiss? Was that not what she had said? Had it been the truth? After all, occasionally people said things they did not mean, even if they did not intend to lie outright. Yes, sometimes people said things to put another at ease, to ease a guilty conscience, to be generous, to be a friend.

"Talk to me!" Grasping the sides of his face, Nora gave him a slight jerk. "Tell me what happened! Is Christopher...? Is he returning to Ireland?" She shook her head in disbelief. "I cannot believe he would leave without...without speaking to me." Something utterly sad flashed across her face, disappointment and regret...and loneliness.

Inhaling a deep breath, Troy braced himself, knowing he needed to tell her the truth, to let her know that Christopher's thoughtlessness did not mean he did not care for her. "Yes, I suppose something did happen between them," he began, searching for the right words. While he had been furious with Christopher at first, Troy understood that his friend had never truly meant to hurt Juliet. Perhaps it had merely been a misunderstanding.

"A few days ago," he said, willing himself to meet her questioning gaze, "just after the rest of my family arrived at Whickerton Grove, we spotted Christopher carrying Juliet in from the garden. It seemed she had fainted."

Concern darkened Nora's face. "Fainted? Why? Is she alright?"

Troy nodded. "Yes, she is all right. As she was not in any condition to provide an answer, I asked Christopher to join me in the study. There, he told me that apparently Juliet had fainted because...he had tried to steal a kiss." He shifted uncomfortably from one foot onto the other, barely able to hold her gaze.

Yet the look in Nora's eyes did not change, did not turn accusing. "I'm confused," she said, her brows drawing down. "Honestly, I always thought she would welcome a kiss. Are they not in love? Have they not always been? Why would she faint? What happened between them?"

Troy shrugged. "I don't know." He raked a hand through his hair. "All I do know is that Christopher felt exceedingly guilty for what he had done, and he...he left this morning."

A heavy sigh left Nora's lips, and as though no time had passed, she let herself sink into his arms once again. Oddly enough, it felt natural and wonderful and...

...a thousand other things Troy could not even begin to list. He held her in his arms as she mourned the loss of her brother yet again. Indeed, while he, Troy, was part of a close-knit family, Nora only had her mother, a woman who had never shown much affection to any of her children.

"I'm glad you're here," she whispered, wrapping her arms around his middle and resting her head against his shoulder once again. "Don't ever leave me again."

"I won't," Troy heard himself say, shocked by those words because he knew they were far from wise, that it couldn't possibly end well, that the day would come when he would cross that invisible line once more. And what would she do then?

A part of him wanted to ask her about the letter, about why she had never even answered him. Yet he did not. He could not. Afraid of what the answer might be.

Chapter Sixteen
WITHOUT OPTIONS

Nora returned home with a wide smile upon her face, a smile that felt true and genuine and that made her heart sing with joy. How long had it been since she had last smiled like this?

Unfortunately, a dark cloud descended upon her perfect day the moment she strode across the front hall. The door to the drawing room flew open and out walked Mr. Clarke, his expression dark and somewhat agitated. His eyes flew over her as he called her name in a way Nora could not help but dislike, as though he had a claim on her, as though he owed him an explanation. "My lady, may I ask where you have been all morning?" His shoulders rose and fell with rapid breaths, and Nora glanced down to see his hands clenched into fists at his side. The moment he noticed her attention, he swung his arms behind his back, linking them.

Straightening, Nora met his gaze unflinchingly, surprised by his demeanor but equally unwilling to allow him to intimidate her. Why he should wish to do so was beyond her! "I went for a ride, Mr. Clarke." She finished her answer with a sweet little smile, needing him to understand that she owed him nothing.

Not even an explanation.

His jaw ground together, and Nora could not shake the feeling that he wanted to lash out at her but knew better than to do so. "I assure you, my lady, I am only asking out of concern. I am not certain if it is wise for you to ride out unchaperoned, unaccompanied. What if something were to happen? Believe me, all I am thinking of is your well-being."

A few weeks ago, Nora would have believed him. He had always been kind and considerate to her, and yet his voice suddenly possessed a sharper edge to it. "I thank you for your kindness and consideration; however, I've grown up here and I know these parts quite well. I assure you nothing will happen to me." Again, she smiled at him and then turned upon her heel and strode away.

Still, as she ascended the stairs, she could all but feel him stewing down there in the hall, his dark gaze following her. Did he truly think it his duty to see to his late cousin's widow? Or was her mother correct and what he wanted from her was far more? Her hand in marriage?

Nora shuddered at the thought. She quickened her steps and retreated into the sanctuary of her own chamber. Once there, she tossed her gloves and hat aside, drawing a deep breath into her lungs. Oh, if only he would leave! He was ruining a perfectly good day! The first in so long! The first in too long!

As though the universe meant to spite her, a sharp knock sounded on her door in that moment.

Nora heaved another deep sigh, knowing without a doubt that it could be no other than her mother. "Enter!"

Without a moment's hesitation, her mother strode into the room, closing the door behind her a bit more forcefully than Nora would have expected. Indeed, the look in her mother's blue eyes seemed tense, the expression upon her face agitated, not quite unlike Mr. Clarke's.

Nora knew without a doubt why her mother was here.

"I cannot help but wonder," her mother addressed her, crossing her arms over her chest, "if it is your brother's influence that has you acting with such disdain for common courtesy." Her brows rose meaningfully.

Exasperated, Nora threw up her hands. "Mother, would you

please stop blaming Christopher for everything? I know why you're upset, and I'm telling you now I will not marry Mr. Clarke." Sealing her lips shut, she lifted her chin and met her mother's gaze without flinching.

A long moment ticked by before her mother finally exhaled a deep breath, a hint of exhaustion in her gaze. "Why ever not?" she asked, stepping toward her daughter, her hands reaching out to her. "He is a decent man, and he will see you well-settled. Why would you refuse him?"

Nora felt her mother's hands settle upon her arms, her blue eyes sweeping over her face. "Did you love Father?" Nora asked abruptly, surprised to feel a tremor shake her mother's delicate frame and travel along her arms into Nora's body. "Did you?"

Dropping her hands, her mother took a step back, unease suddenly painted all over her face. "I did," she finally said, lifting her eyes off the floor and meeting Nora's. "Why would you ask me that?"

Nora shrugged. "I simply wish to know." Watching her mother carefully, Nora moved closer, aware that her mother's unease grew with every step she took. "If you truly loved him as you say you did, why can you not understand that I have no desire to wed a man I do not care for?"

Her mother swallowed; her hands suddenly clasped together tightly. "Affections can grow after marriage," she said, her words clipped and unemotional. "You might come to—"

"No, I will not," Nora replied with vehemence. "You forget, Mother, that I have been down this road before. I married a man I thought I cared for, and I hoped we would develop affection for one another. I kept hoping year after year. And yet," she closed her eyes and heaved a deep sigh, "the time of my marriage was the worst time of my life." Her eyes opened, and she looked into her mother's face, now almost blank as though with shock.

Nora felt her limbs begin to tremble as she remembered moments of her marriage, moments that had robbed her of hope and joy. "You do not know what it's like, Mother, to be tied to someone who does not care for you, who does not see when you're hurting, who is a stranger in every way. You were lucky to have had Father, to share your life with him." Tears pricked the backs of her eyes. "Will you not grant me the same?"

"You wish for a love match?" her mother asked tensely, still wringing her hands. "Is that what you're saying?"

Nora scoffed. "Does it come as such a surprise? Have I not always wanted a love match? Did I not believe that I had found it when I married Hayward?" Indeed, she had...at least until Troy had kissed her that day.

"If that is the case, then choose another," her mother suggested, as though it were only a small matter, barely worthy of consideration. "Far be it from me to insist you marry Mr. Clarke. However, after you yourself said that another man would not have you, I am merely suggesting that you contemplate all your options carefully. How do you picture your future, Nora?" An inquisitive expression came to her mother's face, her brows raised in challenge.

"What I want and what I can have are not necessarily the same thing." Nora wiped a tear from her cheek. "If I cannot have love, does that then mean I must marry for convenience?" Slowly, Nora shook her head from side to side. "No, it does not! My greatest regret is marrying Hayward. There are...dark memories in my past now, and I will not make that mistake ever again. I will not marry a man I do not want."

For a long time, her mother looked at her carefully, something resembling suspicion sparking in her blue eyes. "May I ask? Is there a man you *do* want?"

That one simple question felt like a slap in the face to Nora. Because, of course, there was a man she wanted. A man she had wanted for the past five years. A man who had always been her friend. A man who had always noticed when she had been hurting. A man who had always stood by her side.

Troy.

And the fact that she could not have him did not mean that she did not want him.

"If there is," her mother continued, her voice suddenly almost gentle, "then marry him and be happy. However, if there is not or if he will simply not marry you, then please consider Mr. Clarke's offer." The hint of a smile flashed over her face as she stepped toward Nora, reaching out to grasp her daughter's hands. "Believe me, you do not want to waste your life alone, to have no one to share it with. As surely as love can grow after marriage, it can also wither. It is not a guarantee for anything. Do not rob yourself of this chance. I beg you." Squeezing Nora's hands, she then released them and stepped back. "Think about it." Then she turned and left, closing the door behind her.

Staring after her mother, Nora knew not what to think. As rationally minded as her mother had always been, now, for the first time, Nora thought to see another side of her. It had been barely a glimpse, but she knew she had seen regret and sorrow on her mother's face. Nora had never thought of her mother as a happy woman, and yet she did not know enough about her life to pass judgment, to be certain of how her mother felt. However, in that moment just now, Nora could have sworn that her mother cared for her and worried about her, not wanting her to repeat the mistakes she herself still regretted.

Only what could those mistakes be? Had she lied about loving her husband? Had their love ended at some point?

Sinking down on to the edge of her bed, Nora heaved a deep sigh, wishing she knew what to do, aware that her options were severely limited. Despite her mother's entreaty, Nora knew she would not marry again. She did not want a man she did not love, and she could not have the man she did love.

Ultimately, she was without options.

Chapter Seventeen

COUNSEL OF SISTERS

A hum of voices drifted to Troy's ears, and he stopped short outside the drawing room. He could make out his grandmother's calm voice, offsetting Christina's rather agitated reply. Frowning, he stepped forward, then knocked on the door.

"Enter!"

Stepping inside, Troy found not only his grandmother and Christina within but also the rest of his sisters and his cousin Anne; all except for Juliet. He hoped she was all right. "Is there a problem?" he inquired, his eyes coming to linger upon Christina's flushed face, her eyes flashing with anger or impatience or both.

"It's about Sarah," Anne finally replied with a sideways glance at Christina. "We wish we knew what to do for her."

Troy nodded knowingly.

Miss Sarah Mortensen had grown up in the townhouse next door to their own in London. She had always been Christina's dearest friend, but she held a place in all their hearts. Unfortunately, her father's gambling habit had bankrupted the family, forcing them to sell their townhouse. As far as Troy knew, they were struggling to evade debtors demanding payments Lord Hartmore simply could not afford.

In consequence, Sarah's parents had made it their life's mission to marry off their youngest daughter to the highest bidder, so to speak.

Naturally, Christina—as well as the rest of them—was concerned; however, perhaps the word *outraged* described her feelings better. Thus far, to Troy's knowledge, his sisters and grandmother had managed to protect Sarah from two or perhaps even three possible unions her parents had tried to force her into. Of course, they were all aware that eventually there was nothing they could do to protect Sarah...except see her married to someone of her own choosing.

However, with her parents' reputation ruined, young, decent gentlemen of the *ton* showed no interest in the shy, good-hearted girl Troy had known years.

"There is no use in discussing this again, is there?" Christina exclaimed with a sigh before dropping into an armchair, exhaustion playing over her face. "Decent gentlemen do not just materialize out of thin air, do they?"

Leonora cast her younger sister a compassionate look. "I'm afraid not." She turned toward the others. "Is there perhaps someone we might have overlooked? Someone we didn't think of?"

Heavy sighs echoed through the room, and Troy could all but feel the hopelessness slowly settling upon all their shoulders.

"Christopher?" Louisa asked with a grin.

The other four young women all rolled their eyes at her. "Very funny, Lou," Christina exclaimed with a chiding look and an answering grin. "Unfortunately, he is taken." Something imploring came to her eyes. "As you well know."

Troy frowned. Was he?

"Juliet would never forgive us," Leonora remarked, "if we matched him with Sarah. Teasing her with it is one thing; however,..." Her eyebrows rose meaningfully.

Louisa heaved a deep sigh, one hand resting protectively upon her rounded belly. "I know. Yet he is exactly the kind of man that would be good for Sarah, is he not?"

Harriet laughed, her red curls dancing around her head. "I suppose that's true. Perhaps he has a twin!" She grinned at Christina.

Christina traced the tips of her fingers along her eyebrows. "Not that I know of."

Troy frowned, almost certain that his sisters shared a secret he was not privy to. "Where is Juliet? Is she feeling all right?"

His sisters exchanged meaningful glances before his grandmother cleared her throat and turned to speak to him. "She is accompanying Keir on...an errand," she said cryptically, ending that statement with an amused chuckle.

Troy could have groaned.

Since first arriving at Whickerton Grove, these mysterious errands had repeatedly made Keir disappear for days, only for him to return with the vaguest of answers as to where he had been and what he had been doing. Clearly, their grandmother liked to keep her secrets; however, this was growing to be ludicrous.

"What errand?" Troy asked in a hard tone, fixing his grandmother with a pointed stare. "Why did you see fit to send Juliet along? Is it only the two of them?" His brows rose. "You know that is not suitable. How could you—?"

His grandmother stopped him with a wave of her hand. "Do not worry, dear boy. She is perfectly safe. You do not think that I would intentionally place her in a situation that could see her harmed, do you?" She looked at him with a challenge in her eyes; yet a teasing smile played across her lips.

Troy shook his head, knowing that reasoning or arguing with his grandmother was absolutely pointless.

"Wait!" Harriet exclaimed all of a sudden as she turned around to face him, the look in her eyes deeply unsettling. "Why don't *you* marry her?"

Troy felt his jaw drop.

"Marry who?" Anne inquired as she reached for her cup of tea.

Harriet rolled her eyes. "Sarah, of course! Who else?"

Troy felt all eyes turn to him as a cold shiver crawled down his spine.

"You have to admit he would be perfect for her," Harriet continued, her words directed at her sisters, completely undeterred by her brother's dark glare. "He is kind and sweet and respectful. He has a sense of humor; although, he knows how to hide it." She grinned at him. "He is good-looking and comes from a respectable family...well, mostly respectable, I suppose." Chuckling, she seated herself next to Anne. "Well, what do you think?"

Christina frowned. "I don't know. He might be a bit too serious for her."

"I vote yes," Louisa exclaimed with a wide grin flashed in his direction. "It's about time you marry, and there is no one sweeter in the world than Sarah."

Before Troy could respond to that, Anne remarked, "But he does not love her, does he?" She held his gaze for a moment, then turned to look at his sisters. "Should they not both have the chance to marry for love?"

Sighing with disappointment, Christina, Harriet and Louisa nodded while Leonora turned to them and suggested, "Perhaps we should ask his opinion on the matter."

In a heartbeat, all eyes turned to Troy. "Well?" Harriet prompted, that dauntless spirit of her lighting up her green eyes.

Clearing his throat, Troy faced his sisters with a stern look. "How very kind of you to ask my opinion," he remarked dryly; however, as his eyes fell on Christina's face and saw the worry and concern she felt for her friend, his anger waned. "I wish I could help Sarah, truly; however, I cannot marry her."

"Why not?" Harriet asked promptly, something thoughtful in her gaze, as though her line of questioning served a very specific purpose. Troy knew from experience that his youngest sister might appear free-spirited and careless; her mind, however, was as sharp as their grand-mother's.

"I care for Sarah, yes," Troy admitted, looking around the room at each and every one of them, needing them to understand. "But I care for her as I care for all of you. I look at her and see the little sister who went along with you on all of your ludicrous ideas." He cast a mean-ingful look at Harriet and Christina in particular. "I'm sorry. I cannot marry her. If there's anything I can do, please, do not hesitate to ask it of me. But not that."

Feeling a new wave of hopelessness fall over the room, Troy

excused himself and left, hoping with every fiber of his being that somehow his sisters and grandmother would find a way. Indeed, he could not imagine his grandmother ever failing at something she had set her mind to. No doubt, some kind of plan was already underway to protect Sarah from whatever scheme her parents saw fit to bestow upon her.

Chapter Eighteen

WHAT IT MEANS TO BE SELFISH

This time, when Nora arrived at the ruins, Troy was already there waiting for her. The moment she caught sight of him, her heart leaped with joy and a heavy weight dropped off her shoulders. Only then did she realize how afraid she had been that he would not come, that she would not see him again.

And then Troy turned and saw her, and his whole face transformed.

At least for a moment.

For one precious moment, he allowed his emotions to show, a dazzling smile coming to his face that almost made Nora slip out of her saddle. Then, however, he quickly composed himself, that mildly interested, kind expression once more upon his face that Nora remembered so well.

Pulling on her reins, Nora slowed her mare, her eyes not for a second straying from the tall man standing by the crumbling wall of the watchtower. She knew—or at least suspected—that he had not wanted to see her again after their first encounter. She had seen it upon his face, the doubt and concern. Despite her words, he was still afraid that he had overstepped a line; she could tell.

Yet he was here. Why? What did that mean? Had he simply

changed his mind? Or was he here against his better judgment simply because…he could not stay away?

As much as Nora's heart cried out at the knowledge that they could not have a future together, it also danced with joy at every precious moment—every precious, *stolen* moment—they had with one another.

Being the gentleman he was, Troy stepped forward and offered to assist her down. As he reached up to catch her, Nora's mind instantly flashed back to that moment five years ago. It had happened this way, had it not? He had helped her from her horse, and then somehow…

Everything had been different.

A hint of nervousness lingered upon Troy's face, and yet he did not change his mind. He did not step back. He held out his hands to her, and Nora smiled.

"Don't drop me," she teased, torn between the old familiarity of their friendship and this new, heart-stopping tingle that threatened to overwhelm her every time he stepped near.

A wide smile came to his face, and Nora was certain she saw the hint of an eye roll. "Have I ever?"

Nora looked down into his eyes, all thoughts of teasing him gone. "Not once," she whispered, then she leaned forward and slid into his arms.

And Troy caught her.

With his hands upon her waist, he gently set her down onto the ground, his gaze locked upon hers, his breath coming suddenly faster, mingling with her own. They stared at one another, unmoving, his hands still upon her waist, her own settling upon his arms.

"I was worried you wouldn't come," she admitted freely, surprised to see a spark of doubt come to his eyes.

"I shouldn't have," Troy replied, and despite the mask he kept in place, Nora thought to see longing blaze in his blue eyes. Then he released her and stepped back. He cleared his throat and forced his gaze from hers. "How have you been?"

Nora shrugged. Then she felt a smile tug upon her lips. "As my brother once described my day: embroidery, tea, more embroidery." Grinning, she looked up at him.

Troy chuckled, the expression on his face suddenly less intense, more relaxed. "How do you stand all the excitement?"

Nora feigned an exhausted sigh. "Oh, I hardly know." Then she chuckled, delighted when he joined in. "And you? And your sisters? Are they all busy with preparations for the ball?"

Troy looked as though about to nod when he paused, and a thoughtful expression came to his eyes.

"What is it?"

He cleared his throat, looking uncomfortable. "They are worried for a friend," he answered her, though clearly reluctantly. "Her parents intend to see her married without regard for her happiness."

Nora felt something inside her darken, and for a moment, she felt the urge to cower down and roll herself into a tight little ball.

"Are you all right?" Troy asked gently as his right hand reached out and then settled upon her arm.

Swallowing, Nora nodded. "How awful for her," she murmured. "What will she do?"

"My sisters hope to see her married to a good man before her parents' scheming comes to bear."

"Good. Do they have someone in mind?"

A muscle in Troy's neck jerked. "They asked if I would——"

"No!" Shocked by her own outburst, Nora clasped her hands over her mouth, staring up at Troy with wide eyes, wishing she could sink into a hole in the ground.

To her utter surprise, the right corner of his mouth twitched, as though he wished to smile, but was uncertain if he had reason to. "Why not?" he asked in a quiet voice, and Nora thought to hear hope clinging to those two words.

It made her heart soar...and ache.

"Did you agree?" she demanded the moment that awful thought entered her mind.

Troy held her gaze for a long moment, every second of it—purest torture. "No," he finally said, and Nora exhaled a deep breath. "Why...?" He hesitated, eying her with apprehension. "Why do you not want me to marry her?"

Heat surged onto Nora's face. *Because I want you for myself. Because I love you. Because you belong with me. Because...*

"Because we should all marry for love, do you not agree?" she said instead, trying her best to meet his eyes the way a friend would, knowing that she could not tell him how she felt.

If he knew...

For a moment, Nora allowed herself the fantasy of a shared future. She imagined joining him at Whickerton Grove. She imagined a beautiful wedding with all the people they loved. She imagined seeing him every morning the moment she opened her eyes. She imagined those strong, warm, gentle arms enfolding her whenever she needed them to. She imagined many, countless wonderful things...

...until reality came knocking, urging her to remember the one reason why this fantasy could never come to pass, could never be real.

Never would they have children. She could never be a mother, and if he married her, he would never be a father. And Troy *should* be a father, Nora had decided. Whether he wanted to right now or not, did not matter. He was the kind of man who should have children, who would be an amazing father. She could not take that from him.

Yes, she could be selfish right now, right here, and enjoy a few precious moments. However, she could not be selfish in the long run and rob him of a life that should be his.

No, he could never know that she loved him as much as she suspected he loved her as well. What a tragedy! Everything could be so perfect if only *this* was not standing between them.

"Promise me you will not marry her." Lifting her chin, she held his gaze, well aware of the way his eyes narrowed, contemplating her words most carefully. "Promise me you will not change your mind." Nora knew she had no right to demand this of him; yet there was still time for him...to seek a bride. Right here, right now, she wanted him to be hers...if only for a little while.

Nora felt his gaze sweep over her face as though seeking to unearth her reasons for asking this of him. She could see that he was surprised, confused even, and on the verge of requesting an explanation. Then, however, he merely nodded. "I can give you this promise without regret or hesitation," he said calmly, the look in his eyes still thoughtful, watchful, gauging her reaction. "Although I love Sarah—Miss Mortensen—dearly," Nora heard herself draw in a sharp breath, "she is like another sister to me. I could never marry her. As much as I wish I could protect her, it wouldn't feel...right."

Relieved, Nora nodded. "Good."

His jaw hardened suddenly. "Yet one day I will have to marry," he reminded her. He reminded them both, it seemed, for a mildly shocked expression momentarily widened his eyes. "It is my duty to..." He broke off, leaving the rest unfinished.

Again, Nora nodded, understanding him perfectly. "I know. We all have our duties, responsibilities, and are faced with expectations we cannot simply ignore." An image of Mr. Clarke flashed through her mind, and Nora shuddered involuntarily. Still, if she refused him—of which she had every intention—she would spend the rest of her life as her mother, alone; worse, lonely.

Seeing her reaction, Troy's brows drew down. "What is it?" he asked, an edge to his voice. "What expectations are you facing?"

Nora wanted to wave his question away; yet she could see that he would not allow her. "You were right," she finally said, trying her best to smile at him. "Mr. Clarke wants to marry me."

A jolt seemed to go through Troy, and the expression upon his face darkened, hardened. It pained Nora to see him like this, and yet her heart soared at the knowledge that he cared, that he did not want her to marry Mr. Clarke any more than she wanted to see him wed to Miss Mortensen.

"Will you?" Troy gritted out, his shoulders tensing. "Marry him?"

Nora shrugged, surprised by her own reaction. Only yesterday she had been adamant in refusing Mr. Clarke. Yet every time her eyes swept over her mother, she wondered if she would be a fool to do so. She knew she could not have Troy, but did that mean she would have to be alone for the rest of her life?

"I'm uncertain," Nora finally replied, her selfish heart delighting in the way Troy's gaze narrowed. "My mother insists I consider him. She is quite adamant." Pressing her lips together against the sudden urge to weep, Nora turned away from him, a few, unsteady steps putting distance between them she did not want.

Nora never heard Troy move. She never heard the sound of his footsteps upon the cold ground. She never heard any sound leave his lips.

And yet, a moment later, he was simply there. Right behind her, his hands grasping her arms and spinning her around. With a quick tug, he pulled her into his arms, his gaze thunderous, in turmoil, and yet screaming with longing as he stared down at her. "I gave you a promise," he snarled, his breath hot against her skin, "and now I'm demanding one from you."

Nora wanted to weep with joy, yet the tears that rolled down her cheeks nearly broke her heart.

"Promise me," Troy demanded, his voice harsh and uncompromising, "that you will not marry him. Promise me!"

For a brief moment, Nora closed her eyes, allowing this feeling of their shared longing to wash over her, wrap around her and hold her close. She breathed in deeply; yet her breath came shuddering back out when she felt the touch of Troy's knuckles graze the line of her jaw.

Nora's eyes flew open as he pulled her closer, his blue eyes flaring with intent. His hand slipped to the back of her neck, and then he slowly lowered his head, his gaze darting to her lips. "Promise me," he whispered, and she felt his breath tease her lips.

A gasp escaped Nora, and more than anything, she wanted to forget the world around them and accept his kiss. After all, she had been determined to be selfish! At least, for a little while, had she not? What had happened?

Yet the truth was, one day, Troy would marry. If not Miss Mortenson, then another. And once that day came, Nora's heart would shatter into a thousand pieces. Would it feel even worse if she kissed him now?

"Promise me," Troy urged again, and she felt his hand upon her neck tightening, something demanding in the way he held on to her. Oh, if only she could give in! If only—!

"I won't ever marry again," Nora heard herself say as she looked up into his eyes. "My marriage to Hayward was awful, and not a day passed that I did not regret it." She swallowed, fighting to keep the sobs at bay that fought to escape her throat. "I will not marry again. Not ever." Was that the truth? Nora no longer knew.

For a long moment, Troy simply looked at her, the expression upon his face almost unreadable. "Good," he said then, and his gaze dropped to her lips.

Nora drew in a sharp breath, shocked by that one word, for it was the most selfish thing he had ever said.

And then he dipped his head, and his lips brushed against hers. The feather-light touch sent a jolt through Nora, erasing all doubts, all apprehension. Pushing up onto her toes, Nora reached out to pull him closer as her mouth opened beneath his.

And then Troy froze.

He froze.

In the very second Nora wanted to forget the world around her and live in the moment, he pulled back, no doubt cautioned by his own doubts. Nora could sense it.

Lowering herself back down onto her feet, Nora opened her eyes. Troy's were an echo of the regret that pulsed in her heart, and she knew he was just as torn as she was. He wanted her but knew it would not be wise because there was no future for them. He had to know that she could not give him children, did he not? After all, Hayward's bastards were not a secret. Of course, everyone knew.

Releasing her hold on him, Nora took a step back, her muscles fighting to resist, trying to remain close to him. Tears shot to her eyes, and this time, Nora did not try to hide them. No, this time, she let them come because this...

...this was goodbye.

"I wish," she sobbed, staring into his face, that familiar face of his, now contorted with sorrow and regret, "I wish you had never kissed me that day."

Pain blazed in Troy's eyes and, unable to look at him, Nora spun around and rushed to mount her mare. She never once looked over her shoulder but fled the ruins as though chased by an unseen force wanting to do her harm.

Perhaps it would have been better if they had never met again. If he had never kissed her again. If he had never kissed her...

...in the first place.

Chapter Nineteen

TWO FRIENDS, TWO HEARTS, ONE PAIN

All but in a daze, Troy returned home after Nora had fled from the ruins and from him. He was furious with her, and yet he was not. He knew that there was pain deep down inside him, and yet he was not certain if he truly felt it. He knew he had wanted to kiss her, and yet he knew it would not have been wise.

Hanging his head, Troy allowed his gelding to carry him onward, back toward home, as his thoughts circled in his head, replaying all that had happened. In the end, however, it was one thought that remained.

One thought that made him cringe.

One thought that made him feel like a fool.

He had known better, and yet he had gone to see her. He had kissed her. He had allowed himself to entertain a faint hope that perhaps...he could have his own happily ever after.

A dark chuckle left his lips at the thought. Indeed, he was a fool! Nora had not wanted him five years ago, and she did not want him now. All she wanted was his friendship, especially now in a time of need for her. Her marriage had turned out disappointing to her, and she felt alone and sad, and so she had turned to him, hoping for solace and comfort.

And Troy had misunderstood. He had known better, and yet he had allowed himself to be fooled. Not that she had intended to fool him. She had made it perfectly clear that she wanted his friendship, nothing more.

Troy knew he had no right to feel the anger he did; yet he was unable to extinguish the fire. It burned and blazed, blistering his skin until he almost cried out in agony.

If only he had never stumbled upon her by the ruins the other day! If only they had never met again! If nothing else, the past five years had taught him how to continue on, how to push down this longing and regret and move forward. Now, everything was different.

It was as though an old wound had opened again, and he was shocked at the intensity of the pain it caused him, wondering if it hurt that much when it had first been inflicted. He could not be certain. Was this worse?

After handing his gelding to a groom, Troy made his way back inside. He changed quietly, his thoughts turned inward, reliving the moment by the ruins again and again.

I wish you had never kissed me that day.

Nora's words had cut deep, and Troy felt compelled to remain in his chambers and avoid the world around him. He remembered that feeling from years ago. He had felt it then, too. Yet he had not been able to, not in a house full of his family, his nosy, awfully inquisitive family. And so, he had left.

He had spent weeks drifting from one place to another, drowning his sorrows and trying to forget, trying to ignore the fact that Nora had married Hayward. It had taken a long time for him to realize that he could not continue on like this. He had a responsibility, and he needed to pull himself together. And so, eventually, he had rejoined the world, become the man that he was today, done his utmost to forget the girl who had stolen his heart with a single kiss.

A long time passed before Troy felt strong enough to set foot outside his chamber. He went downstairs, intending to seek out the study, wishing for solitude, when excited voices drifted to his ears. He frowned at the sound of footsteps rushing across the front hall, and he stepped back out of the corridor leading to the study, surprised to spot his sisters and parents, closely followed by Grandma Edie, rushing toward the front door. The poor footman on duty there barely managed to open it fast enough before the sisters reached his side. The man looked a bit flustered, but he quickly composed himself.

"What is going on?" Troy asked his father as he moved closer. "Has someone come to visit?"

Exchanging wide smiles, his parents walked on arm in arm. "*Returning* might suit the situation better," his father replied as they reached the door.

Outside, in the drive, Troy spotted not only Juliet and Keir on horseback but also Christopher. Troy frowned. "What is he doing here?" he murmured, exchanging a glance with his father. "I thought he left."

His father chuckled. "I'm afraid, Son, I know as little as you do."

Gritting his teeth against the wave of anger he felt overcome him —anger Troy could not quite understand nor even begin to make sense of—he stood back, knowing that if he were to say something—anything!—he would only regret it. And so, he remained in the background, watching his family, following as they came back inside and settled in the drawing room. He listened as eager questions were posed, curious glances moving from Juliet to Keir to Christopher.

Eventually, Keir said, "As much as we would like to tell ye all what's happened, we're afraid we canna." The usual grin upon his face, he darted a quick glance at Troy's grandmother. "'Tis not our secret to tell as we were sent on an *errand* by another."

Even though Keir had not given a name, every head in the room instantly snapped around and stared at Grandma Edie. As always, though, their grandmother bore a most innocent expression upon her face, and Troy knew without a doubt that she would not volunteer any information. "I do not have the slightest inkling what you're talking about. All I do know is that there is a ball here tomorrow night and a lot still needs to be done."

Still, another glance at Juliet and Christopher made Troy wonder if indeed Keir had been speaking the truth. What had happened? Where had they gone? And why were they returning with Christopher?

Deep down, Troy knew the answer, though. After all, he understood well the looks exchanged between his sister and his oldest friend. He understood the glow upon their faces, the smiles they cast at one another and the longing that stood in their eyes. It tore at something deep inside him, and his anger reawakened. Despite everything, Juliet and Christopher still had a chance at happiness. If they simply spoke honestly to one another, they could still procure their own happily ever after.

If only Troy could hope for the same.

Watching his sisters jump up with excitement at the impending ball, Troy waited for them to leave and then stepped over to where Christopher sat. The moment his friend looked up, he said, "We need to talk."

Christopher nodded, then he rose to his feet. "Of course."

Turning around, Troy left the drawing room and headed toward his study. He knew he needed to find a way to get to grips with his emotions. He could not blame Juliet and Christopher for something that was outside their control. Of course, their happiness only reminded him of what he had lost, what would never be his. Yet of course, they had a right to it, and he was happy for them, was he not?

At least, he should be.

Still, he knew he needed to make certain why Christopher had returned. He needed to know what his intentions were. As much as he loathed the thought of discussing their possible nuptials, Troy knew it was his responsibility to ensure his sister's happiness. After all, he was her brother...and he loved her!

Holding open the door, he waited until Christopher stepped across the threshold, then closed it. "You left," Troy finally said, regarding his friend with open calculation.

Christopher nodded. "I did."

Troy could sense that something had shifted between them. Once, they had spoken honestly to each other, holding nothing—or very little —back. Yet, now, there was a new caution in Christopher, as though he weighed his words most carefully.

"And yet here you are," Troy remarked, leaning against the mantle of the fireplace in what he hoped to be a relaxed posture.

For a moment, the look in Christopher's eyes remained contemplative, as though he had not yet decided what to say or if to speak at all. Then, however, his chin lifted a fraction, and he approached. "What is it you wish to know? Ask it, and I shall tell you honestly. I promise."

Christopher's words, so open and trusting, reminded Troy of the many years they had been close friends. He had always thought of Christopher as a good man, had always trusted him without hesitation. And he wanted to again.

A deep sigh left Troy's lips as the tension in his body slowly began to wane. All of a sudden, he felt tired, exhausted, unwilling to deal with the world and all it threw at him. "I am not your enemy," he told Christopher with a sigh of relief, "nor do I wish to be. I need you to believe that."

The look upon Christopher's face relaxed as well, and he nodded. "I never thought so. Not for a moment." He moved a step closer. "Neither do you believe that I hold any ill intentions toward your sister."

Again, it was Troy's turn to agree. "You are correct; yet I have been wrong before. Tell me here and now what it is you want. Why did you come back? Why did you not leave? What," he urged a hint of warning into his voice, "are your intentions?"

"I love her." The words flew from Christopher's mouth without a moment of hesitation. "I've always loved her, yet I never knew how much until I thought her lost to me."

It took every bit of willpower Troy possessed not to flinch at that simple statement, a statement that echoed within his own heart. "And?"

"I wish to marry her. Yet more needs to be said. We—"

"Does she know of your son?" Troy blurted out, surprising himself by throwing obstacles into their path. A part of him argued that it was simply his way of ensuring his sister's well-being; yet another part knew that it was envy. He envied them their love, their future, all they could have. It was petty of him and awful, and he hated himself for speaking these words.

Christopher's jaw dropped. "You...You know?" He blinked, then asked, "Who told you?"

Oh, how Troy despised secrets! Yet, they were everywhere! How had this happened? "Am I correct to assume that my grandmother also knows?" He shook his head, wondering why he was surprised. If anyone knew, it was her. "No, she did not tell me," Troy assured his friend, seeing the questioning expression upon his face. "When you left without a word back then, I watched my sister torture herself for weeks, months, wondering what she had done to drive you away, to lose your friendship." He fixed his friend with a pointed stare. "So, I made some inquiries."

Christopher nodded his head. "I never meant to keep this from you, from her. It was a mistake, and yet the thought that my son had never been born is pure torture. I cannot look at him and see a mistake. I cannot say I'm sorry for what happened because a part of me simply is not. It cannot be." Something that looked like relief stood upon his friend's face, and Troy realized that not unlike himself, Christopher had longed to speak to someone about this. "It was one moment, one single moment, and it changed everything. I did not plan it. I did not see it coming. It simply happened, and afterward, I felt like such a fool. Do you know what that's like?"

Troy almost groaned at the question. Did he know what that was like? Yes! He knew exactly what that was like. Odd, how similar their two lives were. Troy had never realized the regrets and doubts that had sent Christopher from these shores. He had never known that his friend had loved Juliet for so long, doubting his own worth, doubting whether she would want him. The thought pained Troy all the more because it felt so familiar. He did not need to imagine what it would feel like because he knew.

Still, Troy had never been one to share his innermost thoughts and emotions with another. Nora had been the first and only, and even she did not know all the thoughts that lingered in his mind whenever he looked at her, whenever he thought of her. And so, as he was wont to do, he schooled his features into a mask that would reveal nothing, or at least not much, and simply nodded.

Yet despite Troy's efforts, an inquisitive frown came to Christopher's face, and he took a step forward. "Nora?"

Troy had never known how much pain the mere mention of her name could bring him. He barely managed to hold on to his composure, feeling all the blood drain from his face. Shaking himself, he tried his best to chase away any lingering emotions, any lingering thoughts of her. His gaze hardened and fixed upon Christopher, determined to steer the conversation back to where it had begun. "Speak to her, and do it quickly," he told Christopher sternly. "You are my friend, but if you hurt her again, I will end you." The words came out as a growl, and he felt an unbearable stab of pain at the thought that Juliet might be experiencing the same emotions he was. No, he did not want that for her. "Is that understood?"

Without a moment of hesitation, Christopher gave him his word, and Troy believed him. He was glad when the door finally closed behind his friend and he could return to his solitude or whatever was left of it. He hoped to stay out of everyone's way, to make no more than a brief appearance at tomorrow's ball and otherwise remain away from everyone and everything. It would be for the best as he was not good company at present, and he did not wish to spoil their mood.

Yet before the ball the next day, Christopher stepped into his study once again. "Do you have a moment?" His hands seemed to shake as he closed the door behind himself. "There is something rather...important I need to discuss with you."

Closing the ledger in front of him, Troy regarded his friend carefully, certain he had come to ask for Troy's blessing to marry Juliet. "Is it about my sister?"

Christopher's face tensed as he came to stand on the other side of Troy's desk. "No, it is about mine."

Shock slammed into Troy, and once again, a battle was fought within himself. One side of him wanted to confide in his friend while another cringed away from the mere thought of it. As always, the side that liked to hide away won out. "There is nothing to discuss." He dropped his gaze to the ledger before him. "I would appreciate it if you—"

"No!"

Troy's head snapped up at the vehemence in his friend's voice.

"No, I will not remain silent any longer," Christopher insisted, and Troy knew that nothing he could say would deter his friend. "There is something you need to know, something I've been meaning to tell you for years." He drew in a deep breath to fortify himself. "I kept quiet before because I saw your reluctance to discuss her and knew that even if I told you, there was nothing that could be done...for either one of you."

Troy glared at his friend, feeling his composure slip away bit by bit. "Whatever you think I need to know—"

Christopher shook his head in defiance. "I will not leave this room until I've said all I need to say. I've kept quiet for too long with regard to so many things. Nothing good ever comes from not telling the truth."

Exhaustion swept through Troy's body, and he felt his shoulders slump. "Why? Why now? Why can you not simply leave it be?"

"Because things have changed. She's no longer married, and she cares for you as you care for—"

Slamming his fist down onto the tabletop, Troy snarled at his friend, "It does not matter! Whatever you think I need to know will not change that she—"

"I never gave her your letter!"

If Christopher had in that moment punched Troy in the stomach, he would have felt less pain, less shock than those few words elicited. *I never gave her your letter!* The words echoed through Troy's head as he stared at Christopher, shock almost throwing him backward as his head began to spin.

"I'm so sorry." Anguish stood upon Christopher's face. "Please let me explain. I never meant for this to happen."

Unable to answer, unable to catch a clear thought, Troy dropped back down into his chair, barely remembering when he had risen. His mind was muddled and confused as Christopher's words continued to bounce around inside his skull. *I never gave her your letter!*

"When you handed me the letter and asked me to give it to Nora," Christopher began, "I had no idea what it said."

An awful thought entered Troy's mind in that moment, and he glared up at his friend accusingly.

"I did not read it!" Christopher assured him swiftly, clearly guessing Troy's thoughts. "I assure you. I don't *know* what it says even now, but from what I have observed, I assume—"

"Why?" Troy growled, unable to keep silent a moment longer.

"Why did you—?" He broke off and gritted his teeth as his hands began to tremble.

"I assure you I had every intention of giving it to her. I was on my way to see her, but then a servant approached me with some problem. Apparently, my mother had failed to give specific instructions and now they were uncertain how to—"

"Get to the point!"

Christopher drew in a slow breath and nodded. "Anyhow, I spoke to my mother, and when she went off to see to matters, I glimpsed... something on her writing desk. It was a letter informing her of my son's birth. It was dated a few weeks back, and yet I had never seen it."

Despite his own pain and shock, Troy could see how deeply that moment had affected Christopher, how it had shocked him.

"Everything changed for me in that moment. All I could think about was that...I had to see him." Raking a hand through his hair, Christopher strode over to the window. "I almost ran out of the house then and there, my only thought for him, my son. As Fate would have it, it was my mother who spotted me hastening through the foyer. She called out to me, and...I confronted her." He scoffed. "She could not understand why it bothered me, why I would want to see him. She told me not to be foolish, berating me for my poor judgment and flawed behavior. But I didn't care. I knew I needed to go. I needed to see him." Turning back around, Christopher met Troy's gaze. "She tried to stop me, and the only thing that gave me pause was the reminder of my sister's wedding." Troy felt his fingers dig into the armrests of his chair, his emotions all over the place, ripped apart and directed in every possible direction. He felt it all. Shock, confusion, anger, regret, and he did not know what to focus on first.

"I left the moment she was married," Christopher finally said, sadness darkening his face. "Your letter completely slipped my mind. I had no idea how urgent it was or what you wished to tell her. At least not at that point. Later, much later, when I returned home and learned of your disappearance, how you had vanished the day of Nora's wedding, when I saw her face upon my next visit, the pieces slowly began to come together. Suddenly, I remembered your letter, and I realized what it must contain." Something helpless and frustrated came to Christopher's face, and he threw up his hands. "But what was I to do? She was married, and any chance you might have had was lost. I wanted to tell you, but I wondered if perhaps it would simply make things worse for you. For the both of you. So...I never said a word, not to you. Or to her." He inhaled a deep breath. "Until now."

Unable to look at his friend any longer, unable to hear more, Troy buried his face in his hands.

Still, Christopher was not finished. "So, you see? Things have changed in a way that matters. She never refused you, chose another over you. This truly is a chance for the two of you to find out what you could have. I don't know what happened between you both. I don't know how you suddenly... I never saw you be anything else but friends and never for a second thought that that could change one day. But if you care for her, as I suspect she cares for you, don't let this chance slip through your fingers. Go to her. Tell her everything you wanted her to know that day all those years ago."

Troy felt dead inside as he stared at his friend, stared at him without seeing him. His words continued to echo in his head, their meaning twisted and confusing. He could not tell up from down or light from dark. All Troy could do, was sit there and stare his friend.

Chapter Twenty

MISTAKES

The moment Nora left the ruins, left Troy's side, she already missed him, and each step that carried her away made it worse. She walked Fartherington Hall like a ghost, eyes unseeing, her mind drifting back to the moments they had shared. They made her smile and then brought tears to her eyes in the next moment. She fought to push them away, but they kept returning, insistent she give them her attention.

"Is this to be my life?" Nora murmured to herself, feeling despair encroach upon her because what was she to do?

As always, when it was least convenient, Mr. Clarke came upon her as she stood in such a desolate moment by the drawing-room windows, her gaze directed outward at the darkening sky. "Do you wish to be alone?" he asked in a gentle voice that surprised her.

Nora shook her head, knowing that many lonely moments lay ahead of her. She might as well skip this one. "There is no need. Please, what do you wish to say?"

Gesturing for her to sit, Mr. Clarke took the seat opposite her. For a moment, he seemed uncertain about what to say or how to begin. Then he smiled at her and folded his hands in his lap. "I don't know if I ever told you this, but my first marriage was one of convenience," he said, surprising her. "She was a kind girl but distant. I suppose we both tried our best but..." He shrugged, regret marking his features. "Our delight, our joy, came from the child we were expecting." He sighed. "And then she died."

"I'm so sorry," Nora whispered, surprised to see this vulnerable side of him. It reminded her of the moments he had spoken to her before her husband's passing. She had thought him kind and considerate, decent and gentle. Indeed, this last fortnight, he had appeared like a different man to her.

Mr. Clarke drew in a slow breath. "I love my son, but he never knew his mother. I...I want him to have a family, parents who love him."

Of course, Nora understood instantly what Mr. Clarke was trying to say. How could she not? She saw the look in his eyes, hopeful and almost pleading, matching the tone in his voice that whispered of someone reaching out a hand toward a dream. Nora knew that feeling. She knew it well.

Troy.

Instantly, Nora's heart grew heavy, and she determinedly pushed all thoughts of her own love away, returning her attention to the man sitting across from her. Was it possible that Mr. Clarke truly felt for her? That his reasons for seeking her out, for wanting her to become his wife went beyond a sense of duty or even friendship? Was it possible that he felt for her the way she felt for Troy?

It was that thought that softened Nora toward him. Indeed, the look in his eyes almost broke her heart. A part of her wanted to stop him, to keep him from saying more, while another wondered if it truly was time for her to bury all hopes for a family of her own.

As a heavy sigh left her lips, Nora remembered Mr. Clarke's little boy. Hubert—Hugh—had always been a quiet, somewhat fearful child with wide blue eyes that had always made her wonder what lived in his heart. Could she be his mother? Would it bring them both happiness?

Nora did not know. How could she? Yet it was something to consider, was it not?

However, the moment she thought it, her mind strayed back to another day spent at the ruins. She remembered the way Troy had grasped her arms; his face contorted into a snarl as he had demanded she promise him she would not marry Mr. Clarke. Had she given him that promise? Nora wondered. She could not quite recall. Then, she had been certain she would never marry again. If she could not have Troy, she did not want another. Yet Nora had never once considered the possibility of becoming a mother to a child not born to her.

But now, here it was.

Mr. Clarke heaved a deep sigh, wringing his hands nervously. "I know you are still in mourning," he assured her with a hint of a smile. "Of course, there is no rush. I would never dream of dishonoring my cousin's memory. Yet I cannot help but voice my admiration for you and tell you I've always held you in the highest esteem." He swallowed.

Nora dropped her gaze, touched by his words. She remembered how he had always smiled at her, always had had a kind word to say to her. Once or twice, she had even overheard him urge her husband to be kinder to her. Had he felt for her even then?

"I believe your mother would approve of a union between us," Mr. Clarke remarked with a hint of hesitation in his voice. "However, I would never want you to be my wife if that decision goes against your heart's desire." He cast her a sad smile. "Take all the time you need, but please, think on it. I assure you I will always do my utmost to make you happy, to ensure that you will never know another day of sadness." He heaved a deep breath. "Please, consider what I've said." He cleared his throat. "I will travel to London in the morning in order to claim my cousin's title. Perhaps some time apart will do us both good."

Unable to hide the tears that collected in her eyes, Nora nodded. "I shall," she replied in a choked voice, seeing Troy's contorted face before her inner eye the moment these two words tumbled from her lips. "I wish you a good journey."

Nora fought to hold on to her composure until Mr. Clarke had left the drawing room. Then, the moment the door clicked shut behind him, the dam broke...

...and so did Nora.

All but crumbling to the floor, she wept for the mistakes she had made, for everything they had cost her, as well as for the mistakes she might yet make. If she married Mr. Clarke, would that be another mistake? Or would it at least grant her a sliver of happiness? What was the alternative? To remain alone forever? To lead her mother's life all over again?

Nora did not know what to do. Had life always been this complicated? She remembered in her youth she had dreamed of falling in love. She had imagined meeting someone, knowing right away that he was the one, marrying him and living happily ever after. Back then, it had not seemed like a fairytale, like something impossible to obtain. It had seemed like the normal order of the world. Had she simply been too young to see the truth? Yet few people in life truly ever found happiness. What most found were disappointment and regret.

Drying her tears, Nora heaved a deep sigh, her body aching from all the many emotions that seemed to wrack it lately. She knew she could not go on like this forever. Troy had told her unmistakably that one day he would have to marry, and they both knew he could not marry her. As much as he might care for her—and Nora could not help the smile that came to her face as she thought of it—he had never once spoken of marriage. Clearly, he had always known that despite their feelings for one another, the future would see them separated. That was simply the way of the world.

If Nora could not find love in marriage, perhaps she could still have a mother's love for a little boy who had always looked in desperate need of a mother. Was that where her path would lead her?

Nora did not know, and she did not have the strength to think about it now. Perhaps tomorrow would bring clearer thoughts.

Perhaps.

Chapter Twenty-One

IN THE FACE OF HAPPINESS

Troy did not feel like celebrating as he stood among a myriad of guests in Whickerton Grove's enormous ballroom. The orchestra played a lively tune, and many guests streamed onto the dance floor. Laughter and cheerful voices echoed through the vaulted room, standing in stark contrast to the dark cloud that hung over Troy's head. His gaze swept from those attending tonight to his own family gathered not far off.

Seeing them, Troy felt the familiar urge to join them, and yet he could not. His legs simply would not move, rooting him to the spot. Indeed, they looked so happy as they whispered to one another, laughed, and embraced each other. He watched his sisters step onto the dance floor with their husbands, watched them smile and sigh, and felt his own heart wither away a bit more.

Juliet and Christopher stood a little apart, and yet the way they continued to glance at one another left no doubt as to how they felt about the other. They were in love. Troy had always known this to be true. He had feared for his sister's heart, and yet he knew he should not have. Indeed, they would be married soon, would they not?

Troy knew that this thought ought to fill him with joy, with relief at the very least. Yet what he felt was something different. Something dark and petty. Something a brother should not feel. Something that made him feel even worse.

Was it envy? Was it fury? Troy could not be certain, could not put his finger on it, yet it seemed to tense every muscle in his body, his jaw clenched, his teeth grinding together as he fought to remain calm. He felt ready to explode, burst into a thousand pieces right here in the ballroom, and for a moment, it appeared there was nothing he could do to prevent it.

And then he saw Christopher lead Juliet onto the dance floor. He saw his sister's face light up in a way that almost brought him to his knees, and for a split second, his eyes swept the dance floor in search of Nora...before he remembered.

Troy could not recall ever having been so focused on what he wanted, and what he could not have. Yet lately, it seemed all he could think about. It was selfish of him, certainly, and yet every time he thought of his sisters, the four youngest now happily married—with Juliet undoubtedly soon to follow—he could not help but think, *Why can I not find the same?*

Troy willed himself to tear his gaze away, to walk through the ballroom and greet their guests, exchange words here and there. He did his utmost to smile, to at least appear to be in a good mood. Perhaps this was nothing more than a matter of willpower. Perhaps if he tried hard enough, he could simply ignore how he felt. After all, what else was he to do?

Time seemed to move slowly, agonizingly so, as Troy fought to maintain a tight grip upon his emotions. He felt like a machine, doing what it had been designed to do without any thoughts of his own, without any motivations or concerns. For a time, it felt good to distance himself, to finally receive a reprieve from these overwhelming emotions. However, with every minute that ticked by the effort it took for him to ignore how he felt grew and grew. Before long, Troy felt exhausted, close to collapsing, when he turned and suddenly realized that Juliet and Christopher were nowhere to be seen.

Of course, there was no good reason for him to be concerned. After all, they loved each other. They would no doubt be married soon. And yet, Troy found himself stalking from the ballroom, his eyes sweeping the hallways, darting from door to door as he moved. Anger boiled beneath his skin, irrational, utterly misplaced anger.

Troy knew he was acting like a madman; yet he could not seem to stop. Perhaps it was simply easier to focus on his sister and Christopher instead of facing his own lonely future.

His steps drew to an abrupt halt when the soft sound of murmured voices drifted to his ears. He strained to listen, tried to make out from whence they came. Step by step, he moved down the darkened corridor until he came to stand in front of the library doors.

Inhaling a deep breath, Troy silently slid open the door. He moved to step inside when his gaze fell on what he had expected: Juliet and Christopher.

It seemed they had been sitting on the floor in front of the fireplace, their faces flushed, and their eyes misted with tears. No doubt aware that someone had come upon them, they now quickly scrambled back onto their feet and turned toward the door, their eyes widening when they beheld him.

"Troy, please, let me explain," Christopher said tensely, a hint of guilt upon his face.

Unlike the man by her side, Juliet looked simply confused by the infuriated look upon Troy's face. Out of the corner of his eye, he watched her brows draw down ever so slightly as she looked from Christopher to him and back.

"What did you do?" Troy snarled, despite his better judgment. In truth, he had no blame to lay at Christopher's feet, and yet there was a part of him that simply could not stop. If only Christopher had given Nora his letter—

If only he had—

All of a sudden, all the thoughts that Troy had not allowed himself to think since Christopher had revealed the truth to him the day before flooded his mind and unleashed his anger in a way he had never known possible.

Christopher swallowed hard. "Nothing untoward happened, I assure you. We were merely talking and—"

I assure you? Those three little words made something inside Troy snap. "You will excuse me if I do not take your word for it."

"Troy," came Juliet's soft voice, and Troy blinked, shocked to find her standing in front of him, her hands placed upon his rigid arm, her eyes seeking his. When had she moved to stand in front of him? He could not recall. "Please, do not place blame on Christopher. He speaks the truth. Nothing happened." A smile tugged upon her lips. "Well, perhaps that is not entirely true. We are betrothed. We truly are. Will you not give us your blessing?"

Troy could not bear the utter joy that stood upon Juliet's face, that lit up her eyes and made her shine in a way that gave her an almost ethereal appearance, as though she were not from this world.

Again, fury slammed into him, mixed with envy and an almost unbearable fear of his own future. "You accepted him?" he snarled, glaring down at her in a way he had no right to.

Juliet's brows drew down farther as she searched his face. "Of course, I did. I... I love him."

So, this was it, Troy thought as her words echoed in his mind. She, too, would soon leave him, walk away and begin a life all her own.

With Christopher.

To Juliet, the past did not matter, the mistakes Christopher had made, the fact that he had a child. None of that seemed to matter to Juliet. She loved him, and she wanted a future with him. "I never forgot him," she whispered, the look in her eyes imploring as they looked up into Troy's. "I tried, but I never could. Who we love is not our choice." Gently, she cupped her hand to his cheek. "This, here, now *is* my choice. I want him. *He* is my choice, and I need you to be happy for me."

Her words—spoken so gently and compassionately—undid him. Troy felt his anger wane, dissolve into nothing, until all he was left with was deep, soul-crushing sadness. It was what he had been running from, what he had known he could not bear, diving into his anger instead—as misplaced as it had been. "You should return to the ball," he gritted out through clenched teeth as the weight upon his shoulders increased and his knees threatened to buckle.

As he turned back to the door, Juliet called out to him. "Have you... Have you never been in love?"

Troy froze.

A part of him wanted to laugh—hysterically. Another wanted to sink to the floor and weep. Yet another was still tempted to plant his fist in Christopher's face.

Instead, Troy forced a deep breath down into his lungs. "You should return to the ball," he said once again and then slipped from the room, unable to remain in the face of happiness a moment longer.

Chapter Twenty-Two
THE DAM BREAKS

Before the ball had even ended, Troy slipped out of the house. A distant part of his mind reminded him of his duties, and yet to attend to them in his current state of mind would be beyond foolish. Who knew what would happen? What if he lost control and...?

Standing outside in the dark, Troy shook his head to chase away the murmur of voices and music that seemed to follow him wherever he went. His gaze moved to the stables, and before he could call himself to reason, he had already taken two steps.

Nora.

He snapped to a halt, cursing himself, the world and all those in it.

I never gave her your letter.

Upon first hearing Christopher's admission, Troy could not cope with those six little words. He had heard them, and yet he could not make sense of them. He had not even dared, pushing them to the back of his mind, determined not even think of them. After all, the annual autumn ball had demanded his attention and...

He closed his eyes and inhaled a deep breath. Opening them again, they came to rest upon the stables once more.

Nora.

A jolt went through him like a lightning strike, and Troy whipped around and marched down the lawn in the opposite direction of the stables.

I never gave her your letter.

The words rang in his ears as he tried to understand their implication. Nora had no idea that he loved her. She had no idea that he had asked her to break off her betrothal. She had no idea that he had wanted to marry her.

Raking a hand through his tousled hair, Troy quickened his steps. He tore his cravat free and tossed it aside, ripping buttons off his shirt as he yanked on the collar, unable to bear the feel of it.

Like a noose slowly squeezing the life from him.

He could barely see where he was going—round and round in circles, most likely—but he did not dare stop. He saw light streaming out of the windows into the dark of night, saw guests dance within and heard the echo of their voices drift through closed doors.

On the fringes of his mind, Troy could sense thoughts begin to form. Thoughts that terrified him. Thoughts that would break him if he allowed them close. A part of him wanted to flee from them, but they would not let him. They chased him until he finally stopped and turned to face them.

If Christopher had given Nora his letter, would she have still married Hayward?

Troy closed his eyes.

If Nora had known how he felt, would she have agreed to become his wife instead?

Troy sank to his knees, feeling the cold seep into his limbs.

Could they have been married these past few years?

Troy's heart felt as though it was being ripped from his chest.

Or was he perhaps...fooling himself? Did he dare hope?

Hours passed as Troy kneeled in the grass, contemplating all that had happened since that fateful day five years ago as well as all that *could* have happened if only...

When his muscles began to ache, he finally pushed to his feet, frowning when he found himself near the back of the stables. He could not recall walking in this direction, but he did not care. His gaze fell on the dim outline of a stack of firewood, and he instantly shrugged out of his jacket, tossed it aside and rolled up the sleeves of his shirt. He moved back around toward the front of the house, snatched up one of the torches that lined the drive up to the front door, and then stalked back to the rear of the stables. There, he grabbed another, unlit one, used a hammer to drive it into the hard ground and then set it aflame, illuminating the small yard and the stump used for splitting wood.

Then he went in search of an axe.

The icy night air felt like sharp pin pricks upon his heated skin; yet Troy's steps never slowed. He glanced inside the small shed situated at the rear of the stables, quickly located what he was looking for and then strode back outside. The smooth handle of the axe felt good against his skin, the tool's comfortable weight somehow reassuring.

The first swing of the axe brought an odd sense of relief. Troy's breath rushed from his lungs, and he felt his muscles tighten with purpose. He swung again, savoring that satisfying *thwack* of metal on wood as he watched the log being split in two.

Again and again, Troy struck, swinging the axe high and bringing it down quickly. Each strike reverberated up his arms, and he felt beads of sweat slowly trickle down his temples.

Yet, unfortunately, as his movements became familiar, his mind less and less focused on what he was doing, his thoughts inevitably returned to Nora. Gritting his teeth, Troy clutched the handle tighter, willing his mind to abandon its pursuit. He doubled his efforts, his muscles tensing as he brought down the axe upon the log.

I never gave her your letter.

A groan slipped from Troy's mouth, and he almost gave in to the impulse to toss the axe across the yard. Instead, his fingers tightened upon the handle, and he swung again and again as his mind seemed to all but chant her name.

Nora. Nora. Nora.

Exhaling deeply, Troy closed his eyes, momentarily resting the head of the axe upon the stump before his feet. He knew if he could see himself in this very moment, he would appear like a raving madman, like a man devoid of all faculties, driven by a single need.

Nora.

Once again feeling that desperate longing for her spark to life, Troy once more focused his gaze, reached for another log and immediately brought down the axe.

Thwack!

The sound was satisfying, and yet the moment it vanished, Troy once more felt, as though he were drowning.

Thwack!

Sweat ran down his face, and he raised his left arm to wipe at it with his sleeve.

Thwack!

As Troy reached for yet another log, he suddenly felt the little hairs in the back of his neck rise. His eyes narrowed as he peered into the shadows, his movements continuing without thought.

Thwack!

He kicked the two pieces aside with his foot, wondering who had abandoned the ball in favor of this icy darkness. In truth, there was only one person who would follow him here.

"I know you're there," Troy called in to the night, once more lifting the axe, and bringing it down with a forceful swing. "What do you want?"

As expected, it was none other than Christopher, who stepped out of the shadows near the stable wall. "I came to speak with you. I came to apologize." Even in the dim light of the single torch, Troy could see contrition upon his old friend's face.

It pained him to see it, but he pushed the feeling aside, steeling himself. He did not want to feel. Not now. "It is too late for apologies," he growled, his gaze focused on the next log, his hands moving to split it.

Thwack!

Something in Christopher's expression changed, and he threw up his hands. "Bloody hell, Troy, talk to me! Don't pretend that—"

Troy's head snapped up, and he stared at his friend as his pulse thundered in his veins. "You ruined my life!" he accused in a roar. His hands gripped the handle of the axe ever tighter as his measured steps carried him toward Christopher. "You ruined everything!" The words flew from his lips, and Troy felt something deep inside open, anger and resentment and all those emotions he had done his utmost to ignore flowed out, like the curses that escaped Pandora's box.

"And now," Troy continued in a snarl, "you come here after all these years and want my blessing to marry my sister?" Glaring at his friend, Troy shook his head. "Well, you cannot have it." His jaw felt as though it would break apart at any moment, and yet it did not counteract the pain that burned in his chest. He tossed the axe aside and balled his hands into fists as a sudden surge of violence seized him. "Never."

Shock now marked Christopher's face. "You would truly withhold your blessing? You would deny us that? You would deny *her* that?" He shook his head in disbelief. "Juliet has done nothing wrong. She loves you and has been a loyal and devoted sister all these years."

The mention of his sister instantly cooled Troy's anger, and he raked a frustrated hand through his hair, desperate to hold on to it. "And you?" he snarled, fixing Christopher with a hard stare. "What have you done?"

His friend's face fell, and he heaved a deep sigh full of regret. "I didn't know," he murmured. "Why did you not tell me? Had I known I..." Another sigh. Again, full of regret. "I still have the letter."

Shock slammed into Troy. "Did you read it?" he thundered as every muscle in his body tensed anew.

"Of course not!"

"Then hand it back to me," Troy demanded, glancing at the flickering torch to his right, "so I can burn it."

Shaking his head, Christopher stared at Troy's outstretched hand. "No, even if it is years too late, I will give it to my sister. She deserves to know how you—"

"No! You will not!" Troy heard himself roar. Then he charged toward his friend and grasped him by the collar. He barely recognized himself in that moment. "You will not! Do you hear? You will not!"

Not even trying to free himself from Troy's grip, Christopher lifted his hands. "Why not? She is no longer married. You are both free to do as you please, to love whom you ch—"

"No!" Troy heard himself roar before he felt his hand curl into a fist, his arm draw back and...

The moment Troy's knuckles connected with Christopher's jaw, his friend was flung backward.

Troy stared in shock. He felt pain shoot up his arm. He watched Christopher land with a dull *thud* on the hard ground, his face contorted and his eyes pinched shut.

For a moment, nothing seemed real, the world almost frozen...and then time resumed, and Troy recognized a familiar part of him reawaken. Guilt assailed him, mingling with the anger still simmering in his veins. He could still hear that little voice whispering, *Why do you get to be happy and I don't?* Only it had not been Christopher's fault, had it? He had forgotten to hand Nora Troy's letter, yes, but he had not known. It had not been his fault. Not truly.

Troy knew that.

Deep down, he knew that.

And yet it had been easier to lay blame at Christopher's feet.

"Are you...Are you all right?" Troy forced out through gritted teeth as he tried to even his breathing and calm his heart.

A groan slipped from Christopher's lips as he sat up and touched his jaw. He moved it and winced. "More or less." Lifting his head, he met Troy's eyes.

Troy exhaled a deep breath while the blood still rushed in his ears. "I'm sorry," he murmured, holding out a hand to Christopher, then he pulled him to his feet. However, the moment he made to turn away, his friend stepped into his path.

"I'm not angry with you," Christopher stated with raised brows, his eyes holding Troy's. "Whether you like to admit it or not, I know you care for her, and I know that the past few years have been hell for you."

As anger and guilt vanished, replaced by crippling pain, Troy closed his eyes, feeling his teeth grind together. Would this ever stop? In that moment, he wished he could return to that sense of oblivion, of detachedness he had clung to these past few years. It had been easier to bear, had it not?

"Believe me, I know what it feels like," came Christopher's voice before he stepped forward and clasped a hand on Troy's shoulder. "I hesitated far, far too long, held back by doubts and fears I should never have allowed to dictate my actions." He sighed deeply. "I regret that today because I will never get back the years I've lost." He stepped back, looking almost imploringly at Troy. "If you care for her as I believe you do, then...do something about it."

At the pleading tone in his friend's voice, Troy blinked, then raked a hand through his hair, afraid to contemplate the options he had, the path Christopher was urging him to explore.

"You never once spoke to her, did you?" Understanding shone in Christopher's gaze, and the right corner of his mouth twitched ever so slightly with what might have been a smile under different circumstances. "You should. Think about it." Then, without another word, Christopher turned and walked away.

Troy stared after him as something else awoke deep within. It was not anger or regret or pain. It was something gentle and sweet, something teasing and alluring, something warm and soothing.

Nora.

Turning upon his heel, Troy surged toward the stable doors.

Chapter Twenty-Three

TO HELL WITH TOMORROW

Tossing and turning from one side onto the other, Nora squeezed her eyes shut as her thoughts continued to circle in her head. One thought, in particular, she could not seem to shake. One that terrified her.

I'm back in my old bedchamber.

Why that particular thought had not occurred to her with such vehemence before or why it chose this night to frighten her so, Nora did not know. Yet when she opened her eyes and looked at the dim outlines of her chamber, she could not help but remember the last time she had lived here.

Then, she had been full of hope and dreams, looking forward to a future of her own, a family of her own.

Love.

Heaving a deep sigh, Nora turned onto her back, staring up at the darkened ceiling. And now? Now, there was nothing.

No hope.

No dreams.

No future.

Perhaps it was because of the Whickerton's autumn ball tonight that Nora's thoughts had decided to torment her. When she closed her eyes, she could all but see the large ballroom, illuminated by countless dancing flames, swaying to the soft notes of the music. She could see a sea of colors, gowns sparkling in azure and emerald, mingling with soft tones of peach and violet.

Was he dancing? A taunting voice suddenly whispered, and Nora flinched.

Oh, she could so easily imagine Troy among the throng of guests. But was that wise? She had bid him farewell, had she not? However, so long as her mind continued to conjure his image, was there any use in staying away from him?

Even now, Nora felt that odd pull, urging her to his side. She had felt it ever since their first kiss years ago. It had never waned; yet since returning home, it had grown stronger. It was no longer a mild hum, always there in the back of her mind. No, now, it was almost deafening, like someone shouting their demands and expecting to be obeyed.

Pushing upright, Nora slipped from the bed. The embers in the fireplace were still glowing in a deep red, sending their warmth across her chamber. She pulled on her robe and tied the strap in the front before stepping up to the window. A crescent moon greeted her far above the woods that led in the direction of Whickerton Grove.

Nora sighed...then stilled as the muffled sound of footsteps drifted to her ears from out in the hall. Her head flew around, and she stared at her door, wondering if she had misheard or if someone else was truly up at this time of night.

Scarcely daring to draw breath, Nora listened, then flinched when the sound came again. Barely audible, but there. Indeed, someone was out in the hall, moving closer. But who? And why?

For a second, Nora wondered if it could be Mr. Clarke, but why would he be up in the middle of the night when he planned to leave early the next morning? It made no sense. Perhaps—

Nora's breath lodged in her throat when the sound suddenly vanished...right outside her door. She stared across the darkened expanse of her chamber and felt her heart almost leap out of her chest when she saw the door handle move.

Slowly, it was turned downward.

Whoever had come was here to see her. But now? In the middle of the night? Was there some kind of emergency? But if so, Nora would have expected to hear voices, commotion and not this...this eerie silence.

If this was indeed Mr. Clarke, come to press his suit once more, to...to..., she would—

The door slowly swung open, and Nora frantically glanced around for a weapon, anything to defend herself with. She had heard of men who would not take *no* for an answer, who... "Who...Who is it?" Her voice sounded feeble and weak, even to her own ears. "Whoever you are, leave. You have no right—" Nora's voice broke off when Troy suddenly appeared in the door frame, shocking her nearly witless.

For a long moment, they simply stood there, almost motionless, staring at one another.

With one glance, Nora could see that something was wrong, that something was different.

Usually, Troy's clothes were spotless, and while he seemed to be in his evening attire, he appeared to have lost not only his coat but also his jacket and vest. His shirt's collar stood open, and its sleeves were rolled up to his elbows. On top of that, Troy's hair looked like a wild mess, as though he had been running his hands through it all night.

"What are you doing here?" Nora exclaimed, her heart hammering wildly as she contemplated what could have possibly happened to bring him here this night. "What happened?"

Inhaling a deep breath, Troy stepped inside and then closed the door behind him, his eyes never leaving hers. They shone dark in the dim light from the window. "Do you want me to go?" His voice was hoarse and deep, almost like a growl.

Nora had been about to shake her head no when she paused. Indeed, something *was* different. *He* was different.

Always—even in moments of great upheaval—had Troy appeared controlled, calm, rationally assessing the situation and then responding to it with care and foresight. Now, however, the look upon his face was far from controlled.

Nora could see the tension that held him rigid, his body hard and unyielding beneath the thin shirt. Yet even with winter around the corner, Troy did not seem cold. Far from it. Even from the other side of the room, Nora could all but sense the heat that radiated off of him. Sweat glistened upon his forehead, and his hands were balled into fists as his eyes looked into hers.

Dark and thunderous.

Nora drew in a shuddering breath, now absolutely certain that there was no emergency. At least not of the kind she had first thought. Yet, something had brought Troy here this night.

In this state.

If only she knew what had happened, why he was here, what he...wanted.

"Do you want me to go?" he asked once more, his hands clenching and unclenching as he stared into her eyes.

Nora swallowed, knowing that if it had been Mr. Clarke who had come to her chamber at this time of night, his eyes burning with quiet hunger, she would have screamed the house down, terrified to her core.

But this was Troy.

He would never harm her. He was here because...

"No," Nora heard herself whisper into the stillness of the room, feeling her own resolve to keep him away dissolve into nothing. Every reason she had told herself, she had convinced herself to believe went away, leaving her with an almost desperate need to find herself in his arms once more.

As though Troy had read her thoughts, he suddenly pushed away from the door, prowling toward her with single-minded intent.

Perhaps the look of him ought to have frightened her, but instead Nora felt her heart warm with longing and love. Yes, the truth was she wanted him as much as he wanted her, ill-advised or not. She ought to send him away, just as he ought not be here. But she could not.

Not tonight.

Large strides carried him closer, his dark gaze fixed upon hers, revealing all that he felt, every weakness that lived in his heart, every fear that had kept him away. Nora recognized them easily before they suddenly disappeared, replaced by a stubborn insistence to have this one moment.

Yes, tonight would be theirs...and to hell with tomorrow!

Impatiently, Nora flung herself into Troy's arms, meeting him halfway. A desperate growl escaped his lips before his mouth closed over hers with an urgency that made her head spin. Indeed, never would Nora have guessed that Troy possessed such a passionate side, that he would ever give in and forgo every rational objection and reach for what his heart desired.

The thought chased away every last doubt, and she pushed closer, desperate to forget what was and live in a dream...at least for one night.

A gasp was torn from Nora's lips when his hands touched her, their sizzling heat raising goosebumps on her chilled skin. Yet they were gentle, tenderly trailing the column of her neck, tracing the line of her jaw.

Then Troy lifted his head, and his dark eyes looked down into hers as he breathed in deeply, as though wishing to commit this moment to memory. The tips of his fingers brushed along her temple, and his eyes flicked to the side, tracing the movement. Nora could feel his heart beat wildly beneath her palm, and yet he remained perfectly still, the soft touch of his fingers slow and savoring. Brushing a curl back behind her ear, Troy pushed his hand into her hair, cupping the back of her head as his eyes returned to hers. Urgency and the need to give in to a longing too long denied blazed in his eyes. His breathing quickened, and she could feel his hand on the small of her back tighten, urging her closer against him.

Yet he waited.

Nora smiled up at him, cherishing his consideration, the way he cared for her heart, for what she wanted, giving her a choice—one her late husband had never seen the need to offer her. Perhaps it had been Hayward's disregard for her feelings that had prevented a closer attachment on her part. Perhaps there could have been a chance for them if only he had ever looked at her as an equal partner in their marriage.

Perhaps not.

Never had her late husband been the kind of man Troy was.

Warmth filled Nora's heart, and she reached up to cup a hand to Troy's cheek. She felt tears slowly blurring her vision and noted the faint crease of a frown come to his face: concern.

Troy was concerned for her. He always was. Concerned that he was overstepping. Concerned that she did not want him. Concerned that he had been mistaken.

Oh, dear Troy! Nora thought. *Sweet, dear Troy!* Her smile widened and her gaze held his for a second longer, needing him to know that she was choosing this freely, before she pushed herself up onto her toes and kissed him.

She kissed him softly and almost hesitantly at first, determined to experience every facet of this moment. Their previous kisses had often caught her off guard, and they had ended before she had even truly realized what had been happening.

Not now.

Now, she wanted to feel every brush of her lips against his, every soft touch, every breath that passed between them. She felt his skin hot against her own, his pulse as it beat in tandem with hers. The moment was so utterly perfect that she wanted to weep.

If only the thought of tomorrow did not insist on lingering, over-shadowing this one perfect moment.

As though Troy could sense the sadness that threatened to sneak into her heart, he tightened his arms around her, pulling her farther into his embrace, and deepened their kiss. His hands undid her plait, and she felt his fingers running through her tresses.

Nora lost herself in Troy's embrace, in the way he cradled her in his arms, safe and cherished, as though she were a rare treasure. It was an utterly foreign sensation; one she would never forget.

Never.

Chapter Twenty-Four

LOST IN A DREAM

Troy was uncertain what woke him, for when he cracked his eyes open, the world was still dark. He listened for the familiar sounds of Whickerton Grove, but he found them strangely absent. Instead, a dream lingered.

He closed his eyes again and felt a deep sigh rush from his lungs as a sense of utter joy tugged the corners of his mouth into a deep smile.

Nora.

A soft sigh drifted to Troy's ears from right beside him, and his eyes flew open once more. He turned toward it, and his heart slammed to a halt when his gaze fell on the dim outline of Nora's sleeping form.

She lay on her belly, arms thrust beneath her pillow and her wild hair draped over her back. She breathed softly, contentedly, and every once in a while, a smile tugged upon her lips, as though she too were lost in a dream.

Perhaps she was.

Staring at Nora in utter disbelief, Troy slowly began to recall the events of the night. Indeed, it had not been a dream.

He now recalled it with clarity, how he had left the ball and fled out into the night, how he had tried to distract himself by chopping wood like a madman; how Christopher had found him and urged him to... speak to Nora.

Troy's gaze swept lovingly over her sleeping face, and he felt his heart leap and dance and trip at the mere sight of her, at the emotions that surged through his body at being near her.

Indeed, they had not spoken last night. Few words had passed their lips, and yet Troy could not recall ever feeling this...happy. Was this what happiness felt like? He wondered. Countless questions remained unanswered, but now at least he knew what Nora's heart felt for him. She did not look at him and see only a friend. He had not crossed a line when he had kissed her. Indeed, she had made that abundantly clear when she had pulled him into her arms.

Belatedly, Troy realized that he was still smiling, that the muscles in his cheeks were, in fact, beginning to ache from the strain. It felt wonderful, though.

A part of him wanted to wake her and talk about everything that had happened, everything they had never spoken of. Yet he did not dare. The sight of her sleeping so peacefully tugged upon his heart, and he reached out tentatively and brushed an errant curl behind her ear.

A contented sigh left Nora's lips at the touch of his fingertips against her sleep-warm skin, and she snuggled deeper into her pillow.

Troy could have watched her sleep for hours, but then the soft sounds of a house awakening drifted to his ears. Servants were leaving their beds and setting to their tasks. Soon, it would be nigh on impossible for him to sneak out of the house unseen.

Reluctantly, Troy slipped from the bed, doing his best to ignore the shiver that snaked down his back at the cool morning air, and bent to the task of retrieving his clothes. In the dim light, it took him a good while to locate everything he had worn the night before, but eventually, he was dressed.

With a sigh, he looked back at Nora, still asleep, then moved over to lay her night rail and robe next to her on the bed. Unable to help himself, he bent down and placed a tender kiss on the side of her temple. "Until we see each other again," he whispered near her ear and then added, "Soon." Then he quietly slipped from the room.

Fortunately, few servants were up and about and Troy only had to duck into a darkened corner once to avoid being seen by a maid, her eyes half-closed and her mouth wide open in a yawn. He moved swiftly and quietly and soon found himself outside. As he strode toward the back of the stables, he felt the little hairs on the back of his neck rise, as though he were being watched. However, when he turned around, no one was there.

His gelding greeted him with an annoyed nicker after having spent the past night bridled and saddled in one of the stable's empty stalls. Yet the night before, Troy had possessed not even a sliver of patience. "I'm sorry, old friend," he murmured, leading the gelding outside. "Let's head home." He swung himself into the saddle and they were off.

The morning air felt freezing, and yet an unfamiliar warmth lingered in Troy's bones that kept him from shivering uncontrollably in his thin shirt. Once at Whickerton Grove, he handed his gelding to a somewhat surprised-looking groom and then rushed inside, determined to change before anyone spotted him like this.

Unfortunately, wishful thinking rarely panned out.

"Good morning, my boy. You're up surprisingly early."

At the sound of his grandmother's voice, Troy froze in mid-step. Cursing her highly inconvenient timing, he inhaled a deep breath and then turned to face her, wondering what on earth *she* was doing up so early. However, he knew better than to ask. "Good morning, Grandmother," he greeted her with a nod, not failing to note the amused twinkle in her pale eyes. "How are you this morning? Is there anything I can do for you?"

The look upon her face told Troy loud and clear that he could not fool her, that she knew precisely what he was up to. How that was possible was beyond him. Had she perhaps seen him leave? But even so, how would she know where he had gone and...?

"You missed the ball last night," his grandmother remarked with a raised brow, completely ignoring his question.

Troy nodded. "I suppose I did."

For a long moment, his grandmother's narrowed gaze lingered upon his face before a warm smile came to her face. "I am glad you did," she remarked with a slight chuckle, as though she truly knew. Troy knew not what to say; fortunately, it was wholly unnecessary. "Your sister and

Christopher will announce their betrothal any moment now," she told him, happiness shining in her eyes. "Will you accompany me to the breakfast parlor?"

Troy did not even bother to ask how she knew they would be announcing their betrothal today—not that he doubted it after what had happened the previous night; however, he was fairly certain it would cause quite a stir if he walked into the breakfast parlor dressed like this. "I'm afraid I'll need to change first, Grandmother." He glanced down his ruined clothes, wondering where he had left his jacket and vest. And his tie.

A wicked grin came to his grandmother's face as she stepped forward and patted his arm. "You certainly do, my dear. You certainly do." Then she turned and walked away in the direction of the breakfast parlor, her walking cane clacking along on the parquet floor.

Fleeing to the safety of his own chamber as quickly as his feet would carry him, Troy breathed a sigh of relief once the door closed behind him. As much as he loved his family, they were quite an intrusive lot—all of them. And his grandmother was the worst!

Never before had it taken Troy quite so long to change, for his thoughts continuously returned to Nora, to all they had shared the night before. He loved her. He had known so for years, but now, for the first time, he had hope. Of course, neither one of them had spoken of love. They had not spoken at all! But...

Was it possible? If Nora felt nothing for him, she would have sent him away. She *did* care for him. He knew she did!

Looking into the mirror, Troy was taken aback by the odd-looking man smiling back at him. Never had he seen his face quite like this. At least not in the past few years. Perhaps before that day by the ruins, but he could not recall. He had not paid attention to it then.

When Troy finally left his chamber and headed down to the breakfast parlor, loud cheers echoed to his ears. It seemed Grandma Edie had been correct—not that that came as a surprise. Juliet and Christopher had announced their betrothal—finally!

Troy heaved a deep sigh, remembering his rude behavior the night before. Had he truly threatened to withhold his blessing? Heat shot to his face at the mere thought of it.

So, instead of joining his family, Troy kept his distance, waiting for the right time to speak to his sister and future brother-in-law. It took a good deal of patience until he managed to catch them alone. They were strolling through the gardens yet again when Troy caught up to them, glad that for once the coast seemed clear. He supposed with no more secrets begging to be revealed, his family no longer saw the need to crowd around them.

"I shall miss you," Juliet whispered to her fiancé, their hands entwined, a shimmer of tears glistening in her eyes.

Christopher pulled her close. "I shall hurry back as fast as I can, and then we shall be a family."

Troy cleared his throat. "Do you have a moment?" he asked, watching their faces as they turned to look at him. He saw tension but also a spark of hope the moment they beheld him.

"Of course," Juliet exclaimed, exchanging one of those meaningful looks with Christopher. Would he and Nora be able to do that, too, one day? "Are you all right? We were worried when you didn't come to breakfast."

"I'm all right," Troy said without going in to detail. Still, he could see speculation in Christopher's eyes; after all, he had been the one to urge Troy to go and speak to Nora. How would he react if he knew... what had happened between his old friend and his sister last night?

Troy knew if their roles were reversed, he would be furious, mad with outrage and concern for his sister. At least, Christopher had possessed the good sense to ask for Juliet's hand before...

Troy swallowed. "I came to apologize," he began, seeing the look upon his sister's face soften. "I did not mean what I said last night. I was...out of sorts, and I am deeply sorry." He felt his head bob up and down to his words. "Of course, you have my blessing." He smiled at his sister, aware of how deeply his words touched her. "All I ever wanted was to see you happy, Jules, and if you are, then I am happy for you." He glanced at Christopher. "For the both of you."

A sob escaped Juliet's throat before she threw herself into Troy's arms, hugging him tightly. "Thank you. Oh, thank you, Troy. You have no idea how much this means to me."

Holding her close, Troy brushed his hands up and down her back.

"Believe me, I do," he whispered into her hair. "I do. Promise me you'll be happy with him."

A relieved smile came to Christopher's face as he watched them, his own features now more relaxed than Troy had seen them in a long time. *Thank you*, he mouthed to Troy.

Still holding on to her brother, Juliet nodded. "I promise. I promise I'll be happy." Then she pulled back and met his eyes, her own still misted with tears. "Perhaps one day I'll have a chance to return the favor," she pinched his chin affectionately, "to give you my blessing as well." The hint of a question lingered in her tone, as though she wished to ask something but did not dare.

Troy was glad for it. "Perhaps," was all he said, well-aware of the speculative look upon Christopher's face. Still, it would be too soon to say anything. First, he needed to speak to Nora and pray that what had been between them last night would survive the light of day.

Never had Troy wanted anything more.

Chapter Twenty-Five

A LETTER DELAYED

S tanding by the windows of her bedchamber, Nora watched Mr. Clarke ride away. She was relieved to see that he did not bother to wait for after breakfast but had decided to set off as soon as dawn began to peek over the horizon. Even on a good day, conversing with Mr. Clarke had become somewhat of a chore. It was not something that came easily to her, and she could not truthfully say that she enjoyed his company. Yes, the day before his words had touched her, and, yes, in that moment she had truly believed it wise to consider his words.

Now, however, she knew that to be impossible.

As Mr. Clarke disappeared from view, Nora sighed, for her thoughts instantly drifted back to the night before. Oh, how she wished she had been awake when Troy had risen! Indeed, when she had woken only minutes earlier, there had been a moment when she had feared their encounter had merely been a dream. She had opened her eyes and found him absent, and her heart had ached with such regret and sorrow that she had felt tears shoot into her eyes. And then her gaze had fallen on her neatly folded night rail and robe...

...and she had known.

From one second to the next, the corners of her mouth had been pulled upward into such a smile as she had never known before. A wave of relief and utter joy had washed over her, instantly soothing the ache in her heart, as though it had never been. She laughed, buried her face in her pillow, and laughed again, hoping that no one would hear but equally unable to stop herself.

Again, everything that had passed between them the previous night drifted through Nora's mind and she closed her eyes, savoring those precious moments. Indeed, barely a word had passed between them, and yet the depth of Troy's feelings for her had been unmistakable. He loved her, did he not? He loved her just as much as she loved him.

Even though Nora tried her best to hold on to the joy that thought elicited, she could not quite keep at bay another that followed. Yes, it seemed they loved each other, and yet nothing had changed since the day before.

Not truly.

Troy still needed an heir, and she still could not provide one. It was as simple as that. Heartbreaking but simple.

Yet last night would forever be hers. No one and nothing could ever take that from her, neither those beautiful memories nor the knowledge that Troy truly loved her.

And so, Nora spent her morning dreaming dreams that would never come true but that painted a smile on her face and made her all but oblivious to the world around her. She barely said a word at breakfast, dimly aware of the slight frown that came to her mother's face. Yet her mother did not ask beyond a general inquiry after her wellbeing, and of course Nora did not volunteer anything.

No, last night was hers and hers alone.

And then Christopher arrived.

Nora saw him from the window, heard the distant echo of his voice, and wondered why he had come. Silent steps carried her out of her chamber and downstairs as she continued to listen, making out the faint sound of his voice as it drifted over from the drawing room. As she knew, her mother usually spent most of her days there, diligently tending to her embroidery. Did the woman never feel bored? Nora wondered in that moment.

"I have no wish to quarrel with you, Mother," came Christopher's voice, for once not placating at all, but resonating with a determination that quickened Nora's steps. "I came here today to inform you of my impending marriage," Nora drew in a sharp breath as she stopped outside the door, all but pressing her ear to it, "and of my intention to bring my son home. We shall be a family, and if you wish, you may be a part of our lives," a warning tone came to Christopher's voice, "if you bury this hatred you have within yourself. One word against my son, and I will send you from this house." Nora silently applauded her brother. She was shocked by his sudden vehemence but pleased, nonetheless.

Their mother hissed something under her breath that Nora could not make out; however, she had no trouble picturing her mother's shocked face.

"I can, and I will," Christopher assured her, not allowing for any doubt of his sincerity. "You will not poison my son's life the way you poisoned mine."

"Christopher," their mother exclaimed, her voice louder now than Nora had ever heard it, "he is a bastard. He can never inherit. He—"

"I don't care!" Christopher bellowed back, and Nora all but danced on the spot. "He is my son, and he means more to me than your silly notions of standing and reputation." He paused, and Nora could all but picture him drawing in a deep breath. "But you've never been able to understand that, have you? A son is more than an heir, and, yes, I was a fool to ever hide him away. He deserves better as I deserved better." Nora pressed her ear tighter against the wood. "I've made my choice, Mother. What is yours? If you cannot accept him, me, then I suggest you leave before we return."

Nora almost flinched at her brother's daring and then held her breath, waiting for her mother's reply. Instead, though, she heard footsteps echoing closer.

"Oh, no," Nora whispered as she spun away from the door and rushed to hide around the next corner. A moment later, the door flew open, and her mother rushed out, her face pale and her hands clasped together as she fled the ultimatum Christopher had presented her with.

The second she vanished from sight; Nora stepped toward the

drawing room. Christopher stood near the pianoforte; his eyes closed as he drew in a deep breath. Traces of regret lingered upon his face; yet Nora could not help but think that he felt relief.

"Bravo!" she exclaimed, stepping into the room.

Christopher's head snapped up, and he spun around to stare at her, something contemplative in his gaze. Yet he said nothing.

"It was about time," Nora said, smiling at him as she moved closer, glad to see her brother finally reach for what he wanted, for what he had always wanted. "I feared you never would." Despite her own sorrow, Nora felt her smile deepen. "I'm happy to be proven wrong."

Christopher nodded. "You overheard?"

A chuckle left Nora's lips. "It was hard not to." Indeed, he did look different. "I've never seen you so angry. It suits you."

Christopher laughed. "Anger suits me?"

"Not anger," Nora corrected him. "It's that...that fire I see in your eyes." She lay her hand upon his arm, giving it an affectionate squeeze. "You look as though you've woken up from a long sleep, Christopher. Before, you never seemed quite here, you know? You do now, though." She chuckled at the image that came to her mind. "It seems as though Jules kissed you awake."

Laughing, Christopher embraced her. "Thank you," he murmured into her hair.

"For what?"

He stepped back and looked down at her. "For being you. For being happy for me." His eyes searched her face, and again, Nora saw a contemplative look upon his face. "I wish I could see the same fire in your eyes."

Ah! Nora thought, and she instantly dropped her gaze. *Troy.* Did her brother know Troy had come to her last night? She doubted it; yet he seemed aware of...something.

Reaching inside his jacket, Christopher pulled out a letter and held it out to her. "This is for you."

Confused, Nora grinned at him, surprised by the lightness she felt in her heart. "Whatever you have to say to me, you can just say it now," she teased. "There is no need for formalities."

Smiling in response, Christopher shook his head. "No, the letter is not from me. The truth is, I was to deliver it to you...five years ago." Something akin to anguish now overshadowed Christopher's face.

Nora frowned, utterly confused. "Five years ago? What delayed you?" Laughter bubbled from her lips, for she did not care for the tortured look in her brother's eyes. What was this about?

Instead of smile or laugh, Christopher bowed his head, and Nora felt a cold shiver snake down her spine. "I am deeply sorry for not giving you this sooner. I know I should have. I had every intention to, but..."

"What is this about?" Nora asked, uncertain if she truly wished to know. Judging from the look upon her brother's face, this letter—whatever it contained—was...devastating. "It is only a letter, nothing that ought to concern you this deeply."

Closing his eyes, Christopher breathed in deeply before looking at her once more. "Troy gave it to me the day of your wedding."

Shock froze Nora's limbs, her heart, her breath. What was he saying? What was this letter? What did it...?

"He asked me to give it to you as soon as possible, but then I learned of my son's birth and the letter slipped my mind." He grasped her chilled hands, holding them gently within his own. "Back then, I did not know what this letter contained. Neither do I now; however, I have my suspicions and I think you should read it." Again, he urged her to accept the letter.

Overwhelmed, Nora slowly extended her hand, her eyes fixed on the piece of parchment that she ought to have received five years ago. What did it say? Was it possible that...?

Her breath lodged in her throat as she remembered that day. Her wedding day. She had been torn between fulfilling her promise and following her heart. She had hoped and prayed that Troy would come to her, but he had not. He had not even attended her wedding. Was it possible that...?

"Read it," came Christopher's whispered voice, the same vehemence ringing in it she had heard before when he had spoken to their mother, "and make of it what you will. I simply thought you should know." He gave her shoulder a gentle squeeze. "I shall see you soon, Nora. Be well." And then he was gone.

For a long moment—a seemingly endless moment—Nora simply stood there, staring at the letter in her hands. She could not bring herself to move, to open it, to think any thoughts beyond disbelief; yet something stirred in her heart, an odd mix of hope and despair.

Eventually, somehow, she found her way to the armchair in the corner and sank into it, her eyes still fixed upon the letter. What did it contain? Why had Troy asked Christopher to deliver this to her the day of her wedding? Why not before? What did it mean?

Nora knew that opening the letter was her only way of receiving any answers, and yet she feared knowing them...

...because deep down, she knew what this letter was. How could she not?

A tear dripped down onto the parchment, and only then did Nora realize she was crying. She wiped it away, then finally turned the letter and broke the seal. Her fingers moved swiftly, for she was afraid if she hesitated, she might not do it. Oddly enough, she feared knowing what this letter contained.

And then it lay in her lap, unfolded, the dark ink in stark contrast to the soft beige of the parchment. Yes, it was unmistakably Troy's handwriting.

Nora drew in a shuddering breath and read the words that had been meant for her eyes five years ago.

My dearest Nora,

I cannot stop thinking about you, about the day by the ruins, about our kiss. These past few days have been torture, for I have been at war with myself about what to do. All of a sudden, the thought of you married to another turns my stomach and sets my blood on fire. I know the day is fast approaching and that I have no right to prevent it. Yet I find it is my dearest wish.

Forgive me for penning these jumbled thoughts. I have barely slept since the day by the ruins, and I fear my mind is far from able to express itself clearly.

. . .

All I know is that I love you. I do. Truly. Please, call off your wedding. Do not marry Hayward. Marry me instead. I know it will cause a stir. I know it is wrong of me to ask this of you, but I must. I know I would regret it for the rest of my life if I did not.

Please, Nora, send word and I will come to you. Please!

Troy

Silent tears rolled down Nora's face as she stared at Troy's letter. Her jaw was trembling, and she heard the faint sound of her teeth clicking together. Oh, how different her life could have been!

A part of Nora could not help but doubt that she was truly sitting here, Troy's letter in her hands. Was this a dream? Or had he truly penned these beautiful words? Had he truly loved her even then?

Nora's limbs went slack, and the letter slipped from her fingers as she all but slid off the chair and sank onto the floor. Her whole body began to tremble, and she pulled up her legs and hugged her arms around them, her chin coming to rest on her knees. "He loves me," she whispered to herself, staring into nothing, barely aware of the curtain of tears that obscured her sight. "He truly loves me. If only I had known, I..."

Nora stilled. Indeed, if she had known, she *would* have called off her wedding. She would have married Troy, and she would have been happy...at least for a while.

At least until they would have been forced to realize that they would never have children. What then? What would have happened then? Oh, Troy was not the kind of man to blame her for it, to feel anger toward her because of something that was not within her power. Yet he would have been saddened. It would have been a strain on their marriage. She would have seen regret upon his face every day, not about having married her, but about the consequences of that choice.

At least, *then*, Nora had not known that she could not have children. But she did now.

As much as she wanted to believe that there was a chance for them, it was selfish of her to think so. She could not marry him, no matter the love they felt for one another.

She could not.

And that knowledge broke her heart all over again.

Chapter Twenty-Six

SIMPLE WORDS

Troy had never been one to stroll through the gardens. Whenever he needed to think, he usually retreated to the study, perhaps the library; however, he had never felt the need to leave the house, to breathe fresh air and stretch his legs. Oddly enough, though, he did today.

His warm breath billowed out in little clouds as he walked without direction, his mind occupied and not focused on a specific destination.

With Christopher gone to Ireland to fetch home his son in anticipation of his marriage to Juliet, Troy could not help but picture his own future. At least, he tried to. Soon, all his sisters would be married. Happily married. Would he be able to count himself equally lucky one day? Only the day before, Troy would not have thought that possible. Now, however, hope blossomed in his heart. Out of habit, he shied away from it, afraid to trust it, afraid to let it grow. Yet life was different today, was it not?

"Have ye found yer way home?"

Troy drew to a halt at the sound of the Scotsman's voice. He inhaled deeply, then turned to face the man. "Pardon me?"

A few long strides carried Keir closer, his blue eyes watchful and oddly knowing. "I saw ye ride off after the ball." He chuckled. "Or

164

perhaps it would be more accurate to say during the ball." His brows rose. "Ye seemed quite out of sorts, looked the part, too."

Troy eyed the man curiously, taken aback by the familiarity that resonated in Keir's voice. After all, they hardly knew one another. Even if Troy were the kind of man to share his innermost thoughts with others, he would not have confided in Keir...would he? Indeed, it seemed easy to speak to the man. He had a way about him that promised understanding and counsel. Troy doubted Keir would ever judge another for their choices. He was simply not that kind of man.

Exhaling deeply, Troy nodded. "How did it come to be that when you and Juliet left here a few days ago, you returned with Christopher?" This time, it was Troy who lifted his brows, demanding an answer before providing one of his own.

No doubt understanding perfectly, Keir chuckled. "Yer sister needed to speak to the man," he shrugged, "so I suggested she do so before 'twas too late."

Troy frowned. "You convinced her to go after him," he mumbled, knowing it to be so. Juliet had never been daring, always concerned with adhering to etiquette, with doing what was expected of her. It was something the two of them had in common. Troy understood it well, understood that following one's heart did not come easily to everyone. Indeed, Juliet had needed someone to urge her to take that leap of faith, and it seemed Keir had done so. "Thank you."

Keir shrugged. "'Twas nothing. I only helped her realize something she already knew."

Troy nodded, surprised how easy it felt to speak to Keir. He hesitated only for a moment, then he said, "I've been in love these past five years." Indeed, the words shocked Troy more than they shocked Keir, and yet it felt liberating to speak them out loud, to say them to another soul. Perhaps the fact that Keir was not a confidant, not someone he had known his entire life, made it easier to speak the truth.

So, instead of gaping at him or laughing or asking a thousand questions, Keir simply nodded, understanding marking his features.

Troy swallowed. "With a married woman."

The Scot grimaced in compassion but said nothing.

Closing his eyes, Troy chuckled. Then he breathed in deeply, exhaled slowly and said, "Only she is not married anymore."

A wide grin came to Keir's face. "If that is so, then I'll tell ye the same thing I told yer sister: right now, ye're standing at a crossroad, and the choice is yers. What will ye do?"

Troy nodded, grateful for the counsel. As simple as it was, it helped. "Thank you," he told Keir. "Thank you."

The Scot nodded. "Anytime." Then he strode away, as though his sole purpose at Whickerton Grove had been this moment, these few words he had spoken.

"My choice," Troy mumbled to himself as he continued down the path, his feet carrying him onward as his mind drifted elsewhere. "And hers, of course."

Yes, Troy knew what he wanted. He had always known. Only up until yesterday he had thought her heart could never be his. But now? Now, he knew Nora cared for him, that she perhaps even loved him. Of course, she was still in mourning, but...was there a chance for them? If he proposed to her, would she accept him? After all, she had not refused him five years ago, had she? She had never received his letter.

Hanging his head, Troy sighed at the thought of all that could have been if only she had read his letter back then. What would have happened?

Like Juliet, Troy had never been one to act on an impulse. He knew he needed to think, look at this matter from all angles, be certain that he was not misinterpreting something.

"I need to speak to her," he murmured to the wind as he stopped atop a small slope where leaves whirled through the air like dancers, determined to dance the night away. "I need to tell her..."

A smile came to Troy's face. He felt it approach slowly, felt it tug up the corners of his mouth, felt it in every muscle of his cheeks and jaw. It reminded him of earlier that morning, of when he had looked at Nora's sleeping face. The memory almost brought him to his knees, and he knew he wanted it to be more than a memory. He wanted to see her like this every morning. He wanted to hold her every night.

And he did not want to sneak out of the house like a common thief.

No, he wanted her to be his, as he had always been hers. He wanted the whole world to know. He wanted his parents to see his happiness. He wanted Nora here at Whickerton Grove. He wanted her to be his wife. He wanted her to be the mother of his children.

He wanted all that and more.

Chapter Twenty-Seven
RETURN TO WHICKERTON GROVE

The past two days were a blur to Nora, for she had barely left her chamber. Feigning a headache, she had kept to herself, reading and re-reading Troy's letter until she knew it by heart. Tears continually flowed from her eyes as she contemplated what could have been...but also what now never would. Her heart teetered back and forth between treacherous hope and crushing despair until she felt utterly exhausted. At night, she slept fitfully, often waking to the conviction that Troy's letter had been nothing but a dream.

Two days had passed since their night together, and thus far, Nora had not heard from him. Of course, neither had she attempted to contact him. A part of her felt an almost desperate need to speak to Troy, to hear him say the words he had written, even if there was no hope. Another, however, urged her to accept the hopelessness of their situation and not torture herself further. She needed to bid Troy farewell.

For good.

Yet on the third morning, Nora rose with the knowledge that she needed to see him. It was like a physical need, like the one for air or water. Something that was not debatable. Something that was necessary for life to continue.

And thus, she found herself in a carriage not long after, Troy's letter in her hand and her lady's maid across from her, as they passed through the familiar landscape of her youth. Trees grew in abundance, and expansive meadows stretched far and wide. The sky was overcast, and a harsh wind blew. Winter was on its way, and Nora wondered when the first snow would fall.

And then Whickerton Grove came into view.

Staring out the window, Nora momentarily felt as though a lifetime had passed since she had last been here. Everything seemed foreign and different and strange, her eyes detecting small alterations here and there that offset her familiarity. Then, however, her mind absorbed the scene at large, comparing it to years past. Indeed, nothing had changed, not truly. The house still looked as inviting as ever, warm and welcoming, her thoughts imagining the Whickertons inside going about their day. Countless times she had come here in the past, eager to see the sisters as well as Troy, to spend an afternoon in blissful companionship. What would await her here today?

Nora drew in a deep breath, bracing herself for what lay ahead. She could not even quite say what she was hoping for or what she feared. Indeed, the letter had told her everything she needed to know. Troy loved her. He had loved her ever since that day, and he still did. Nora knew he did. It had been in every look, every touch, every moment they had spent in each other's arms.

Nora could not remember that night without smiling, without feeling her heart grow to at least twice its size, without dreaming and feeling her thoughts carried away to a place where no rules, no restrictions existed, where everything was possible, where dreams still came true.

Yet, eventually, *that* voice always piped up. It reminded her of her mother, something she would say and had said in the past. Of course, there were rules. Life was defined by them, and it served no one to pretend that that was not true.

Yes, all Nora could hope for today was to hear Troy say those beautiful words; yet they would inevitably be accompanied by heartbreak because there simply was no future for them.

There could not be.

Alighting from the carriage, Nora slowly, almost reverently, climbed up the few steps to the front door. Excitement hummed beneath her skin, slightly dulled by a touch of dread that continued to linger. The door opened as she approached, a diligent footman always on duty, and Nora stepped across the threshold when the sound of footsteps suddenly echoed in her ears.

"Nora?"

A jolt went through her, and her mind snapped back from her contemplations to focus on the here and now. "Jules!" she gasped as her eyes fell on Troy's eldest sister, Christopher's betrothed. "Oh, you surprised me." Her heart beat almost thunderously in her chest, and for a moment she felt almost lightheaded. "Of course, I shouldn't have been. After all, I'm the one coming to your home." She heard herself chuckle, overcome by this unexpected moment. Indeed, like Troy, Juliet had not been a part of Nora's life these past few years. They had not seen each other beyond a few glimpses at an event here and there, and the short time Christopher and Nora had stayed with the Whickertons last year. Yet, once, they had been friends. Could they be again? Was that even wise?

Lately, too many questions existed in Nora's head, too many things to be considered, to be weighed and measured. Had it always been this hard to make a decision? Had there always been so many things to take in to account?

Indeed, life felt exhausting.

A frown lingered upon Juliet's face. "Are you all right? What brings you here today?"

And there it was, another question without an easy answer. Yes, what had brought her here today? Quite frankly, Nora had no words.

"Is it about Christopher?" A crease of concern came to Juliet's forehead. "He said he wanted to speak to his mother before leaving for Ireland. Did he?" Her hands clamped together.

"He did," Nora assured her old friend quickly. Indeed, a smile touched her lips at the memory of how Christopher had stood tall and strong and faced down their mother. "He told her off," she told Juliet, reaching out to grasp one of her hands. "I've never seen him like that. You made him very happy. Thank you."

Utter relief showed on Juliet's face. "He has made me very happy as well," she replied with a wide smile...before her eyes ventured lower and came to rest upon Nora's hand, a contemplative look coming to them.

Belatedly, Nora realized she was holding Troy's letter clutched in her hand. Was it possible that Juliet knew of the letter? Of course, Christopher would have told her. He would not keep anything from her, would he? After all, the look in Juliet's eyes was proof enough.

"It is... Is your brother here?" Nora asked, and suddenly, her voice was trembling, her hand tightening upon the letter, as though somehow it could protect her.

Protect her heart.

Juliet nodded. "He's in the study. You still know your way around, do you not?"

"Yes, I believe I do," she whispered and allowed her gaze to sweep over the large foyer, not surprised in the least when memories jumped up from every corner. "It has been some time, but I remember this place well," she mumbled with a deep sigh. Then she smiled at Juliet and turned to head toward the study.

Behind her, Nora dimly heard the soft footfall of her lady's maid; yet her mind was singularly focused, her eyes straining to see around every corner. And then, her gaze fell on a familiar door and the knowledge that Troy sat on the other side of it nearly made her heart beat out of her chest. Her steps faltered, and for a second, all courage vanished. What was she doing here? This could only end in disaster! Worse, heartbreak!

Still, she could not turn back now, and so Nora proceeded onward. Just outside the door, she paused and ordered her lady's maid to wait for her here, ignoring the look of disapproval that came to the woman's face. Her right hand rose, her fingers curled into a fist, and she gave the door a few quick knocks.

Holding her breath, Nora waited until Troy's voice drifted through the closed door. "Enter."

Not daring to hesitate even for a moment, she stepped inside, closing the door behind her.

Clearly, Troy had not expected to see her, for the look on his face for once was utterly unguarded. Surprise and something resembling stunned disbelief showed there a split second before he surged to his feet, his eyes fixed upon her. "Nora!" he exclaimed, then he quickly rounded the desk he had been working at and strode toward her. "What are you doing here? I had not expected to..." His voice trailed off as his gaze swept over her face in such a tender and loving way that Nora felt her heart ache.

Nora drew in a shaky breath. "I had to see you," she said simply, knowing it to be the truth. "There's something...I wish to speak to you about." She swallowed, glancing down at the letter still clutched in her hand.

Briefly closing his eyes, Troy nodded. "Yes, I suppose there is something we should speak about." He exhaled a deep breath, and she could see a touch of shame coming to his eyes.

Nora tensed, for a second terrified that perhaps he had come to regret their night.

Reaching out, Troy gently took her hands within his own, a soft smile upon his face as he looked down into her eyes. "Though I have no regrets," he said with a hint of chagrin, "I cannot deny that my conduct that night did not befit a gentleman." He pressed his lips together; yet the smile upon his face lingered, giving him an adorably sweet expression. "Indeed, I should not have come to you in such a state, in the middle of the night," he closed his eyes and shook his head, "or even at all." He exhaled deeply and looked at her again. "I should not have," he whispered, pulling her closer, "yet I'm glad I did."

Nora felt her heart sigh with longing and delight and, yes, hope. Of course, she should have seen this coming. Of course, he was saying such beautiful things, making it even harder for her to leave this room and return to her life of solitude.

Of loneliness.

But first...

"Did you mean this?" Nora said quietly as she pulled her left hand from his and uncurled her fingers, revealing the crumpled-up piece of parchment she had clung to these past three days. "Did you mean what you wrote?"

Confusion drew down Troy's brows as his gaze fell from hers and drifted down to the piece of parchment on her palm. However, the moment only lasted for a split second before understanding widened his eyes and dropped his jaw. "Where...?" He swallowed hard, his blue gaze returning to hers.

"Christopher gave it to me," Nora explained, deeply touched by the vulnerable look that came to Troy's eyes. "He urged me to read it. He said you gave it to him to give to me...the morning of my wedding day."

Troy nodded. "I told him to burn it," he whispered, heaving a deep sigh, "that night before I came to you." He closed his eyes. "But he wouldn't. Instead, he urged me to seek you out. He told me to speak to you and find out where your heart lies."

Nora smiled up at him as tears began to snake their way down her cheeks. "Did you mean what you wrote?" she asked once more, needing to hear him say the words. "Did you... Did you truly love me? Did you—?"

"Yes!" The word was spoken without hesitation but with vehemence instead. His blue eyes blazed with something Nora had rarely seen, something that always lay hidden beneath that calm exterior of his. "Yes, I meant every word."

Closing her eyes, Nora knew she ought to leave as her heart urged her to reciprocate. It would be foolish to do so, and yet she could not prevent it. Dropping the letter, she reached for Troy and pulled him down into a kiss.

Chapter Twenty-Eight

IF ONLY

The sudden sensation of Nora's lips against his own stunned Troy momentarily, and he wondered if perhaps the day had not yet begun and he was still abed, lost in a beautiful dream. Yet the woman in his arms felt so warm and alive that he doubted his mind could have conjured such sensations.

Returning her kiss, Troy held her close, delighting in the soft touch of her fingers against his skin as they skimmed down his neck and then back up into his hair. She kissed him eagerly, almost desperately, and he wondered at the tears that lingered upon her cheeks. "Are you all right?" Troy whispered, wrapping his arms around her as she rested her head against his shoulder.

"I don't know," Nora whispered, her voice heavy with emotions. "I never expected any of this. After you kissed me that day, I... I did not know what to do." Lifting her head, she looked up into his eyes. "All of a sudden, I no longer wanted to marry Hayward. I knew it right then and there, and yet..." She shrugged almost helplessly.

Troy nodded. "I know," he replied because it was the simple truth. "I felt exactly the same. A part of me could not believe what had happened, how my feelings had suddenly changed. I told myself it was just...a moment, that it would pass, that everything would go back to normal." He shook his head. "But it didn't. In fact, it got worse and worse every day, every minute that passed. I thought of you married to him and—" He gritted his teeth at the memory of those days, those awful, life-shattering days.

Closing her eyes, Nora once more laid her head against his chest, her arms wrapping around him and holding on to him tightly. "I should've said something," she murmured, reproach and regret in her voice. "I wanted to, but I did not dare. I had given my word. Everything was arranged. I could not imagine how..." She exhaled a deep breath, and he felt her fingers curl into his lapels.

"I know," Troy said yet again because, as it seemed, they had both experienced that moment in exactly the same way. If only they had known! "That day five years ago changed everything for me, and...and your marriage to Hayward destroyed me. I kept hoping that something would happen to prevent it, that you would send for me." He closed his eyes and hung his head as the despair of those few days washed over him anew. "When you did not, I thought..." He gritted his teeth to swallow the lump in his throat. "I thought you didn't feel the same. I thought it had only been me, and I told myself I had to let you go."

Heavy sobs now shook Nora's shoulders. "I wish I had known," she wept, her face still buried against his shoulder. "Life could have been so...so different." Suddenly, she looked up at him, her face tear stained. "I would've married you in a heartbeat."

The air rushed from Troy's lungs in one swift whoosh as he stared down into Nora's face. Joy flooded every fiber of his being, and he gently grasped her chin. "In a heartbeat?"

Nora nodded. "In a heartbeat."

Holding her gaze, Troy slowly lowered his head and placed a soft kiss upon her lips, then one on her nose, on her cheeks, first left then right. He kissed her again and again, holding her to him and reveling in this unexpected sensation of knowing that her heart was his.

And had always been his.

"As much as I wish it," he murmured, "we cannot change the past." He looked deep into her brown eyes. "Yet we can still determine our future. It is ours to take and do with as we wish." A flicker of doubt came to her eyes, and Troy sensed she wanted to drop her gaze. "What is it?"

Nora swallowed. "I... I..." she stammered, either reluctant to speak or uncertain what it was she wanted to say.

Troy, however, felt no such doubts or hesitations. Finally, he knew what he wanted, and he saw it within reach. He would not hesitate now. "Marry me, Nora! Please, marry me and let us have the life we should've had five years ago."

Nora's eyes closed. She hung her head, as though his words had been the last thing she had wanted to hear. Then she shook her head. "I cannot. I'm sorry, Troy, but I cannot."

Feeling her rejection like a punch to the stomach, Troy almost doubled over in pain. He stared at her, disbelieving, doubting his own ears. "Why?" Troy gasped as his hands grasped her arms. "Why?"

Nora's eyes were wide as she stared at him. "I...I do not wish to marry again," she replied in a weak voice, her lower lip trembling, as though she spoke the words against her will. "I w-will n-not marry again."

Unable to form a coherent sentence, Troy simply stared at her.

Nora blinked her eyes, dropping them again and again before glancing up at him in a way that belied her words. "I simply... I simply want my freedom, to be in charge of my own life."

Troy felt his hands tense upon her arms. "That sounds like an excuse," he all but growled, feeling as though he stood facing an enemy, he thus far had had no knowledge of. "Look at me, Nora."

Slowly, reluctantly, she lifted her head, a hint of fear in her eyes Troy did not understand.

He swallowed hard, gathering his courage as every fiber in his being screamed at him to take a step back, to not risk his heart any further. "Do you care for me?" He closed his eyes and inhaled a deep breath. "Do you...love me?"

Again, Nora's eyes blinked rapidly, looking everywhere but into his. "Of course, I love you. You are my friend." She tried to smile but failed. "We'll always be friends, won't we?"

Troy wanted to shake her. Nothing she was saying made any sense. Had she not a moment ago been in his arms, crying, wishing she had known about his letter, saying that she would have married him in a heartbeat? Why then was she retreating now? What made her so afraid? Because she clearly was!

"Friends?" Troy growled, unable to keep his frustration out of his voice. "We were not friends three nights ago, were we?"

A soft blush darkened her cheeks as she dropped her gaze.

Unwilling to let her slip away, Troy once more grasped her chin, forcing her to look up at him. "Why would you allow me into your bed," he asked with a calm he did not feel, "if you feel nothing for me?"

A shiver shook her delicate frame. "I did feel something," Nora finally admitted, "but it was not enough. Not enough for marriage."

A fearful part deep inside Troy urged him to retreat, warning him that if he continued on, heartbreak would find him anew. However, another rather rational part argued that, at this point, heartbreak was inevitable no matter what he did. "After what happened," Troy growled, desperate to find something, anything to change her mind, "we ought to be married." He looked into her eyes, his brows rising meaningfully. "I compromised you."

Nora drew in a trembling breath, then slowly shook her head. "No one knows. Nothing has to change."

Shaking his head, Troy frowned. "Why are you doing this? Why are you all but looking for an excuse not to marry me when, a moment earlier, you said you would do so in a heartbeat? What is going on, Nora?"

A sob tore from her throat, and she hung her head, resting it against his shoulder. "You're a wonderful man, and you deserve to marry someone...someone better...than me."

Utterly confused, Troy stared at her bent head, uncertain if he had truly understood her right. This made no sense! "Why would you say such a thing?" he asked gently, urging her to look at him. "I...I love you." Oddly enough, it was still hard for him to say the words. "And you love me. You cannot deny that. We are perfect for each other. We should have been married these past five years. The fact that we weren't is something that I will regret for the rest of my life. However, we have this chance now. Why will you not take it?"

Nora swayed on her feet so Troy felt compelled to grasp her by the shoulders. "I can't. I simply cannot marry you."

Troy could not help but think that Nora had stressed the last word, meaning she could not marry *him*. But someone else? "What about Mr. Clarke?" Troy growled, his patience running out as he found himself at his wit's end. "Will you marry *him*?"

Nora shook her head, and Troy exhaled the breath he had been holding. "No, I will not. I know that now."

"Now?" Troy dared her, loathing the doubt that clung to her voice.

"He asked me, and I promised him I would think on it." She drew in a sharp breath as Troy's hands tightened on her shoulders. "But I now know that I cannot." She sighed, the look in her eyes heartbreaking. "But neither can I marry you."

"Why?" Troy demanded. "At least, tell me why. You owe me that."

Her lips parted.

"The truth!" Troy said in a warning tone. "The truth, Nora. Not an excuse."

Swallowing, she nodded, and the air rushed from her lungs in one swift breath. "I cannot have children."

Troy blinked. Perhaps deep down, he had not truly expected her to speak plainly, truthfully. Perhaps it was the simplicity of her reason, free of long explanations. Perhaps it was Lord Kinsley's voice echoing in his head, *Damn shame! Young and fetching, she would have no trouble finding herself another husband. If only she weren't barren.*

"So, you see," Nora continued, shaking her head, "we cannot marry because I cannot give you children. I wish it weren't so but it is."

"I don't care!" Troy blurted out, reaching for her once more as she tried to slip from his grasp. He brought her closer, looking deep into her eyes. "I. Don't. Care." He stressed every word, needing her to hear him.

A soft smile played over her lips, and she reached up to cup his face. "I love you for saying that," Nora whispered, "and I know you truly believe it right now, here, in this moment." She heaved a deep sigh. "But one day, you will care. Believe me, you will."

Troy shook his head. "You're wrong." He exhaled a sharp breath. "I want you, and I already know what it is like to be parted from you." He pulled her deeper into his arms, so she had to crane her neck to hold his gaze. "I cannot do it again. It was hell." He shook his head vehemently. "No, not again. You're mine, and I will not give you up."

Nora's lips trembled, and he could see that she fought to hold on to what remained of her composure, that she fought to resist the promise he made. "You need an heir, Troy," she whispered, as though it pained her to speak the words. Slowly, she slid out of his arms. "Your family needs you to have a son, an heir, to carry on your father's title, to inherit Whickerton Grove." A wistful smile played over her lips as Troy continued to stare at her in shock. "You need to ensure that this beautiful place will forever remain with your family...for all the generations to come. This is your home, your family's home, and they need you."

Troy closed his eyes as that awfully rational voice deep inside piped up once more, arguing that Nora was right. Indeed, he was his father's only son. If he did not have a child, a son, his father's title and everything connected to it would eventually pass out of their family. Once his father was gone, if something happened to him, Troy, his mother would lose everything.

Was it selfish that a part of him did not care? That even now, he wanted nothing more than to marry Nora and ignore his responsibility?

And then Troy heard the door close behind Nora, a soft sound, almost inaudible, as though she had never even been here. As though all of this had merely been a dream.

Opening his eyes, Troy looked at the empty space where Nora had been only a moment earlier.

How had this happened?

Chapter Twenty-Nine

THE TRUTH OF THE MATTER

The days following her visit to Whickerton Grove, Nora spent in solitude. She was not fit for company, not even her mother's. She walked the gardens, welcoming the stinging cold wind upon her cheeks or sat indoors, a book forgotten in her lap as she stared into nothing. Her heart still ached but slowly acceptance was sneaking in. After all, there was nothing to be done, was there?

Nora knew it was dangerous to even ask herself that question, and so whenever it surfaced, she flinched away from it, turning her attention elsewhere, hoping to chase it away. Yes, she had done the right thing. Again and again, she kept reminding herself of that, hoping to one day find herself truly believing it.

And then, one afternoon, Nora spotted a carriage arrive from an upstairs window. The moment she saw the Whickerton coat-of-arms, Nora felt her knees buckle, and she had to brace herself against the icy windowpane. Still trembling, she watched as Juliet and Grandma Edie alighted from the carriage, her eyes going wide at the sight of them.

For a moment, Nora was confused as to why they were here. After all, Christopher was still in Ireland. Why had they come?

Dimly, she heard voices echo upstairs as the two were shown inside to the drawing room. Moments later, Nora could make out the sound of a door opening, then closing, before it opened once more, and the sound of her mother's footsteps echoed to her ears.

Nora's heart sank as the longing she had felt was replaced by despair. Oh, how she longed to see them! To have Grandma Edie's knowing eyes look into hers the way they always had and understand!

Before Nora knew she had made up her mind, her feet were already rushing to carry her down the stairs. Turning her head at her daughter's sudden appearance, her mother cast her a questioning look, but she did not comment upon Nora's company as they strode into the drawing room to greet their guests.

At the sight of Grandma Edie, Nora felt a deep smile transform her face, one she had not thought herself capable of in her current state.

Greetings were exchanged and refreshments offered as they all took their seats. Her mother expressed her delight with the impeding nuptials between Christopher and Juliet. However, instead of leaving it at that, she felt compelled to voice her disapproval of Christopher's intention of bringing his illegitimate son home.

Juliet—bless her heart!—however, made her own position unmistakably clear. "In fact, it was I who urged Christopher to bring his son back home. A child belongs with his family. Do you not agree?"

The look upon Nora's mother's face stated quite clearly that she did not. However, Juliet would not be deterred and made it abundantly clear that she would not tolerate her future mother-in-law rejecting her son—born to her or not, Christopher's little boy would now be hers as well!

Nora loved Jules for the way she spoke, for the conviction and vehemence in her voice. "Let me make this perfectly clear, Lady Lockhart. If you reject Sebastian, if you treat him without respect, we cannot permit you to be a part of our lives. I will not allow an innocent child to be subjected to the kind of treatment you have bestowed upon your own son since the day he was born."

Inwardly, Nora cheered.

Her mother, on the other hand, looked awfully uncomfortable, clamping her hands together and fidgeting in her seat, as though she wished she could simply disappear into thin air.

Nora heaved a deep sigh. "Mother, you should think this through carefully," she advised gently, bothered by the thought that her mother might continue the solitary life she had led thus far because of a misguided sense of pride and reputation. "You know," she continued as her hands began to tremble, "that Christopher's children will be your only grandchildren." She tried to look into her mother's eyes, but her mother kept her gaze averted. "Do you truly wish to spend the remainder of your life alone? Would you not rather be part of a loud and loving family?" Nora felt tears shoot to her eyes, not only for her mother's sake but also for her own. Was that not exactly the future that now lay ahead of her? Loneliness? The absence of family?

Although her mother tried her best to hold on to her composure, Nora could see that the ice was slowly melting from her heart. There were cracks in her armor, revealing glimpses at a woman who had known her fair share of misery. Nora could not help but wonder what had happened in her parents' lives. Something had to have happened, didn't it? Now and then, she had glimpsed love in their eyes, deep devotion to one another, only to see it replaced by something...she couldn't quite identify, sending her parents in separate directions. They should have been happy together. Why had they not been?

"Nora, dear," Grandma Edie suddenly addressed her, "I need to move my old bones. Will you accompany me?"

Nora frowned, surprised by the request and even more so by the conspiratorial spark that briefly lit up the old woman's eyes. "Of course," she replied, rising to her feet, certain that Grandma Edie knew what she was doing. Indeed, perhaps it would be wise to allow her mother and Juliet to speak to one another confidentially.

Offering Troy's grandmother her arm, Nora escorted the old woman into the hall where they both donned their winter coats, hats and gloves before stepping outside into the cold.

An icy wind blew, and Nora shuddered as the cold trailed across her skin. "Let us head over there to the small grove," Nora suggested. "The wind will not blow as harshly there."

Grandma Edie nodded. One hand held on tightly to Nora's, while the other gripped her walking cane. Slowly, they made their way along the path, keeping their heads slightly lowered until they reached the grove, finally breathing a sigh of relief at the absence of wind here. "Ah, this is much better."

Nora regarded the old woman carefully, wondering why she had insisted on a walk when the cold weather clearly caused her great discomfort. "I am so happy to see you again," she heard herself exclaiming, a deep longing in her voice that made her own heart ache. "It has been some time."

Warm eyes looked into hers, and a deep, affectionate smile came to Grandma Edie's face. "Oh, my dear sweet girl, I missed you terribly these past few years." A wrinkled hand reached out and gently cupped Nora's face.

Closing her eyes, Nora heaved a deep sigh. It had been a long time since anyone—apart from Troy—had reached out to her like this, had offered a small comfort, attempted to ease the loneliness in her heart. "I missed you as well," she whispered, remembering the years when Grandma Edie had been a fixed presence in her life. "Thank you for the tea you sent me over the years and all those kind words. They meant the world to me. I don't know what I would've done without them."

A shadow fell over Grandma Edie's face. "Loneliness is hard to bear," she mumbled, a touch of anger in her voice as she shook her head. Then her pale eyes looked into Nora's. "And these days? How is your heart?" The ghost of a smile played over her face. "What happened between you and my grandson?"

Nora froze. "You...You know?" she asked without truly knowing what it was she was asking. Always had Grandma Edie known things, and in truth, Nora was not surprised that she was here today, asking these questions. Yet how much did she know?

An affectional chuckle drifted from the old woman's lips. "Oh, dear girl, he has loved you these past few years. Did you not know?" She heaved a deep sigh and then reached for Nora's hands. "I'm afraid even I realized it too late, and for that I am truly sorry. Had I...known, I assure you I would have interfered."

At Grandma Edie's words, Nora's heart suddenly seemed to warm and grow and almost dance with joy. "I suppose I should not be surprised, should I?" she chuckled, tightening her grasp on the old woman's hands.

"We cannot leave everything up to Fate," Grandma Edie stated with a hint of annoyance. "Too often things go wrong. Too often people make mistakes, blind to what is truly before them." She huffed out a deep breath. "Sometimes, it is wise to interfere."

"So, I've heard," Nora replied, cherishing this moment of speaking her mind openly and without holding anything back. "Four of your grandchildren are already happily married, and Juliet is on the verge of it. Am I right to assume that you had a hand in all their unions?"

A sly grin came to Grandma Edie's face, but she merely shrugged. "Now, only Troy remains," she stated, a question in her eyes as she looked at Nora.

Sighing deeply, Nora closed her eyes. "Yes," she whispered then. "Yes, I do love him. I have these past few years." She opened her eyes once more and found a deep smile upon Grandma Edie's face.

"Then why do you hesitate, child?" Grandma Edie inquired, something searching in her gaze. "I've watched my grandson most carefully these past few weeks. Clearly, you are his choice. He should be happy as you should be happy, too." Her brows rose in question.

Grandma Edie's words reignited Nora's longing for Troy, for a life with him. She wanted nothing more than to give in, to ignore all that was and simply be happy right now, here, in this moment. "I... I cannot have children," she finally admitted, feeling tears run down her cheeks and chilling her skin as the wind swept over them.

Grandma Edie frowned. "Is that so?"

Sighing heavily, Nora nodded. "I was married to my husband for five years, and yet I never once conceived while he—"

Grandma Edie's eyes darkened, and she nodded knowingly. "Perhaps you were simply not meant to have his children."

"I wish I could believe that," Nora replied with a heavy heart. "I wish things could be different. But they are not. Troy needs an heir. He needs a wife who can give him a son." Nora hung her head in defeat. "He deserves someone better than me. He deserves someone who will not cost him his future, his family's future."

"Is that what you truly believe, child?" Grandma Edie inquired, her brows drawn and a look of incredulity in her eyes. "That there's someone better suited for Troy out there?"

As the world before her eyes began to blur, Nora nodded. "You know how he is," she whispered as the crack in her heart grew deeper. "He always thinks of others before he thinks of himself. He knows his duty to his family, and he would forever blame himself if something were to happen and he could have prevented it."

Gently, Grandma Edie brushed the tears from Nora's cheeks. "You see the world in a dark light, my dear. Trust me, my grandson would choose you no matter the circumstances."

A sad smile came to Nora's face as she remembered the last time she had seen Troy. "I told him," Nora whispered, only now realizing that his reaction had confirmed what she had feared. She had told him, and he had let her go. "Yes, he loves me, but...even that cannot make him look past the fact that if he were to marry me, he would never have children. Love is not enough, and perhaps it simply should not be." She heaved a deep sigh. "He will do what is right for his family, and he should. It is better this way. If he were to marry me...I know that one day he would come to resent me for it. It's a thought I cannot bear."

Understanding lingered in Grandma Edie's eyes as she nodded her head. "Perhaps you're right," she whispered in a way that made it clear that the last word had not yet been spoken. "Perhaps, however, he will come to resent you for robbing him of the woman he loved." Gently, she patted Nora's hand. "Think on that." A shiver shook her, and she exhaled a deep breath. "Now, let us head back inside. I'm beginning to feel like an icicle."

With a heavy heart, Nora escorted Grandma Edie back to the house. Every fiber of her body ached with loss and longing, and yet it had felt good to speak openly, to confide in another. Was that why her mother always looked so distant? Because she had kept to herself these past years, never daring to share her pain, her regrets? What did it do to one to be truly alone in the world?

Chapter Thirty

A WEDDING TAKES PLACE

T roy had always been one to keep to himself. He liked solitude. He liked being alone with his thoughts. And yet, ever since Nora had left his study that day, things had been different.

Now, instead of interacting with his family at normal times throughout the day; he was actively avoiding them, barely speaking to anyone. Of course, his family had noticed that something was different. More than once, Harriet had tried her best to tease an answer from him. They all seemed to be watching him, curiosity and concern in their eyes, waiting for something to happen, for him to say something, to explain.

Yet Troy never said a word. He could not. As much as he wanted his sisters to confide in him, to be their rock, to help them whenever they needed him, somehow, he felt reluctant to see their roles reversed.

And then Christopher returned from Ireland.

The moment Troy's gaze fell on his oldest friend's son, he once more heard Nora's voice echo in his head. *I cannot give you children.*

He had snarled into her face that he did not care that he wanted her no matter what.

One day you will care.

Was that true? Troy could not help but wonder as he looked at

Bash and Samantha, bundled up warm as they ran across the leaf-covered ground, their parents watching with joyful eyes.

Thus far, Troy had never truly thought about being a father. Of course, he had always known that one day, it would be his responsibility to have a son, an heir to the family's title. But that thought had been far in the future, an almost abstract concept, something of the mind alone.

Now, that was different. Now, he looked at Bash and Samantha, saw them snuggling into their parents' arms, whispered words of love leaving their lips, and knew that becoming a father was so much more than simply providing an heir.

Yet the thought of marrying a woman who was not Nora seemed impossible, *felt* impossible. He could not imagine courting another, proposing to another. He wanted Nora. But if he married her, he would never have children. What was he to do?

The day of Juliet's wedding, Troy wanted nothing more but to remain inside, locked away in the study. He knew Nora would attend—in mourning or not!—and the thought of seeing her now, knowing that their day would never come, nearly brought him to his knees.

"Why do you look so glum?" Harriet remarked yet again as the rest of his family gathered in the foyer headed toward the pavilion where the ceremony was to take place. "Quite frankly, you've been looking glum for a while." She stepped closer, her green eyes sweeping over his face. "What is it, big brother? Why can you not tell us?"

Troy swallowed hard. "It is nothing," he insisted, well aware of the hard tone in his voice.

Sighing, Harriet shook her head at him. "Keep telling yourself that," she replied before stepping into his path and meeting his eyes. "One day you might even believe it." Her hand reached out and touched his arm, and he could see how much his pain saddened her. "I know it is not easy to change course," she whispered, then stepped closer as her eyes drifted sideways toward her husband.

Troy watched her face, saw her eyes light up as they swept over Jack, standing in conversation with Drake and Thorne. A deep smile tugged upon the corners of her mouth, and she exhaled a shuddering breath, as though the mere sight of her husband overwhelmed her.

Troy knew that feeling, and he closed his eyes, wishing to be elsewhere.

Harriet's hand squeezed his arm. "You know how determined I was never to marry," she told him the moment he dared open his eyes and meet her gaze. "You know I had my reasons, valid reasons, and it was hard for me to let them go, to realize that other things mattered more." She smiled at him. "Whatever you are running from, whoever you're running from, please, stop and ask yourself if this is truly what you want or if, perhaps, the day has come for you to change course." Pulling him into her arms, Harriet hugged him tightly. "I want you to be happy, big brother. Please find a way to be happy."

Troy held her tightly, tempted to do as she asked. "I'll think on it," he finally mumbled, wondering if he truly would.

After all, thinking things through was torture. He knew that from experience. Also, it never led him anywhere. The facts were what they were, and no matter how often he considered them from all angles, they remained the same. All he could do was make a choice, and he knew that the man he had always been would do right by his family.

And then Nora arrived, and Troy's world once more turned upside down.

Still dressed in black, she stepped into the foyer, her brown eyes wide as she was welcomed by his sisters and parents. Hugs and kisses were exchanged, and for a moment, Troy felt himself transported back in time. How often had Nora set foot into this hall? How often had she been here with them?

Countless times.

Yet years had passed since.

A shuddering breath left Troy's lips as her eyes met his across the foyer. He could see her lips move as she spoke to his sisters, answering their questions and asking her own. Yet her eyes always returned to him, her own breath just as unsteady.

"It is good to have her back here, is it not?" came Grandma Edie's voice and Troy flinched.

Wrestling another breath down his lungs, he turned to look at her. "Pardon me?"

A sly grin came to her face. "Don't pretend you didn't hear precisely what I said." She poked her walking cane into his arm. "Why did you let the girl get away? I thought you loved her."

Dumbfounded, Troy stared at his grandmother. "That is... We... I..." He swallowed hard. "It is none of your concern."

His grandmother's gaze narrowed. "I disagree," she finally said, once more poking him with her cane.

Troy gritted his teeth as he watched the rest of his family step outside and head toward the pavilion. "I am well aware that you've meddled in my sisters' affairs lately, however..."

Yet, one glance at Juliet these days was enough to make one smile, even him. She radiated such happiness that Troy felt choked up and jealous to the bone each time he laid eyes on her. "You look happy," he had said to her this morning, aware that the words fell far short in describing the look upon her face.

"I am," Juliet had breathed in that quiet way of hers, her voice soft and almost inaudible. "Thank you, Brother. I know it was not easy for you to give us your blessing. I know it is not easy for you to be here today." She had smiled at him then, placing her delicate hands upon his chest. "Thank you for doing this, for being here for me. This day wouldn't be perfect without you." She sighed, a hint of sadness sparking in her eyes. "It would be even more perfect if I could see you just as happy. You deserve it, big brother. Don't ever doubt that. Don't ever—" She broke off and swallowed, a contemplative look coming to her green eyes. "Sometimes it takes great patience...but it'll be worth it. I promise."

Before Troy had been able to inquire what she had meant by that, Juliet had been swept away by their sisters to see her dressed for her wedding.

"Meddled?" his grandmother asked with a huff of annoyance, and Troy snapped back to the here and now. The way her pale eyes flitted over his face gave Troy pause. "Granted, I might have...brought certain situations about; however, the decision was always theirs." She looked out the window to where her granddaughters were walking arm in arm with their husbands. "Each one of them made their own choice." Her brows rose meaningfully. "As you now need to make yours, my boy. I only hope you'll make the right one." She slipped her arm through his. "Come, help an old lady outside."

Fortunately, today, the sun shone brightly overhead, offsetting the chilled wind that blew across the gardens as they slowly made their way toward the pavilion. It was a small ceremony with only family in attendance, and as Juliet and Christopher whispered their *I dos*, Troy could not help but look from one happy couple to the next until his gaze locked with Nora's.

Tears lingered in her eyes, and she bit her lower lip as though fighting down a sob. Instantly, Troy felt the urge to hurry to her side, and he had to clench every single muscle in his body to keep from doing so.

"You clearly love her," his grandmother whispered beside him. "Why will you not admit it?"

Troy hung his head. "It is not as easy as that," he replied openly, for there was no use in pretending otherwise. His grandmother knew, and she seemed determined to make her point.

"Neither is it as complicated as you think," she retorted with a sideways glance.

Troy gritted his teeth as the priest declared Juliet and Christopher husband and wife. "There are...circumstances you're not aware of, circumstances..." Cheers went up around him, and the newly-weds were showered with congratulations and well-wishes.

"Speak to your father."

Frowning, Troy turned to look at his grandmother. "Pardon me?"

Grandma Edie nodded. "You heard me. Go and speak to your father. He'll know what to tell you." She patted his hand. "Don't worry. All shall be well." And with that, she hobbled over to Juliet and drew her granddaughter into her arms.

Troy stared after her, wishing he could believe her.

"Are you all right?"

At the sound of Nora's voice, Troy flinched. He had not even heard her approach, his thoughts helplessly overcrowded.

"You look pale," she remarked, her gaze barely meeting his as she continued to twist a handkerchief in her hands. "Is something wrong?"

Troy swallowed hard, noting that his family was heading back toward the house for the wedding breakfast. "Everything is wrong," Troy told her, not caring how he sounded or what such a harsh statement would do to her.

This time, it was Nora who flinched. Her brown eyes rounded, and she drew in a shuddering breath. "Why—?"

"Don't pretend you don't know," Troy snarled, surprised by the sudden anger that boiled beneath his skin. He could lash out at her...or he could walk away.

Neither option would change anything.

"I'd better return to the house," Nora remarked, her eyes once again not quite meeting his. She made to step away, then paused. "I'm sorry, Troy," she whispered as her gaze slowly rose from the grass beneath her feet. "Truly. I wish things could be different. I wish..." Her voice broke off.

It seemed she, too, knew that wishes never changed anything. They only made it harder to accept what was.

Bowing her head, Nora stepped away, quick steps carrying her back to the house and away from him.

Chapter Thirty-One

A MOTHER'S REVELATION

Frost lingered in the air as Nora stood by the drawing-room windows, her gaze directed outward. How long she had been standing here she did not know, her thoughts circling around Christopher's wedding, that look of utter happiness on his face that she would never forget. Oh, how truly happy he had looked!

Closing her eyes, Nora sighed deeply. That day had made her heart ache, ache for more than simply existing from day to day. Yet it seemed the moment she had married Hayward five years ago, she had unknowingly set foot on a path that led her nowhere, that simply continued to run across the land, never intersecting with another's, never quite taking her anywhere.

The true tragedy was that Nora knew very well what she wanted. She wanted Troy, and he wanted her as well. Indeed, he had made it as clear as a man like him ever would. As was his way, he had been hesitant, uncertain of how to approach her, of what to say and how much to risk. It was something Nora could understand. Yet what now stood between them was no matter that could be solved. She had no right to force a life on him that would rob him of children, of being a father, of seeing his line continued. Yes, he had told her he did not care, that he wanted her despite these circumstances. Yet since the day she had walked out of his study, telling him she could not force the sacrifice upon him, he had not approached her again. Had he realized that he had spoken in haste? Had he changed his mind?

Of course, Nora did not blame him if he had. She could not. He had every right to want children, to seek a wife who would bear him a son. Yet she could not deny that it hurt. It hurt so very much!

As Nora leaned her forehead against the ice-cold windowpane, the sound of hooves and carriage wheels drifted to her ears. Instantly, her head snapped up, her eyes gazing outside, searching for the approaching carriage. Instantly, she knew what her heart was hoping for, whose face it hoped to see, completely ignoring her mind's objections that it could not possibly be Troy.

And it wasn't.

It was Mr. Clarke, returning from London, which meant he was no longer Mr. Clarke, but the new Lord Hayward.

Feeling exhausted, Nora hung her head. Would he once again approach her? Would he now demand an answer? Of course, she was still in mourning, and yet Mr. Clarke had proved to be a rather impatient man.

Dimly, she heard his footsteps climb the few stairs to the front door and then step inside. His voice echoed across the foyer and in through the open door of the drawing room. She could hear him inquire about her and wished she could simply disappear, never to be found again.

Unfortunately, that was not an option. He knew where she was and he was coming for her as she had known he would.

"My lady," came his voice from the doorway. "It is good to see you again. I hope you are well." Eager footsteps carried him closer.

For a moment, Nora wished she didn't have to turn around, didn't have to face him. Would it be rude to simply pretend she had not heard a word he had said? That she had not even noticed his entrance? What a silly question! Of course, it would be! Yet one could dream, could one not?

With a heavy sigh, Nora turned around, willing a polite smile on her face. "Mr. Clar—Lord Hayward, it is good to see you. I hope you had a pleasant journey."

He nodded, his eyes sweeping over her face in a far too familiar way. "I must admit," he said, his voice almost dropping to a whisper as he slowly approached, "the thought of you hastened my return."

The look in his eyes made Nora want to flee the room. The way he gazed at her, the way he spoke revealed loud and clear that in his mind she was already his wife, that it was only a matter of time until she would accept him, and they would be married. There was this self-assurance, this overbearing confidence in his demeanor, that tempted Nora to slap that sickeningly sweet smile off his face. How had she never noticed this side of him before?

"I do not believe it appropriate," Nora remarked in a chiding tone, "for you to speak to me in such a way." Her brows rose meaningfully, and although his presence made her more than uncomfortable, she did not flinch away.

At her words, the look in Mr. Clarke's eyes darkened and his lips pressed into a thin line. "I apologize, my lady," he forced out through clenched teeth, "for making you uncomfortable. I assure you it was not my intention."

Nora could not quite tell whether he spoke truthfully. A part of her could not help but think that the side of him she saw now was only the one he wanted her to see. What was it he kept hidden? And why?

Something stirred at the edge of her vision, and Nora glanced behind Mr. Clarke, surprised to find his seven-year-old son Hubert hovering in the doorway. He held his green eyes downcast, as though he did not dare look at the world around him. Never had he seemed comfortable in new environments, and Nora could see a slight tremor run through him.

"Hubert, Hugh!" she exclaimed, relieved to have this moment interrupted. With a sideways glance, she hurried toward the child. "I had no idea you were here. It is truly good to see you."

Hugh peeked up at her, a shy smile tickling the corners of his mouth. "Good day, Lady Hayward. It is a pleasure to see you again." He offered her a formal bow, and it made him seem far older than his years. Nora could not say she liked it. He was far too serious for a child. Children ought to be loud and happy and safe in the knowledge that life was beautiful, ought they not?

Stepping up to them, Mr. Clarke placed a hand on his son's shoulder. "As you said," he remarked, seeking her eyes, "it is never easy for a father to be parted from his child. Therefore, I thought to bring him along, knowing how close the two of you have always been."

Nora frowned. Indeed, she had always liked Hugh—he was a sweet boy!—and yet, they had never spent much time together. "How good of you," she replied, nonetheless.

Mr. Clarke cleared his throat. "Have you given any thought to the proposal I put before you before my departure?" Watching her intently, he moved closer. "After all, we are already family, and it would bring me great joy to know that our paths would continue in this way."

Casting an uneasy glance at Hugh, Nora swallowed hard, knowing with every fiber of her being that she had made up her mind. That she did not want him! Of course, she did not want him! And yet a small part of her hesitated.

Again, Nora saw Christopher's little son run across the leaf-covered ground, chasing after Samantha, Christina's adopted daughter. Indeed, both children had found parents they had not been born to. Both children were now loved and had become part of a family by nothing more but another's choice. It had not been destiny or Fate, but simply a choice that one had made.

It was the image of that day that made her hesitate; of Christopher's wedding day, when she had come back to Whickerton Grove and had once again been among the family that had once been like her own. It had been a wonderful day, full of joy and laughter, and it had made Nora ache even more. This was what she wanted! This precisely! A household full of people she loved, children running about, turning everyone's lives upside down.

Noise.

Laughter.

The absence of silence.

After returning from the wedding festivities, Nora had been overwhelmed by the oppressive silence of Fartherington Hall. It suddenly seemed like a tomb, devoid of life, her mother a ghost hovering in the corner, floating from room to room, never quite there. Was that to be her future as well? Nora wondered, and the thought sent an ice-cold chill down her back. She would never be a mother, would she? She knew it to be true, and yet the thought filled her with disbelief. It seemed impossible!

And heartbreaking!

Not until this moment had she truly, deep, deep down accepted that fact. She could almost feel that small crack in her heart grow and slowly begin to stretch across its entire surface, knowing that one day the *dreaded thing* would split in two.

Again, Nora glanced at Hugh, suddenly wondering why Mr. Clarke had brought him along. Was he simply a father who did not wish to be parted from his child? Or had there been another motive? Had he brought Hugh in order to sway her?

"I have thought on your proposal," Nora replied, for it was the truth. "Indeed, I have given it great thought." She sighed deeply, well aware of the eager look in Mr. Clarke's eyes.

"And?" he prompted, another step carrying him closer, a look of imminent triumph sneaking onto his features. "Have you come to a conclusion?" He reached out a hand and caught a stray curl of hers between his thumb and forefinger, giving it a gentle tug.

Shocked almost witless by this small and yet intimate gesture, Nora did not quite know what to say or do, how to react. She merely stared up at him as her mind pictured a future in which he would have every right to reach for her, to draw her close. A shudder snaked down Nora's back. "I... I..."

"Nora, dear, do you have a moment?"

At the sound of her mother's voice, Nora flinched, relief shooting through her body as Mr. Clarke stepped back, his fingers releasing the strand of her hair. "Of course, Mother," Nora croaked, brushing the curl back behind her ear as she stepped away from Mr. Clarke and her eyes fell on her mother.

Nora could not quite say what it was, but somehow the look upon her mother's face gave her pause. It no longer held that distant, faraway expression, as though nothing and no one mattered, as though her mind had long since retreated to another place. Instead, what Nora saw there warmed her heart, and for a split second, she thought that perhaps her mother had come simply because Nora had needed her to.

Was that possible? She could not recall her mother ever coming to her aid, not even in small matters. Grandma Edie had. The Whickerton sisters had. But never her mother. Her attention had always been focused on some unknown thing, making it impossible for her to become aware of her daughter's need for support.

Pulling Nora's arm through the crook of her own, her mother smiled at Mr. Clarke and Hubert. "If you'll excuse us; there is an urgent matter I need to discuss with my daughter. Please, make yourselves at home. We are most glad to welcome you here once more." She gave a quick nod of the head and then escorted Nora from the room.

Without a word, her mother urged her up the stairs and led her to Nora's chamber, closing the door behind them once they were inside.

Completely taken aback, Nora stared at her mother, uncertain what to make of this unusual behavior. "Is something wrong?" Nora inquired as a new chill settled in her bones. "Did something happen? To Christopher? Or—?"

Her mother shook her head as she stepped toward Nora, her hands reaching for her daughter's. "No, it is nothing of the sort. I'm sorry for worrying you. It was not my intention. I simply wanted to..." Her voice trailed off as she groped for words, then shook her head as they eluded her. For a moment, she closed her eyes and then inhaled deeply as though gathering strength for whatever it was she was about to say. "Were you about to accept him?"

Nora blinked. "I don't know," she whispered in reply as her hands warmed in her mother's gentle hold. "I know you want me to accept him, but I simply don't know—"

"I was wrong," her mother interrupted her, and for the first time in as long as Nora could remember, she saw tears gathering in her mother's eyes. "I was so wrong." Tears spilled over and ran down her cheeks as she shook her head at herself.

Nora stared. "But... You said that..." She frowned, not quite certain what she wanted to ask. "Mother, what's happened? Why are you...?" She shook her head in confusion.

Inhaling a deep breath, her mother urged her to the settee in the corner, and together, they sat down, their hands still linked. "Please, I urge you," her mother said in an almost broken voice, "do not make a choice against your heart's wishes. If you do not care for Mr. Clarke, then don't marry him."

Nora blinked, certain that she had strayed into some kind of daydream. Her mother could not possibly be sitting here right next to her, saying these things. "Why would you...? But I thought..." Surging to her feet, Nora reclaimed her own hands. "Mother, what's gotten into you? Why would you suddenly advise me not to marry him? What has changed? Why would you—?"

Stepping forward, her mother's hands grasped her arms, her pale eyes looking deep into Nora's. "It has taken me long years to realize my mistakes," she whispered as fresh tears shot to her eyes. The woman Nora had always known her mother to be would have done her utmost to hide them, to wipe them away, to pretend they had never even been there. However, the mother currently standing in front of her, let them fall without another thought. "Please, listen to me, for I cannot bear the thought of you following in my footsteps."

Nora nodded. "Very well."

Relief showed upon her mother's face as she guided her daughter back toward the settee. They sat down, and for a moment, it seemed her mother needed to collect her thoughts, for her gaze became distant, as though she was not quite certain where to begin. "When I married your father," she finally began, and for the first time that Nora could remember, deep emotions shone in her mother's eyes, "I loved him with all my heart." A wistful smile tugged upon the corners of her mouth. "And he loved me as well. We were so happy." Her voice broke, and she bowed her head.

Nora felt her hands begin to tremble, and yet she reached out and placed them upon her mother's.

A brave little smile showed upon her mother's face as she looked up at her daughter once more. "Life was good then, and foolishly, I thought it would remain so. I suppose I took our happiness for granted when I shouldn't have."

Nora swallowed hard, uncertain if she truly wished to know what had destroyed her parents' love. "What...What happened then?"

Her mother's hands tensed upon hers. "Sebastian was barely two years old at the time when your father and I decided to slip away for a few days. You see, his mother had always been rather overbearing, dictating our lives, always watchful, always criticizing. We simply wanted a few days to ourselves, and so we decided to spend a little time in a hunting cabin out in the woods. We thought it would be a wonderful opportunity to rekindle our love, to simply be us, to do as we pleased without watchful eyes observing everything."

Longing lingered in her mother's voice, and yet Nora could sense a dark foreboding that promised an awful end to the story she had begun to tell.

"Sebastian loved the outdoors, and your father took him out hunting every day, teaching him to be quiet and stealthy," she laughed, "or at least as quiet and stealthy as a two-year-old can be. I enjoyed preparing meals myself and doing all those little things that are usually done for us. It gave me a different sense of purpose, and I remember being utterly content during those few days. At night, we would sleep in each other's arms, Sebastian between us, his little hands curled into my hair. I would often lay awake at night and simply watch them sleep, so peacefully, wishing to commit this moment to memory, to never forget it and hold on to it forever." She closed her eyes and exhaled deeply. "Everything was perfect."

A shiver traced itself down Nora's back, and she almost urged her mother not to continue. Yet whatever had happened had been the very reason for this drastic turn in her parents' lives, had been the reason why her mother seemed more like a ghost than a woman of flesh and blood.

"I did not know someone had entered the cabin until I heard a door slam shut." Her mother's voice trembled, and Nora could hear the reluctance to continue on in each word she spoke. Yet beneath the anguish and sorrow etched into her face, Nora saw courage flare to life, the determination to not back down, but continue on and face this evil. "There were five of them." She swallowed hard, her eyes downcast and unable to meet Nora's. "They were after valuables, I suppose. They ransacked the cabin; however, when they did not find much, they turned their anger on us." Her eyes closed, pinched shut. "I still remember the way they looked at me. I still remember the moment I realized what they wanted."

An ice-cold paralysis fell over Nora as she stared at her mother's face, contorted in anguish and pain. She heard her words, and yet they echoed like the retelling of a story that was not founded in truth. It couldn't be! Things like those did not happen, did they? And yet, the look upon her mother's face made her cringe.

"I will not tell you everything that happened that night," her mother finally continued on, a sharp edge to her voice as she sat up and straightened her shoulders. "There are some things children should never know about their parents." She lifted her chin and met Nora's eyes. "Yet I can see that you understand what I speak of. You know what it is like to have to endure another's touch, do you not?"

Closing her eyes, Nora inhaled deeply as memories of her marriage returned.

Her mother's hands tightened upon hers. "I'm so sorry, my dear. I should never have urged you to marry Hayward, and neither should I have urged you to accept Mr. Clarke." Tears glistened in her eyes as she tugged upon Nora's arms, pulling her closer. "Your father and I lost each other after that night. Whenever I looked at him, I saw guilt. He could not stop blaming himself for what had happened, for being unable to protect me." She exhaled a deep breath. "And then I realized I was with child."

Nora's eyes flew open, and she stared at her mother. "Are you...Are you saying Christopher is not...?" Of course! All of a sudden, everything made sense! Her parents had always treated Christopher differently, perhaps not intentionally, but... How did one handle such a tragedy?

Her mother nodded. "We didn't know what to do," she whispered, the look in her eyes once more distant as she recalled those days. "The only one who ever knew was your father's mother, and she made it very clear that the family name had to be protected, that no scandal was to come from this. She told us never to speak of it, to pretend it had not happened, to continue on as before." A heavy sigh left her lips. "But we could not, neither your father nor I."

Drawing her mother into her arms, Nora held her close as tears streamed down both their faces. She could not recall the last time she had embraced her mother like this, and yet despite the tragedy that had brought them here, Nora cherished this moment. For the first time, she felt close to her mother. She felt a bond grow between them, and only moments later, words spilled from her own lips as well.

As they held on to one another, Nora told her mother everything that had happened in her life, beginning with that day by the ancient watchtower, when all of a sudden, she had come to look at Troy in a different way. Of course, confiding in her mother did not solve anything, did not present a magical solution, but it felt good.

So very good.

Chapter Thirty-Two

A FATHER'S REVELATION

R unning a hand through his hair, Troy stared out the window, his gaze glued to the young woman walking at her mother's side down into the gardens. Snow covered the ground, and little flakes still danced in the air as the Whickerton clan enjoyed a blissful afternoon out-of-doors. It was the first snow, and it had drawn the two children outside without a moment's hesitation. Bundled up warmly, Bash and Sam chased each other up and down the snowy slope, here and there picking up snowballs and flinging them at one another. Their laughter echoed to Troy's ears, and yet he could not bring himself to move his gaze to them and away from the young woman now standing amidst his sisters, a rosy glow upon her cheeks.

More than anything, Troy wanted to join them outside, to hasten over to her and look into her eyes. He missed her! As much as he knew that there was no future for them, that Nora had made her choice, his heart simply would not comply. Not that that was a surprise! After all, he had spent the years after her wedding to Hayward in a similar state. Was this what his life was to be? Would it always be thus?

Watching, Troy noticed how Nora lifted her head and then glanced over to the house. He could almost feel her gaze coming to rest upon him, even through the window that hid him from her eyes. Perhaps she simply knew that he was there. After all, Troy had always been a rather predictable man, who enjoyed his solitude. Did she long to see him as well? Did it matter?

Raking his hands through his hair, Troy forced himself to turn from the window. It would not serve him to dwell on what could not be. He had told her he wanted her for his wife, that he did not care that they would not have children; and yet she had turned away from him.

Nora had made her choice, and he needed to accept that.

Over the next few days following Nora's visit, Troy did his utmost to adhere to his resolution. He tried to keep busy, working long into the night, for whenever his head touched the pillow, his thoughts inevitably returned to her as though to torment him. He barely slept, kept awake by the fear that perhaps, just perhaps, she might accept another. He could not forget how she had told him of Mr. Clarke's intentions. Now that Nora was vulnerable, would her late husband's cousin use that to his advantage?

Troy reminded himself that he ought not care that Nora could do as she pleased; yet the reminder fell far short, never managing to convince him for even a second. Before, it had been easier because they had rarely crossed paths. Now, however, she was only a quick ride away, their families forever connected through their siblings' marriage. Juliet's and Christopher's children would be both their nieces and nephews, and Troy imagined what it would be like to have her so close and yet so far away all the years to come.

A sharp knock sounded on the door, and Troy looked up from the ledger he had been working on. "Enter," he called, rising to his feet when he saw his father step over the threshold.

"Do you have a moment," his father asked, then chuckled, "or perhaps two?"

Troy nodded. "Of course." He stepped around the desk, wondering at the watchful expression upon his father's face.

Clearing his throat, his father moved into the room, his right hand grasping his chin in a thoughtful gesture before he looked up and met Troy's eyes. "Once again," he began rather solemnly, "I find myself wanting to speak with you."

Troy frowned. "What about?"

His father's brows rose meaningfully.

Troy swallowed, then he bowed his head. "There's nothing to say," he insisted, stepping around his father and moving over to his familiar spot by the window. Yet in his mind's ear, he could hear his grandmother's voice, *Go and speak to your father. He'll know what to tell you.*

Behind him, his father inhaled a deep breath. "It is Nora, is it not?"

Troy turned to stare at his father, completely caught off guard.

His father chuckled. "One has to be blind, deaf and dumb not to notice the way you two gravitate toward each other." Measured steps carried him closer, his dark eyes fixed upon his son. "What is it that stands between you?"

Closing his eyes, Troy ran a hand through his hair. "She cannot have children," he murmured as all fight left his body. As much as he wanted to keep this to himself, he could do so no longer. Perhaps his grandmother was right. Perhaps his father's words would help him make his peace with the situation.

With losing Nora.

"And?" was all his father said, his hands linked behind his back as he considered Troy rather curiously.

Troy frowned. "And...I need a wife who can give me a son." The words felt wrong upon his tongue, and more than anything, Troy wanted to take them back.

An indulgent smile came to his father's face. "And so, you decided not to marry her?"

Troy huffed out a deep breath. "I did no such thing. However, Nora refused...me." He bowed his head, remembering that shattering moment. "I...I tried to convince her, but she was adamant."

Another chuckle drifted from his father's lips as he moved to stand beside Troy, his gaze now directed out the window. "The moment I saw your mother, I knew she was the one," he said almost reverently, awe and admiration in his voice. Then he looked over his shoulder at Troy, and a smile came to his face. "She, on the other hand, told me in no uncertain terms that I was to leave her alone." He chuckled. "She was quite *adamant*."

Curious, Troy looked into his father's face, wondering if he, too, had once felt so disheartened. "I know what you're trying to do, and I do thank you for it, Father. However, you and Mother had no such insurmountable obstacle standing between you as we do now."

Clasping a hand on his son's shoulder, his father laughed. "That is what you think." A deep sigh rushed from his lungs, and he briefly closed his eyes. "You all know that your mother and I went against our parents' wishes when we married."

Troy nodded. "Of course, you've told us so many times."

"And did you ever wonder," his father began, "why our respective parents were so determined to keep us apart?"

Troy frowned, trying to remember the many times he had heard the story of his parents' love. Everyone told it a little differently, and so, over the years, he and his siblings had done their utmost to piece together the individual snippets they had heard. "As far as I remember, grandfather had a better match in mind for you, whereas mother was already betrothed, was she not?"

His father nodded. "Yet there was more to it, something we've never told any of you."

Looking at his father most intensely, Troy wondered what precisely he was trying to say, what point he was trying to make. The look in his eyes seemed almost hesitant, and yet a touch of relief came over his face, as though he had wanted to share this for a long time but never quite found the right words.

"Before I met her," his father began as he turned back to the window, "your mother fancied herself in love with another. She dreamed of marriage and children, expecting a proposal any day, while he," the tone in his father's voice darkened, "had less honorable intentions." Over his shoulder, he met Troy's gaze. "When it all fell apart, her parents quickly arranged for her to be married to an old family friend in order to avoid the scandal."

Troy shook his head, unable to make sense of his father's words. "What scandal? Why should there be a scan—?"

"Because your mother was with child."

The blood froze in Troy's veins as he stared at his father.

"Of course, I had no idea," his father went on, his dark brown eyes fixed upon Troy's. "And then one night at a ball, I came upon her in tears. She tried to send me away, but...I wouldn't go." He smiled. "As adamant as she was, I was even more. Eventually, she broke down and told me everything."

Troy swallowed as his father's words slowly found their way underneath his skin.

"She cried, and I held her." Turning toward him, his father grasped both of his shoulders, his gaze intent. "And when her tears ceased, I asked her to marry me."

Troy felt his jaw drop as shock jolted through his body. "The...The child?" His mouth opened and remained so, unable to put into words what echoed in his chest.

His father nodded, his grip upon Troy's shoulders tightening. "The child was you," his father confirmed without a moment of hesitation. "You see, when something feels right, nothing else matters. I loved your mother, and I wanted her by my side until the end of my days." He chuckled, and Troy wondered how his father could be so truly at peace with himself after what he had just shared. "Of course, our parents disagreed. They forbade us to marry, insisting she was betrothed. Your grandfather lectured me for an hour on the pitfalls of jumping head over heels into something. He told me I would come to regret this decision."

Troy simply stood there, his heart all but silent as his mind tried to make sense of all he had learned. "And Grandmother?" he asked, remembering the many creative ways she had found to see her grand-daughters happily married.

A wide grin came to his father's face. "For a long time, she remained quiet. Not a word passed her lips. You know how she is." He chuckled. "And then one night, she led me outside to the stables where a carriage, unmarked and inconspicuous, awaited me with your mother inside. She sent us off to Scotland, said that everything was arranged," he shrugged, "and we were married."

Aghast, Troy stared at his father. "But she...she loved another, did she not?" he asked, focusing on his parents, and pushing aside the unsettling questions that slowly dug their way into his heart.

His father sighed, a wistful look upon his face. "Love is an odd thing. Sometimes it blooms slowly, and sometimes it finds us lightning-quick. It can be forever or it disappears in the blink of an eye. There are no guarantees, and we must never take it for granted." He squeezed Troy's shoulders. "Your mother sharing her heartbreak with me that night brought us closer than anything else possibly could have. We learned more about each other in a single night than we could have in months of courting." He nodded. "Her heart changed, and what at first seemed impossible turned into a wonderful life."

Troy felt a shuddering breath leave his lips, a part of him utterly certain that this was a dream. In all likelihood, he was upstairs in his chamber, in his bed, his eyes closed in slumber, his mind conjuring this moment in order to...

He frowned. Why would his mind imagine something as life-shattering as this? What was the point?

"You are my son, Troy," his father said into the stillness of the moment, his voice strong and certain, matching the look in his warm brown eyes. "Do you hear me? You are my son in every way that matters! I need you to know that I do not have a single regret when it comes to the choices I've made in my life." He smiled at Troy, a hint of tears in his eyes. "Do not ever doubt that I love you! I assure you; you would be wrong to believe so. Not only women can love children not born to them."

Immediately, Troy thought of his two sisters, Christina and Juliet, who had both recently become mothers to children not their own. Only now, Bash and Sam *were* their own. Troy had seen it in their eyes. He had seen the way they looked at them, the same way his mother looked at him.

Blinking away the images in his mind, Troy focused his gaze once more upon his father's. "Why...Why are you telling me this now?" It was the first question that came to his mind, and yet there were so many more, pressing in on him, making his heart ache and his mind doubt.

His father inhaled a deep breath, his gaze distant for a moment as he considered most carefully how to reply. "We didn't say anything before because we wanted to protect you from a world that would see something wrong in the way our family came together. You are my son, and I want you to inherit my title, not because I need an heir, but because you're mine and it is your right." A dark growl rumbled in his throat. "To hell with society!" He shook his head, deep displeasure upon his face.

"I'm telling you this now," his father continued, "because I need you to understand something." His gaze seemed weightier all of a sudden, and Troy drew in a deep breath, knowing his father's next words were important. "Life should never be about duty and following someone else's rules. Your mother and I chose love with no regard for reason, and we have been happy ever since." A heartwarming smile came to his father's face. "You are my son, Troy, and I love you. I want you to be happy. I'd rather our line end with you than see my son lose the woman he loves. Do you hear me?"

Troy felt his father's hands almost dig into his shoulders.

"If you love her," his father counseled, "marry her! Be adamant! Don't let her get away! No one should have to live without love in their life, and I assure you that everything else will work itself out. There are always ways. You might not see them right now, but they will reveal themselves to you with time." He sighed deeply. "A broken heart, though, is something that will stay with you for the rest of your life."

Overwhelmed, Troy stared at his father, his thoughts and emotions helplessly entangled. *His father? Yet he wasn't, was he? Of course, he was, but...*

Pinching his eyes shut, Troy hung his head.

"I understand that this came as quite the shock to you," his father said gently, giving Troy's shoulders another squeeze before he stepped back. "Take your time, think everything through, and if there is anything you wish to speak to us about, your mother and I will be happy to tell you everything you wish to know." He stepped toward the door. "We love you, Troy, and we always have." With a last smile, his father stepped from the room.

With trembling limbs, Troy remained behind in the study, his eyes wide and his heart beating fast. *Think everything through*, his father had said, and yet at present Troy's mind seemed only capable of spinning in dizzying circles. For the first time in his life, he could not think. Not one clear thought would come. Not one. He began to pace, his hands balling into fists as a torrent of emotions washed over him.

After a few seemingly endless moments, Troy spun around and

rushed out the door, unable to find peace in the one room that had always been his sanctuary. Large strides carried him down the corridor and toward the door. He snatched up his coat and then stepped outside into the icy cold of early winter, still uncertain where his feet were carrying him.

And then he sat atop his gelding, feeling the animal's smooth movements as they charged across the land, the wind upon his cheeks like pinpricks. The world flew by, and yet Troy's eyes remained blind...

...until they fell upon the ancient watchtower and he felt his heart cry out for Nora.

Here in this moment, he needed her. Her warmth. Her kindness. Her comfort. Her understanding. Everything she was. She would need no more than one glance and understand, wouldn't she? If only—

Rounding the ruins, Troy pulled up short, and the air rushed from his lungs as his gaze fell on a young woman with tear-stained cheeks, her mahogany tresses escaping her pins and dancing wildly upon the winter winds.

Nora.

Chapter Thirty-Three

AGAINST ALL ODDS

Ever since she had pulled herself into the saddle, Nora's heart had entertained a foolish and yet desperate hope that perhaps, just perhaps, she would meet Troy at the ruins. It was what one would call a heart's desire, was it not? Something the very essence of her being longed for, ached for, needed in order to continue on.

Yet after the way they had last parted, Nora doubted he would ever seek her out again, would ever come to the ancient watchtower for fear that she might be there.

Drawing in one shuddering breath after another, Nora stared across the small expanse, her gaze fixed upon him, savoring the moment that had found her so unexpectedly.

Snow lay draped across the world in a thin layer, and ice clung to every blade of grass, every branch, giving the world an almost magical touch.

As though anything was possible.

As though, here in this place, dreams could still come true.

Nora knew she was foolish for allowing such thoughts, and yet one was helpless against one's own heart's desires, was one not? Just as she had been unable to keep herself from riding out, from riding here to this very place. Reason forbade her from doing many things, and yet her heart beat strong in her chest, demanding to be heard.

Pulling to stop only a few paces away from her, Troy slid out of the saddle, his boots flattening the thin layer of snow. He stared at her with wide eyes, the soft blue of his sparkling in the tentative rays of the sun; and yet deep sorrow clung to his features.

Instantly, Nora felt her heart pause in her chest before almost running off at a gallop. Her eyes swept over his face, saw the tears in the corners of his eyes, the hard set of his jaw, and she knew that something had shaken him.

Deeply.

Without another thought, Nora moved toward him, her eyes never veering from his. She saw him draw in a shuddering breath, his shoulders trembling, and forgot all the many reasons why she ought to stay away from him. They disappeared into thin air, leaving behind an almost desperate need to comfort him, to ease his pain and see his burden lifted.

For a long moment, they simply looked at one another, something meaningful, something silent passing between them, before Nora reached out her hand, gently cupping it to his cheek.

At her touch, Troy closed his eyes and leaned into her hand, a trembling breath leaving his lips and dancing away on the chilled winter air. Barely a moment later, his hands reached for her, and they sank into each other's arms.

The feel of him filled Nora's soul, and she closed her eyes, savoring the moment, wishing it could be a happy one, but grateful for it, nonetheless.

Troy all but slumped forward, his forehead coming to rest upon her shoulder as his arms tightened around her, as though he did not trust himself to remain upright without holding on to her. Heavy breaths left his lips, and she could feel him tremble deep inside, as though something had shaken everything he was, everything he knew.

Running her hands onto his shoulders, Nora then slipped them into his hair, brushing them up and down, trying to soothe the tension that lingered. Whatever had happened had knocked his feet out from under him, and her heart ached at the sight of his sorrow.

Endless moments passed as they stood in each other's arms, a comfortable silence settling over them. Slowly, Nora felt his breaths go deeper, his muscles beginning to relax, and yet he held her as tightly as before.

Eventually, Troy lifted his head, and his blue eyes looked down at her face. "Why are you here?" he asked softly, reaching out a hand to gently trace the line of her jaw, the look in his eyes almost mesmerized.

Nora sighed, savoring his tender touch. "I might ask you the same," she whispered in reply.

He inhaled deeply, his shoulders rising and falling. "Yet you were the one to refuse me," he murmured almost absentmindedly, as though reliving the very moment they had shared in his study, the moment when she had told him she could not marry him. "You are the one," he blinked, and his eyes focused on hers once more, "who left, who didn't want anything to do with me."

The pain in those few words almost brought Nora to her knees, and a reply tumbled from her lips without another thought. "You know that is not true." She swallowed hard, aware that she should say nothing, but unable to keep up pretenses. "You know that I have loved you ever since you first kissed me," a soft smile tugged upon her lips, "right here, in this very spot."

A shuddering breath left his lips, and Nora could see how deeply her words affected him. His arm held her tighter, and his hand slipped to the back of her neck as he slowly lowered his head to hers. His eyes danced down to her lips before rising once more. "I have loved you as well," Troy whispered before gently brushing his lips against hers. "I've cursed that day a thousand times, and yet it was the best moment of my life."

Tears gathered in Nora's eyes. "I know," she whispered back, feeling his warm breath upon her skin. "I felt the same." In that moment, her heart beat strong against her ribcage, as though wishing to urge her on, to give her courage and make her daring. "Will you kiss me now?"

At her request, Troy closed his eyes and a deep breath rushed from his lungs before a tentative smile stole onto his face. "I've dreamed of this," he whispered as he inched closer. "You've been from my arms for far too long." A shuddering breath left his lips, teasing her own. "I've missed you."

"I've missed you as well," Nora replied a second before his lips touched hers, her heart overflowing with utter joy at being so close to him.

This kiss was slow and lingering, echoing the depth of their emotions, the longing they felt as well as the fear they could not shake. It rang with truth, opening their hearts and urging them to acknowledge what was truly between them. This was no mere passion, no carnal lust. No, this was life-changing, an exchange of hearts, knowing it could never be undone.

For better or for worse.

Troy's hands trailed over her cheek, the tips of his fingers brushing over the wetness her tears had left behind. "You're crying," he whispered, his blue eyes seeking hers.

Nora swallowed. "As are you," she replied, noting the way his features darkened, as though he wished to hide. "Tell me," she urged, knowing the kind of man he was, knowing that it was hard for him to reveal how he felt, to share his sorrow and accept help and comfort from another. "You're in pain. I can see that you are. What happened?"

With a reluctant look in his eyes, Troy bowed his head. His lips parted, and yet no words emerged.

Reaching for him, Nora cupped her hands to his face and gently tilted up his head until his eyes once more looked into hers. "You cannot carry this burden alone," she told him gently. "Share it with me, and I will help you."

For a long moment, Troy closed his eyes before he finally spoke. "My father told me today that...that he is, in fact, *not* my father." A dark chuckle followed that statement.

Nora stared at him, for a moment certain that she had misunderstood. "He's not your father?" Instantly, her thoughts returned to what her mother had told her only a few days past. Were there secrets everywhere? In every family? Had the world never been what it seemed?

Willing her thoughts to return to the here and now, she held Troy's gaze. "Tell me what happened. Tell me everything."

And so he did.

As they stood together in the snow, Troy told her of his mother's first love, of her predicament when she realized it would never lead to marriage. He spoke to her of his father's certainty that his mother was the one for him, willing to accept a child who was not his in order to secure her hand in marriage.

When he finished, Nora smiled. "What a beautiful story!"

Troy flinched, a deep frown coming to his face. "A beautiful story?" He shook his head, the look in his eyes aghast. "Everything they told us was a lie. The person I thought I was…" His voice trailed off, and again, he shook his head, a look of utter confusion marking his features.

Watching him carefully, Nora asked, "What frightens you, Troy? What is it that sent you here today?"

His mouth opened, as though he knew precisely what to say. Then, however, he paused, and she watched his forehead crinkle into frown lines as he realized he did not.

"I understand you are shaken. Of course, you are. Anyone would be." Still cupping his face, Nora gently ran the pads of her thumbs over his cheekbones in a soothing gesture. "Yet what you must understand is that your father chose you."

Troy scoffed. "He did no such thing. He chose my mother. He accepted me because he wanted her."

Nora sighed. "Perhaps it began like that, yes. But knowing your father, I am certain—"

"He is not my father!"

"Oh, but he is," Nora insisted, determined to make him hear her, knowing that it would destroy him if he left this place believing as he did now. "Do you not remember when you fell ill and ran that high fever? Do you not remember how your father remained by your bedside for days, watching over you? He barely slept. He barely ate."

A flicker of recognition sparked in Troy's eyes.

"And the time, you were furious with yourself because you had not closed the stable door properly and Lord Dunhaven's precious mare… ended up in close quarters with that *old nag*—as he called it—that Harriet saved?" Nora chuckled, feeling encouraged by the hint of a smile that tugged upon Troy's lips. "He took full responsibility and told you that mistakes happen and that you were not to think on it, didn't he? He told Lord Dunhaven to get over himself and to leave if he could not be civil, did he not?"

Closing his eyes, Troy nodded. "He kept retelling the story a hundred times, but in such a way that made me the hero, as though I had released the mare so she could seek out her one true love." He chuckled, then shook his head.

"Your father loves you, Troy," Nora pointed out. "He always has, and he always will. Even if he did not choose you the moment he married your mother, I bet there was a moment for him—perhaps the day you were born—that he chose you the same way he had chosen her."

A long breath rushed from Troy's lungs, his gaze distant, perhaps locked on moments of the past he had shared with his father. Then he suddenly looked at her once more, something hesitant in his eyes before he spoke. "After you married Hayward," Nora almost cringed at his words, "I...I needed to get away. I...I could not stay and pretend that..." He swallowed hard, and his hands upon her waist tightened. "I disappeared. I left without saying a word to anyone. I knew it was rude and thoughtless of me, but in that moment, I..."

Nora nodded. "I know."

"Eventually, my father found me in some tavern, me barely able to remember my name." His lips pressed into a thin line as he remembered the state of disgrace he had been in...because of her; Nora reminded herself. "Later, I learned he had combed London week after week, searching for me."

Nora brushed a tender hand over his cheek. "Do you see then?"

Troy inhaled a tentative breath. "I've watched my sisters become mothers to children not their own, and yet...I cannot help the doubts that linger when it comes to my father." He shook his head. "I'm to inherit his title, even though I am not of his blood. Does that not bother him? Perhaps it does, deep down somewhere, and he simply won't admit it because it wouldn't change anything." He sighed. "I wonder if he ever came to regret his decision."

"I cannot imagine not loving a child," Nora began, feeling her heart contract painfully, "any child, so long as I could be its mother. Now, that I..." She drew in a deep breath as her gaze slid from his. "Now that I will never have one of my own, I understand how insignificant blood is." Involuntarily, her thoughts strayed to little Hugh, with his unruly blond hair, his shy eyes and mischievous freckles atop his nose. Oh, yes, she could love him! If only she did not have to marry his father in order to call him her own!

Nora snapped out of her thoughts as Troy's hands upon her suddenly tensed. She looked up and saw his face suddenly pale. "What is it? Are you all right?"

All but staring through her, he stammered, "It's not only my father. Grandmother, she..." He shook his head and swallowed hard before looking at her again. "She is not my grandmother, and...and my sisters, they're only my half-sisters. We... I..."

Nora could see his need. She could see the upheaval he felt, some-thing that was to be expected when one suddenly learned of such a family secret. He needed time, and perhaps the right kind of counsel. "Go and speak to your grandmother," Nora advised. "She will tell you what you need to know." Again, she cupped his cheeks in her hands. "She will know how to put your heart at ease, I promise." After all, Grandma Edie's kind words had sustained Nora through a loveless marriage. If anyone knew what to say, it was her.

Chapter Thirty-Four

WISE COUNSEL

By the time Troy returned to Whickerton Grove, darkness was already falling over the world. Only a thin sliver of the sun still remained upon the horizon, casting warm colors of orange and red across the darkening sky. Many of the windows were illuminated, and Troy could glimpse people walking past them here and there or standing nearby, their mere outline giving them an almost otherworldly impression.

Dismounting, Troy led his gelding into the stable, grateful for a moment of solitude before his bustling family would swarm him once again. No doubt, they had noticed his absence—his prolonged absence —and would fire a volley of questions at him the moment he stepped across the threshold.

With a shake of his head, Troy waved away an approaching stable boy, sending the lad back to the hayloft where he had been playing with the recently born litter of kittens. Then he led his gelding into a stall in the far back, removing the saddle and bridle before starting to brush his horse down. It felt good to have his hands occupied, to do something worthwhile, something the animal appreciated, its breathing content. Troy, too, began to relax, even though his thoughts still circled around everything this day had brought.

His father's revelation.

As well as Nora's.

She loved him, did she not? At least, she had said so, and in truth, Troy had believed her. Yet his father had said so as well, and Troy could not help but feel a sting of doubt. He did not want to, but he could not help it. *Go and speak to your grandmother. I promise she will know how to put your heart at ease*, Nora had said, and Troy realized he trusted her. If she said so, it had to be true. What did this mean?

At the sound of the stable door swinging open, Troy turned to look over his shoulder, a chuckle drifting from his lips as he saw Keir emerge from the darkness outside. The Scotsman led his dapple-gray mare down the aisle and into the stall next to Troy's gelding. "Another errand, I presume," Troy remarked with a scoff.

Keir laughed. "Ye would presume right," he replied as openly as he dared; after all, Troy's grandmother had sworn him to secrecy.

Regarding the other man curiously, Troy stepped over to the stall wall. "How many days were you gone this time? Four? Five?"

Removing his mare's saddle, the Scotsman grinned at him. "Six, to be exact." He paused, meeting Troy's gaze. "I can see that ye have questions and I wish I could answer them, but..." He shrugged almost helplessly.

Troy nodded in understanding. "I would never ask you to break your word." He sighed deeply as his thoughts returned to his own secrets, and he felt a spark of anger for their existence alone. Never before had he realized how many secrets there were in the world. The weight of them was crippling.

"Are ye all right?" Keir inquired with a narrowed gaze, his arms resting upon his mare's back as he watched Troy intently. "Ye have the look of a man standing at a fork in the road."

Sighing, Troy nodded. "I suppose I am," he remarked, still uncertain how to proceed from here. *Go and speak to your grandmother!* Indeed, he ought to, and yet he lingered.

For a moment, silence wrapped around them, the soft breathing of the horses in their stalls the only noise drifting through the hay-scented air. "Today, I found out that my father is not my father," Troy suddenly blurted out, flinching in surprise at his own words. Yet a part of him remembered he had felt comfortable speaking to the Scot before.

Lifting his head, Troy met Keir's gaze, surprised to see neither shock nor outrage upon the man's face. Indeed, he looked as calm as ever, as though not a day passed without someone confessing such a life-altering occurrence to him.

Then his head suddenly nodded up and down, and a hint of a wistful smile touched his face. "I had a sister once," he whispered with a deep sigh, resting his arms more comfortably on his mare's back. "She was a wee little thing with big round eyes and a daring little heart that made me fear for her every day of her life." He shook his head, though the smile never left his face.

Troy stared across the small expanse, utterly riveted by the Scotsman's tale. He wondered how it might pertain to his own confession, but he could not bring himself to ask.

"I was out riding with my father and brother one day," Keir continued, running a hand through his dark hair, a distant look in his eyes, "and when we passed by the glen and rode higher up toward the cliff face, that's when we found her."

Troy frowned. "Found her?"

Keir's gaze met his, a twitch lifting the right corner of his mouth. "Aye, she was just there in our path, barely three years of age, all alone."

Staring at the Scotsman, Troy tried to imagine such a scenario, still uncertain what precisely the other man was trying to tell him.

"We searched the countryside for hours but never found anyone," Keir explained, and the look in his eyes said loud and clear that even after all these years he still did not know how she had come to be there. "For months, we asked around, sent riders to every village to make inquiries," he shook his head, "but no one ever came forth and claimed her." His eyes turned to Troy, and a deep smile showed upon his face. "And so, she remained with us, became my parents' daughter and our sister, and I couldna have loved her more if she had been of my blood." He nodded to emphasize his words.

Troy exhaled a slow breath, grateful to the Scotsman for sharing this story. Perhaps it was not so unusual for parents to love a child not born to them, for whole families to welcome someone into their hearts who had come to them in a most unexpected way. Indeed, his own heart was already beginning to feel lighter. Perhaps all you needed was time, the time to sort through his emotions, to acquaint himself with the knowledge he had received. Perhaps this truly did not have to change anything.

Suddenly, Troy frowned as his gaze once more focused on the Scotsman. "You *had* a sister?" he inquired, and for the first time, he glimpsed deep sadness in Keir's eyes.

The other man nodded. "One day," he swallowed hard, "she simply disappeared." He shrugged his shoulders helplessly, and yet that simple gesture conveyed the depth of his loss. "The same way she had suddenly come into our lives, she left us again years later." He shook his head, the need to know what had happened burning in his eyes, tempered by the harsh realization that he never would. "It broke my parents' hearts. Ours, too. My brother blamed himself for not accompanying her into the woods that day; yet she had gone by herself many, many times before. No one had ever been able to hold her back. That's who she was."

Troy felt his hands tremble at the thought of one of his sisters disappearing like that. He could not imagine ever continuing on, not knowing what had happened to her. "I'm sorry," he whispered, knowing the words to be inadequate; yet they were all he had.

Brushing a hand down his mare's back, Keir stepped around her, his green gaze seeking Troy's. "The world turns. We canna help that. But we can make the most of the life we have." A slow smile came to his face before he nodded toward the house. "Go on ahead. They surely await yer return."

Exhaling a deep breath, Troy nodded. "Thank you," he said simply, then stepped from the stall and back out into the aisle. "If there's ever anything you need..." He held Keir's gaze for a long moment, hoping the Scotsman could see his sincerity.

That carefree smile returned to Keir's face. "I shall call on ye." He grasped Troy's shoulder and gave it a quick squeeze. "Thank ye, my friend."

Determined to heed Keir's words, Troy returned to the house to seek out his grandmother. However, the moment he stepped inside, the little hairs on the back of his neck rose. An odd tension lay in the air, and he swallowed hard, anxious to learn what had happened in his absence.

"Jules!" he called the moment he spotted her rush by the stairs on the first floor. Hearing her name called, she paused, and her gaze drifted down to him as he climbed the stairs three at a time, rushing to her side. "What's happened? Where is everyone?"

A tentative smile came to his sister's face. "Louisa is having her baby," she whispered, a touch of awe in her voice as she grasped his hands. As though to confirm her words, a bloodcurdling scream pierced the stillness of the house in that moment.

Troy flinched at the sound, even more disconcerted when Juliet's face paled alongside with his own. "Is she...? Is that...normal?" He turned his head to look down the corridor toward Louisa's chamber, torn between rushing to her side and remaining where he was.

Juliet nodded. "It is not easy bringing a child into the world," she told him, a touch of unease in her eyes; after all, she, too, longed to be a mother. "However, it is well worth it." She squeezed his hands and then hastened away, back to Louisa's side.

Remaining behind in the hallway, Troy felt a bit forlorn, uncertain what to do. However, in the next moment, the sound of shuffling foot-steps drifted to his ears, and he turned to find his grandmother approaching.

"I see you have returned," she remarked with a wicked gleam in her eyes. "Come," she waved him over, "let us sit and talk."

Another scream pierced the stillness, and again, Troy flinched, once more looking over his shoulder toward Louisa's chamber. "Should you not...help her?" he asked his grandmother, completely overwhelmed by the situation. Indeed, Louisa was the first of his sisters to give birth and he felt completely out of his element.

Taking his arm, Grandma Edie tugged him along. "There's nothing I can do for her right now. She has your mother and sisters with her as well as her husband," she chuckled, "although I'm not certain how much help *he*'ll be." She grinned up at him. "Care for a wager? I'll say that our dear Phineas will faint at least once before the day is out."

Unable to help himself, Troy laughed, cherishing this moment of reprieve. "You are truly impossible, Grandmother."

"I try to be," she chuckled, as they slowly made their way downstairs. "But it's not always easy."

Once in the drawing room, Troy assisted his grandmother into her favorite chair near the fireplace, then he reached for the blanket she always had wrapped around her legs in winter. "Is there anything else you require?"

Ignoring his question, Grandma Edie pointed her cane at the seat beside her. "Sit," she ordered, then set aside her walking stick and fixed him with curious eyes. "So, your father finally told you."

Troy heaved a deep sigh. "I won't even ask how you know this."

"Perhaps your father told me," she suggested, humor in her voice.

Troy shook his head. "I rather doubt it." Then he fell silent, uncertain how to begin.

"What is it that lingers on your mind?" his grandmother asked after a moment of observing him most intently.

Troy met her gaze, a challenge in his own. "Am I to understand that you do not know?"

His grandmother chuckled. "I like your sass, boy!" She reached out and patted his hand. "Go ahead, ask your questions."

Gathering his thoughts, Troy paused for a moment, uncertain where to begin. "My father, he..." He frowned, shook his head, then began again. "When they married, did he...? Do you know if he...?" Closing his eyes, he hung his head.

After a moment, Troy felt his grandmother's hand settle upon his own. "For your father, it took one look into her eyes and his heart was no longer his own." A sigh left her lips, and a wide smile sneaked onto her face. "You should've seen him. That besotted look upon his face was utterly endearing...and somewhat humorous." She chuckled.

Troy sighed, smiling at his grandmother as he felt himself begin to relax. "And my mother?"

"For her, it was different," his grandmother explained as his father had before. "She needed a bit more time, but once she fell, she fell deeply." Her eyes once more focused upon Troy as her mind returned from moments of the past. "But that is not what you wish to know, is it?" Her brows rose meaningfully.

Troy heaved a deep breath. "I know he loved her. I know that he still loves her. I see it every day." He shot to his feet and began to pace. "I never doubted that. However, I cannot help but wonder if..." Stopping by the fireplace, he rested his hands upon the mantle and hung his head. "If he merely accepted me because he wanted her. I don't doubt that he cares for me, but does he truly love me? As he would love his own son?"

"You are his son!" came Grandma Edie's voice loud and strong, a hint of annoyance mixed within as well. "I know that society has this silly notion that family is made by blood." She scoffed in derision. "I suppose that is because society does not care about love. All it cares about is reputation. So long as everything looks perfect on the surface, society does not care what lies underneath." She inhaled a deep breath, and Troy could feel her eyes upon him. "However, not since your grandfather and I were married have we, as a family, ever believed that to be true." She chuckled. "We are Whickertons. We do things differently, and we like it."

Unable not to, Troy smiled as he turned to look at his grandmother. "I might've noticed that," he remarked as he walked back over to her and took his former seat. "Yet when I was born," he asked hesitantly, "was father not at least a little disappointed that his title would pass to—?"

"No! Not for a second!"

"How would you know?"

Grandma Edie sighed. "Parents simply know," she said with a look of utter wisdom in her pale eyes. "You'll know once you're a father yourself." Smiling, she patted his hand.

Troy cringed at her words.

"Listen," his grandmother said gently. "Love is not something that can be measured or compared, and I suppose it should not be. Yes, your father loved your mother and so he accepted you into his family as well, even though his heart held no love for you yet. How could it have? You hadn't even been born yet!" Her hand once more closed around his, giving it a soft tug so he would look at her. "Tell me truthfully, do you already love the children you might one day have?" A slow grin came to her face.

Chuckling, Troy exhaled a deep breath. "I suppose I do not."

Again, she patted his hand. "See?" Leaning back in her seat, a wistful expression came to her face. "I remember the day you were born." She cast him a sideways glance. "I remember the moment the midwife placed you in your father's arms. I remember the look of utter joy and love I saw upon his face, the same as when your sisters were born." She smiled at him. "You and your sisters are your parents' greatest treasures, and they would not hesitate to relinquish title and fortune and everything that society places such high value on in a heartbeat if it were necessary to keep this family intact. Together. That's how parents feel about their children, not their heirs, but their children. It's all that matters."

Troy's heart warmed at his grandmother's words, every fiber of his being recognizing their truth. Yet there was another that remained. "Nora refused me," he told her, surprised how easily the words fell from his lips, "because she cannot have children." He exhaled, feeling a weight lifted off his heart. "She worries I will come to regret my choice, that I will resent her for robbing me of the opportunity to be a father, unable to provide an heir for my father's title." He scoffed, annoyed with the impact society's rules had upon his life.

"Do you love her?" Grandma Edie asked, a knowing twinkle in her old eyes, as though his revelation had not come as a surprise to her. Of course, it had not!

Closing his own, Troy sighed. "I do." An image of Nora's smiling face appeared in his mind, and he felt his heart beat with more force than before. He saw the soft glow of her rosy cheeks, her warm brown eyes looking into his as she had spotted him earlier that day riding toward her. "I do."

"Then marry the girl," Grandma Edie whispered, "and if you wish to have children, you will...one way or another. I'm certain of it."

Looking at his grandmother, Troy felt a shiver dance down his back. It had been a long time since he had felt utterly certain of anything.

And it felt good.

Too good to ignore.

Chapter Thirty-Five

WHAT IF?

Voices drew Nora downstairs. Agitated voices. Straining to listen, she tiptoed down the corridor once she had reached the ground floor, her heart quickening as she recognized them.

Mr. Clarke—she could not seem to bring herself to think of him as Lord Hayward.

And her mother.

The drawing-room door stood ajar, and Nora carefully inched closer, all but holding her breath, afraid to be discovered.

"Will you not speak to her?" Mr. Clarke inquired, a hard tone in his voice, speaking of impatience as heavy footsteps carried him across the room. "A union between us would benefit us all. I thought you agreed."

A heavy sigh left her mother's lips, yet her voice did not falter as she spoke. "I did agree," she replied, a touch of regret tinging her words. "However, the choice is my daughter's, and I will not persuade her to accept a man she does not wish to marry."

A moment of silence followed, and Nora wished she could see Mr. Clarke's face.

"I apologize for being so blunt," her mother continued, "but perhaps it would be best if you returned home."

Nora smiled as her heart warmed. Never had her mother stood at her side like this, to defend her, to fight for her. It felt wonderful, precious and...made Nora wonder if perhaps...

...dreams came true after all.

At least, upon occasion.

Again, silence lingered, and Nora wondered what was happening in the drawing room as she stood with her back pressed against the wall of the corridor. Were her mother and Mr. Clarke eyeing each other cautiously? Was there hatred in Mr. Clarke's gaze? Or simply disappointment? Was her mother's chin raised or had she bowed her head, unable to meet his gaze?

Oh, Nora wished she knew!

Eventually, her mother spoke once more. "Once her year of mourning is up, you are, of course, free to repeat your intentions." She inhaled a deep breath, and when she spoke again, the tone in her voice brooked no argument. "However, whom she marries will still be my daughter's choice. Is that understood?"

Nora smiled, unexpectedly proud of her mother. Laughter bubbled up in her chest, and she quickly turned away and hastened down the corridor lest they discover her eavesdropping. However, the moment she turned around the next corner, she drew to a sudden halt.

"Hugh!" she exclaimed, staring down at the little boy, his eyes wide and staring at her in a way that sent a shiver down her back.

Inhaling a calming breath, Nora cast a cautious look over her shoulder before stepping toward him. "What are you doing here? Is everything all right?"

His little shoulders rose and fell as he continued to look at her, the expression upon his face disconcerting. "Will you come back to Leighton with us?"

Leaning down to him, Nora gently took his hands. "I'm afraid not," she told him honestly, more certain than ever before that she would never marry Mr. Clarke. Her heart belonged to another! "My home is here, as is my family." The look upon his little face fell. "But I'm certain we shall see each other again. You're welcome to visit any time." Nora did not know where these words had come from, and yet the look upon his face held such disappointment, as though she had just snatched away his fondest dream.

His little hands tightened upon hers, and then he looked up at her again. "Father said you'd be my new mother. Why did he say that if it wasn't true? Do you not like us?"

Shocked beyond words, Nora stared at Hugh. Had Mr. Clarke truly told his son that they would be married? How could he have? Had he been so certain that she would accept him?

Anger surged through Nora's veins, and she was tempted to spin around, stomp back down the corridor and seek out the man who dared raise his son's hopes without first securing her hand. How presumptuous of him!

However, she did not.

"I'm sorry, Hugh," she said gently, smiling at him. "I suppose there has been some kind of misunderstanding. You are quite dear to me," *although your father is not*, she added silently, "but Leighton is no longer my home. It shall be yours, though, and I'm certain you will be happy there."

Putting on a brave face, Hugh nodded. "Very well."

Nora straightened, brushing a gentle hand over the top of his head. "Run along now," she told him as eagerness surged through her veins. "There is somewhere...I have to be." She smiled at him. "I shall see you later." And then she hastened away.

Rushing upstairs, Nora quickly donned her riding habit before cautiously peeking out into the corridor again. When all remained quiet, she took the back stairs to the ground floor, slipping out the back door, her steps eager as they carried her toward the stables. Fortunately, no one saw her depart, no one tried to stop her and only moments later, Nora found herself galloping across the fields...

...toward the ancient watchtower.

And Troy.

The world gleamed in a brilliant white, and Nora had to squint her eyes against the blinding rays of the winter sun. The cold air chilled her skin, and yet breathing in deeply, she felt invigorated. A deep smile sneaked onto her face, and she could feel her muscles ache with the strain, for it would not retreat. Her head swirled with everything that had happened, and she had to blink her eyes a couple of times to focus her gaze upon the horizon.

Indeed, these were tumultuous times. Times full of doubt and regret. Times full of heartache as well. Yet there was something waiting for her upon the horizon, was there not?

Nora could barely glimpse it, but she knew it was there. Her heart knew, and it rejoiced at the mere thought of a possible future with Troy. She had shied away from it for so long, first believing him indifferent and then realizing that she could never be the wife he needed. But perhaps, just perhaps, all the reasons she had recounted to herself again and again did not matter, were not reasons at all.

At least, not good ones.

Perhaps, every once in a while, reward could only be found in following one's heart.

In that moment, Nora felt utterly tempted to throw caution to the wind and marry Troy without another thought. She knew it was what she wanted, and she did not want to listen to that cautious voice inside her head any longer. Of course, it spoke up once more, urging her to reconsider, assuring her that, one day, he would come to regret this decision and resent her for it.

That, one day, she would lose him. Better to let him go now and save herself the heartache.

And then the ruins came in to view, and that cautious voice deep inside grew quieter. Nora's heart rejoiced, almost tripping over itself the second her gaze fell on a lone figure standing near the crumpled wall.

The only one left standing.

Troy.

Kicking her mare's flanks, Nora spurred her on, eager to reach his side, to look into his eyes once more. He heard the sound of her approach and spun around, a dazzling smile coming to his face the moment he beheld her. Indeed, it was these moments when their eyes would meet unexpectedly that made Nora's heart soar. There was something between them, was there not? Something more than passion and friendship. Whatever it was, it had depth. It gave her strength but could also cripple her in a way she would never have expected. It was a part of her, part of who she was, and she could not imagine ever being herself again without that part.

Without him.

Pulling her mare to a halt, Nora slid out of the saddle, her eyes on him, unable to look away. He rushed toward her, a wide smile upon his face. "I'm relieved to see you," he said on a long sigh, revealing how deeply he felt in this moment. "I feared you would not come."

Stepping toward him, Nora suddenly felt her head begin to spin. The world tilted strangely to the side, and she lifted her arms to try and keep her balance.

In the next moment, strong hands grasped her, and the blurred outline of Troy's face appeared before her eyes. "Are you all right?" Deep concern tinged his voice as he pulled her into his arms. "Are you unwell?"

Nora blinked, trying to clear her thoughts, as her fingers curled into his coat, seeking to steady her. "Oh, it is nothing. I simply feel a bit lightheaded." She blinked her eyes again, and slowly his face came in to focus. "Perhaps it is simply the joy of seeing you."

The frown slowly vanished from Troy's face, and the smile that replaced it melted Nora's heart. He truly loved her, did he not? She had known before, and yet in that moment, the realization truly sank in. He loved her!

Slowly, his head lowered to hers, his lips capturing her own in a kiss that was new and familiar at the same time. It felt wonderful and right and precious. It spoke of new beginnings, of hope and dreams within reach. Did she dare believe? Or was she a fool to do so?

"How are you?" she asked, her eyes searching his face. "Did you speak to your grandmother? Was she able to reassure you?"

Smiling, Troy nodded. "I did, and you were right. She knew exactly what to say. I spoke to my father again and to my mother also, and I feel better now. Soon, I will tell them all." A slight crinkle came to his nose. "Quite frankly, I've never liked secrets. I cannot abide them, and I want to be honest with my family, including my siblings." He chuckled, and suddenly, his face lit up. "Louisa had her baby!"

Nora's jaw dropped as her heart danced with joy at the news; yet she could not help the stab of disappointment that swiftly followed, reminding her that such a day would never come for her.

Or for him...if she agreed to be his wife!

Chapter Thirty-Six

WITHIN REACH

J oy stood upon Nora's face, and yet Troy could not help the thought that somewhere a dark cloud was gathering nearby, that there was a shadow hanging over her, dampening her happiness.

As though willing the corners of her mouth back up, Nora smiled once more. "Oh, that is wonderful!" she exclaimed, that light slowly returning to her eyes. "Is it a boy or a girl? How is Louisa? I hope she's well."

Troy laughed at the memory of his new little niece. "It's a girl," he told her quickly, seeing the eagerness in her gaze. "And Louisa is well. It was..." He closed his eyes briefly, remembering his sister's screams. "I had no idea how hard childbirth is for a woman. Honestly, it was awful to hear her pain." He shook his head, trying to chase away the memory.

Nora sighed. "And her husband? How did he make it through the day?" A hint of humor lurked in her eyes.

Troy laughed. "Quite frankly, my grandmother wagered he would pass out at least once."

"And did he?" Nora asked chuckling.

Troy shook his head. "No, he did not. He remained steadfast;

although, I have to admit I've never seen him look quite so pale. Frankly, more than once, I thought he would indeed pass out."

For a long moment, they looked at one another, smiling, imagining the moment of two people becoming a family, adding a next generation, a precious little child. Troy remembered the look upon Louisa's face, utter joy despite her ordeal. Never before had he seen her so happy. It was an image that would stay with him.

"Did you hold her?" Nora asked tentatively.

"I did," Troy whispered almost reverently, remembering the soft weight of his little niece in his arms. "It was incredible...to look at her and..." He shook his head. "There are no words, but I think I understand better now how truly easy it is for a parent to love a child not born to them. Yes, she is my niece, she's family and we share some of the same blood, and yet that is not what matters, is it? It is not why I love her."

Nora grasped his hands. "Does that mean you no longer doubt your father's love for you?"

Troy shook his head, now thinking it foolish to have ever done so. "I think I never truly did. I felt simply unsettled by the news, and it made me doubt everything I thought I knew." He inhaled a deep breath, releasing it slowly and watching the puff of air dance away on a chilled breeze. "In truth, nothing has really changed, has it? Everything that matters is as it always was." He nodded. "I know that now." Gently, he cupped a hand to her face and drew her closer once more. "Thank you. Thank you for your counsel. I don't know what I would've done without you."

Nora's face softened, and he delighted in the gentle smile that teased the corners of her mouth. Closing her eyes briefly, she leaned into his hand and snuggled closer, the wish to hold on to him, to hold on to them painted on her face.

This was it, Troy thought. If he wanted to win her, he needed to take this chance...and he needed to be adamant. He needed her to know that he was certain of what he wanted, that he would always and forever want her.

No matter what.

Troy cleared his throat, and her eyes slowly opened and looked into his. "I spoke not only to my grandmother but also to my father and mother about...about us." He paused, his brows rising meaningfully as he waited for her to absorb every word. "I know you worry that sometime in the future I will regret my choice. However, you need to know that you are the only one who worries about that. There is not a single doubt in my mind that it is you I want and that that will never change, no matter the circumstances."

Tears filled Nora's eyes, and her chin started to tremble, her teeth chattering as though from the cold. Yet she did not say a word, her eyes wide, her heart and mind listening.

Holding her close, Troy brushed his thumb across her cheekbone, wiping away her tears. "My father said that if I truly love you, I am to marry you," he chuckled, "and to hell with everything else."

Laughter fell from Nora's lips before she sank her teeth into her bottom lip, staring up at him with wide eyes.

"He said," Troy continued, his heart feeling hopeful as never before, "that he would rather have his line end with me than to see his son lose the woman he loves." His arm around her middle tightened. "And I agree." He nodded, holding her gaze as tears flowed freely down her cheeks. "I love you, Nora. You and no one else, and I want to marry you."

A sob tore from Nora's throat. "I love you as well," she whispered, her voice choked. "I have loved you for so long, and I..." She closed her eyes and inhaled a deep breath. "I want nothing more than to be your wife, but—"

"No," Troy interrupted, giving her chin a gentle pinch so she would look at him. "There is no *but*." He nodded for emphasis. "There is only you and me. That is all that matters."

Hope shone in Nora's eyes, the desire to charge ahead and ignore the doubts she still harbored. Yet it seemed she could not.

Bowing her head, she stepped back, gently removing his arms from her body. Then she inhaled a deep breath and lifted her chin, meeting his eyes. "Recently," she began, her voice no more than a whisper, "my mother spoke to me of her marriage, of those early wonderful years and of something that happened to destroy it all."

Troy frowned, wondering what she was trying to tell him, afraid that she was truly too afraid to take this chance with him.

"Neither one of them was at fault for what happened, and yet it still ruined their lives. It destroyed everything. It separated them in a way that..." Closing her eyes, she shook her head. "We cannot know what the future will bring, and as much as I wish I could marry you, I'm so very afraid of what might happen. So many things have gone wrong so far. Silly things have happened that I did not see coming. I had such dreams when I was young, but then my choices led me down a different path." With pleading eyes, she looked at him. "I don't want that for you. I don't want you to live with regrets, dreaming of what could have been. I want you to be happy and—"

"But I am not!" Troy insisted, grasping her by the upper arms. "What life do you think I will have without you? If the past five years were any indication, then it is a life I do not want." Holding her gaze, Troy could see her resistance wane, and his heart grew hopeful again. "I love you, Nora, and I need you in my life. You say you want me to be happy," he grinned at her, surprised to be teasing her in a moment like this, "well, then you *have* to marry me because otherwise you'll doom me to a life of regret."

Chuckling, Nora lowered her head, resting her forehead against his chest. "Oh, why would you say this? I'm trying my hardest here not to be selfish," she lifted her head and looked at him, "and you? You go ahead and take away the one thing I have to keep you at bay!" She gave him a playful shove, shaking her head at him, as though he had truly done something unforgivable.

Troy grinned, once more reaching for her. "Does that mean you'll marry me?" he pressed, wanting her to answer, needing her to answer.

Nora swallowed. "I want to," she whispered, then slowly shook her head. Instantly, Troy felt his hopes plummet. "But I..." She inhaled a deep breath, her shoulders rising and falling slowly. "Let me sleep on it," she finally said, reaching for his hands. "Please, let me sleep on it. I cannot make this decision now. I need at least a few moments to consider this."

Releasing a heavy sigh, Troy nodded. "Of course," he finally said, knowing that he needed to respect her wishes. Perhaps it truly was easier for him to make up his mind than it was for her. After all, she was the one worried about disappointing him, about stealing his happiness. If their roles were reversed, how would he feel? Would he give her up willingly in order to ensure her future happiness? It was a thought that felt almost familiar.

"Thank you."

Troy grasped her chin, looking deep into her eyes. "One night," he told her, brows rising meaningfully. "You have one night to think this through, and you better come to the right decision." He cast her teasing smile. "Meet me here again tomorrow morning."

Nora nodded. "I shall," she vowed, and the smile that stole onto her face in the next moment made Troy think he would find himself a husband soon.

Chapter Thirty-Seven

DISAPPOINTED HOPES

S lipping on her riding gloves, Nora descended the great staircase into the foyer, a bounce in her step and a smile on her face. It was true. She had spent the better part of the night thinking about Troy's words, about what to do, about regrets and, most importantly, about happiness. Yet looking back, Nora realized she had never truly needed to think about it. She loved him, and although she could not be certain of what the future would bring, she believed in her heart that they would be happy together.

Yes, courage was needed. The courage to move forward, to risk her heart as well as his and claim the reward they both wanted.

Courage!

"You look happy this morning, my dear," observed her mother as her eyes fell on Nora from where she stood by the landing. "I've never seen you like this before," she added in a thoughtful voice, regret resting in her eyes.

Stepping down, Nora grasped her mother's hands as a deep sigh flew from her lungs. "Oh, Mother, I am so very happy. I could dance and sing and twirl and..." Her voice trailed off, and then she gave in to what others might have deemed a childish impulse and twirled in circles around the entry hall, her skirts billowing outward.

The rare sound of her mother's laughter drifted to Nora's ears. "Have you made your choice, then?" she asked, moving toward her daughter. "Has he finally convinced you?"

Nora nodded, grasping her mother's hands as the world around her continued to twirl, even though her feet once again stood still. "I have, and he has," she confirmed. "I always knew I loved him, but I never thought I had the right to be his wife."

Her mother gently squeezed her hands. "Love is never about right and wrong. It simply is."

Nora nodded. "It took me a while to realize that, but I finally do." She glanced toward the door. "I have to go. He's waiting for me."

Brushing a kiss on her daughter's cheek, her mother smiled at her. "Then go and be happy."

And so, with her mother's blessing, Nora all but charged from the house, her feet almost floating through the air as she hastened toward the stables. She barely felt the icy wind as her mare charged across the meadow, for her body felt warm all over in a way it never had before. Somehow, even the sun seemed brighter, and the snow glistened like diamonds. Had the world always been this beautiful? Or had she simply never noticed?

Suddenly, a harsh voice whipped through the air, and Nora looked over her shoulder to see Mr. Clarke riding up to her. Instantly, the warmth fled her body, leaving it shivering against the onslaught of the temperatures. "What is he doing here?" she murmured to herself as she watched his approach. A part of her had hoped he had already left Fartherington Hall, never to bother her again. It would seem she had been wrong.

Reluctantly, Nora reined in her horse, annoyed with Mr. Clarke's sudden appearance. It ruined her mood, and she was determined to rid herself of him with the utmost haste. After all, there was somewhere she had to be!

As Mr. Clarke reached her side, Nora could see the furious scowl that rested upon his face. Indeed, she had never seen him quite like this. Usually he was quietly disapproving, voicing his opinion with eloquent words. Now, however, he looked like a volcano about erupt.

"Good morning, Mr. Clar—Lord Hayward,"," Nora greeted him

with as much politeness as she could muster. "What are you doing out here? I thought you were making preparations to return to Leighton." The moment she spoke these words, Nora realized she had never truly given Mr. Clarke an answer. Indeed, it had been her mother who had advised him to leave, not her. An unfortunate oversight!

"I had thought you a lady," Mr. Clarke snarled without any attempt at civility. His eyes were narrowed, and anger tinged his face as he glared at her. "And I'm shocked to realize that I was severely mistaken."

Caught off guard, Nora stared at him. "I have not the slightest inkling what you are talking about," she replied, feeling utterly confused...and somewhat disconcerted. "Surely, there has been some kind of misunderstanding. Otherwise—"

A dark chortle escaped Mr. Clarke's lips. "Oh, there has been no mistake. I've seen you with my own eyes. I know what you are."

Shaking her head, Nora stared at him as a cold shiver crawled down her back. "Seen me? What on earth do you mean?" A part of her urged her to end this conversation as quickly as possible. Indeed, there was something dangerous lurking in Mr. Clarke's contorted snarl.

Fixing her with a hard stare, Mr. Clarke urged his mount closer. "Only yesterday, I saw you ride out once more to meet that man in secret. You let him...touch you and kiss you." Disgust contorted his face, and he suddenly reached out and snatched the reins from her hands. "What would you call that? Is that the conduct of a lady? Or rather that of harlot?"

Shock froze Nora's limbs as she realized he had to have seen her with Troy. Had he been following her? Only yesterday or other times before?

A wave of nausea rolled through Nora, and for a moment, she feared she might slip from the saddle. Her hands grasped her mare's mane, needing something to hold on to as she fought the dizziness that engulfed her head. "None of this," she panted, blinking her eyes quickly to focus them, "is any of your concern, Mr. Clarke." She lifted her chin, relieved to see her vision clear, and she fixed him with a determined stare, only now realizing she had forgotten to address him by his title—and glad for it.. "I'd appreciate it if you returned my reins to me. I apologize if I've caused you any distress; however, you knew from the beginning that I was reluctant to consider a union between us. As things are now, I must inform you that I cannot marry you. Now?" She held out her hand, demanding her reins be returned to her.

Unfortunately, Mr. Clarke was disinclined. In fact, his hands upon her reins tightened as he leaned forward in the saddle, bringing his face closer to hers. "How dare you?" In the next instant, his arm shot out and his hand grasped her right arm painfully.

Nora flinched, and her mare stamped her hooves nervously, her ears flattening against her head.

"Is this the thanks I get," Mr. Clarke growled into her face, "for ridding you of your vile husband?"

Nora's jaw dropped, and it felt as though all blood was suddenly draining from her face. "W-What?" she stammered as disbelief filled her mind, closely followed by a sense of overwhelming panic.

Mr. Clarke seemed not to notice, too caught up was he in his own outrage. "I always knew you were the one for me, but I was no one while *he* inherited his father's title." He scoffed bitterly. "A drunkard and a gambler, he was not fit to be called an earl. He was not worthy of you." His hand tightened possessively upon her arm, and Nora's mare tossed up her head and neighed with agitation. "I knew you would be mine if only I could find a way to rid you of your husband. Unfortunately, it proved more difficult than I had anticipated."

Oddly detached, Nora stared at Mr. Clarke's face until a jolt of panic surged through her, aiding her in shaking off this sudden paralysis that had come over her at his words. Instantly, she jerked on her arm, seeking to release it, and in doing so, upended Mr. Clarke's balance.

Where she had found the strength, Nora did not know; however, in the blink of an eye, she saw Mr. Clarke tumble off his horse and land in the snow at her feet. An angry growl tore from his throat, and Nora knew she had to get away, afraid of what he might do should he get his hands on her again.

Quickly gathering up her rains, Nora spurred her mare into a gallop. They all but flew across the fields as the wind tore on her hair and skirts, reaching out with icy fingers and chilling her skin. Her heart beat almost painfully in her chest, and her body still trembled with the impact of the past few moments. Had this truly happened? Had he been the one to...to end her husband's life?

Although Nora had not been there, she had been told that he had been thrown off his horse. He had been drunk at the time, and so no one had thought it unusual. After all, accidents happened. But had it perhaps not been an accident?

Blindly, Nora charged across the field, her only thought to put as much distance between herself and Mr. Clarke. Yet when she turned her head, her eyes sweeping over her surroundings she realized she was not heading toward Fartherington Hall.

She was not heading home.

But in the opposite direction.

Toward Whickerton Grove.

The thought of Troy steadied her heart, and she guided her mare to the east, knowing it to be a more direct path. Soon, a thick forest loomed in front of her, and with a last glance over her shoulder, Nora urged her mare inside. Was Mr. Clarke following her? Or had he given up?

Nora did not know; however, she did not think it wise to slow her steps any more than she had to. Carefully, her mare picked her way through the forest, and Nora wished there were a path right here to speed their journey. However, there was not, for she had turned east too late. But if she kept going, she should eventually come upon it.

Clinging to her mare's back, Nora blinked her eyes as dizziness engulfed her once more. The trees around her began to spin, as though they no longer possessed roots. Nausea settled in her stomach, and her hands grasped her mare's mane yet again.

"Leonora!"

The sound of Mr. Clarke's angry snarl felt like a slap to Nora while a rather distant part of her mind felt annoyed at hearing him call her by her given name. How dare he take such liberties?

Nora shook her head, her eyes drifting back over her shoulder, trying to glimpse his position. Had he caught up? She could not spot him anywhere between the trees nor had his voice sounded close enough for him to be nearby. Still, he was coming for her, and although

Nora knew very little about him, she felt absolutely certain that he was not one to simply give up.

She had to make haste!

Yet her eyes began to close as a heavy blanket settled over her, something dark and smothering. She forced them back open, but it took all her strength to do so, for her limbs felt suddenly weak. What was this? Had he drugged her? Was that possible? After what Nora had learned about his true character in the last few moments, she would not put it past him. But why? And how?

Again, her eyes closed, and she felt herself slump forward onto her mare's neck. The world around her retreated, as though it no longer existed. A welcoming reprieve! Only Nora knew that it did exist and pretending otherwise would only see her caught.

And so, she forced her eyes back open...and glimpsed the blurred outlines of the ancient watchtower in the far distance, somewhere upon the horizon, past this forest and the meadow beyond.

Troy, her mind whispered...before darkness fell once more, dragging her down into the snow.

Chapter Thirty-Eight

A MOMENT OF TRUTH

Every soft crunch of snow under his feet echoed like a thunderclap in Troy's ears. It felt as though an eternity had passed since he had arrived at the ancient watchtower. Again and again, his gaze moved to the horizon, his eyes squinting, trying to see. Yet there was nothing *to* see.

No lone rider.

Troy closed his eyes as a growl of agony slipped from his mouth. She wasn't coming! Nora was not coming!

The words echoed in his head, and yet he could not quite believe them. After everything they had said to one another the day before, after seeing that look of love in her eyes, Troy had felt absolutely certain that she would accept him. He had spent the past few hours, the previous night, in a state of utter bliss, barely able to keep his joy to himself. He had been so certain!

Again, his gaze rose from the white landscape around him and drifted to the far horizon. Would she truly not come? Even if she had decided not to accept him, would she not at least tell him so? Never would Troy have thought her a coward. Or perhaps he had thought she was a coward; however, the letter he had sent her had never been delivered to her hands. He had assumed wrong. But now...

After raking his hands through his hair, his feet still not standing still, Troy felt them ball into fists, the need to hit something shooting through his body. Anger spread to every fiber of his being, demanding to be released after years of yearning for her, after months of temptation, after last night's joy. It was simply too much!

His dream had seemed suddenly within reach, so close, that Troy had dared to imagine what his future might look like, what their future might look like. He had seen them married, surrounded by friends and family. He had all but felt their happiness, seeing that smile upon Nora's face. He had imagined rising every morning, finding her beside him, and falling asleep every night, with her in his arms. And even if they would never have a child born to them, he was certain they would find a way. He had truly come to believe his father, his grandmother, when they had told him that one way or another, they could be a family.

All doubts had vanished, and he had felt absolutely certain.

Looking up, Troy's gaze swept over the white fields, the blue sky. A deep sigh left his lips, and he hung his head. Only a dream, after all!

With a heavy heart, Troy finally turned and walked a few paces over to his gelding. He pulled himself into the saddle, and with one last look over his shoulder, he headed back home.

Alone.

A part of him still could not believe that this was truly happening. It felt surreal, and he repeated the words to himself again and again as his mount carried him homeward. Still, when Whickerton Grove came within view, he shook his head, still unable to believe that she had truly not come.

Like a ghost, Troy walked into the house, his feet moving of their own accord, his mind foggy and unfocused. He wasn't quite certain where to go or what to do. He did not even know if he wished to be alone.

And then he heard his family's voices drift to his ears from the drawing room. They were joyful voices, laughter ringing here and there. It was precisely what Troy wanted, what he had dreamed of the night before. He wanted to be a part of that. All his sisters had found happiness in marriage. All of them would soon have a family of their own. Louisa already held her little daughter in her arms. Only now, Troy knew he never would experience it himself. The closest thing he would ever find to happiness was the echo of theirs.

Whether to torture or remind himself of something his heart wanted, Troy changed direction, his steps carrying him toward these joyful voices. Part of him urged him to turn around, to not submit himself to the sight of their joy, but he could not.

Coming to stand in the door frame, Troy's gaze swept over his family. They were all here, eyes lingering upon Louisa's little daughter as she lay snuggled into Phineas' arm. He walked around the room in an odd skip step, which Troy suspected was to keep the infant quiet. However, since it looked rather ridiculous, the rest of his family barely managed to suppress their laughter at the sight.

Troy sighed as he saw Louisa and Phineas share a meaningful look,

...as he glanced to where Drake pulled Leonora into his arms,

...as his gaze traveled to Thorne, whispering something into Christina's ear

...before coming to rest upon Juliet and Christopher, newly married and such a look of happiness upon their faces that it felt like a punch to Troy's midsection. Yes, this was the future he wanted. He wanted to be one of them. He always had, even if he had never allowed himself to admit it.

"And what about her name?" his father asked in that moment, shaking Troy out of his reverie. "Have you finally settled on one?"

Another meaningful look passed between the new parents before Louisa nodded. "We have, yes."

Impatient as always, Harriet stepped forward, her hand though remained within Jack's. "And?"

"Well," Louisa replied, seated in an armchair right next to a snoring Grandma Edie, "we've decided to name her... Edith."

Various degrees of surprise showed on everyone's faces as Troy slowly moved farther into the room, his gaze curious as it swept over everyone. Something about the scene drew him near—it felt torturous—and yet he could not stay away. He came to stand by the pianoforte, his eyes as watchful as before.

"Why Edith?" Harriet inquired as she glanced from the little girl to her great-grandmother. "Not that I object. I'm merely curious."

It turned out that Louisa and Phineas thought it a fitting name because of their own resemblance to Grandma Edie and her late husband, their grandfather. Indeed, from the way their cousin Anne's betrothal had come about, Troy had to agree. Louisa did have similar meddlesome tendencies as their grandmother. Perhaps the name was quite fitting, after all. Who knew what kind of a person little Edith would grow up to be?

Troy sighed, for he longed to find out.

"Well," Harriet suddenly exclaimed as she turned from the two Ediths and looked at him, her brows rising daringly, "six siblings and five are married."

Troy felt an ice-cold shiver run down his back as all eyes turned to him.

Completely ignoring his dark glare, Harriet asked with a grin, "Any marriage plans on the horizon, Troy?"

Feeling every muscle in his body tense, Troy glared at his sister, feeling his jaw begin to hurt at the pressure. He barely even noticed Juliet's sharp intake of breath before she tried to intervene. "Harriet, perhaps we should not—"

"What about Nora?" Harriet went on, completely unimpressed by either her sister's warning or the murderous look upon Troy's face.

Taking a step toward her, Troy did his best to ignore the way his family stared at him, watched him, curiosity and the desire to know, to understand shining in their eyes. Any other day, their concern and interest would have touched him—but not today. "I would appreciate it," he forced out through gritted teeth, "if you kept your nose out of my affairs." Then he spun on his heel and marched toward the door, determined to leave all this behind him.

It had been a mistake to seek their company!

Unfortunately, Harriet had never been one to give up easily. "I know that you care for her," she called after him. "We all do. Why do you deny it?"

Inwardly cringing at her words, Troy fought to maintain the hard look upon his face. Slowly, ever so slowly, he turned around and faced his sister once more. "I do not care for whatever you think you know," he hissed. "Lady Nora means nothing to me beyond an old acquaintance." Every fiber of his being cried out against this lie. "In fact, I plan on searching for a suitable wife come next season." Did he? He should! And yet...

Every part of Troy felt like weeping, giving up and burying himself somewhere deep and far away from the rest of the world. Yet there were duties and responsibilities to consider. For the first time in his life, Troy hated that fact with a vengeance.

Fortunately, before Harriet could say any more, the door to the drawing room flew open, and a disheveled man stumbled inside, panting under his breath.

"Gerald!" Christopher exclaimed. After exchanging one of these annoyingly meaningful looks with Juliet, he approached the man. "What are you doing here? Is something the matter?"

The man named Gerald drew in a deep breath. "I'm afraid I bring bad news, my Lord. Your mother bade me ride to Whickerton Grove as fast as possible."

Troy frowned as that ice-cold chill from before once again trailed down his back. Clearly, the man had come from Fartherington Hall. Bad news? What—?

"Speak!" Christopher demanded impatiently.

The man nodded. "This morning, Lady Nora went for a ride," Troy felt his heart slam to a halt within his chest as a terrifying sense of foreboding fell over him, "and she has yet to return."

Troy saw all the blood drain from Christopher's face, his emotions an echo of his own. "How long has she been gone?" Christopher asked.

"Six hours."

As shocked exclamations echoed through the room, Troy suddenly felt his body revive. All paralysis fell from him, and without another thought, he hastened from the room, his mind focused on one thing alone.

Nora.

Oh, what a fool he had been! Of course, she would not simply stay away. Something had happened to her! She had never even made it to the ruins! Had she been thrown? Had there been some sort of accident? Yet if there had, would she not already have been found some-where on the way between her home and the ruins?

All but flying out the door, Troy rushed back to the stables. He did not have a second to lose, and neither did Nora. Who knew how long she had been gone? When she had left? And when something—what-ever it had been—had befallen her?

Panic spread through his body, cold and paralyzing, and yet Troy pushed past it. He needed to stay focused. Nora needed him. Her life might depend on him finding her. If only he could! He would give anything to see her safe again.

His life.

Even the future he longed for with every fiber of his being.

Everything.

If only she would be all right.

Chapter Thirty-Nine

IN THE SNOW

Cold.

Icy cold.

It lingered in every fiber of her body, and Nora groaned as she tried to blink her eyes open. Even this small movement hurt. Her jaw trembled from the cold, her teeth clicking together painfully. She tried, and yet she could not stop it.

Finally, managing to blink her eyes open all the way, Nora found herself lying in the snow. For a moment, she could not remember how she had gotten here. Her mind seemed blank, unable to provide information. And then, from one second to the next, everything came rushing back.

A terrified groan slipped from Nora's lips as panic surged through her veins, pushing her into an upright position. Her eyes flew over her surroundings, searching for Mr. Clarke, and terror seized her at the thought that he might have found her. Fortunately, all Nora could see were snow and trees.

Shaking like a leaf, Nora swept her hands down her dress and found it wet. How long had she been lying in the snow? Had she simply passed out? She could not recall. Yet she knew she could not stay here.

She was cold and wet and freezing. She needed to get somewhere warm or...

Nora craned her neck, searching for her honey-colored mare, and her heart sank when she could not spot her anywhere. Had she run back home? Or was she somewhere nearby?

Fighting against the wave of panic that rolled through her, Nora struggled to her feet. Her limbs felt stiff, and the moment she put weight upon her feet, a surge of pain shot through her. Her arms tingled as she moved them, and the shaking simply would not stop, the sound of her teeth clattering together ringing in her ears.

"Leonora!"

As the sound of Mr. Clarke's voice cut through the air, Nora froze, eyes wide. For a moment, she could not move, panic paralyzing her limbs even more than the cold.

"Leonora!"

Instinct took over, and Nora sank to her knees, ducking down, hoping that he would not spot her. She craned her neck from side to side, her eyes searching, drifting from tree to tree.

And then she saw him.

It was no more than a glimpse, and yet it was enough. It sent a jolt of panic to her heart, made her spin around as the impulse to flee his presence gripped her hard. She staggered backward and then...

...her foot sank deep into a hole hidden beneath the snow cover. Her ankle twisted to the side, and pain gripped her.

Nora cried out.

Reaching the ruins, Troy jumped out of the saddle. His eyes swept over his surroundings, but there was no sign of Nora. Not that he had truly expected to find her here. What he did find were his own footprints from before, from earlier that day. Yet he could make out no others. She had not come here. She had never reached this place.

After another quick sweep of the ruins turned up nothing, Troy remounted. His gaze swept the horizon east to west as he considered what to do, where to head. Since she had never arrived at the ruins, he would have expected her to disappear somewhere between her home and here. However, if that had been the case, she would have already been found. Something must have made her leave the path. But what?

His gaze swept toward the forest in the distance. She could be anywhere. His pulse picked up speed, and his heart tightened in his chest. Where could she be? Which way should he turn? If he chose the wrong one...?

Troy gritted his teeth, yet the frustrated growl still made it past his lips.

And then he spotted movement.

His whole body tensed as he squinted his eyes against the bright winter's sun. Had it been a trick of light? No, he was certain he had seen something move. Had it been Nora? He squinted harder, and then he saw a horse trotting near the forest's edge.

A honey-colored horse.

Troy's heart slammed to a halt before thundering along as it had before. Instantly, he jerked on his gelding's reins, ignoring his horse's disapproving snort, and urged him down the field and toward the tree line.

His gelding's large strides ate up the distance quickly, and yet it was not fast enough.

Troy kept his gaze fixed upon the mare, afraid she might run off or he might lose sight of her. Was Nora nearby? Had she been thrown and now lay hurt somewhere on the frozen ground?

Reaching the mare, Troy once again jumped out of the saddle and grasped her reins. "What are you doing here? Where is Nora?" he asked before he shook his head at himself, his gaze moving from the mare to his immediate surroundings.

Unfortunately, he saw nothing but snow.

Snow marked by hoofprints.

Rushing back to his horse, Troy pulled himself into the saddle and then urged his gelding toward the tree line, following the tracks Nora's mare had left behind. Where had she come from?

As they reached the forest, Troy forced himself to slow down. He knew it was not safe to rush through without thought, no matter how much he yearned to do so. His gaze swept left and right before returning to the tracks that guided him onward. He heard nothing aside from the occasional bird or an animal crawling through the underbrush.

And then a scream shattered the silence.

Troy flinched, jerking around in the saddle. His eyes wide, he stared ahead, then immediately kicked his gelding's flanks. "Nora," he murmured under his breath a moment before movement caught his eyes once more. He was about to call out to her but then stopped himself. Something...eerie lay in the air. He could not quite say what it was, but he could not help the thought that there might be danger nearby.

An instant later, his gaze cleared, and he saw Nora lying on her back in the snow, her head raised, her eyes wide as she crawled backwards.

And then Troy saw him.

It was the same man he had seen with Nora before. They had been riding together up upon the hill while Troy had stood by the ruins, looking up, wondering who he could be.

Now, he knew.

It was none other than her late husband's cousin.

The man who wished to marry her.

Had Nora refused him? Indeed, it had to have happened that way, had it not? She had refused him, and he had been unable to accept it.

Despite the fear in Troy's heart, he could not ignore the small spark of joy that found him at the thought.

Slipping out of the saddle, Troy crouched low, silent footsteps carrying him closer as he kept his gaze on the man towering above Nora.

Chapter Forty

JUST IN CASE

Nora's breath came fast, and her pulse thudded wildly in her neck. The cold still lingered, and yet it was no longer as overpowering as it had been before. Fear had taken that place, even now moving her limbs in the hopes of escaping. She blinked and saw bright spots dance before her eyes. Yet her attention was focused on nothing else than the man advancing on her.

A dark snarl contorted his face as he glared down at her. Gone was the man who had spoken kindly, who had inquired after her well-being. No, this stranger was nothing like the man she thought she had known. "Quite frankly," he hissed, "I expected gratitude for ridding you of your vile husband." He scoffed, and it was a dark and threatening sound. "I knew you did not care for him. I could see it in your eyes. Every time I visited Leighton, you were begging me to help you, to free you of him." Gritting his teeth, he shook his head. "And now that I have, this is how you repay me? This is how you show your gratitude?"

Overwhelmed, Nora shook her head. "I never asked you to," she responded, her voice barely more than a whisper, her teeth still chattering. "I would never have dreamed of asking you to rid me of my husband. I can't understand how—"

"He did not deserve you!" Mr. Clarke snarled, advancing another two steps. "He was never good enough for you." Again, a look of reproach came to his eyes, and he shook his head. "And yet you married him. After all, he had title and fortune. I knew it was a marriage of convenience, not one of affection. Still, you did not even look at me then."

Indeed, Nora could not remember ever laying eyes on Mr. Clarke prior to the first time he had come to visit them at Leighton. She did not even remember seeing him at her wedding. Yet the day had been a dark day, and her thoughts had been elsewhere, not even with her own husband.

Troy, her heart cried out silently. Would she ever see him again? How would this day end?

"You do not need me," Nora stammered, trying to think of something that would soothe his anger. "You are heir to the Hayward title and lands. Everything is yours now."

Mr. Clarke sneered at her. "I never cared about these trappings; do you not know that?" Reproach marked his voice. "They were only meant to be means to an end." He moved closer until he stood over her. He braced his hands on his knees, leaning down to her. "I only ever wanted you."

Nora blinked as the spots before her eyes grew larger and then smaller and then larger again. She tried to focus her mind, but a sickening sensation rolled through her stomach, and for a moment, she feared she would cast up its contents.

Yet no matter what happened, there was something she needed to make clear...even if it was the last thing she did. "I will not marry you," she told him, surprised by the strength in her voice. "No matter what you do, I will not marry you."

Enraged, Mr. Clarke lunged forward, grabbed her by the arms, and yanked her up and against him.

Pressing her eyes shut, Nora prayed she would not give in, that she would remain strong. She would not marry him! But perhaps...she could make him believe she would? Could she? Perhaps it would be wiser than antagonizing him. After all, he no longer appeared like the calm and quiet gentleman he had portrayed before. Indeed, there was something in his eyes that spoke of a man possessed, a man no longer thinking clearly.

Yet the decision was taken out of her hands when she felt Mr. Clarke suddenly yanked away from her. His grip vanished, and Nora fell back into the snow with a heavy *thud*.

Again, her body screamed out in pain, and for a moment, Nora simply lay in the snow, dazed, as muffled grunts drifted to her ears.

Blinking her eyes open, Nora squinted at the image before her. Two men were rolling around on the forest's floor, exchanging punches and kicks, their hands trying to grasp the other's throat.

Stunned, Nora pushed herself up and stared, for a moment unable to grasp what was happening. And then her eyes recognized the other man.

Troy.

Instantly, a desperate sob tore from her lips. Relief that he had come mingled with fear for his life as Mr. Clarke delivered a punch to Troy's jaw that flung him backward.

Nora flinched. "Troy!"

For a split second, his blue eyes met hers before he lunged at Mr. Clarke all over again. The sound of bone on bone drifted to Nora's ears, and she cringed, her head beginning to spin as those bright spots returned with full force.

Afraid to avert her eyes, to let Troy out of her sight for just a second, Nora frantically blinked her eyes, then slapped herself hard across the cheek to stay conscious.

Mr. Clarke grasped Troy, then spun him around, and wrapping his hands around Troy's throat, he squeezed. Nora's heart stopped as she saw Troy gasp for breath before he jabbed his elbow backward into Mr. Clarke's middle. Doubling over, the man released his grip and Troy spun out of reach.

"I will kill you!" Mr. Clarke panted. "She is mine! I deserve to have her! I—"

Troy's knuckles collided hard with Mr. Clarke's jaw, cutting off his words and sending him tumbling backward. "Don't you dare come near her ever again!"

And then, Nora saw the dagger. She did not know where it had come from, but she saw it clear as day in Mr. Clarke's hand.

Seeing it, eyes fixed on his opponent, Troy reached toward his right boot...and withdrew his own, the small blade he had always carried for as long as she had known him. Just in case. Nora watched with bated breath as the two men circled one another, wishing with every fiber of her being that this was nothing more than a bad dream.

A nightmare.

And all she had to do was wake up. Oh, why couldn't she wake up?

With a savage snarl, Mr. Clarke flung himself at Troy, the bright winter's sun gleaming off his blade. Nora screamed when they collided, her eyes trying to pierce the fog of jumbled limbs, trying to determine what was happening...

...if Troy was unharmed.

And then, all of a sudden, the two men went still, both their eyes wide as they stared at one another.

Nora felt darkness tug upon her mind once more, yet the wildly hammering pulse in her neck kept her conscious. "Troy," she whispered breathlessly.

With a groan, Mr. Clarke suddenly keeled over into the snow, his blade falling from his limp hand, not a drop of blood upon it.

Staring at him, Nora flinched when Troy suddenly appeared beside her. "Are you hurt?" he asked, his gentle fingers grasping her chin as his eyes flew over her body. "Did he hurt you?"

With his familiar blue eyes upon her, Nora felt the cold drift away. "Troy," she whispered, saying his name again and again.

Pulling her into his arms, Troy held her, almost crushing her in his embrace. Nora's fingers clawed into his arms, needing proof that he was still alive, safe and sound, here with her.

Over his shoulder, she spotted Mr. Clarke lying unmoving upon the ground, the snow stained red with the blood that flowed from a large wound in his stomach. She did not know if he was still alive; neither did she care.

Nora's eyes closed, and she felt blackness tug upon her mind. "I...I feel dizzy," she mumbled, and her head rolled back as Troy tried to look into her eyes.

"You're freezing," he remarked with a dark growl in his voice as he stripped off her coat with swift fingers. Then he replaced it with his own before hoisting her into his arms. "We need to get you home."

As Troy trudged through the snow, Nora nestled into his embrace. The hint of a smile tugged upon her lips, and she felt herself exhale a breath of relief. She felt warmed not only by the simple warmth of his body but even more so by his presence.

Still, her mind seemed to be spinning, her thoughts unfocused. The soft swaying of Troy's steps seemed to aid the tug upon her mind, that heavy blackness that promised relief. Nora's eyes closed again and again, and she felt her hand slide off his shoulder.

"Stay with me, Nora," Troy whispered, alarm in his voice as his arms tightened upon her, holding her closer. "Stay with me."

The soft sound of a nicker drifted to Nora's ears, and as she blinked her eyes open, she saw not only Troy's gelding but also her own honey-colored mare.

With a groan of effort, Troy pushed her up into the saddle, holding on to her arms as he mounted to sit behind her. Again, his arms wrapped around her, and again, her head rolled back against his shoulder. Yet Nora did not feel afraid. She knew he would not let her fall. She knew he was here, and he would always be.

The gentle swaying of his gelding's movements almost lulled Nora to sleep. It became harder and harder to open her eyes and utterly impossible to keep them that way. She heard nothing but the powerful beating of Troy's heart beneath her ear as well as the harsh breath drifting from his lips as he spurred his gelding onward, rushing to get home.

And then, distant voices echoed to her ears, quickly followed by others. Nora's eyes blinked open once more, and she saw riders approaching. Dimly, she saw the faint outline of her brother, his face contorted into a grotesque mask of concern. Never had she seen him like this before. She wanted to assure him she was all right, but her lips would not part and no words would tumble from her tongue.

"What happened?" Christopher inquired in an urgent voice, his hand reaching out to touch her face.

"Later," Troy insisted in a harsh voice, his arms tightening upon her. "She's freezing. We need to get her back."

"Hand her to me," came Christopher's voice, and although Nora loved her brother dearly, she snuggled deeper into Troy's embrace, not wishing to leave.

Troy's arms tensed upon her, echoing her own feelings. "It will be quicker if I hold on to her," he replied simply, then spurred his gelding onward without waiting for a reply.

Nora felt another distant smile dance across her face before her eyes closed once more...and stayed that way.

Chapter Forty-One

AIDING FATE

Reluctantly, Troy relinquished Nora to the doctor's care and then stepped outside her chamber—*his* chamber!—to meet his family's questions. Of course, everyone wanted to know what had happened, where Nora had been, and why she had been missing for hours.

"It was Mr. Clarke," he told everyone, more than one face looking puzzled at hearing that name.

"Who on earth is Mr. Clarke?" Harriet inquired, exchanging a glance with her sisters.

His father scratched his chin. "I cannot say I have heard the name before."

Only Christopher nodded in understanding. "Mr. Clarke is Nora's late husband's cousin and heir to the late Lord Hayward's title and estates."

Deep frowns showed on all their faces. "But why would he attack the lass?" Keir inquired, his watchful blue eyes drifting across Troy's face.

Troy felt every muscle inside his body tense to the point of breaking. "From what I overheard, it was he who caused her late husband's demise." A part of Troy could not deny that he was indeed grateful to

Mr. Clarke for that. "He did it because he wanted her for himself." A sentiment Troy understood. Still...

Shocked gasps drifted to his ears. "Then why would he attack her?" Leonora asked thoughtfully. "If he cares for her, I would expect him to propose and not..." She shook her head in confusion. "What you say makes no sense. Perhaps there's more to the story than—"

"Because she was riding out to meet *me*," Troy growled, knowing it to be the truth deep in his heart. Why else would Mr. Clarke have attacked her if not out of fury over her choice...to be with him, Troy.

The thought that he had been the cause of the danger she had faced today twisted his insides painfully; and yet the knowledge that she wanted him as much as he longed for her was unlike anything he had ever felt before.

Harriet chuckled, a wicked gleam in her green eyes. "See? I told you. Didn't I?" She looked around their family circle, delighted when heads began nodding up and down in agreement. "I knew you cared for her." She slapped his shoulder playfully. "Why couldn't you simply admit that?"

Ignoring his sister, Troy cleared his throat. "As it is, Mr. Clarke is still out there in the woods. I'm uncertain if he was already dead when we left; however, I believe he should be by now."

His father nodded. "I'll send a message to the constable."

Keir ran a hand through his hair. "I'll ride out and see to the body."

"I'll accompany you," Christopher chimed in, a dark look upon his face. "And then I'll ride over to Fartherington Hall...and inform my mother." He exhaled a deep breath before his eyes met Troy's. "Take good care of my sister."

Holding his friend's gaze, Troy nodded. "You have my word."

Drake and Thorne volunteered to accompany Christopher and Keir, and after a few more words were exchanged with their respective wives, the four men left. Troy was incredibly grateful to have all these people in his life, people who did not hesitate to stand by his side, to do what had to be done.

Glancing over his shoulder at the door to Nora's chamber, Troy hoped with every fiber of his being that she would be all right. "I... I have to see to her," he murmured, not daring to meet anyone's gaze.

He simply turned and strode toward the door, opening it in one swift move.

Bright sunlight streamed in through the windows, making Nora's cheeks look pale as she lay upon the bed, a warm blanket covering her to her chin. Yet a soft shiver still shook her frame, and Troy felt compelled to pull her into his arms and offer his warmth. He strode into the room and rushed to kneel at her bedside.

As it seemed, the rest of his family followed immediately, unable to stay away. Worried murmurs echoed through the room as their eyes fell on Nora's pale face. Yet all Troy could see was Nora. Her hand still felt chilled within his own, but it lifted his heart to see her eyelids flutter.

The thumping sound of Grandma Edie's cane preceded her into the room. "How is the girl, Dr. Parker?" she asked before seating herself in the armchair near the bed. Her pale eyes were watchful as they swept over Nora before returning to look at the doctor. "Well?"

Troy looked up and what he saw upon Dr. Parker's face almost stilled his heart. There was reluctance there as well as a deep sense of discomfort, as though he expected the words that needed to be said to be ill-received. Troy's hand upon Nora's tightened as fear spread through his being. Would he lose her after all?

His grandmother's eyes narrowed as she looked at the doctor, and Troy could not help but think that she knew precisely what the man could not bring himself to say. In the next instant, she lifted her cane and swung it slightly in a circular motion. "Out you go! All of you!" She fixed her family with stern eyes.

"You cannot be serious, Grandmother!" Harriet exclaimed, annoyance upon her face. "We, too, want to know how she is."

Grandma Edie nodded. "And you shall but not now." Her brows rose. "Out! Now!"

Although reluctantly, everyone heeded Grandma Edie's words. "Come along," their mother called. "We shall see to her soon. Right now, she needs rest."

After a few more grumbled words, the door finally closed, and Troy turned to the doctor. "How is she? Is it serious?"

As though to answer him, Nora's eyes fluttered open in that

259

moment. She heaved a deep sigh, and he could feel her hand tighten upon his own.

Troy's heart soared to the heavens. "Nora!" he called, immense relief flooding his entire being. His right hand brushed a curl from her temple, then gently traced the line of her cheekbone. "Nora, can you hear me?"

Her eyes met his, and after a heartbeat or two, they focused. He saw recognition before a dazzling smile curled up the corners of her mouth. "Troy," she breathed, her voice faint and without strength.

"How are you feeling?" he asked, uncertain if he wished to hear the answer. How bad was her condition?

"Tired," she replied on a deep exhale. "Still a bit chilled but... better." Another soft smile drifted across her face before it was replaced by the beginnings of a frown. "Why do you look so worried? Is something wrong? Are you all right?"

"Do not worry for me," Troy reassured her with a smile. "I am well." He looked up and met the doctor's gaze. "How is she?"

Dr. Parker wrung his weathered hands, his gaze not quite settling on Troy's before it drifted to where Grandma Edie sat watching him with hawk's eyes. "Well, you see, there..." He broke off, the discomfort upon his face deepening. "Perhaps I should..." Again, his gaze flitted to Grandma Edie.

"Speak!" Troy growled, at the end of his rope and not in the least caring if he offended the man.

Looking shaken, Dr. Parker stared back at him. "She..."

Chuckling, his grandmother leaned forward in her seat, hands rested upon her cane. "She's with child, isn't she?" Her brows rose inquisitively as she met the doctor's gaze. "Is that not what you are trying to say, Dr. Parker?"

Swallowing, the doctor nodded, a look of unease in his eyes deepening.

Rooted to the spot, Troy stared from his grandmother to Dr. Parker, his eyes wide and his mind sluggish. "P-Pardon me?" Abruptly, he turned to look down at Nora.

Her eyes were as wide as his own. "It cannot be," she whispered, still as breathless as before.

Troy cleared his throat. "You...You did not know?"

Slowly pushing herself up into a seated position, Nora shook her head. "Of course not. How...?" Her gaze rose and moved toward Dr. Parker, who was in this very moment closing the door behind himself, no doubt glad to have escaped this rather uncomfortable situation.

"I thought you said," Troy began as Nora's eyes returned to him, "that you could not have children." He raked a hand through his hair as the meaning of these words sank in. "You told me you could not marry me because—"

"Yes, so I believed," she murmured, absentmindedly brushing her hand over her flat belly. "I...I never once conceived during my years of marriage while my husband—" She broke off, swallowing hard. "Well, everyone knows he has children. So, naturally, I assumed..." Closing her eyes, she shook her head. "Perhaps Dr. Parker is wrong. Perhaps—"

"He is not wrong," Grandma Edie assured her from her spot on the other side of Nora's bed.

Troy fixed his gaze upon his grandmother. "How would you know? You cannot possibly—"

"You did this!" came Nora's breathless voice as she stared at his grandmother. "You did this! But how? How could you have—?" Her voice broke off, and her eyes widened. "The tea!"

Troy frowned. "What tea? What are you talking about?" His world had suddenly turned upside down, and he was scrambling to catch up. Was Nora truly with child? And if so, didn't that mean that the child...was his?

Heaving a deep sigh, his grandmother leaned back in her seat. "Yes, it was the tea," she finally confirmed, the look in her eyes one of utter sadness. Troy could not recall ever having seen it before.

Nora looked up at him, a question in her eyes. Troy shook his head, unable to make sense of it himself.

With her hands tightly wrapped around the knob of her walking stick, Grandma Edie exhaled a deep breath. "I always had a tendency to...immerse myself in the affairs of others," she told them with a wistful chuckle. "Quite often, it was not appreciated, to say the least." Smiling, she shook her head, and Troy wondered about the memories that called to her in this moment.

Moving himself closer to Nora, Troy wrapped an arm around her and pulled her close. With their hands linked, they listened.

His grandmother heaved another deep sigh, and for the first time, Troy thought she looked...old. "So, eventually, I stopped. I still saw what I saw, but I no longer...*aided Fate* in its course. I stood back, and I let happen whatever would." She cast them a sad smile, one that showed how hard it had been for her not to interfere. "The world continued to turn, and people continued to fall in love even without my help." A quick laugh escaped her lips. "I admit, for a time, I was rather disappointed that Fate managed without me. However, life kept me busy. I had a husband and children, and for a long time, I all but forgot about *aiding Fate.*"

"What changed?" Nora asked quietly, the tone in her voice as mesmerized as Troy felt.

His grandmother sighed. "I saw my grandson's heartbreak, and I knew I had made a mistake."

"Made a mistake?" Troy inquired, confused. "What do you mean? You didn't do anything."

"Precisely," his grandmother agreed, a note of anger in her voice. "I did nothing. I knew what the two of you felt for one another. I saw it as clearly as I see it now, and yet...I did nothing." She shook her head, clearly still furious with herself. "I sat back and left it up to Fate." She scoffed. "As it would seem, occasionally Fate requires a helping hand after all." She looked from Nora to Troy. "I'm so sorry that I failed you. I never forgave myself for allowing happiness to slip through your fingers, and I promised myself that I would never allow it to happen again."

Running a hand through his hair, Troy chuckled as he remembered all the many ways his grandmother had meddled in his sisters' lives this past year. "And you kept that promise," he told her with a smile. "They're all happily married...because of you."

Almost bashfully, Grandma Edie waved his words away. "Oh, it was nothing. I merely pushed and prodded here and there."

Nora drew in a shuddering breath. "But why the tea?" She looked up at Troy. "After all, it couldn't change anything. I was married and..."

Troy stilled as an icy thought slithered into his mind. His gaze narrowed as he looked at his grandmother. "You didn't, did you?"

Her brows rose in challenge. "Do you truly think I would go so far as to hasten a man into his grave?" She clucked her tongue disapprovingly. "Of course, the possibility occurred to me—as it would to anyone —however, I did not."

Despite the circumstances, Troy breathed a sigh of relief. For a moment, he had truly thought it possible because, quite obviously, there was not much his grandmother would not do for those she loved.

"However, neither did I prevent Mr. Clarke from doing what he did."

Both Nora and Troy flinched at those words.

Chapter Forty-Two
INTO FOREVER

Staring at Grandma Edie, Nora drew in a slow breath, feeling it fill her lungs as she absorbed the implications of the woman's words. "You...You knew? You knew he would...?"

"I did," Troy's grandmother confirmed. "Or at least, I suspected."

"How?" Troy croaked beside Nora's ear.

Grandma Edie shrugged. "I saw the intention in his eyes. It was in the way he looked at you," her gaze met Nora's, "and in the way he looked at your late husband." Again, she shrugged. "I heard about the late Lord Hayward's *mishaps* and made a few quiet inquiries." A devilish grin came to her face. "And then I sat back...and did nothing."

Nora felt Troy's hand upon hers tremble. She knew he possessed a deep sense of honor and wondered how he felt about his grandmother's confession. Yet he did not say a word.

"Some might judge me for what I did...or rather didn't do," Grandma Edie continued, a surprisingly peaceful look upon her face. "I, however, have no regrets, except for...that one." She smiled at them, and Nora felt the overwhelming desire to hug her.

Always had Grandma Edie been in her life. Always had she had kinds words for Nora. Always had she watched over her...even more than Nora would ever have suspected.

"But why the tea?"

"Do you not remember?" Grandma Edie asked, her pale eyes looking into Nora's. "What you told me?"

For a moment, Nora was confused, uncertain what Troy's grandmother was referring to. Then, however, her mind cleared, and she remembered a drizzly afternoon only days after her wedding to Hayward.

Her heart had been broken, Troy's loss and her disillusionment with her new husband too much for her to bear. Unable to speak to anyone about the anguish in her heart, Nora had felt close to losing her mind. Of course, no one knew of her loss, and no one ought to know. She was a young wife. She ought to be happy, thinking about children to fill her home.

Yet she could not. Her heart had ached at the mere thought of it, unable to ask for comfort or counsel from anyone.

And then Grandma Edie had come to her, and her eyes had seen what Nora had been unable to say. Even now, she remembered gentle arms, enfolding her, as whispered words had found their way through her tears and sobs.

All will be well. One day, you shall be happy again. I promise.

"I told you," Nora whispered, seeing that day so clearly in front of her now, "that I loathed the thought of bearing his children." Tears gathered in her eyes as she looked at Troy's grandmother. "I said that I'd rather have no children at all than his." Her right hand flew to her lips, and yet a sob escaped, drifting through the quiet of the chamber like a shot fired from a cannon.

Troy's arms tightened upon her, pulling her against his chest, as he placed a kiss on her temple, murmuring soft words of comfort.

Tears glistened in Grandma Edie's pale eyes. "I granted you your wish as best I could, knowing it might be a while before a chance might present itself to set things right."

"But I still drink the tea!" Nora exclaimed all of a sudden, her hand still resting upon her belly. Was she truly with child? Or was there some kind of mistake? "I drank it only this morning. How...?"

A deep smile showed upon Grandma Edie's face as she nodded. "Indeed, it is the same tea." Nora nodded along to her words. "Yet since your husband's death, it contains one less ingredient." A wicked twinkle came to her eyes that almost made Nora laugh as it swept away all the heartache of the last few years, finally freeing her of a past she had always regretted.

"I can have children," Nora whispered in awe as she looked into Grandma Edie's eyes, needing her to confirm what she already knew in her heart. "I can have children."

Grandma Edie chuckled. "Quite obviously, you can."

Turning in Troy's arms, Nora looked up into his eyes. "I can—" She broke off, and a shuddering breath left her lips. "We can have children."

The smile that came to Troy's face made her heart soar and set her world on fire. He gently cupped her face in his hands and stared into her eyes, as though he could not believe this moment to be real.

"I'll leave you to it then," Grandma Edie mumbled, a smile in her voice, as though her greatest dream had just come true. Nora heard the old woman push herself to her feet, her walking cane tapping on the floor, as she walked to the door and then closed it behind herself.

"Does this mean you'll marry me?" Troy asked, tears misting his eyes.

Joyous laughter rose in Nora's throat and fought its way free. "Yes, I'll marry you! Yes!" She threw her arms around him, and for a long time, they simply held one another, tears streaming down their faces.

Troy's hands rubbed up and down her back, still seeking to warm her, his own skin almost hot to the touch. His pulse beat fast in his neck, and his breath tickled her own.

"I came to tell you that," Nora murmured before pulling back and meeting his eyes. "I know I said I needed time to think," she shook her head, "but I didn't. I knew I loved you. I knew I wanted you." She cupped a hand to his cheek. "All I needed was the courage to say it." She placed a gentle kiss upon his lips. "I love you, Troy, and I want to be your wife. I came to tell you that this morning."

Surging forward, Troy wrapped her in his arms once more. "I was beside myself when you didn't come," he murmured into her hair. "I feared you were too afraid to take this chance. I feared I'd lost you all over again."

"I know," Nora replied, her voice heavy with emotion. "I'm so sorry you had to go through this." She closed her eyes, remembering how Mr. Clarke had come upon her. "He found me. Perhaps he followed me. Somehow, he knew I was going to meet you."

Troy pulled back and looked into her eyes. "Did he hurt you?"

Swallowing, Nora shook her head. "He frightened me. He told me what he had done." She shook her head, a part of her still unable to believe. "I tried to get away, but I was starting to feel lightheaded." A smile tugged upon her lips as her hand once more settled upon her belly. "I had no idea."

Troy joined in her joy, his blue eyes glowing with such warmth that it chased away the last of Nora's chills. "Of course not. How could you?" Closing his eyes, he shook his head. "Today has been a day of many revelations. It will take some time to absorb them all." He placed a kiss upon her lips. "But what matters most is that you're safe and that...our child is safe." He laughed. "Our child." A deep breath rushed from his lungs.

"Our child," Nora echoed, wondering how many times she would have to say the words before she dared believe them.

"I will send for a special license immediately," Troy said suddenly, his gaze drifting to where her hand lay on her belly. "There is no time to wait. Without doubt, there will be rumors. However, the sooner—"

"Not today," Nora interrupted him as she took his hand. "Today is ours." She scooted to the other side of the bed, then pulled back the blanket. "Will you hold me?"

Troy nodded, his eyes never leaving hers as he slid into bed beside her. His arm wrapped around her as she rested her head upon his shoulder. "Sleep," he whispered, kissing the top of her head. "You need rest. The both of you do."

Nora smiled. "Don't you mean the three of us?" Her hand wandered up his chest until the tips of her fingers came to rest upon his neck, right above his pulse point.

A deep sigh left Troy's lips. "I suppose so, yes. I...I'll never forget the moment I saw you on the ground with him advancing on you."

"I'm all right," Nora whispered to reassure him as his hands upon her tensed at the memory. "You came for me, and now we shall never be apart again."

"Never," Troy vowed, a promise that would carry them from one day to the next into forever.

Chapter Forty-Three

COMING HOME

Of course, the idea had been to marry quickly to prevent rumors from spreading once their child was born...less than nine months after their wedding. However, as Nora knew by now, things had a tendency to go off plan.

Although Nora had sustained no injuries beyond a sprained ankle from her encounter with Mr. Clarke that day, she still woke up the next morning with a high fever. Her head throbbed, and icy shivers occasionally shot up and down her limbs.

Troy was beside himself with worry and self-reproach. He never left her side, watching over her day and night. He told her stories of their childhood, placed a cool cloth upon her forehead when she thought she was burning up, brought her tea—her favorite tea!—and simply kept her company in that sweet, caring way of his.

Her eyes would close easily throughout these days, her heart reassured by his presence, and she would dream of the future, of the child she carried. Those dreams were beautiful, easily replacing the fearful ones she had had before. Whenever she would blink her eyes open, she would see him seated beside her or standing by the window or half-asleep with his head upon the bed.

Once Nora started to feel better, Troy finally *allowed* her to receive visitors, instructing each and every one of them not to upset her. Harriet, in particular, received a rather stern look from her brother, but she met it with an annoyed roll of her eyes and continued to do as she pleased. "Out you go, big brother!" she instructed with a shooing motion of her hand in the direction of the door. "If I weren't a lady, I'd suggest a bath." With a wide grin upon her face, she blinked her eyes at him in such an innocent gesture that Nora had to laugh.

Troy fixed his sister with another stern look, but then he relented and left the room.

Seating herself on the bed beside Nora, Harriet heaved a deep sigh. "He loves you dearly, does he not?" A wide smile rested upon her face. "I always knew he did."

"Always?" Christina asked with a frown. "If that were true, I wonder why you never said anything."

Harriet merely shrugged. "A girl must have her secrets."

Her sisters laughed, and so did Nora. It felt wonderful. It had been so long since she had been a part of them. She had felt so alone these past few years, and being here, now, at Whickerton Grove, was like a dream come true.

Slightly bouncing in her step, Louisa walked over and sat on the other side of Nora, little Edith in her arms. "Would you like to hold her?"

Nora's heart skipped a beat as a deep and almost desperate yearning awakened within her. "Yes," she whispered almost breathlessly, then held out her arms to receive the child.

"Don't take it personally," Louisa advised as she gently settled her daughter into Nora's arms, "if she starts bawling in a moment." An exhausted sigh left her lips. "She seems to require this odd bouncy movement in order to be able to sleep." She winked at Nora. "I suppose that is what husbands are for."

Everyone laughed, quietly, of course, so as not to disturb the child.

A wistful sigh left Anne's lips as she placed her hand upon her round belly. "Oh, she looks so sweet! So adorable!"

Louisa cast her a meaningful glance. "She is slightly less adorable when she starts screaming in the middle of the night."

"As far as I know," Harriet remarked, "that is what nurses are for." She lifted her brows pointedly.

Looking at her sister, Louisa slowly shook her head. "I cannot imagine her sleeping far away," she replied in an unusually calm tone. "No, I want her with me. With us."

Her sisters nodded in agreement, and Nora felt herself nod along with them. Indeed, she could not imagine handing her child off to someone else. She wanted to be there every moment of every day, treasuring this life that she had for so long thought to be impossible.

Leonora smiled. "I believe it is these early years," she said in that wise tone of hers, "that create a deep bond between parents and their children." Her blue eyes swept over little Edith.

"I think you're right," Louisa mumbled, reaching out a hand and brushing it over her daughter's head. "Honestly, I am perfectly happy just looking at her, watching her sleep, seeing that soft smile tugging on the corners of her mouth every once in a while."

Looking down at the infant in her arms, Nora felt her heart open in a way she had never expected before. Little Edith's gentle weight felt wonderful in her arms, her body warm and soft, that newborn scent tickling Nora's nose. "She is so beautiful," she murmured. "I cannot wait to hold my own."

"Neither can I," Anne exclaimed in utter agreement before Harriet suddenly straightened, her eyes narrowed as they fixed upon Nora's face. "Your own?" she asked with obvious suspicion in her voice.

Looking up, Nora found numerous sets of eyes looking back and forth between Harriet and her, understanding dawning on all their faces. She saw shock, but also sparks of joy, more than one mouth opening and closing without a single word uttered.

Feeling heat flush her cheeks, Nora bit her lower lip. Still, a wide smile wrestled its way onto her face.

Harriet clapped her hands together. "Are you saying...that my brother is to be a father soon?"

Apparently, the look upon Nora's face was enough because a moment later, all the sisters erupted into cheers, causing little Edith to stir in Nora's arms. The girl waved her fists as though threatening mayhem should they not all quiet down.

"Does this mean you will get married?" Leonora asked tentatively, concern in her wide blue eyes. "I mean, I hope this means you will—"

"Of course!" Christina interrupted, a joyous chuckle falling from her lips. "It's not as though they have a choice now." Yet despite the seriousness of her words, she seemed to glow with utter delight.

"Of course, they have a choice," Harriet interjected, that familiar look of defiant independence in her green eyes. "No one should be forced into—"

"Calm down," Louisa soothed her youngest sister, placing a calming hand on her shoulder. "No one is being forced into anything. They're clearly in love," she smiled at Nora affectionately, "and they're getting married because they *want* to get married." Her eyes met Nora's. "Right?"

Grinning from ear to ear, Nora nodded. "Right." She could not remember the last time she had felt such happiness as she did these days. She loved the laughter, the cheers, the voices echoing through the house at every hour of the day. She loved the companionship, the closeness, the honesty. But above all, she loved the family that was now truly to be hers.

Bash and Sam often poked their heads in, bringing her pictures they had painted or twigs they had collected or even snowflakes that melted in their little hands. The sisters, too, often stopped by, and Nora loved it when Louisa brought little Edith along with her.

And then, a sennight before Christmas, Nora's wedding day finally arrived. The whole house was decorated for the season, green garlands everywhere, glittering with red and gold ornaments. The scent of fresh-baked bread and pastries wafted from room to room, mingling with laughter and children's voices singing Christmas songs.

As Nora walked toward Troy, standing up front with the parish's priest, she experienced a strange flashback to her first wedding. She remembered, clear as day, how her hands had trembled, how dread had settled in her stomach, how her heart had cried out.

But she had given her word, and her mother's watchful eyes had been upon her, urging her on, urging her to walk the path she had so foolishly chosen.

Nora blinked, and her gaze found her mother's, standing next to

Lord and Lady Whickerton. A smile lay on her face, one that spoke of silent joy, one that whispered of affection rather than duty, and Nora felt her own heart grow lighter. Her gaze swept over everyone assembled here today, Troy's family as well as her own—not to mention the tall Scotsman with the dancing eyes with whom she had only exchanged a word or two thus far.

Still, she already knew she liked him. He was...family somehow.

Everyone looked happy.

Troy in particular.

His otherwise pale eyes shone in a startling blue, and Nora knew she had made the right choice. Child or no, this was where she was meant to be...

...by his side.

And the moment, they were declared husband and wife, Nora felt the world right itself. Every wrong turn her life had taken before no longer mattered. Indeed, all of a sudden, every obstacle seemed worthwhile because in the end, it had led her here.

To this moment.

To this man.

To her true self.

She was finally home.

Chapter Forty-Four

A NEW LIFE

For so long, Troy had been certain that his wedding day would never come. Or if it would, that it would be a dark day, his life forever tied to a stranger, their union based on rational factors rather than the all-consuming love he felt in this very moment.

At the thought of his new wife, Troy's steps quickened, and he hastened up the stairs two at a time. Eagerness hummed in his veins, the need to reach her side spurring him on. Somehow, he no longer felt at peace on his own. Now he needed her.

The thought made him smile.

Happy voices echoed to his ears from downstairs where some of his siblings still celebrated today's union. They all had been overjoyed to welcome Nora into their family. Troy would never forget the way his father had come to him after the ceremony as the rest of his family had been heaping well-wishes upon them. He had said nothing; still, the look in his eyes had spoken volumes.

Troy had understood in that moment just how deeply his father loved him and how relieved he was that Troy had chosen a path that would bring him happiness.

Indeed, it had been the right choice.

The only choice.

Reaching his chamber, Troy drew in a deep breath and then stepped inside. Nora was seated at the vanity that had been brought over from Fatherington Hall. After all, the Whickertons did not hold with separate bedchambers. Troy supposed that was something that could be said for all spouses who had chosen to marry out of love.

And it was a Whickerton tradition.

Closing the door, Troy smiled at her. "Are you all right?" he asked, wondering about the shadow that seemed to have passed over her face just now.

For a moment, Nora hesitated as though reluctant to answer. Then, however, she turned to look at him, her eyes meeting his. "I was thinking of my first marriage." She shrugged. "My first wedding. I suppose it was inevitable." She rose to her feet and came over to him. "I'm sorry."

Troy shook his head, tugging on a loose curl dancing down her temple. "Don't apologize," he murmured, relieved that she had told him instead of hiding her thoughts from him.

Reaching up, Nora brushed the tips of her fingers along the line of his left brow. "It was a dark day for me, nothing like today." Her smile broadened, and Troy felt it all the way to his toes. "Today was...the way I always dreamed it would be. I shall never forget it." She sighed. "And although I still wish things had gone differently, you...you were worth the wait."

Dipping his head, Troy kissed her, slowly at first and then with more ardor. He felt her body lean into him, felt her pulse beneath his fingertips skip a beat and whole-heartedly agreed with her words.

She, too, had been worth waiting for!

"I love the way you smile," Nora murmured against his lips. "Over the years, whenever I caught a glimpse of you at an event, you always looked tense and earnest and almost devoid of emotion. It seemed as though your light had gone out." Her hands slipped over his shoulders, up the sides of his neck and into his hair. "Now, you smile again as you used to...long ago." Her warm brown eyes searched his face, and a deep smile full of joy and love came to her own.

"That is your doing," Troy whispered back, delighting in the way her face lit up. She seemed to glow like the sun, the moon and all the stars in the night sky together. "My world was dark without you." He brushed his lips against hers, his hold on her tightening possessively. "Now, everything is different. Be assured that I shall never let you go again."

Nora laughed, a wonderful, heart-warming sound. "I will hold you to that, Husband."

"I would expect nothing less, Wife."

Again, their lips met and the world around them fell away. Troy still remembered that feeling of longing in his chest, the hopeless distance between them, and to have her here in his arms now was utterly over-whelming. "You're truly here," he whispered. "You're truly mine."

A melodious chuckle fell from her lips. "Hold on to that feeling of wonderment because before you know it, our own little bundle of joy shall keep us up all night."

Troy felt the corners of his mouth stretch into a wide grin. "I can hardly wait," he told her, surprised by his own words. "Truth be told, I never thought much about becoming a father, for I hardly allowed myself to think of becoming a husband." He sighed. "Every year, my family travels to Lord Archibald's Christmas house party, and last year—"

"Except this year," Nora threw in.

Troy nodded. "Yes, except this year." He paused. "In fact, I think it might be time for a new tradition. With more children being born into the family, perhaps Christmastime spent at home would suit everyone more."

"A wise thought," Nora said with a smile, then nodded to him. "You were saying?"

"Last year, when Louisa and Phin became betrothed, my sisters wondered if yet another one of them would receive a proposal next time around. Suddenly, they were all speaking about marriage, and I saw the way they would look at me every once in a while. I realized I needed to choose a wife and yet..." He shrugged, remembering that sense of dread that had fallen over him at the thought.

Nora grinned up at him. "Harriet told me that the day of her wedding, your grandmother gathered her and her sisters together, asking for their assistance in seeing not only Juliet and my brother matched...but us as well."

Staring at his wife, Troy was momentarily too stunned to draw breath. "I...I know I shouldn't be surprised and yet..." He shook his head. "I suppose it was all her doing, seeing them—us!—all married within a single year."

Nora laughed. "Your grandmother does know what she is doing!" A deep sigh left her lips, and Troy could see her own relief at the turn her life had taken. Neither one of them had truly believed they would find happiness, that they would ever see themselves married to the one they loved. "We should thank her."

Troy nodded. "We should."

"Do you think," Nora paused, frowning, "with all her grandchildren happily married, she will miss meddling in another's affairs?"

Troy laughed. "Honestly, I don't for a second believe that my grandmother will now keep her nose out of other people's business. Oh, no, she will find a way to get involved." He chuckled. "I wonder who her next victim will be."

Nora cast him a chiding look. "Don't pretend you don't appreciate her help. After all,..." Her brows rose meaningfully.

Troy nodded. "We would not be here without her." He pulled her closer. "I missed you," he said in a suddenly choked voice, echoing the words they had first said to one another by the ancient watchtower.

"I missed you, too," Nora whispered back, tears shimmering in her brown eyes. "Never again."

Troy nodded. "Never again."

As the snow fell silently upon Whickerton Grove, Troy and Nora took their first steps into a new life.

A life they both wanted.

A life they would never take for granted.

Epilogue

Whickerton Grove, January 1804 (or a variation thereof)
A few weeks later

"Have you ever seen this much snow?" Nora heard Harriet ask the three children, their cheeks glowing with excitement.

Bash, Sam and Hugh shook their heads, eagerness making their little feet dance upon the spot.

"Are you prepared?" Harriet asked like a general, marching up and down in front of them.

All three children nodded.

"Hats?"

More nods.

"Scarfs? Coats? Mittens?"

Their little heads bobbed up and down.

"Shovels?"

Their little faces froze, mouths agape as they stared at Harriet.

Nora could barely keep from laughing, her hand pressed to her lips. It seemed the rest of the Whickertons fared no better.

"Then how do you expect to build a snow fort?" Harriet demanded in mock outrage. "But not to worry, I procured one for each of you."

Utter relief came to the children's faces as they finally exhaled the breath they had been holding. A moment later, Harriet shooed them outside, bellowing instructions.

The moment the door closed behind them, laughter erupted in the drawing room. "Harriet will never grow up, will she?" Louisa asked, her cheeks flushed red from laughing.

Leonora shook her head. "I'd say it's highly unlikely."

A warm smile came to the face of Harriet's husband. "It will make her a wonderful mother one day," Jack declared with a dazzling smile, clearly not in the least put off by his wife's exuberance.

While Thorne, Drake and Tobias helped their wives into their winter coats, Louisa and Phineas bundled up their little daughter in thick layers until one could barely spot the child.

"Air holes might be good," Nora joked, peering at the sleeping infant. Beside her, Troy laughed.

Louisa looked up, an oddly serious expression upon her face. "You think it's too much?"

"Perhaps one layer less," Nora suggested.

"Or ten," Troy chimed in, laughing.

Louisa cast her brother an angry look.

And then, they all stepped out into the cold, delighting in the warm rays of the sun, glittering off the ice and snow. It was a beautiful day full of joy and laughter, snowball fights and collapsed snow forts. And by the time they all returned inside, everyone was exhausted.

After a cup of hot tea—or warm cocoa—a contented silence fell over them all as they sat in pleasant companionship in front of the fire in the drawing room. The three children were asleep, snuggled into their parents' arms; little Edith the only one suddenly wide awake.

Nora's gaze drifted to Hugh, Mr. Clarke's now orphaned son. Every time she looked upon him, her heart constricted painfully. No child deserved such a fate. He had never known his mother and now also lost his father. As awful a person as Mr. Clarke had been, he had always doted upon his son.

As no immediate family remained, Nora had considered taking the child in herself. However, in the end, it had been her mother who had taken the decision out of her hands. As much as she had cut herself off from the world before, her recent reconciliation with Christopher and Nora, too, had brought about a drastic change. She was no longer satisfied with drifting from one day to the next. No, now, she wanted a purpose.

And that purpose was Hugh.

Indeed, Nora could not remember ever seeing that utterly devoted and affectionate side of her mother. It made her heart ache whenever she thought of her own childhood. And yet Nora knew better than anyone that sometimes Fate led one the long way around. The same was true for her mother, and Nora was relieved that she had received that chance.

That Hugh was now receiving it as well.

After all, with his father dead, he was now the new Earl of Hayward...and he would need someone formidable at his side.

Nora had to admit that there was no one more suited for that task than the woman her mother had so recently become.

"Has anyone seen Keir lately?" Juliet asked into the stillness as her gaze swept the room. "He seems to have disappeared again."

Instantly, all eyes moved to Grandma Edie, sound asleep in her favorite chair.

Harriet laughed before a wide yawn contorted her face. "She probably sent him on another errand."

"I wonder," Phineas chimed in, "if we'll ever find out what these errands are." He looked from one to the next. "Any ideas?"

Everyone shook their heads.

"It's been going on ever since he arrived last summer," Troy remarked, pulling Nora tighter into his embrace. "He once told me it was to aid a friend but could not say more as he had been sworn to secrecy."

"A friend?" Leonora echoed before her blue eyes moved from her husband Drake to her brother. "A friend of his? Or of hers?"

"Hers," Troy replied with a sideways glance at his grandmother.

"What could she possibly send him to do?" Thorne wondered out loud, rubbing his chin.

In the next instant, Christina burst into the room, her eyes wide and her cheeks pale, the shawl she had gone to fetch dangling forgotten from the crook of her arm.

"Are you all right?" Thorne exclaimed, extricating himself from his sleeping daughter before hastening toward his wife. "What happened?"

"I just received this letter," Christina gasped, the pulse in her neck hammering wildly. "It's from a friend in London. She writes that... that..." Her eyes returned to the parchment, disbelief upon her face.

"That what?" Harriet demanded impatiently.

Christina's head snapped up, and her eyes met her sister's. "That Sarah was kidnapped out of her parents' rented townhouse the night before her wedding." She shook her head as a collective gasp echoed through the room. "I didn't even know her parents had arranged for another match. I..."

Nora shivered at the thought of Sarah's fate. She did not know the girl well, but over the past few weeks had heard the sisters speak about her as well as their desire to see her safely settled.

"She was kidnapped? Truly?" Anne asked, turning to look at her husband, Tobias, who bore a similarly disbelieving expression upon his face. "Out of her home? Who would...?" She shook her head, her arms wrapping around her rounding belly.

"N-No one knows," Christina stammered, passing the letter to her husband, who read it and then passed it to the next. "We have to find out what happened! We have to find her! We have to get her back!"

"Who was she to marry?" Phineas threw in. "Does it say?"

Christina was about to answer when another voice spoke out, "Lord Blackmore."

Once again, all eyes snapped to Grandma Edie before a myriad of questions and comments was fired at her simultaneously.

"How do you know?"

"He's old enough to be her father!"

"Was he the one who kidnapped her?"

"When did this happen?"

Rapping the tip of her walking cane upon the floor, Grandma Edie managed to silence everybody. "Now," she began, a stern look in her eyes. "One at a time. You people sound like a beehive."

Christina stepped forward. "Did you know?" she asked, tears glistening in her eyes and a snarl upon her lips. "Did you know she was to be married?"

Grandma Edie nodded.

Christina's jaw dropped. "Why didn't you say anything? We could've... We could've...done something!" Her voice grew louder with each word she spoke.

"There was nothing you could have done to prevent it," Grandma Edie replied with a kind look.

"How can you possibly know that?" Christina shrieked before panting breaths forced her to stop talking and focus on calming herself. Thorne wrapped an arm around her and pulled her close, murmuring something into her ear.

"Why would anyone kidnap her?" Harriet threw in, her voice hard but a puzzled frown upon her face as she looked from her sister to her husband. "It cannot be for ransom. Everyone knows her father gambled away the family fortune. Why then?" Jack nodded along to her reasoning.

Christina shook her head, sufficiently recovered. "I don't know. But we have to do something!"

Harriet frowned before her gaze once more moved to Grandma Edie. "Do you know who kidnapped her?"

"How would she know?" Troy inquired, looking from his youngest sister to his wife.

Nora frowned, unable to shake the feeling that they were missing something vital.

Harriet shrugged. "The same way she seems to know everything else! I don't know! I simply thought I'd ask!"

"We need to return to London immediately," Christina exclaimed, suddenly unable to accept the comfort her husband was offering. "We need to find out what happened. We need to find her! Now! As soon as possible! Who knows what—?"

"Not to worry. Sarah is perfectly fine."

For the third time that day, all eyes snapped to Grandma Edie, her own looking suspiciously innocent.

Harriet chuckled. "I knew it!"

"What are you saying?" Leonora asked. "Do you know something?"

A wicked smirk came to Grandma Edie's face as she merely shrugged her shoulders.

"Grandmother!" Troy exclaimed. "You cannot say something like that and then not elaborate. Do you know who took Sarah?"

A rather indulgent look came to the old woman's face, and Nora had to suppress a laugh. Indeed, Grandma Edie would never know boredom because, even after seeing all her grandchildren happily married, there were still countless people in this world who could do with a bit of help.

"Let's just say," Grandma Edie finally replied, "that it'll be best for Sarah if she is not found...just yet."

As numerous voices erupted around them, demanding an answer, more of an answer, Nora let her gaze sweep around the room. Indeed, the tall Scotsman was nowhere to be seen. Had Grandma Edie truly sent him on another *errand?* Could he have been the one to *kidnap* Sarah in order to protect her from the threat of yet another forced marriage?

Nora could not help but think that it was so, and her heart felt lighter at the thought, knowing that the young woman would be all right. Perhaps it would truly be good for Sarah to remain *lost* a little while longer. Perhaps she would find herself in love soon. After all, Grandma Edie was not known to be wrong.

Ever.

THE END

Of course, this is not truly the end! Of course, Sarah deserves her own story...as does Keir. Might it be one and the same? And what would we do without Grandma Edie and the wicked Whickertons?

Stay tuned! More stories are to come!

In the meantime, have you read all Whickerton books, including the prequel? Check them all out here!

THE WHICKERTONS IN LOVE

If you have read all 7 books of the *Whickertons in Love* series browse other books by Bree Wolf or check out one of WOLF Publishing's latest releases of Jennifer Monroe: The Sisterhood of Secrets Series!

SISTERHOOD OF SECRETS

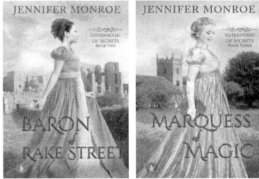

HAPPY EVER REGENCY SERIES

LOVE'S SECOND CHANCE SERIES: TALES OF LORDS & LADIES

LOVE'S SECOND CHANCE SERIES: TALES OF DAMSELS & KNIGHTS

LOVE'S SECOND CHANCE SERIES: HIGHLAND TALES

For more information visit www.breewolf.com

About Bree

USA Today bestselling and award-winning author, Bree Wolf has always been a language enthusiast (though not a grammarian!) and is rarely found without a book in her hand or her fingers glued to a keyboard. Trying to find her way, she has taught English as a second language, traveled abroad and worked at a translation agency as well as a law firm in Ireland. She also spent loooong years obtaining a BA in English and Education and an MA in Specialized Translation while wishing she could simply be a writer. Although there is nothing simple about being a writer, her dreams have finally come true.

"A big thanks to my fairy godmother!"

Currently, Bree has found her new home in the historical romance genre, writing Regency novels and novellas. Enjoying the mix of fact and fiction, she occasionally feels like a puppet master (or mistress? Although that sounds weird!), forcing her characters into ever-new situations that will put their strength, their beliefs, their love to the test, hoping that in the end they will triumph and get the happily-ever-after we are all looking for.

If you're an avid reader, sign up for Bree's newsletter on www. breewolf.com as she has the tendency to simply give books away. Find out about freebies, giveaways as well as occasional advance reader copies and read before the book is even on the shelves!

Connect with Bree and stay up-to-date on new releases:

facebook.com/breewolf.novels

twitter.com/breewolf_author

instagram.com/breewolf_author

amazon.com/Bree-Wolf/e/B00FJX27Z4

bookbub.com/authors/bree-wolf

Printed in Great Britain
by Amazon

32729914R00169